I don't want to go to jail

BOOKS BY **JIMMY BRESLIN**

Can't Anybody Here Play This Game?

The World of Jimmy Breslin

The Gang That Couldn't Shoot Straight

World Without End, Amen

How the Good Guys Finally Won

Forty-Four Caliber (with others)

Forsaking All Others

He Got Hungry and Forgot His Manners

Table Money

The World According to Breslin

Damon Runyon

I Want to Thank My Brain for Remembering Me

I Don't Want to Go to Jail

I don't want to go to jail

a good novel

Jimmy Breslin

Little, Brown and Company

BOSTON   NEW YORK   LONDON

First Edition

This is a work of fiction. All characters and happenings are completely
imaginary. The opinions expressed by the characters are not always
those of the author.

Library of Congress Cataloging-in-Publication Data

Breslin, Jimmy.
I don't want to go to jail / by Jimmy Breslin. — 1st ed.
p. cm.
ISBN 0-316-11845-1
1. Italian American families — Fiction.   2. New York (N.Y.) — Fiction.
3. Organized crime — Fiction.   4. Criminals — Fiction.
5. Clergy — Fiction.   6. Mafia — Fiction.   I. Title.

PS3552.R39 I15 2001
813'.54 — dc21
00-058880

10 9 8 7 6 5 4 3 2 1

Q-FF

Book design by Fearn Cutler
Printed in the United States of America

For my aunt, Harriet Arnone

"There is nothing like being in the Mafia at sundown. You got all the money you need, custom clothes, a big new car, jewelry, the finest women, stay out all night. Then they put on the bracelets."

— *Sal Meli*

of Ozone Park, Queens, New York City;
and Federal Penitentiary, Lewisburg, Pennsylvania;
Federal Penitentiary, Sandstone, Minnesota; Federal Correctionals, Jessup, Georgia,
and Ashland, Kentucky,* and Loretto, Pennsylvania;
Myrtle Avenue, Brooklyn, Half-Way House for releasees with low boiling points.

*Considered worst federal prison in United States.

I don't
want to go
to jail

Prologue

The rooster in the chicken market downstairs woke up mad that day. He let out a scream that brought the kid in the bedroom upstairs tumbling onto the floor. He got dressed while the rooster shouted in distress, as if he had a throat filled with broken glass.

The kid, Fausti Dellacava, was in the kitchen before the sky outside the kitchen window turned into summer steam. He could not wait for any day to start because he spent time with his father, who wasn't at home.

"Buon giorno!" he called out.

His mother, Gina, groaned from the bedroom.

"Buon giorno!" he called again.

"Buon giorno!" his mother called, wearily.

"Mangia!" he said.

He took out cereal to start the day.

After this he sat and watched cartoons on television. And now, in the bright hot light of a summer day here is Fausti, six now, chubby, with black hair brushed straight back, coming out of his building. The narrow entranceway to 235 Bleecker is alongside a bar and the chicken market with angered rooster. Fausti walks down to the corner of the main street in his village, Sullivan Street in Greenwich Village.

He is the only one in the family allowed to carry the name Fausti, other than the famous dark Boss, his uncle Fausti Dellacava, known as The Fist. This uncle originally got the name because he had twenty-five professional fights and had his picture in the barbershop window on Spring Street in trunks and with bare fists threatening anybody walking past. The caption on the picture said, "Fausti Dellacava, heavy-fisted middleweight. Tommy Ryan Manager." Many times, he shadowboxed in the club and threw his fists all over the air. Over the years, as the circle of fear and fantasy intensified, this would take on an article and he would be known as The Fist. His name in headlines, however, always was Fausti Dellacava. He ran two families, the mob outfit and his own, with the use of about ten words.

When Fausti was in a carriage and he made fists with his hands, the old guys on the block called him "Little Fist!" Later on, that was dropped when The Fist said he didn't like his name being copied. So they called him "Little Fausti." Usually, he was just Fausti. But the world knew he was something to The Fist, most figuring him for a son.

"Buon giorno!" Fausti calls to Olga the seamstress.

She looks out the door of her small shop.

"Buon giorno!" she says.

Fausti smiles proudly. He is speaking Italian and he believes that this makes him an Italian, like the old men who stand in front of his father's place. He can be American when he plays with other kids, Italian if he feels like it, or an immigrant speaking broken English.

He would always be an open, laughing contrast to the brooding, silent threat of his family on the streets on which he lived. He was at first a mascot, then thought of as considerably more serious than that. Let a kid walk enough streets and he could grow up to be anything. Maybe make him a monster. But here at the start, all he wanted to do was exult in each day.

Which he does now, as he calls out to two old women with shopping carts.

"Buon giorno!"

They answer.

"Come sta?"

"Bene."

"Ah sure," Little Fausti said.

He passes the candy store in the middle of the block.

"Caramella!"

The man inside waves.

Little Fausti struts past a delicatessen and calls out proudly, *"Carne!"*

The counterman nods.

Now Little Fausti goes past the woman pushing babies past the redbrick Children's Aid Society building.

"Buon giorno!"

"Buon giorno."

He didn't even glance across the street at the five-story tenement at number 250 Sullivan Street, where black iron banisters went down one short flight of basement steps to the clubhouse of the Concerned Lutherans. Nobody alive today is sure of where the name came from, although oral history of the block states that German Lutherans who survived the *General Slocum* disaster, which killed 1,021 in the East River, moved out of sorrow from their East Side housing and occupied two buildings on Sullivan Street following the catastrophe in 1904. The clubhouse, originally housing the civic group called Concerned Lutherans, changed hands when the Lutherans moved out to Ridgewood in Queens and Italians from Naples, their hair matted from the ocean crossing, moved in. The name on the basement club remained as "Concerned Lutherans." It happens that if a Lutheran ever set foot in the place since 1920, which is improbable, it was either for purposes of paying the Italian loan shark or for being killed by the Italian loan shark for not paying him. It is the central office, the powerhouse, the seat of the boss of crime, the Boss. On the brass mailbox alongside the door, there is scratched the name "Luthrans." Nobody refers to it as anything other than "the Club." If you have to ask what club, then you belong living in Sweden.

At this time, the Italian blocks of Greenwich Village were overcrowded with gangster clubhouses, with two and three to a block; one block of Thompson Street had three clubhouses and Sullivan also had three. A couple of the names were common in news stories, the Ravenite on Mulberry Street most prominent. All clubs were under the rule of the Concerned Lutherans club, which neither newspeople nor, for long years, lawmen could find.

Now, walking the street in the bright morning, Little Fausti drops into silence because he doesn't know any more words in Italian. Oh, he does know *"Buona sera"* for good night, but it would be many hours before he could use that. And he could answer if somebody asked him how he felt, but nobody had so far.

So he uses immigrant English that he has picked up from his grandmother, who lives around the corner on West 3rd Street. She speaks only a few words that are not Italian. When the grandson, Fausti, first came to see her, she tried to teach him her Italian. This infuriated her son, Little Fausti's father, Larry, who came in from the gambling and shylocking storefront clubhouse he ran next door and shouted, "What are you turning this kid into?"

From then on, the grandmother spoke broken English to the grandson.

On the street on this morning, Little Fausti calls to Jimmy from the Carvel stand, "Where you go?"

"Subway."

"Soobaway!" Little Fausti says.

The woman coming out of the building next to the Children's Aid and starting for work smiles, and Little Fausti says, "Boosa!"

"That's right," she says, walking to the bus on Sixth Avenue.

After that he called out, to no one in particular, "I can no understand."

His father usually was no farther than a door away from the grandmother's.

In the front room of his storefront club, Little Fausti's father, Larry, booked bets, loaned money, and ran card games. The back room was a kitchen, which he used for cooking, fish mainly. Sometimes he disappeared for a week. When Little Fausti looked for him at the club, either Little Fausti's older brother, Larry Jr., or one of the men playing cards would assure him that the father would be back soon.

On this morning, Fausti thought he would stop by his father's club. Larry Dellacava was the rare mob guy up early because he took horse bets in person, and regulated cash and credit with common sense. He was a lifer in gambling. When horse betting would be nearly erased from the streets and politicians got their fingers on racing and started off-track betting stores of such filth and filled with so many derelicts that it cried for the Mafia, Larry remained.

Fausti usually went to his grandmother's at sundown. As his mother was sick, he ate every night at the grandmother's. Her time and menus never changed. At five each night, she had dinner for Fausti. On Monday it was steak. Tuesday, chicken cutlets; Wednesday, macaroni; Thursday, roast beef with rice and spinach; Friday, fried fish. After dinner he would take a plate of food home to his mother, who was in bed.

Now, almost turning the corner to the father's club, he saw there was suddenly an uncommon daytime gathering across the street in front of the steps to Concerned Lutherans. A crowd of men, their eyes smarting in the first daylight many had experienced for months, clapped enthusiastically as a car stopped on the narrow street. A man as wide as a boar slipped out of the car and went down the steps to the clubhouse at number 250. The men followed, going down the steps and through the doorway one at a time, as if boarding a plane.

This was homecoming day for Big Fausti Dellacava, also known as The Fist. He was coming home from the usual Mafia sentence of the time, five years at Lewisburg, in Pennsylvania, during which time any inquiring party was told that he was "away in the army."

Little Fausti's father, Larry, appeared in the doorway of the club. He called to Fausti:

"Your uncle is here."

Fausti walked across to the club, but with no excitement. He didn't know if he knew his uncle.

"Here he is."

Larry Dellacava is standing in the doorway of the club with Fausti, who seems uncertain.

"What's the matter with you?" his father says. "You know your uncle, don't you? This is your godfather from when you got christened. Say hello to your uncle."

"*Buon giorno,*" Fausti says.

Big Fausti, The Fist, has a crooked smile as he looks at his godson. "I get confused by his size. I ain't seen the kid in four and a half years."

The chubby, handsome boy stands there with his father and uncle, neither of whom could look to the heavens and receive a single vision that would tell them of the danger of mixing good and bad in the same saucepan. The mixture of humans can take on the properties of nitroglycerine and can be set off by the tiniest outside agent, even the air in the room.

"He's Mama's favorite in the whole family," Fausti's father said.

"You a good boy?" his uncle asked the boy.

"*Bene. Molto bene,*" the boy answers, using up his reserve of Italian words.

"Buy him a dog," the uncle says.

On homecoming day from prison, The Fist returns to start governing America's organized crime from a card table in the Concerned Lutherans. The inside was a slum. There were two large lounge chairs, a refrigerator, couch, a small bar to serve coffee, a television set, and a large round table for cards and death sentences.

On the wall over the table were signs, one a poster from World War II with a sailor calling out, "Loose Lips Sink Ships." The others read, "Tough Guys Don't Talk" and "Don't Talk. This Place Is Bugged."

On the wall right behind The Fist's permanent seat was a hand-lettered sign saying:

"No Kissing. Due to Strep Throat."

Growing up, The Fist had chronic throat trouble. Little Fausti had the same trouble, and most people said it was evidence that he was born to follow the uncle. One of the earliest memories of his uncle, and the one that lasted forever, came out of a day when Little Fausti came up with a sore throat and The Fist, a hypochondriac, suddenly felt his throat tighten, too. He and the nephew went in a car with Baldy Dom to the Ear, Nose and Throat Hospital on Second Avenue. They were examined, given tests and prescriptions.

"All right," The Fist said to the secretary.

He took a huge roll of money out of his pants pocket.

"What do I owe?" he said.

"Oh," she said, startled by the size of the bankroll. "Aren't you afraid, carrying that much money around? Somebody might mug you."

"Nobody fucks with me," The Fist said quietly.

At the time, Fausti had no idea of what his uncle was, except that he caused a feeling of admiration.

The club had a sweet sound to it — the slot machine, cards slapping, cartoons on television, murmurs, the hiss of men exhaling cigarettes.

The club was the most important single solitary property of the mob. Just standing in the one-flight-down smoky club tells people that you do absolutely nothing for a living; that you are not some slob citizen living on a time clock.

Herewith, the list of reasons why men become gangsters:

1. to 10. Don't want to go to work.
11. Being Known.
12. Broads, aka women.
13. Big new cars.
14. Stay out all night.
15. Killing is fun.
16. Hated father.
17. Trouble reading and writing.

The Fist put on a black cap that was as big as a flying saucer. It came down almost over dark eyes that were suspicious of the dust. He had full lips and a broken nose. The hands go with his name. They were large for his size and covered with lumps and black hair. They were hands that fit best around a large, dangerous club, as they often were.

He sat at the table to play his first hand since coming out of prison. The Fist glanced at the cards and threw them in.

"Gin."

On the next hand, he wouldn't even look at the cards. He pushed the cards to the center of the table.

"Gin."

One of the first things that Fausti remembers was the uncle calling out from the clubhouse on a dull and chilly Sunday afternoon:

"Fausti. Go up to Bleecker Street and get Joe Joe. You know who I mean?"

"Yop."

Fausti found Joe Joe in a doorway on Bleecker Street. He ducked in and out of a building to snatch Super Bowl football bets from guys walking up or pulling up in cars.

"He wants you!" Fausti called happily.

Joe Joe was instantly nervous. He had a nice small bookmaking business and suddenly, for some reason, he was being dragged into an arena in which he always chose not to play. To Joe Joe, going up to the club was similar to exposing himself to pneumonia.

Upon stepping into the smoky club, Joe Joe found his new client eager for the late afternoon game. While The Fist ran the nation's sports betting, he couldn't regard himself as a true sportsman unless he had a bet on the playoff game, and all the big playoff games. He had missed the last four due to locked doors. Now, he wanted to bet with a neighborhood bookmaker; the head of the phone company using a streetcorner booth. The first betting game since his coming out of prison was this playoff game of Kansas City against Oakland.

Joe Joe said Oakland was minus six. This meant Oakland had to win the game by at least seven points to make up for the six-point handicap.

"I want Oakland ten dimes," the Fist said.

Joe Joe nodded, warily. He left, carrying the bet in his stomach.

Joe Joe knew that The Fist grows violent if he loses at anything. There is no initial disappointment. Just a murderous surge. He also blames everybody else. If he loses this bet, he would pick on Joe Joe right out of the box. At the same time, Joe Joe knew that if word spread that he was The Fist's personal bookmaker, the suckers would be flooding in from Jersey and Great Neck to bet personal with The Fist's own bookmaker. So you'll take a chance, Joe Joe told himself. Either I count money on a Sunday night or I get choked to death. That's only fair.

Late that afternoon, the Oakland–Kansas City game was a 24–24 tie. In The Fist's bet, the handicap meant that Kansas City was ahead by 30 to 24. Then late in the game somebody on Kansas City throws a long pass. They win the actual game by six points. With the six-point handicap, The Fist loses his bet by twelve points.

The Fist is sitting at the card table when Joe Joe walks into an ominous barrage. "You fuck. I owe you ten thousand. You're here to collect, you fuck."

"You don't owe nothin'," Joe Joe said.

"Are you crazy? I watch the game."

"You have it wrong," Joe Joe said. "You took Oakland and six points. That means you had a tie score game. Nobody pays."

"I thought I was minus six."

"You don't remember me saying you had to get six points, that the home field was good for Kansas City?"

"Geez, you know, maybe you're fucking right."

"I got to be right," Joe Joe said. "You had a push," Joe Joe said.

"I don't owe you ten thousand?"

"Never!"

"Fuckin' great. I hate to lose on football."

From then on, he was known as Tie Score Joe Joe. Which was nice, but on all those Sundays after that Joe Joe was found standing outside the club in the darkness, pounding his fist on his forehead as he tried to come up with a way to turn a 33-point loss into a tie score for The Fist. Joe Joe never got out of elementary school and now his very life depended on pure mathematics. He had to make touchdowns out of cold air.

The Fist believed that all money he saw everywhere was his. No amount was too small to shoot somebody over. The reason why he loved small money so much was that it made him think of big money.

He thought that money had eyes and ears. That money had hands and feet. That money had a nose for breathing. After that you didn't need anything.

"You don't need a mouth because how could you get hungry

when you got money?" he asked. "Why would you need brains? To think? Money does all the fuckin' thinking."

On this one ominous day, The Fist dispatched Buster Greco to the federal court in Manhattan, where there was a major problem. The jury verdict against a group of gangsters from all over was being announced at 2:00 P.M. The Fist told Buster to inquire about a hijacked truck with which Paschal Horan was involved. Horan owed him two hundred thousand. It was a trailer truck that had been hijacked from a parking lot on the Jersey Turnpike by two thieves who then sold the truck and its contents to Horan for fifteen thousand cash. Horan hid the truck in the Bronx. The shipper in Elkhart, Indiana, let out an enraged howl. The truck was loaded with musical instruments, worth about $1.5 million. They were going to colleges in the South for all uses, including outfitting their 300-piece bands for big football games. One school, South Carolina Technical and Agricultural, was expecting thirty-three piccolos.

Horan was a trucker who alluded to heavy weapons platoons moving in. He caused customers to beg for his exorbitant services. "Fear is fucking beautiful," he said. At the same time he believed he was legitimate. Upon his arrest in this case, he told the judge, "How could I commit a crime? I live in a house."

From that moment on, he did not as much as whisper. He spoke to nobody, his visiting wife included, because he feared tapping that would be used at his trial. His last possession was the hijacked truck and he would give it to The Fist for the two-hundred-thousand-dollar debt the moment he could tell somebody where it was.

The Fist loved the idea of musical instruments. He had a fantastic feel for music. His all-time favorite song was "My Boy Lollipop." He loved the whole thing, including the millions he got on the recording.

Buster Greco also liked music: "Anyplace I go into got a juke box, I play it."

Buster was known as a prizefighter, a decent welterweight, although The Fist said he was "too small for his size." He also received great respect from all mobsters for the amount of work he did; the word *work* a synonym for *murder.* Buster had a reason for every single body; "Long overdue." He stuffed these bodies into large orange oil barrels that he kept in a neat line at one end of his junkyard in the Bronx.

He then weighted the drum with either cement or chains and dumped it into some water of his choosing that day.

This time, he arrived in court in time to see all six defendants seem to step on a third rail when a great big black woman called out, "They be guilty!" The guys rattled like stacked cups.

Buster took advantage of the confusion. He rushed to the gate in front of the pews and hissed to defendant Paschal. Paschal stepped backward and was within hearing distance. Buster said, "He wants to know."

Paschal turned his head and told Buster out of the corner of his mouth how to get the truck.

"No talking," the nearest marshal said. He waved at Buster, "You got to step back."

Paschal kept mumbling. "Fuck this. I don't want to go to jail. Anybody wants me to talk, I'm talking. I don't want to go to jail."

Soon afterward, two days later, Buster walked up to a loose tile in a service station in the Bronx, pulled it off, and took the many keys from behind it. He went to an abandoned commercial garage, with weeds growing in front. In the dimness inside was the gleaming trailer truck from Elkhart, Indiana. He worked the truck locks and opened the back doors to a solid wall of boxes, with the first row labeled "Beuscher Bari Sax."

He thought Bari meant the Italian region on the Adriatic, and this familiarity caused him to tear the box open and be confronted by a baritone saxophone that was a couple of inches taller than he was. The yellow sales tag tied to it said the instrument cost $2,250. He was thrilled. "I wonder who you sell these to?" he said. The second row of boxes were labeled as Selmer US Buescher trumpets. He took out one of them. The tag was for $550. "Beautiful!" He held it up to his mouth. "I wonder how long it takes to learn how to play this thing." Then he reminded himself that it all belonged to The Fist.

A day later, on appointment, Buster came to the clubhouse. Fausti was playing the pinball game.

He gave Fausti a shove and Fausti turned around with his hands up. Buster bobbed and weaved and had his hands flailing the air. Fausti threw a punch back and was blocked and Buster held on to him, laughing, when The Fist growled. Fausti went outside.

"What'd you see in court?"

"Nothin'."

"You didn't notice nothin'?"

"I saw him, you know, and I says to him —"

"He turned rat the minute he heard guilty," The Fist said. "He don't even get into the pens and he is crying to the fucking law.

"Fuck owes me two hundred thousand. They took him away and he rats."

"I didn't hear nothin'," Buster said. "Tole me nothin'. He was standin' there with all the bulls around him. Like I say, I tried to say something to him, but all the bulls and that."

"So you got nothin' from him?" The Fist said.

"I tole you. I tried. But not a fuckin' word."

"Owes me two hundred thousand. He got a truck someplace. Fuck. We're liable never to hear about it again."

When Buster came out, he passed Fausti, and when Fausti put up his hands to fool around, Buster took a swipe at him and walked on. Simultaneously, he was in fear and exultation. "How many trumpets they got in that truck," he wondered. "A couple of hundred, I bet."

1   You would never think that Greenwich Village, whose streets are famed for palette and pen, would be the home of the nation's biggest and most dangerous Mafia outfit. The Village daylight is an artist's assistant. Perhaps it is the metallic content of the old buildings that causes a reflection seen nowhere else in the city. Unlike so many other parts of New York, the Village sky has not yet been stolen. Stand on a Greenwich Village street in the early morning and see the night sky lighten and break into streaks of rose, and you envision life with an unclouded eye. The light and the artists using it made the Village famous, and deflected attention from a criminal mob that was started by Lucky Luciano and went through homicidal maniacs like Albert Anastasia and Caesar De Francisi and into the hands of the silent, deadly Fausti Dellacava, or The Fist.

The tenement streets of the Dellacavas' end at Washington Square park, where the sun glistens on the park's white marble arch — 77 feet high, 30 feet wide, and built in 1895 at a cost of $128,000, which at the time was enough to buy the Ukraine. Rosetta Dellacava and Gina Lauretano used to take their infants in carriages to the park and sit on benches alongside the arch as the children slept. Little Fausti was in one carriage. In the other was Concetta Lauretano. The two were never to get much farther apart.

The arch stands over the first signpost of Fifth Avenue, which begins its long stroll northward through the city's splendor. In the park around the monument, sunlight splashing onto lawns between walks turned the grass blinding green.

This glory is tarnished immediately by the history of the pin oaks, oriental planes, yellow locusts, ash, and American elm trees in the park that once were used as gallows, and people thronged to the park to see men swing for such heinous crimes as burglary, pickpocketing, and skin color.

The Village that became famous to America was formed by three migrations, the Italians first, then a second from the west of Ireland, and the third, Americans calling themselves bohemians. Into the narrow crooked streets of Greenwich Village, alleys really, came artists, philosophers, poets, writers, loungers, and air inspectors.

Washington Square is lined by buildings of New York University, many of them two-story Greek Revivals. The Greek Revivals form the north side of the park. On the east side is a bronze statue of Garibaldi, donated by the Italians of New York in 1888. On the ground floor of 100 Washington Square East is the Museum of Living Art, with Picasso's *The Three Musicians,* Léger's *The City,* and Mondrian's *Composition in White and Red.*

And there is a large, ugly NYU building, with a painful history: Sing Sing Prison convicts were used to cut the stones. On the east side of the square, number 22 Washington Place, now college buildings, was the address of a building that was hailed as completely fireproof in 1911. It housed the Triangle Shirtwaist factory on the eighth through tenth floors. One Saturday, thin paper hanging over blouse-making machines caught fire on the eighth floor. One hundred and twenty-six women and twenty men between the ages of thirteen and twenty-one were locked inside the factory to prevent them from leaving during the day's work. A sign on the wall read "If you don't come to work on Sunday, don't come on Monday." The fire then moved to the ninth-floor workroom, and the lint in the air exploded. Women in flames began jumping from the windows.

Some leaped into the elevator shaft and landed on the roofs of two small elevators. The bodies of young women slammed with the force of steel atop the elevators, driving the elevators into the basement, where they remained immobile.

As the fire engines had no ladder that could go over seven stories, all the young women on the higher floors jumped from the windows. Three held hands and leaped into the sky together. All these young women hitting the sidewalk caused a famous lead in the *World* newspaper:

Thud, Dead.
Thud, Dead.
Thud, Dead.

At Madame Blanchard's Rooming House, number 61 Washington Square South, the roomers at various times included Theodore Dreiser, Adelina Patti, Frank Norris, Stephen Crane, Willa Cather, John Dos Passos, James Oppenheim, Henri Matisse, René Dubos, and Alan Seeger. The Village is where Henry James wrote *Washington Square,* Washington Irving wrote "Legend of Sleepy Hollow," and Edgar Allan Poe wrote "The Fall of the House of Usher." Around at 133 MacDougal Street, there were Eugene O'Neill and Edna St. Vincent Millay. John Masefield scrubbed floors in Luke O'Connor's barroom up on Greenwich Avenue.

Once, in the NYU buildings, faculty member Morse experimented with telegraphy. Walt Whitman was in an upstairs room. This was more than well balanced by another faculty member, Samuel Colt, who perfected a revolver to shoot people. They call it the gun that won the West, but it came from two blocks off the West 4th Street subway.

When The Fist took over the streets only yards away from Colt's old housing, he decreed, which is the right word, that anybody caught with a gun on the block would be summarily executed. "A gun proves you got bad intentions." One of which could be to shoot The Fist. Anybody leaving his gun in his car, under the seat or in the glove compartment, also dies.

In other places they talk of gun control. On The Fist's street at all times there is nothing to control because there is no gun or there is no you.

The streets of Dellacava began as a black neighborhood. In 1860, number 218 Sullivan Street was the First African ME church. By 1879, it became the Colored Bethel church. The buildings were called tenements, with rooms no larger than packing cases. There were six and seven people in two small bedrooms, with a bathroom for the floor in the hall and a tub in the kitchen. The blacks held the buildings for only so long. In the annals of the city, blacks arrive, whites flee. Except in this succession, Italian immigrants took Sullivan and Thompson streets, with Lutherans slipping into two buildings, and the Italians said they were theirs forever. If you don't like it, then watch out. Exit Lutherans.

The Village, however, was worthy of its beginnings by the way bohemians were able to live and grow famous amidst Irish and Italians, the breeds most suspicious of outsiders, and capable at any odd moment of exploding into uncommon violence. Italians were comfortable with bohemians because they had less money and did not protest. Poor people rise in fury at any worthwhile protest. Always, the striker is despised.

The Irish living along the West Side docks were too naïve to believe that two men would share a room for any reason except to save rent. As for two middle-aged women living together, it was unthinkable, it was desperately sinful, for anybody to have a trace of suspicion of them being lesbians, about which the Irish knew nothing.

2

Rose Lopresti, the founding mother of the Dellacavas, came to these streets in 1920 from the nastiness of Naples. She came with a spirit and stubbornness that spilled out of her, and almost covered her scars from terror while young.

She was ten in Naples and she walked home from school along the narrow crooked streets to her home at Via Del Grande, 14. She went up five flights of stone steps to her apartment and walked cheerily into an explosion of grief. Moans and low screams came from every part of the large apartment. Her mother stood in the living room with arms flailing.

In an instant, Rose's childhood was gone.

The day before, her father, Antonio Lopresti, and a man named DioGuardia, who was with his wife and three children, had been in the doorway of the Lopresti Brothers pharmacy when three men ran up to a horse wagon on the near corner and blew the driver off his seat with shotguns. As the killers ran away, one glanced back and saw the DioGuardia family standing in terror in the pharmacy doorway. Directly behind them was Rose's father, Antonio Lopresti. He was as terrified as the people standing with him. He and they were eyewitnesses. The guy had his shotgun wrapped in a red shirt. That was visual proof of his insanity. The surviving baby could recall in open court seeing him run away with that color. The guy stopped and yelled to the two others. He pulled the shotgun out of the red cloth, reloaded, and started to run up to the pharmacy, the gun barrel rising. One of the others shouted the word *police*. The man put the shotgun and red shirt under his arm, shook his fist at the gray faces in the pharmacy doorway, and fled.

That night, the DioGuardia family, parents and children and an old aunt, were murdered as they slept. In the morning, when Lopresti was on his way to the pharmacy, groups of people were on every street corner talking in whispers about the murder in the daytime and the murders that followed at night. The newspaper, *Il Giornale di Napoli*, had a headline size used for war or famine: "ROSSA LUPARA!" The red shotgun.

Lopresti could not get enough breath to walk properly. At the corner in front of the pharmacy, a customer told him that strangers were around asking where Lopresti lived.

"I did not tell them the house where you live," the man said. "I only told them the street."

Instead of opening the pharmacy, Antonio Lopresti walked the narrow crooked streets with wash waving from all floors, up to the yellow brick Regina Pacis elementary school. A nun in the office said that a man who said he was a distant cousin of Rose's had come to pick her up, but the nun refused because Rose could not recognize him. Lopresti left his daughter in school, went to the pharmacy, wrote a note to his family saying he was doing this to save their lives, then put a shotgun into his mouth and blew his head from his body.

Now in the afternoon his family wailed in despair and pain that would show itself in many ways over a century.

At eighteen Rose Lopresti married Michele Dellacava. In Naples at this time there were no jobs and no social services and people begged for meals. For $165, they booked passage to New York on the steamship *Castel Gabriel* in the winter of 1920. The ship left Naples on an outgoing late afternoon tide, with the light blue water darkened by the long shadows of the mountains surrounding the harbor. On the third night out, in the North Atlantic, Rose and Michele were awakened by the crashing of a tin trunk, while baggage, clothing, and other belongings were flying off shelves and bunks. Rose slid from her bunk and tried to stand. The ship lurched, and the sudden bucking knocked her down. The deck tilted swiftly and by too many degrees to the starboard. There was another lurch and the bulkhead on the port side of the deck was tilting up to hit the roof and the starboard bulkhead was tilted so far down that it seemed only a few degrees from being vertical and plunging forever into freezing dark water. Rose was trying to hang on to the deck, the floor, and suddenly the gray metal ceiling over her head fell like a counterweight to the port side. The starboard climbed quickly. With the sound of a train accident the ship and the dormitories inside righted.

Suddenly, it all tilted again to starboard. The waves had the ship turned so that they pummeled the port side, and several times the ship almost capsized into the black water.

Rose got on her knees and promised the Lord that she would send her first son to the priesthood.

She said this aloud and had her husband repeat the promise.

Then the huge wave rolling under the ship lifted the rear of the ship so high the propellers churned wet air.

The storm lasted ten days, during which Rose and Michele Dellacava repeated their promise to their God to have their firstborn son become a priest.

The last angry roll of the ocean hit the ship as close to shore as the channel off Rockaway Beach. It stopped rolling in the great harbor. Rose Lopresti Dellacava saw the land of freedom from fear on the streets and opportunity, and she grabbed her husband's hand. It was here that she would raise her family.

She assured the Lord that calm waters did not mean that she would forget her promise to deliver a son to his ministry.

She and her husband went to cousins on West 3rd, which was a line of five-story tenements with three-room apartments of tiny rooms with ten and eleven people living in them, and the streets below packed with people from Naples.

Her husband, Michele Dellacava, had worked in a boot factory outside of Naples. Here in New York he worked as a tile setter. His wife took whatever work she could get in shops, a fruit stand, and then had her family.

Rose and Michele had three girls and two boys. The boys slept in one bed in the bedroom. They were the firstborn, Fausti, to grow up as The Fist, who had strep throats and yet a body that grew to become filled with danger for others. Larry was the second. The Fist and Larry were to last over half a century without having any significant brushes with the legitimate.

The three girls slept in the small living room. The parents slept in the space between the kitchen and the front door.

At the outset, to keep her promise made on a stormy sea, she encouraged her firstborn, Fausti, The Fist, to study for the priesthood.

"I'd rather join the army," The Fist said, and did. Actually, he was drafted. He was listed as doubtful at the Whitehall Street induction center when a doctor told him not to smoke during an examination and he attempted to put the cigarette out on the doctor's hand. He lasted three days at Fort Dix, during which time noncommissioned officers held a meeting and said they would not report for duty on the firing range if at any point in basic training The Fist was given a weapon that could shoot. An officer gave him discharge papers that said he had "Anti-Social Behavior" and put him on a troop bus going back to New York.

Rose then asked the Lord to accept the second son, Larry.

"Mama, I don't want to be a priest. I want to steal." She thought he was being puckish, which he was not. He gambled and stole all his life.

3 The Fist's children called him "Daddy." Fausti and all nieces and nephews called him "Uncle Fist." Suddenly, he announced that he didn't want to hear this Uncle Fist anymore. He stopped his tirade only to spit on the floor. That ended The Fist as a proper noun.

He passed a new law for anybody out on the street: Mention his name and lose your life. Just look up quickly, as if searching a rock ceiling, when you mean The Fist. Not a long look, either, for that might cause you to think you're appealing to God, and The Fist did not want to mix things up. Early, he had rationalized this: "I got my thing here, you got everything else," he told the sky. Therefore, no imploring looks at high altitudes. Just a quick flick.

Over the years, when needed, the mother would keep him in her apartment and line up shelves of medicine to prove he was too sick to commit crime. She listened to none of these stories coming off the streets about her son being around with Caesar De Francisi.

De Francisi had his headquarters for drugs, gambling, murder, and extortion at 178 Thompson Street. That was three blocks away from the Dellacava house. The Fist had to put a little legwork into starting in crime and during the walk actually had to resist the temptation of honesty. Those who lived close only had to tumble out of their beds and cross the narrow street to greet the devil. De Francisi was the Boss, from Naples and Palermo in Italy to New York, Philadelphia, Chicago, wherever gangsters congregated. An appearance by De Francisi on his home street, Thompson Street, caused people to run up and kiss him. If there had to be Italians in crime, then they had the most fearsome in the whole world.

"I am in the funeral supply business," De Francisi always said.

4 The Fist made it despite the most famous miss in the history of New York crime. They sent him out one Sunday night in 1957 to get Ernesto Basile Brady, the Boss of the De Francisi and Dellacava crew. Brady had a last drink on a Sunday night in a place called the Mount Etna on East 55th Street and then left for his home, the Monarch Apartments on Central Park West, from 71st to 72nd streets.

By now, The Fist had pulled up on the 72nd Street side of the Monarch building in a big new black limousine. You drive a broken-down car, the Monarch doorman locks the doors at first sight. The Fist parked in a bus stop because it was illegal. Always, your first obligation is to break the nearest law. Second, it also happened to be close. What do you want, he's on a shooting, not out delivering cartons of toothpaste to the drugstore when it would be all right to park half a block away. Leaving a murder, a short direct run with a minimum of commotion is advisable. Any sudden movement turns heads and produces fifty people telling a grand jury the color of your shirt.

The Fist is inside the Monarch with his gun. Outside, a common foot patrolman, Officer George Clarity, comes along 72nd Street and puts a parking ticket on this limousine in the bus stop. Officer Clarity resumes patrol.

Brady goes into the lobby. The Fist, as big as an elevator, appears in front of him and says, for all to hear, the doorman most prominently, "This is for you, Ernesto."

He fires once, Brady reels, and The Fist leaves.

But he had violated Mafia Street Rule One:

You do not say anything to the victim. You never give him an opportunity to take any evasive or defensive action. You don't shoot at anything over a foot away because then it becomes like golf putting, you miss more than you hit. What you do, you get as close as possible, preferably from behind, unseen, where you can get off a point-blank shot to the back of the head then turn and walk away. Just like that.

Practically the whole city knew that when The Fist walked out of the building he announced:

"I took him out in one."

He was off to the Village, with the parking ticket still on the limousine windshield.

The doorman, Norville, first said he could identify the shooter, after which he thought of his life and he announced he was legally blind and, as a matter of actual fact, he had trouble finding the front door handle, much less see a man shooting Ernesto Basile Brady. But he was clear on the aftermath. He remembered Brady shaking his head like a wet dog, taking a handkerchief from his breast pocket and patting the blood on the scalp over his right ear.

Going off-duty at midnight, Officer Clarity placed his traffic ticket in the pouch that went to the Central Traffic Administration. Homicide detectives would have it soon enough, don't worry. A traffic ticket is the number one reason major crimes are solved.

You could tell how much they thought of The Fist that nobody got mad when he missed like this. The Fist went on the lam. When he shot Brady, he weighed 340 pounds and figured that if he could lose fifty pounds, witnesses wouldn't recognize him if he sat in their living room. The Fist fled to Livingston, New Jersey, on the estate of Tony Scalfaro, who had the largest outdoor barbecue pit in the Americas. As you can't barbecue macaroni, The Fist wondered why he had such an enormous grill. He found that out on his second morning at the estate. Black smoke came from the grill.

"What are you cookin' this early?" The Fist asked two guys from Newark, who were standing many yards away from the barbecue.

"Bodies," one of them said.

This only helped The Fist pass up eating. When he was thirty-four pounds lighter, he took a cab over to the Manhattan headquarters on 36th Street and swaggered up to the desk. "Somebody tells me you was lookin' for me." The lawmen had the parking ticket waiting, but not the witness. "I never seen him," Brady testified.

5

One hot afternoon in 1968, just before Fausti was born, the cops raided a card game on MacDougal Street and arrested the Dellacava father, Michele.

Michele's son Larry, who was to be Little Fausti's father, ran around the corner as the police were about to yank Michele and several others into a wagon.

"Officer, let me take his place," Larry said. "He's my father. He's old. What's it matter, you get one guy, you get another."

"Yeah, yeah. Take my son," Michele, the father, said. "He's strong. Take him in and let me go."

The moment Larry saw this, his father grasping with great excitement the idea of his son going into a jail cell on his behalf, he walked off. The father went to the station house.

Later, Larry shouted at his father, "I'm going to name my next son Michele and smack him around every day." The father shrugged. "Go ahead. It won't hurt me." Larry never named either of his two sons Michele, although it was unheard-of in any family not to have a male named after the grandfather. When Fausti was born, Larry told The Fist, "I'm naming him for you."

"Don't do that," he told his brother.

The Fist thought it was a dangerous name. Right up to Fausti's baptism, The Fist insisted the name Fausti Dellacava had a bad history to it, and shouldn't be used.

"The name got a curse on it," he said.

There had been a Fausti killed in Reggio, in Calabria, and unfortunately for a good reason, and then here in New York Fausti, also known as The Fist, popularized the name in every paper that was printed.

"I'm naming him for you," Larry said.

In the pale late Sunday afternoon light of Miraculous Medal Church, The Fist promised on Fausti's behalf to renounce the

Devil and all his evil and pomp. He made no such claim about his own intentions, although he did see the danger in falling for pomp. Evil was all right, but pomp destroys. Still this royal name of the underworld went through the air like a chant to herald Fausti's approach wherever he was.

Growing up, wherever Fausti went, the name caused people to look. Vinny's grandmother shopped at the Grand Union on Bleecker Street, and Vinny came along to carry packages. Everybody on Bleecker Street knew who she was and who her sons were. In the store, she ripped off all outer leaves of lettuce. Going deeper, tearing and ripping, until she was absolutely sure there was nothing left that either was tinged, or wasn't such great lettuce to her touch.

"*Pago solamente per quello chez mangio,*" she told the checkout women. "I only pay for what I eat."

Fausti, carrying packages home, was happy when people pointed to his grandmother and whispered, "Dellacava." That means me, too, Fausti told himself.

The sidewalks always were light under his step. Going past Cardinales's Meat Market, he would wave and call to the two Cardinale brothers, "Mister." One of them would wave and say, "That's Larry's son — and the other guy's nephew."

Then here was Mickey Jap's candy store.

Wave, smile, and Mickey saying, ". . . And the other fellow's nephew."

And Mario the butcher and the woman in the fruit store and on through the smiles and greetings that had gladness on his face through all early years. Fausti, nephew, bursting with energy, made his grandmother proud.

6

Larry Dellacava came to Sullivan Street with the dog that the uncle had promised to nephew Fausti. It was a German shepherd who already weighed one hundred pounds and had a head as big as a front end. "His name is Malocchio," The Fist said. Fausti's father sent the dog for paper training and the like to Captain John's dog school way up on First Avenue in East Harlem, the headquarters of the Army of the North of The Fist's organization. Knowing the dog's connections, John slept in the office in order to be close at all times to his client. Malocchio's left ear was up, the right ear permanently folded in half at the top. There was no way to change that.

The dog came back and ran around Little Fausti's apartment with his tongue hanging. He flew with joy onto Fausti's chest, covering it with his fur. Almost immediately, Fausti had to go into the bathroom and throw up. The allergy would not subside. The doctor had Fausti walk the dog to the Concerned Lutherans. The dog jumped all over The Fist, who ruffled the bristly hair fondly. His friend Natale Grassi had two German shepherds at his house in New Jersey, and The Fist liked to wrestle with them.

The effort and details that The Fist put into this dog caused many to assume that Fausti was the favorite and his future said "Boss."

Every Monday, which was steak night at his grandmother's, Fausti brought a steak bone up to Malocchio. The dog slept in smoke so thick in the clubhouse that he had to be tied up outside so he could breathe. He instantly hated any black he noticed on the street. In this, Malocchio only reflected the street. Tied to the railing of the entrance to the clubhouse steps, he would watch blacks with insane anger. It now was apparent that the dog had a sociological makeup that, while delightful to The Fist — "He wants to chew up moulognones" — was not conducive to getting along in a pluralistic society.

Let a black so much as tiptoe onto the street and Malocchio would be off the sidewalk faster than a bird, and in furious anger, fighting leash or anybody holding him. To be somewhat fair to the dog, he hated anybody in uniform, too. A uniform was strange, and therefore an enemy. When the mailman arrived each day, the fear and hatred of uniform was instant.

One chill midmorning, Malocchio bit a quiniela: a black delivery man in a gray uniform.

When he complained to the club, the delivery man was told that he could go and fuck himself.

When the delivery man came back with the police, there were apologies and some money paid to the delivery man, who was sent to Dr. Leonard Warren, the official family doctor for the De Francisi organization.

And Malocchio went back to duty in front of the club.

Whites could stream by. Malocchio dozed. He awaited uniform or black.

A black guy with a big box radio walked on the same sidewalk where Malocchio was crouched like a guerrilla. Wild tan-black eyes riveted on the black with the radio. When the guy got close, Malocchio bit the guy's leg.

A city Department of Health inspector came and issued a summons for Malocchio. This was the second assault charge against him. The inspector said that the next bite would be the dog's last; any dog found guilty of biting three times must be destroyed.

He now bit a black woman on the leg. She had a name, hospital records, and a lawyer. She said she absolutely could identify the dog because she remembered vividly that his right ear was folded in half.

Two health department inspectors and an animal shelter veterinarian arrived with a warrant for Malocchio's arrest.

At the club, the veterinarian put a leash and muzzle on Malocchio.

"Preventive detention," the inspector said. "He goes on trial next week."

"Who trial?" Natale Grassi asked. He was a real man who was born on Houston Street and spent his life with one foot in Atlanta.

"Capital punishment trial," the inspector said. "Three bites and you're out. Exterminated. That's a city law."

The Fist stuck out his hand, which had bills crushed inside. The inspectors backed away. "You wouldn't believe the heat on this case," one inspector said.

"This is to turn off the radiator," The Fist said.

"I can't risk nothin'," the man said.

When they left, The Fist made Grassi repeat three times exactly what he had seen and heard. Of course he was there for all conversation. He still wanted to be certain that he had missed no nuance. Fausti came running into the club with harsh tears running down his cheeks. The Fist never was quick to comfort. Besides, this was more important, a matter of mob history. He and every single gangster worth his life knew the names of the seven who were blown away in the St. Valentine's Day massacre. "There wasn't a one of them wasn't long overdue," The Fist told himself. But the whole squad of machine gunners that day did not touch the German shepherd who was in the garage. They had no trouble killing the seven bastards, but there was no way they were going to shoot the German shepherd. Why would you do that? What did the dog do that was so wrong? Nothing. Fuck these seven guys. Blow them away. But give the dog a pat on the head and leave.

If they had shot the dog, The Fist always pointed out, the dog wouldn't have been able to bark so much that people came and discovered the massacre. If they had shot the German shepherd, nobody would have heard of the St. Valentine's Day massacre, he figured. They'd find skeletons ten years later. If they didn't shoot the dog then, in the biggest hit in American history, that means you're supposed to take care of all German shepherds.

"You know the name of the German shepherd?" The Fist asked the club.

"Lucky," somebody said.

"The name was Hi Ball. You know where he got it from? The garage mechanic, Murphy. He used to work in the railroad yards. The trains used to Hi Ball it out of there."

In the matter of Malocchio, the extent of The Fist's efforts made many think that the kid was the future chief.

The Fist began by strolling up to the New York University Law School rear entrance on West 3rd Street. It happens to be about seventy-eight feet from the club to the back of the law school, a redbrick wall with trees and bushes hanging from a long balcony. The building's front entrance faces the splendor of Washington Square park.

The law school is considered a good one. One graduate, Giuliani, was at this time a clerk for a judge. Whenever a black came in to deliver coffee, he shook like a clothes dryer. Many go on to become assistant United States attorneys. Wearing the three-piece suit of an old man, they proudly prosecute members of the De Francisi crime family, Fist Dellacava, official Boss.

Following which, and this is why The Fist knew right from the start that they were all no fucking good, most of them would turn around, become defense lawyers, and take all the money from The Fist and his people.

At the same time, just by looking at the law school building, he knew they never would stop coming, one year after the other. So you stop them one year, the fuckers come back with more the next year.

Every night, as he did now, The Fist urinated on the wall of the law school.

"I piss on lawyers," he said.

This time, he used a pay phone inside the law school that he believed was untapped, to call Feinstein, the lawyer who had walked him in a big attempted murder case. Feinstein now said, "You want me to cross-examine people over a dog? That is an insult."

The Fist told Feinstein that he would die.

"I'm only thinking aloud," Feinstein said. What he really meant to say was that if he appeared for a dog it would so diminish his stature that the next time he was called upon to defend The Fist, he would be markedly weakened in the eyes of judge and jurors. For this dog case, he recommended a new lawyer, Lawrence Sloane, who took the case because he felt morally compelled to feed his family. Not only would The Fist pay this time, but if he won there would be many cases in the future.

Even if it was a dog, it still was a capital punishment case, the first of his life, and along with the opportunity to become a star, Sloane also knew that if he lost, the dog might be the least to die. He felt his best defense would be to have Malocchio put in a lineup with other German shepherds. Sloane hoped that it would be virtually impossible for the woman to pick out the right dog. Unless Malocchio had distinguishing marks. "I think I'll take a look at my defendant," Sloane said.

The Fist mused. Malocchio had that right ear that flopped in half. The black broad could fucking remember that.

That night, the lone security guard at the animal shelter on the East River strolled to answer the bell. At the door, glaring at him from beneath his black cap was The Fist. With him were Baldy Dom, Quiet Dom, and Dom Dom, a mob afterthought in a Texas Western University jacket.

"He can't sleep account of his dog," Baldy Dom told the guard. "His dog is named Malocchio."

The guard looked at his roster. "He's on death row. Nobody can see him. We don't want people visiting him. It makes it harder on everybody if he loses the case and we have to kill him inside."

The Fist whispered to Baldy Dom, who said to the guard, "He says he don't want to see anybody die around here, including right now."

The security man's eyes opened wide. This was not a time of beepers and cell phones. If you wanted help, you screamed. A man strangled could not do this. The guard could figure that out. Baldy Dom put fifty dollars into his hand and that made it even easier. When the guard brought Malocchio out, Baldy Dom told him, "We're good people. We'll have him back in an hour."

In the car, all the Doms pounded Malocchio hello.

They drove the dog over to the house in New Jersey, where Natale Grassi's wife gave them one of her German shepherds, Tony, who had two good ears. They left Malocchio with the one ear down.

Tony was a stand-up German shepherd. He did not whine

when he was walked into the shelter under the name of Maloc-chio and was put on death row for a crime he never committed.

The Fist decided it was better that Sloane didn't know about the switch. "Never tell a fighter he's going to win a fixed fight. Let the guy think he's King Kong, he scores a knockout."

On trial day, Father Paul of St. Joseph's said a prayer. He was ancient and smirked when his pastor told him to steer clear of these mobsters. "O Lord, what would you have us do with this dog Malocchio. He bites people and has no soul or conscience so he doesn't even know what he does. But if he gets the chair it would wound young Fausti terribly. I know I shouldn't be asking for a dog to be saved. But I must for this kid."

Only a tearful and fearful Fausti, with Baldy Dom as escort, was allowed to wait in the lobby of the Health Department building on Worth Street.

Inside, there was a hearing officer at the desk in a bare room. The female complainant was there. The hearing officer had ASPCA men bring in three German shepherds. One was supposed to be Malocchio, with the prominent folded ear. Actually it was Tony of New Jersey, of the two stand-up ears. The other two lineup dogs, each with normal ears, were brought by the Health Department veterinarian.

Sloane asked the woman three questions.

"Were you bitten in front of 250 Sullivan Street?"

"Yes."

"Do you realize that if the defendant Malocchio is determined to be guilty, he will be executed?"

"Yes."

"Very well. I ask you to identify the dog who bit you."

The woman looked for some time at the three dogs. They were triplets to the eye.

"This is a cheap trick," she yelled.

"Thank you."

The innocent Tony was returned to Jersey and Malocchio, excited by Fausti's presence in the backseat, rode back to the Con-cerned Lutherans. There, Fausti presented Malocchio as a heroic figure. He was put on a shortened chain leash so he couldn't bite anymore, although he tried and would continue to do so.

7

Con, for Concetta, who came from the carriage in the park next to Fausti, saw him only sporadically in the Miraculous Medal school, which had separate entrances and lives for boys and girls. She was twelve now, and she was one flight up from her apartment at 331 Thompson Street, at her aunt Rosie's, watching television, when the kitchen erupted. It was over the discovery of another woman. Aunt Rosie's husband, who had gone out for a walk after dinner on the night before, returned in the brightness of the noon hour as if the world owed him love. "I went over to the library and read something," he said.

"You went over to see your whore," she said.

She did not realize that she was insulting his second wife. Ten years ago, he had gone to Maryland somewhat surreptitiously and married the second woman. That was before The Fist opened things up. What right did Rosie have to call this woman who was his wife a whore?

He hit her. Nice. She broke a big green glass soda bottle on the sink. Two long glass splinters stuck out from the shattered bottle. Con came running in just in time to see the aunt grip that bottle with two hands and go after this fuck of a husband with those long green fingers of broken glass. Con thought she should shriek. She shrieked. Then again. The husband put a hand out to stop the aunt. The aunt bent and went for the groin. He spun and had his back to Rosie. She took what she could get. She wasn't sure what she was hitting, but she knew that broken glass was going into something. One, two, three times. He howled so loud that Con no longer felt any need to add her own. The aunt's bottle was stuck onto something. It took eighty-six stitches to close the back.

He said to Rosie, tearfully, "I'll never do it again."

"No kidding," Rosie said.

Con told everybody she knew. She stood in front of Miraculous Medal school, on the last day of the term, and told the story slowly and in a hushed voice that rose dramatically when she came to the great part, the bottle going into the back, and had everybody around her shivering with glee.

When she saw Fausti crossing Carmine Street to make it to school, she ran up to him and said she had something confidential to tell him. She then repeated the story.

A week later, the aunt took Con to a house a cousin was renting in Bradley Beach, New Jersey. After dinner, Aunt Rosie gave Con ten dollars and sent her with the other kids to the amusement park, hoping she would forget what had happened up in the city. Con told everybody about how her aunt had almost sliced through the husband's neck so that the head was about to fall off.

One morning a year and a half later, Aunt Rosie's sainted husband, Peter, was down in the living room. Rosie yelled down the stairs for help and Con came running up from downstairs. Rosie felt for his pulse. His wrist was as lifeless as a shirt cuff. She put a hand on his heart. Nothing. She took a makeup mirror from the bathroom and held it to his mouth. Nothing. No sign of even a good-bye sigh.

"I guess I know what this is," she said to herself.

She left Con with the dead body. "Don't look at him, look at a television show." Then she ran down to West 3rd, past the tree where she shot dice when she was young, ran past the law school, on an errand that was basic to all of law: get to the bank before some rat put a brick on the cash and said that because of death, the box could be opened only by the probate court and the state tax collector. The clerk gets a $1,000 bounty, and somebody like Aunt Rosie is left with forms to fill out.

In a safe deposit box there was $264,000 in cash, and bearer bonds worth $30,000, along with several pieces of jewelry, a couple of them so hot you could cook over them, and the rest, big ones, too, legitimate. Now she could call 911 for her husband.

At eight o'clook on the funeral morning, the aunt took Con to the coffee shop and got two containers of coffee, a hot chocolate, and a pack of Marlboros. She walked in her black dress up to Bleecker, and Palumbo's Funeral Home.

She gave Johnny Palumbo one of the containers of coffee and the hot chocolate to Con. Rosie took a chair alongside the casket and lit a cigarette. She stared through the smoke in the empty dim chamber at her husband. Then she told Con to go out to the lobby and wait for her.

She turned to the casket. "Peter, you're a fucking moron."

"I guess he fucked you," Palumbo said.

"Look what you did, Peter," she said. "You fucking died and left me alone. You're a dirty filthy bastard."

"I got to agree with her," Palumbo said.

"You got no fucking class at all," Aunt Rosie said. "Look at you. Fucking dead. Peter, you prick you, you leave your wife alone for the rest of her life and you call yourself a man?"

They buried him out of Miraculous Medal with pallbearers trudging and old women saying rosary beads. Except for Con, there were no kids there, including Fausti. "They'll have enough of fucking funerals," Fausti's father said.

On the way to the cemetery, Aunt Rosie talked as she smoked. "Doesn't he come up with another wife. He'd go out early Sundays, I'd say, 'Where the hell are you going?' He'd say, 'Oh, I got big players I got to meet up with.' So I say, 'How come you got a suit and tie, you never do that with me.' He says, 'It's Sunday, maybe I go by a church, I stop in, show respect for the Lord.' Some respect. Lousy bastard had his girlfriend on Sunday. Girlfriend? Huh. Don't Peter go and marry her down Maryland. You know how long ago? Ten years. Con, remember this filthy rotten bastard. These men, you think you're really married to them."

At the graveside at Oak Grove Cemetery on Queens Boulevard, Rosie was looking around as the priest intoned. "I'm waiting. I'm just waiting for this wife to come around, she needs money."

She did not wait long. A woman with tear-darkened cheeks walked up hesitantly and stood on the fringe of the small crowd.

She was a couple of steps away from a new grave ready for the morning's next funeral.

When the ceremony was over, Rosie talked to the fresh dirt. "Peter, you die and leave me alone. You never let nobody know you had another wife. You lousy fuckin' bastard."

She seemed distracted as she walked away from the grave, going right past the other wife. Or almost. Suddenly, Aunt Rosie bumped into the other woman and pushed her right into the open grave.

"Die with him!" she yelled.

Con couldn't wait to get home and tell everybody. She told Fausti about this, and it was fine gossip that held his attention for fifteen minutes, after which he was off and moving on his street, Sullivan Street, which gave him so much excitement.

8

Then, deep of a summer night, Con's mother was upstairs sick and her aunt Lucille, unnerved by her niece's stricken face, told the kid to go out for a while. Con and Fausti were sitting in front of the house when Fausti's father, Larry Dellacava, came by in a car.

"You ever been to the fish market?"

They shook their heads.

"Go tell her aunt the two of you are with me."

He drove them crosstown to the bulkhead over the night-black East River. The lights from two bridges splashed diamonds onto the water. They were on South Street, where Franklin D. Roosevelt shook hands with men in mackinaws, held up fish for pictures that went into a nation's schoolbooks, including those of both young people in the car.

As Larry led the kids through the narrow spaces between the fish stands, workers called him and he waved. Of course they knew the Mafia. The street was closed to traffic at 10 P.M. and there were

· 36 ·

a thousand or so fish handlers under outdoor lights as big as spotlights, with fish on sparkling beds of ice. Selling wholesale orders until midmorning.

A man with a fedora turned a large brown paper bag upside down on a wet metal table and shook money out as if emptying it into a coffee grinder. Larry waved his hand at Ralph. The man put it all back into the paper bag. Larry handed it to Fausti, who held it like groceries. "Breaking him in," he yelled. The guy at the table said, "It's all there."

Larry said, "If it ain't, then we'll count you out."

Of course Fausti was not shocked. His father's assurance to him that there was no Mafia, and he certainly wasn't in it, had died with time. When you don't go to work on a job for three years running, the son no longer questions. They walked through stacked boxes of Atlantic salmon from Peru and fresh tilapia from Costa Rica, king crabs and snow crabs from Korea, brought in by air freight planes and trucks.

Larry led them over to the river bulkhead, where the last of the commercial fishing smacks sat in the water along the bulkhead. The fishermen polluted the water with so much waste that most had been banned. One old smack sat rusty and greasy, with a table piled with the silver bellies of fish.

"Stripers?" Larry said.

A man in rubber overalls held up a large shining silver fish with green lines running from mouth to tail. Larry took it.

On the way back to the car, Larry stopped at a heavy kid in a Yankee baseball cap and a lot of sweatshirts. Plunging his raw red hand into a mound of ice, he felt around, deep in the ice, and brought out a salmon. His hand was flaming red and wet in the freezing night air.

Fausti's father shook his head no. The bare hand plunged the fish back deep into the ice. Fausti shivered. He would remember it forever.

Driving home, Larry had the paper bag on the seat next to him. "Once a week off him. Then there's a hunnert others. It's good, isn't it?" he said.

In the backseat, Con said very quietly, and aimed at Fausti: "Jail."

Larry stopped at the Village Garden, which was closed, and he tapped on the window. A woman looked out, nodded, and came to the door. The two spoke animatedly.

"Girlfriend," Con said in the car.

"Not my father."

"All the fathers," she said.

"No, not my father."

"All of them, my aunt and my mother say."

Her mother died and her father married a woman who had been at the cemetery. Con went with him and his new wife to Yonkers. She and Fausti were in different universes through high school, although every time Fausti saw her brother he asked for her.

9

The Mafia lived in the most powerful of illusions, that a Family at home existed with church and Sunday dinners, without shattering discords. You shriek in delight for a baby. You kill for an aunt. You love your wife and her mother and they love you and everybody lives in joyous shouting, good people at a dinner table. Their belief that this was their life was total. This was fable enough, but then they went and carried Family and its meaning to their underworld life. Every time the guys got together in a restaurant, somebody was missing and had been for a couple of days due to strangulation. But this only meant that there was one less Family member at this particular meal and his absence was unmentioned during the hearty uproar.

The Fist made one shift in the lives of the Mafia warriors that could not have been accomplished by an earthquake.

This started when The Fist was blindsided by love. One warm night in 1963 he went to the Feast of San Gennaro, a street carnival on Mulberry Street, in Little Italy, and met a woman named Carmella Bella, who lived on the block. That she had the same first name as his wife intrigued him. He asked her out and she answered no, he was married. That is all that he had to hear, somebody telling him no. He pursued the second Carmella until she went out with him, and did many more times. Soon, he ran a rough hand across his life to make room for what was surely going to be a long and large romance; he would have it no other way. They moved into an apartment on Mulberry. Ten blocks away, on Bleecker, the married Carmella and what would become their three children lived. He had three children on Mulberry Street with Carmella Bella. Their love was their wedding license. He had no better plan at first than to shuttle back and forth like a bus between families in cramped apartments.

All the time living in illusion that one family or two families, it still meant Family. When the first child of this new union, a boy, was born, some people on Sullivan and on Bleecker heard about it, but had no proof and therefore did not talk about it. To die over a rumor is a total waste. They never heard of other births.

And The Fist put all craftiness and effort into keeping his double life secret.

It fell apart on the day when Fausti's Aunt Dolly took him shopping with her, so he could carry bundles. He was nine. They were on Hester Street, which had great fabrics, but one obstacle that bristled with unfathomable danger. Hester crossed Mulberry one block below Grand, which was all right except Mulberry and Grand was the home of the second Carmella and *fils,* a family and nest that was supposed to be secret. After shopping for cloth, Dolly took Fausti into a store that had a tray full of peppers and egg. "Yeah!" Fausti said. Aunt Dolly ordered two peppers-and-egg sandwiches. While she gave the counterwoman a ten-dollar bill, Fausti grabbed his sandwich off the counter and immediately took big bites.

"Fausti, wait until we get to the park. All you Dellacavas eat like savages."

The woman behind the counter stopped counting out Dolly's change. "Is he Dellacava? Fausti?"

The woman came out from behind the counter excitedly.

Dolly was just this little bit late in putting her foot atop Fausti's to silence him.

"Yeah!" Fausti said.

"Fist Dellacava?" Dolly said, playing immigrant, and thus ignorant of the rule about using the name.

"From Sullivan Street. Are you from Sullivan Street?" she asked Fausti.

"No, Bleecker. Sullivan is the next corner."

Dolly's foot pressed harder. It made no difference.

"You know Dellacava? The Fist? Larry Dellacava?"

"My name is Fausti Dellacava."

"Whose son?"

"No, Larry's my father. The Fist is my uncle. Why, who are you?"

Dolly cut in and said in Neapolitan that she was only here from Naples for two months and that she didn't know anybody with such a name as Dellacava or The Fist.

The woman said to Fausti, "Carmella Bella is my daughter. You know her?"

"I know my aunt Carmella," Fausti said. "Carmella Dellacava. Sometimes she uses Fist." Dolly summarily ended the talk by pulling Fausti out. Walking home, Dolly told the kid, "People want to know your business. So you tell them nothing. If the sun is out, say it's raining."

Three days later Stefano Geraci came to Dolly's door.

His eyes flicked quick up and down. "He wants to see you."

"He can see me here anytime."

"No, he wants to see you at the club."

"At the club? Why?"

"He makes it an official sitdown."

"A sitdown. Are you fuckin' crazy?"

"I'm sorry, Dolly. You got to come."

Just for a moment, Dolly became frantic. What could she have done to be called to a sitdown?

She went with Geraci down to the club and he stayed outside

while she walked down the basement steps. Oh, of course these people would kill their own mothers, why do you think everybody fears them?

"Siddown, Dolly," The Fist said.

"What the fuck for?" she said. Tension did not dissolve her spirit.

The Fist ordered everybody out of the room. None could recall such a scene as this, a woman walking into the smoke and sinister silence of the headquarters of all crime in the nation.

Still, Dolly would not cower. "You better have a fuckin' reason for this," she told The Fist.

"You went to Hester Street," The Fist said.

"And?"

"You was in the store there."

"What do you have, a spy?"

"I know everything," The Fist said. "I know you was with Fausti and you both had peppers-and-egg sandwiches."

"Yeah, so?"

"And the woman behind the counter was talkin' to you."

"She tried. Nosy fuckin' bitch. She got nothin' from me."

"From the kid?"

"You got to ask him."

"I better never hear that you go over there and start talkin' to that woman. That better never fuckin' happen ever."

Dolly was angered. "I know you all my life. You put the bull on me? Who the fuck do you think —"

"Dolly," he said, suddenly softening, "you have to do me a deep, personal favor. It's important for my whole life. You got to promise me from the heart that you won't never go nowhere near Hester Street again."

When she hesitated, he leaned over and gave her a kiss on the cheek.

"Please. You got to do it for me."

"All right. But what's so important about it?"

"Dolly, please. Don't ever ast me that. Don't ever say nothin' about us talkin' here."

Dolly said, "The trouble starts with the kid's name. The second she heard 'Fausti' she was all over us."

He shook his head. "I said the name was no fuckin' good."

The Fist thought he could live his life surrounded by smoke through which nobody could exactly see, and if the smoke parted a trifle, and they did happen to catch a glimpse of his life as it was, they would look away and pretend they had noticed nothing. Yet in the next instant, he could feel a cold wind blowing every wisp of smoke away and leaving him open for all to see. Particularly his mother, who, upon hearing a story about her son's behavior, cried out, "A girl, all right. But a baby!"

He pretended not to know that he had no protection at all from somebody from anywhere asking in passing a question like "Does The Fist have two wives?"

The Fist had to accommodate two smiling families at Christmas, one on Grand and Mulberry, the other on West 3rd Street, where he observed Christmas Eve, with its fish dinner and cases of Tattinger's kept in the cold in the bare courtyard outside the kitchen window. On Christmas morn, he would go to his second family at Grand and Mulberry. Everybody loved him, and he loved them, and at times such as these he felt supreme. His illusionary power as the Boss of crime gave him a belief in nothing beyond himself.

10

Fausti walked into his uncle's club one day to find boxes of candy bars stacked against all the walls. There were maybe a couple of thousand Best Ever candy bars. The candy bar, long and heavy with nuts and chocolate, is made almost exclusively for fund-raising events of Catholic grammar schools. There are supposedly only 320 calories in each bar. This is like weighing only the front end of a truck. City Catholics, most prominently great big fat Italians and Puerto Ricans, seem to be the only strains interested in eating something like this. Except that a crew-cut Polish kid from St. Stanislaus in Greenpoint ate a record entire box of them one night.

The market for the Best Ever chocolate bar is mainly religious halls, and the wrappers are marked for the specific church. The candy bars this time were marked for the fair at St. Luke's School, where The Fist had three children nobody knew about by his girl-friend, Carmella Bella — the second Carmella of his life.

St. Luke's was one of the four Catholic churches and elementary schools within a few blocks of each other in the Village. Every morning, Baldy Dom Cataldo came around in a Cadillac and picked up the three Bella kids at Mulberry, where The Fist lived with the second Carmella, and drove them to St. Luke's. At three o'clock each day, Baldy Dom picked up the three kids at St. Luke's and brought them home to Mulberry Street.

The Fist's official family attended Miraculous Medal Church, west on Bleecker Street, in the heart of the old Italian Village. The church is Italian by look, light yellow brick and with two gold-domed steeples that can be seen for blocks. St. Anthony's, on the corner of Houston Street, is a huge gloomy building that serves all faithful living to the south of Houston.

As Fausti lived north, he was sent to Miraculous Medal grammar school, where all the neighbors' children, as Italian as a vowel, shook the remnants of Naples out of their speech.

At lunchtime, he roamed for an hour, often to a pizza stand on Sixth Avenue, which was a block and a half from the Miraculous Medal school and about twenty-five yards from St. Luke's, which, particularly at lunchtime, was to become forbidden ground for Fausti.

"Don't ever go over to St. Luke's," his father told Fausti one day. "The worst rats in the world are over there. There are all bad people. Terrible people there. Don't you dare ever go there."

For an Italian, that was a fair description of St. Luke's parish, which took its religion with a great dose of middle-class Irish snobbery. Fausti could understand why they told him to stay away from such miserable people. Irish snobs at St. Luke's. The other Irish church, St. Veronica's, was on the waterfront and served longshoremen and their families, and therefore they could look down on nobody.

However, the stencil on the side of all these Best Ever bars on The Fist's clubhouse floor said they were for delivery to St. Luke's.

Fausti said to the uncle, "I thought you said we shouldn't go by St. Luke's."

"You better not. Why are you saying that?"

"Because the candy," he said, pointing.

When The Fist realized that he had convicted himself on his own evidence, he put his head down and looked at the cards and talked no more.

What good was anything if you did not have secrecy? He saw in his mind a barricade collapsing with a great noise, leaving two families, each with three children, standing for all to see.

There seemed no way to nullify this kid's curiosity, which had everybody wary at all times.

"He stands here and he listens to two, three conversations at once," Baldy Dom said in the club one day. "He could be dangerous." Later, Fausti's father told him, "We tell you about St. Luke's, didn't we? So I'm telling you again right now. Go over to St. Luke's, you'll get your ass kicked."

Of course on the first night of the church fair at St. Luke's, Fausti was there early and he was talking to a kid in the church basement and the kid said, "Your name is Dellacava? The Fist's son goes here."

The kid pointed out a dark-haired young man.

Fausti walked right over to him. "My name is Fausti Dellacava. What's your name?"

"I'm Robert Bella," the kid said.

"Then why are you telling people that Fausti Dellacava is your father?"

"Because The Fist is my daddy."

When the kid said this, said aloud the name most feared, The Fist, Fausti felt as if he had both feet on the third rail.

"And I know who you are," Robert said. "You're Larry's son."

Fausti was bewildered and angry to find this kid was experiencing great pleasure by knowing more than he did. How could anybody know more than he did? His new cousin, Robert Bella, now explained that The Fist was his mother's partner, and that there were two younger girls out of the union. He said they lived on Mulberry.

The next day, Fausti walked into the club, took a Best Ever bar out of his pocket, with the St. Luke's wrapper, and said:

"I saw this kid Robert Bella last night and he told me we were cousins."

The Fist said nothing. He stared at Fausti once, and scared him forever. Fausti never thought it was the same with his uncle after that.

Fausti thought he had done nothing wrong, but he realized the uselessness of this. If The Fist was certain that you had crossed him, then you were guilty. Instead of using the sidewalk in front of the Concerned Lutherans, he began hanging out at Nini Scalfaro's candy store, which was hunched down in the presence of Miraculous Medal, towering, ominous, only a few steps across the narrow street. In the front of the store were two pay phones. On the corner was Sixth Avenue, wide and from the din came exhaust as thick as a carpet. On the far side, up at the corner of Houston, was a playground of asphalt that ran a block long, running up from Sixth Avenue. Fausti's West Side team played Sundays in a touch football league at the park. The West Side team wore blue shirts bought at Johnny's T Shirt City on Bleecker Street. On this Wednesday before the West Side team and the hated Sixth Ward, or East Side, were scheduled to play, city workers came into the park at Houston Street to do some kind of work. Fausti noticed them, thought nothing of it, and went into the candy store.

It was a candy store out of the past, crammed and disorderly, a business of pennies made in a haphazard arena. Snickers candy bars, flip-top Marlboros, fashion magazines, a paper container of coffee and a bagel, cases of Coke and Evian water. Nini carried Evian because he figured that made him new, and also because he knew that these fools bought drinking water when they lived in a city that had the best water on earth, and therefore he would take them with a good marked-up bottle of nothing. Newspapers were inside the front window, magazines along the wall, and the narrow space between magazines and counter was made only for the young. They could sway back or forward to make room for somebody trying to squeeze past. Let an old guy stand there and the smallest child couldn't get by.

At the back of his store, almost hidden by stacks of Evian water boxes, was a slot machine that one of the steady players, Liliana Angela, was working. She and her sister, Marie, split their times on the machine, each playing for hours, betting in multiples of two dollars a try. One played, the other stayed home. Usually, one would win $200, the other would replace her and lose $400. There was one day when Liliana let her mind fly out the window and, betting eight dollars at a time, she blew $1,500. She was still at it when Nini closed the store. Under house rules, she was the only one permitted to play the next morning. In she came, wary but brave. She caught the machine when it was programmed to pay and soon won back twelve of the fifteen hundred.

When he came to the store on Friday, Fausti saw that workers had dug up one end of the playground, cutting off most of the end zone at the Sixth Avenue end. The teams decided to play over on the East Side, on Baxter Street, right behind the Criminal Court building.

Fausti was excited about playing against his new cousin, Robert Bella. When Larry Dellacava heard this, he went up to the club and told the brother. Who then called for Fausti.

"You can't go to no East Side to play," The Fist said.

"So I don't go," Fausti said.

"Tell everybody else they can't go there."

"Where they supposed to play the game?"

Fausti told him about the end zone. After hearing three slow recountings, The Fist drew on a pad a new field that made a right turn on the ten-yard line. "You pretend you're turnin' a corner," The Fist decreed.

The right turn was an interesting idea, although the turn was into the basketball courts. Standing ominously after the turn were three baskets mounted on heavy metal poles.

When the East Side team arrived, Fausti looked for his new cousin, Robert Bella.

His father told Fausti, "He won't be here. He got told not to be here. You can't go there and he can't come here."

Everybody hated the playing layout, but nobody could complain. The East Side had a button man in charge of each block and the kids were used to taking directions. And the West Side kids knew enough never to use The Fist's name, much less complain about his edict.

The winning touchdown came when Willie Vaughan, the top West Sider, threw his pass as if carrying over trees on a golf course, high over the fence where it became a right angle. The ball hit the top of a basketball backboard, kicked off into the air and dropped right into Fausti's arms.

The Sixth Ward team shrieked that the play did not count. The West Side said that all that counted was that Fausti's feet were in bounds when he caught the ball.

Fausti had his arms up, signaling a touchdown, but it really meant the start of hostilities. The fight used the entire playground, including The Fist's right turn.

11

The Fist now diagrammed new living arrangements. He had to be extraordinarily careful because even with only nominal federal investigations he was sure, by some rumors and paranoia, that every time he went into a place and bought a pack of cigarettes an Internal Revenue Service agent walked in afterward. He said a favorite uncle had died and left him $30,000, which he used as a down payment for a house in Briarcliff Manor, New York, for Carmella Dellacava and their children.

After this, he was secretly building a great house in Pound Ridge in which he intended to live with Carmella Bella and their three children. He changed directions. A partner in private carting, Vincent Tortorello, had the first three stories of an old Embassy building on East 68th Street, between Fifth and Madison. The triplex, a house really, was owned by Stanley Sunshine of the music business, whose partner was The Fist. Sunshine sold it to Tortorello, of the private hauling, because everybody is together here. Tortorello moved in. Suddenly, The Fist, in the midst of his personal turmoil, decided that his second family would live there. He looked at the house and said, "Mine." The house was worth $2.5 million at that prehistoric era of Manhattan real estate. The Fist paid Tortorello $16,000 and told him to take the new house that was being finished in Pound Ridge. That was nice. Tortorello's wife was a spirited Village woman who was not going to like the suburbs. Which meant she didn't like the suburbs when she moved to the suburbs.

The Fist was unknown to anybody on East 68th Street except two families in a town house at the end of the street closest to Fifth Avenue. They were the Guariglia brothers, who ran trucks in the garment center with John Gotti's cannons behind them. They had stayed out of trouble for so long that they thought of themselves as more than legitimate, as actual compatriots of such as the Bergdorf Goodman people. "Who are these hoodlum to move here?" one of their wives said. While the husband let her do what she wanted, for she was invited to social luncheons that could lead to respectability for all of them, he had to tell her not to talk like that unless she wanted him to die.

The Fist decreed from the start that the lawn in front of the house would be his family's life. His street world, his crime, was closed to them. It was the same for a Dellacava son living in the Manhattan town house. He ruined the kid's fun by making him go to school. This was one reason why many disbelieved him later when he was presented as not only crazy, but incompetent. On a bug, John Gotti boasted of his son being a "made man" and The Fist said quietly, "I'm sorry to hear that." Everybody knew that was The Fist, as clear as noon.

As Fausti was his brother's son, The Fist could neither deny nor encourage. If the kid wants to shoot people, let his father say yes or no. Fausti's father had conservative views about his son. "You want to wear an earring? Go ahead. I won't say anything. I'll just cut your ear off." One day he found Fausti with football betting pool slips. Just a few. The father regarded this as huge and dangerous. "Do you want to live like me? A common fucking patrolman can get pissed off at me and I do a fucking year. Do you want that for a life?" At the same time, his father was in the street one day smacking around a man who was late paying on $5,000. The violence confused Fausti, as did the excitement and laughter and the atmosphere of money nobody worked for, the ego of mobsters, the accents that came out of the sidewalk. You live in a place like this, it all finally comes down to money or the chance of years in jail, and almost all will go for the money.

Fausti didn't have to ask for anything or shout the name. At Thanksgiving, he wanted to get two big pumpkin pies from Venero's on First Avenue and when he called, the woman answered by saying, "We're only taking orders for next year. Thank you."

Fausti cut in. "No, no, I just want my name on a list in case somebody doesn't come."

"That never happens. But all right? What's the name?"

"Fausti Dellacava."

"What time are you coming?"

"I guess seven o'clock."

"That's fine."

"Do you want my father's credit card number?"

"No, we don't need it. You can pay when you get here. It's fine. See you tonight."

The way he did it was the best. There was not even a hint of threat as he gave the name, so the place wouldn't embarrass him by handing him the store. They just don't treat you like a common customer. He paid, but didn't have to wait. Fausti loved it. The name could take him the other way, too. When he took his test for a driver's license, he got in with the Motor Vehicles guy on Pitt Street under the Williamsburg Bridge. The examiner got in the car, with the papers on his lap, and coughed. "Let's see now, you're . . ." His head bucked back in fright.

"You pass."

The Motor Vehicles man slipped out of the car. He put his head in the window and said, in a mixture of good fellowship and fear, "Tell me the truth. Would you have had me killed if you failed?"

If some catastrophe occurred to The Fist, the fear engendered by the mere whisper of his name would be gone in a half hour. What would be left would be an immediate resentment of your having the name and not the power.

This time, he was at his aunt's house in Briarcliff Manor and a cousin threw Fausti the keys to a Mercedes convertible and asked him to get cigarettes. Driving to the store, he grew inches. When he pulled up at the store, he got out and swaggered. No conqueror arrived with so many trumpets. Nearly eighteen with a Mercedes convertible. Later, his aunt told him, go for a drive, go down to the Jersey shore. Fausti got right back in that car and drove to Bradley Beach. He was in the Seaspray Club when the comic called out, "I'll show you what a big guy I am. I got a bookmaker named Larry. I owe him my living room couch. If it was important, he'd smack me in the face. But you can see what he thinks of me. He sends his kid down here to get paid."

He pointed at Fausti and everybody laughed, including one topless dancer who was instantly intrigued. She put her eyes on Fausti the rest of the night.

Walking out of the club with her on his arm, Fausti felt he had arrived. Eighteen, I got a topless dancer. That's it. That's me.

When the topless dancer saw the Mercedes convertible, she gasped.

"What do you do?" she said.

"What do you mean, what do I do? You know my name, don't you? What more do you have to know?"

She is not in that car five minutes when she throws her arms around him.

"Fausti Dellacava, I think I'm falling madly in love with you."

Fausti had never taken a dollar from anybody on the street. He decided that he couldn't do that, kick around some poor weakling, teach him not to pay late. Already he knew that he couldn't shoot anybody. At the same time, as the comedian showed, he had a known name that impressed people. That gave him a warm feeling. A gangster's gold. How can it not be the greatest life? An instructor in school liked his paper. But he didn't get a check, he couldn't go that way anymore. He thought, "They can't ever say I didn't start out legitimate."

At first he thought that maybe somehow he could always drive a Mercedes without doing crimes and attending prison.

Coming home from his aunt's house in Jersey, in something somewhat less than a Mercedes — the bus — he stopped at Lester's clothes store on Sixth Avenue because Mike Tyson supposedly had been in a fight there the night before. Lester took a hat off a shelf, a snap-brim wise guy hat.

"He was buying this when somebody says something to him and he punches the guy and don't stop," Lester said. He slapped the hat on Fausti's head. "It's yours."

Fausti walked from the store to Sullivan Street with his hat on and chest out. Malocchio was in a deep sleep. He went into the club, which was empty in the daytime except for Jerry, who serves as porter and coffee maker. Jerry was dozing when Fausti walked in, leaving the door partly open. Right away, Fausti lit a cigarette with disdain. Fausti's index finger pointed to Jerry. His mouth went into his uncle's best sneer.

"Are you crazy . . .

". . . . are you fuckin' crazy?"

Then he rocked back and forth on his heels.

"We don't make no idle threats. You hear me? You hear what I say? You hear what I'm telling you?"

He began to whoop and make old man Jerry laugh. He never heard Concetta outside on the sidewalk. She could see him, but he couldn't see her. She turned on her heel and walked toward the corner.

About a half hour later, Fausti was cavorting in the hat, threatening a whole imaginary mob, when in church silence The Fist shuffled in.

"Take off the hat," he said.

Fausti took it off.

"Don't ever let me see you with the hat again. Get rid of it."

The Fist also allowed nobody from the neighborhood to get into the mob. He was sure that if the neighbors' children got into the mob there would come days when the wives or mothers would be screaming out the windows that their made man didn't get enough money for his part in the last murder. Of course, everyone in the neighborhood said The Fist was keeping them out because he didn't want to share anything.

At the same time, a mob clubhouse could flourish only in neighborhoods of enthusiastic and thrilled Italians. The Mafia presented themselves to the Italian neighborhoods as protectors against an outside world that despised them and called them dishonest and dangerous. That the Mafia was the reason that Italians were maligned, that their children were turned down by colleges, that boys lost girls and girls lost boys, was overlooked. The Italians were shunned and despised and worked in the most filth, the highest danger, and were paid the least. When they died on dangerous jobs, work didn't stop a quarter of an hour in their honor.

The Italians felt protected by living in neighborhoods with the Mafia, who could beat up anybody. Many Italians in neighborhoods were secretly proud of having a Mafia.

Their heroes were restricted to singers like Caruso and, in another form, Sinatra, to lovers like Valentino and to athletes like Joe DiMaggio. There were no intellectuals or important political people past a district leader. The day soon would come when Italians burst forth with Italian governors of states like New York and Ohio and Italians in the House and the Senate and governing the

Stock Exchange and dominating advertising. As the number and influence of Italians in daily life rose, the Mafia declined. The canard is that the Mafia buys and owns big-name Italian politicians.

12 "All your trouble starts with some shirt with a high collar," The Fist insisted. He was pointing at Sal Meli, who walked up the street in a shirt that in the 200th Anniversary Sale at Lee's made-to-order on Coney Island Avenue cost $199, a dollar off for America. A dark blue shirt with a white collar that went three inches above the top of the jacket. A red Countess Mara tie finished dressing of the upper neck region. The rest of him was draped in gray double-breasted silk from Morning After on Broadway. This was the official uniform of the crew from Ozone Park, headed by John Gotti. The Fist hated Gotti and his clothes. It was mutual.

His daughters bought all The Fist's clothes. His favorite was a black "Boss" zipper jacket with the inscription "For Members Only." The Fist regarded it as made for his crew, and everybody wore one. Whistling, the bartender from Coogie's Bar, arrived for work at six P.M. one night wearing a "For Members Only" jacket. The Fist told one of his people, "Go over and tell him don't ever wear that again."

The shadows fell on the street at the beginning of a Friday night, which was the most important night in the Concerned Lutherans. On these Friday nights, anybody would want the mob to last for all time. When the building shadows met and covered Sullivan Street with the first of night, The Fist strolled down the street, back from the barbershop with his new shave and in his "Boss" jacket. There was a crowd outside the club and, as the noise indicated, a larger one inside. They were at the club to celebrate the end of the week, to give thanks for not having done five minutes of legitimate work all week.

The guys on the sidewalk formed an alley and murmured, "Thank you, Boss," while glancing upward briefly. The Fist walked through like a hero.

Inside, all talking stopped and everybody rose and stood in reverence, as if The Fist were delivering a sacrament. The Fist greeted them with a face whose lines were arranged pleasantly, although his eyes had the usual complaint: Is that all you got for me? The men formed a line and each man came up and from a step away, blew him two kisses. This was obeying The Fist's strep throat rule on the clubhouse wall. All were acting like they're at a swell occasion. The men hugged each other and applauded and kissed and shouted joyously. These Friday night gatherings were a pep rally for gangsters. They provided an hour of warmth when they could imagine themselves as people from another life, a place where people didn't whisper as you passed, but who tolerated you, or maybe even loved you as a neighbor. "Overlay" of Middle Village, Queens, hugged and kissed little fat Pepe Sabato. "I love you," Overlay said. Pepe said, "This is my guy. I love him!" For this moment, Overlay and Pepe envisioned themselves to be happy next-door neighbors, who had the approval of all, for they were upstanding citizens on the block. Or at least this is how they imagined legitimacy.

Now Friday night started with whiskey and cigarettes and after that came waiters in white jackets and huge smiles carrying trays with silver covers. They were from Joe's Restaurant, a block away. They entered the club with great cheer and many cries of "Bon appetito" and turned an empty table into a sweet-smelling Italian garden, whose beauty excites the eye.

The Boss loved all the food colors and the intoxicating smell of garlic in sauce. His fist came out to each waiter, handing him a twenty-dollar bill. The Fist was not famous for being a tipper. Aside from here, and a few diners, he never was anywhere where he had to tip. For a moment, he gazed at the platters of sausages and peppers, bright green and bright red against the black crust of the sausage. Then there was lobster fra diavolo, lobster tails, clams oreganata, veal scallopine, chicken parmigiana, and a cauldron of No. 10 macaronis with filet de pomador sauce.

This vision suddenly was disturbed by the big fat hand of Joe Mop as he pulled a crescent of lobster from the dish.

"Can't you wait?" the Boss said.

"I couldn't help myself." He was a huge slob of a man who had had open-heart surgery a few weeks back, and who now took a drag on his cigarette as he chewed the lobster.

Fausti came in beaming and carrying two large trays sealed with tin foil, which when removed let delicious steam dance in the air. Many in the room seemed overcome. Fausti announced, "I cooked it myself. Spaghetti carbonara." This is spaghetti with many bits of bacon in it and a sauce that has been soaked up by the spaghetti. The sauce had started out as white cream. Fausti was coming straight from the kitchen of Luciano's, a famous Italian restaurant only steps down the sidewalk from Fausti's father's club. For special occasions, the Luciano's chef cooked for any Dellacava, this time the youngest, Fausti.

Fausti thought the restaurant was so nice to him because they liked him. And if this is what the Mafia is, this Friday night feast, then it can't be bad, he decided. Fausti got a plate and filled it with all in sight and sat down at the table with his uncle. Next to Fausti was a slim dark-haired guy, who seemed all right until he smiled. Fausti did not like the smiles. The guy was pandering to The Fist so openly that Fausti wondered about his uncle keeping him around.

As Fausti was eating, the dark-haired guy ruffled Fausti's hair.

"How are you, son? You're the nephew, right?"

"I'm Larry's son," he said firmly.

"Yeah, but you're his nephew," he said, nodding to The Fist.

"Domenico," The Fist mumbled to Fausti.

That the uncle introduced him was recommendation enough, and nobody in the room was uncomfortable when Domenico's voice became so earnest as he said to The Fist, without using any name, "Ah — can I get you anything?"

"Bring me all of it," The Fist growled.

Getting up to be a waiter, Domenico smiled at Fausti. It was obvious that he would break into bitter tears if he thought that would win people over. A subject bowing, totally obedient. If this did not please, he immediately walked onto other paths — sincere, silent, sadistic, a ceaseless probing of the people with him to find the way to approval. This was his unseen strength. He never despaired — he was a murderer who shot people in the back, but he arrived with an innocent look. No back is turned on somebody hated.

Joe Mop took the seat alongside Domenico's. He was prepared to eat himself to death. He had the most crowded fork. He dragged on his cigarette. Another forkful.

Somebody watched Fausti eating the spaghetti carbonara.

"I think he eats more than all of yez put together," the guy said.

The Fist growled. He had a forkful of spaghetti in his right hand and a lobster claw in his left hand.

"I got fifty that the kid eats the most," Pepe Sabato said. He was another of Fat Tony's men. The Dellacava kids said he looked like Simon Bar Sinister from the cartoon show *Underdog.*

"I like the Boss."

"You're covered."

"Domenico got no belly. He eats all the time. I figure he got real good digestion. I put fifty on him."

"I'm not in nobody's league here," Domenico said.

"Just have the money up," The Fist said. "Don't worry who wins. I win."

Several fifties were put on the table. Now The Fist held a finger up for those at his table.

"No pushers. You can't push with your thumb. You can't use bread for a pusher. You got to eat clean off the fork."

The Fist took a forkful of spaghetti carbonara.

Fausti finished the carbonara. He took a plate of No. 10 macaroni as high as his chest.

Domenico said, "I got to say, fellas, the food is beauty."

The Fist ate by fork in a deep crouch, his face bare inches above the plate. He looked around only to say he wanted veal scallopine. He was into that when out of the corner of his eye he saw Domenico sitting with a poncetta, a large veal chop, the largest in the universe, stuffed with grapes and rice.

"Why does he have what I don't have?" The Fist said. Domenico pushed the serving plate to him.

Fausti went to the table and with large eyes and fast hands, grabbed chicken parmigiana, peppers and sausage, then a second peppers and sausage, which required another plate.

He reached for the bread and ripped the end from a long loaf.

"No pushers," The Fist said.

"No, sir. I just eat it," Fausti said, stuffing it in his mouth.

"No pushers!" The Fist reminded Domenico, whose left thumb was suspiciously close to the plate.

The Fist brought his left hand down like a file divider. Then the left hand moved across the plate, a snow shovel, pushing every bit of food, the last of veal, even the macaroni gravy. Now that he had it in one place on the plate, he picked up the plate, tilted it and let the whole thing go into his mouth like he was a storm drain — veal, macaroni, peppers, cheese.

After a while, The Fist saw Joe Mop chewing thoughtfully. Soon, he would have enough. He looked at Domenico. Not a word about the food now. Lugging in.

Joe Mop, the pig, now gave up on utensils. He put both hands on a plate of spaghetti.

"No pushers," The Fist said.

"I'm not pushin', I'm going to do the same as you." Joe Mop's tongue went out. He began jamming in food by hand.

"Eat right off the plate like a cannibal?" The Fist said.

The Fist looked at Fausti. The kid now was pacing himself. Fausti raised the fork on a sloping motion, then gently brought it down to his mouth. He then broke the rules of an eating contest and chewed.

"You can't win eatin' if you chew," The Fist said, between swallows.

Fausti sat with broccoli rabe and soft-shell blueclaw crabs.

First he had one forkful, then he ate another. The pace was maddening to The Fist. He wanted to pick up another plate and swallow it all, but the bottom of his throat said no.

Fausti continued, one fork after the other. Soon, The Fist's hands were clasped in front of him. He could go no more. With a huge burp, he signified that he was through.

Fausti was finishing a lobster tail. He liked them. He got up for another.

"He wins," somebody said, pushing the money.

Fausti's father slapped a hand over his son's. It would be unseemly for a boy in his teens to be taking out of a pot of money. He has to prove that he knows his place. He was showing Fausti by loud example how to behave around this mob.

The Fist then showed how the Boss acts.

"Give me the money," The Fist said. "Give me all the fuckin' money."

He lit a cigarette, took one drag, then put it out. He sat uncomfortably.

"Bene!" Fausti announced. He swaggered out of the club and over to Jimmy's Carvel stand. He bought a supercone, with caramel and chocolate swirled and topped with multicolored sprinkles. He walked back into the club licking the ice cream.

The Fist's eyes widened and he gagged. Joe Mop wouldn't look.

Domenico, who felt his life depended upon his showing no weakness, retched. Moisture came to his eyes. Seeing the fucking ice cream.

The Fist whispered to Baldy Dom, who suddenly told Fausti to leave.

When he walked out, he glanced back and saw Domenico, Natale Grassi, and his uncle going to the side door that opened onto the hallway next door. One moment The Fist had been sick from eating. Now without a pause he had on his business face, a cold, dark face that threatened.

Fausti went into the doorway of 250 and ate his ice cream. Of course he was there to hear something. He did. He heard a tremendous burp from his uncle. Then Domenico said, too loudly, "This Louis Napoli, he's only a kid, I don't think he's past seventeen. Can't you give him a cha —"

"Keep your voice down. You take him."

When Domenico came out of the club, he saw Fausti and his smile turned into a wince. "Did you hear us in there?"

"Me? Never."

For Domenico, this would be a clear memory twenty years later.

After dinner, there arrived at 250 Sullivan Sal Meli and Norman Heller. Sal Meli was president of Local 295, Teamsters, and Heller ran Local 851 at Kennedy Airport. Sal was a made man, whose earnings for the mob went to Dellacava and the Ozone Park clubhouse of the Gambino organization. Heller was Jewish, but they still took his money. He had a brother who was away in the army. A third brother died in a saloon holdup. He was everybody's pet gorilla, a main event fighter who once fouled an opponent fifty straight times in the ring at Madison Square Garden and started a riot that required eighty cops to clear the ring.

That not one of the Hellers was allowed in the Mafia, but instead had to hang around the stage door of crime is indisputable evidence that the Mafia wanted only ruffians with Italian names and backgrounds, Naples, Calabria, and Sicily. In Italy there was no room for organized criminals in Rome, due to a traditional overcrowding of political thieves. By keeping the outfit in America open only to those with Italian backgrounds, the mob felt safe from infiltration. You ask a stranger for the name of his cousin from Reggio in Calabria, and if he comes up short, he is a suspect. The other requisite for admission wasn't bad, either: A candidate had to murder somebody before he could fill out an application.

But keeping out Jews meant the Italians did all the counting themselves and this was a disaster. After so many years of crime, only three or four mobsters left money that showed in second and third generations. At the end, the great Al Capone had as much money as a moderately successful insurance man. And on the day the president announced his death, Caesar De Francisi had $1,100 willed to his brother, a thoroughly legitimate man.

The only outfit to make money was the De Francisi mob after The Fist took it over. He didn't throw any money into the incinerator of Mafia night life and he didn't like any of the other usual splurging. He believed in taking and saving.

Norman Heller, Hebrew, and Meli, as the necessary Italian

partner, were reporting on their businesses, allowing big companies like Air Stream to have 40 percent of a job non-union. The companies paid one hundred dollars a week to the Mafia for each non-union man working a union job. A non-union man on that job cost the company $300 a week (plus the $100 to the Mafia). A union man cost $840 a week, or $440 more than the non-union guy. You have one hundred non-union men on a job, the company saves $44,000 a week. (And while paying the Mafia only $10,000 to allow non-union workers.) It's nice. Of the $10,000 each week handed to Sal and Heller, they gave The Fist $5,000 and the Gambino family $2,500. They split $2,500 between themselves, which doesn't sound like much. But you pick up $2,500 in the afternoon and another $2,500 at night someplace else, seven times a week, it adds up to money.

The mob gambling and moneylending at the airport freight terminals brought in more and more money, even in bad times, but it all was based on control of freight terminals.

Any working man with a legitimate complaint about these tactics was given a hearing consisting of a pistol stuck into his ear.

John Gotti of the Gambino family, as new killer on the scene, came out of a clubhouse on 101st Avenue in Ozone Park, only five minutes from the airline freight buildings. For residency, he wanted a huge raise.

Meli and Heller were called in by The Fist. Before being allowed to sit at the table, they had to present a neat package of bills, $500 apiece rent for their seats at the table. You do this ten times a day, it tends to add up. Then they outlined the dispute. The Fist made them repeat it four times. Now The Fist decided: "Fuck John Gotti — from now on bring all the money to me. I want every fuckin' dollar."

Sal said to Heller, "Now we got nothing to worry about. We don't have to go through all the trouble of money. It's nice. We just give it all to The Fist and go on our way."

13 The Fist could see no snipers on the roofs as he roamed through his life with two families. As usual, the enemy was on the ground alongside him. He imagined that each family lived in bliss and with no idea of the other. This was disrupted by a Westchester mailman. Of course a letter arrived at Carmella Della-cava's house in Briarcliff Manor; any one of a thousand people could have written it. It was addressed to Carmella and said that her Fist man had another family and here were the names of the mother and her children and the home address, East 68th Street. There wasn't even time to make up a list of suspects who could have written a letter that had a stiletto in every paragraph. There could have been a thousand chief suspects. Any woman betrayed by a man wants to destroy everybody else.

The Fist never realized that he was without his smoke screen. Everybody in The Fist's mob interpreted what they saw and heard as the new official way of life. Just as they imitated him by dressing loading platform, anybody who did not have a second wife and family went out and got one. Where once a second family was a desecration, it now was a show of respect for The Fist.

That The Fist had tried to keep his worlds hidden was ignored. That he was silent about it was taken as a Silent Command. Any reverence for loyalty and chivalry was diluted to make way for the new way of life. For anybody to remain with one wife meant she was so dangerous that discovery meant death. Otherwise, anybody who did not marry twice was considered a walking insult to The Fist, a condition that was always temporary. They all tried to live somewhat openly like real guys while simultaneously not allowing the wives and families to know each other. Of course this was trying to have it both ways, but The Fist saw nothing wrong with this. The second wives were not the trophy wives that people in a less moral society take on for lust and ego. The Fist married two women in his own age range and from similar backgrounds; his first wife came from the street where he was born, Thompson, and the second from Mulberry. Both walked up a couple of flights to their apartments. They were presentable and each had the attitude of someone who had just looked up from the stove. Strangers cannot be brought in to do housework; the possibility of hearing or seeing something not meant for them is too great.

Always, the first wife, married before God in a church and with a huge reception afterward, alone has an official paper to prove her position. Second wives have to rely on the guy's word at first. Everybody knows the word isn't worth hearing. As soon as possible the women have children to throw a rope around the great sire.

There is no divorce. How could you do that when you need every wife you have?

The fact that there are two wives doesn't stop decent mobsters from running around with women whose faces indicated they just looked up from the bar.

Nobody dared mention how The Fist himself, whose social order had been busted by a common letter in the mail, handled what historically was a catastrophe. He intimated that only powerful love could last. But the wrath he was facing could only be smothered with plain money.

The money had a rapid, noiseless, and totally effective movement under each of the roofs he supported. It kept the rage of betrayed wives muted. The outsiders, the cousins and beyond to mere close friends, rather than look on matters as scandalous, were so jealous of the money that they wished they had both feet in the rich mess.

In all living arrangements, good big money is the winning emotion. Any imbecile can give the woman a greeting card from a store. The man who truly understands that money talks is the one to change hearts and minds.

"I like you a lot," says Andrew Jackson from his twenty.

"I am in love with you," says Ulysses S. Grant from a fifty.

"You are beautiful and I am hopelessly in love with you," says Benjamin Franklin from a wonderful hundred.

The arms of Salmon P. Chase reach out from his ten-thousand-dollar bill and clutch the woman and pledge love through the entire century.

And poor fools lead with a Hallmark card and think they are impressing.

Because money can buy love, The Fist by example turned his personal travail into a Reformation of Mafia life. Henry the Eighth had to kill and change religion to have a few marriages, proof that he was an imbecile in a small country who had no conception of what his money could do. The Fist threw cash before anybody even had a chance to complain. An entire culture, revered and recounted through the last hundred years, was shattered. Before this, nobody ever wanted to examine the myth of Family, other than to regard it as if it were real. Toast it at dinner and extoll it in conversation. "Family." Tears and big noisy loving dinners and weddings. Do not disturb the illusion. The real life existed in secrecy and absences and girlfriends. And when The Fist, foiled by a letter, had to openly live with two wives and families, the followers followed. There were no orders or suggestions. Not a word or a nod. The Fist had two wives. Then I am going to have two and maybe three wives. Any conflicts in their hearts were kept hidden.

The Fist's aide, Baldy Dom Cataldo, had one wife, the former Angelina Rocco, and one child so far and lived in a great yellow brick house in Bensonhurst, in Brooklyn. She was a good-looking neighborhood girl who loved the excitement of a gangster. They had been married at Regina Pacious Roman Catholic Church and had a huge reception at the Oriental Ballroom, also in Bensonhurst. He had no idea that he ever would leave her or cut their lives in half, but if The Fist has two wives at once then I, Dominick, his aide, must have two.

His second wife lived in Kingston, Ontario, right across the bridge from Niagara Falls. She was one of two women he met at the bar of a disco owned by a wise guy out of Buffalo. Baldy Dom was in Buffalo for a conference on killing people. The first woman was about sixteen and was dressed in flesh. She said she loved him. The second woman was Marie Pandolpho and she was his age, in her forties, and looked it, which he knew would impress The Fist. Ms. Marie Pandolpho had no marriage license but had a powerful brand-new ranch house from Dominick. The house came with a hungry lawn.

Baldy Dom served both marriages by leaving Sullivan Street and rushing off for Kingston at 3 A.M. on Saturday, informing his first wife that she didn't have to know what he was doing because it was too dangerous. He had no traffic all the way up. On the seat next to him as he drove up was the last of the night's food from his late-night places, Rocco's on Thompson Street, Two Toms in Brooklyn. It was cold mussels, cold spaghetti with heavy sauce, cold veal piccata, cold garlic, and by Albany he was bent in half. He got to the second wife, Ms. Marie Pandolpho, at midmorning Saturday. The second wife always wanted to go for a drive. He remained in Ontario in wedded bliss until 2 A.M. on Monday morning, when he rushed back to Manhattan for the start of his week's crime. Driving down on Monday morning he had a breakfast packed by his wife. It was big sausages that turned cold on the drive, fried eggs that became coated with grease, and big cold solid chunk butter on toast. On three occasions, he got to Utica and pulled over to throw up by the same low pine tree.

Each trip was 411 miles. He was a tree branch sitting in the car with the spinning Texas asphalt road surface whittling the bark from him. And then within days, wife Angelina called him during dinner in Rocco's to inform him that she was pregnant with their second child. "You make me feel like a hero," he said.

Two days later, Marie Pandolpho called him at his other place, Two Toms.

"I have to tell you something important," she said.

"Yeah, what?"

"Guess."

"I can't do that."

"I'm pregnant."

"You told me that."

"What do you mean?"

"You told me the other night."

"I what?"

Baldy Dom just did pull himself together. "I mean I had a dream. Isn't that somethin'? I dream of a real thing."

Some thirty-nine weeks later, Baldy Dom was pushed awake by his wife at 4 A.M. "Dom," she said, calm and urgent. He drove her to Methodist Hospital in Brooklyn. He went out for coffee, brought back the newspapers, and was through with them and asleep with his chin on his chest when the doctor came down to tell him he had a baby girl. He went upstairs for a moment and kissed his wife and peered at the baby. His wife said he must be exhausted and he should go home to sleep. "Boy, can you see what's wrong with me," he said. "I need sleep bad. I'm going home and turn off the phone."

He drove over to Manhattan and parked the car in the garage on Thompson Street, around the corner from The Fist's clubhouse. On a whim, he went to the pay phone and called Ontario collect, which was his usual style — why not, he paid the bills. Marie Pandolpho was excited on the other end. "I was just trying to figure out where to find you. Can you get up here? I'm having contractions. The doctor says this afternoon. You better hurry."

Dom got back in the car and started for Buffalo. He had hot tired eyes and was dazed by noon-hour traffic in lower Manhattan and on the West Side Highway. Trucks and buses and fumes and traffic funneling slowly past construction. He got on the Thruway and started straight for Ontario, a nice 411 miles up. He used the men's room at the first Thruway stop. Afterward, he bought salami pizza and a big black coffee. The salami worked. It killed his digestion. The coffee did not. His eyes grew sandy and the lids heavy and he had to pull off at Albany and sleep for a half hour. He then made the rest of the run to Ontario with bleary eyes and indigestion. He pulled in front of the yellow brick ranch house at 8 P.M. The woman next door was on the sidewalk waving at him.

"She just went a half hour ago. My husband took her."

The woman got in the car and directed him to the hospital.

The baby arrived at 9 P.M. Again he went to the room, kissed his wife and newborn, and after that went downstairs and fell asleep in the car.

"Two babies in two countries on the same day," he announced upon waking up. "I am a real fucking hero."

He planned to move the second wife and baby down to the Westchester. He knew that he would die at the wheel if he had to make the commute to Canada.

But the first thing he did was get the guys in Buffalo to set up a priest and church for the baptism of his new son. They escorted Baldy Dom and his party to St. Barbara of the Cataracts in Niagara, where on a Sunday Father Phil Napolitano stood in vestments. He reverently, and in a voice that all could hear, brought the child into the Roman Catholic religion.

"What's that?" he growled as Baldy Dom slipped an envelope into his hand.

"It's you know."

"No, I don't know anything like that." The priest took the envelope, folded it, went to the poor box, and jammed it in.

"I tole you," one of the mobsters told Baldy Dom. "This guy is the greatest."

After that, Father Phil brought everybody to the rectory, where he opened red wine that tasted like it came from Heaven.

"We got to get you down with us," Baldy Dom said.

"Oh, I'll be down," Father Phil said.

14

Phil Napolitano came out of a family of nine in a two-and-a-half-story frame house on Grant Street in the old West Side of Buffalo. The neighborhood was as Italian as anything in New York, about which he knew very little except that he had a cousin who had married into a family that caused him deepest envy. She was a Dellacava, but only by marriage. Still, she had the name and he wished he had it.

He did have two brothers who were unfamiliar to anything legitimate. One, Tony, who was known as Tony the Dispatcher, because he dispatched taxis for owner Buster Wyoming, whose name is self-explanatory. Tony had conflicts with police over his hours. One night, he took off unexpectedly. His replacement was shot eight or nine times as he sat in the broken-down dispatcher's chair. He did die. When detectives came to the house, Tony told them that he had taken off to see a movie. "I don't remember it, I fell asleep," he said. Phil had been awakened when his brother came home at 4 A.M. He knew the movie was a lie and he had sudden fear. But then a detective violated everybody's rights by going through the house without a warrant. He even went through Phil Napolitano's sports magazines. Forever after, he never thought of the lie about the movie. He despised anybody with a badge.

At home, he prayed with the mother at the kitchen table. Then in school, the nuns noticed right away that he prayed and did not merely recite. His class marks were extraordinary and after school, he went to the St. Pius rink. From his first days skating around the place, his quickness and enthusiasm for knocking people down showed he was one of several who were going somewhere.

He played hockey at St. Pius High and the first time he scored in a game he took the box score down to the *Buffalo Courier* sports department and whirled in front of the desk of the schoolboy editor. "Right in the crease. Goal! Napolitano!"

The editor laughed and put it in the paper. "Napolitano Scores for St. Pius."

The headline started him off to a hockey scholarship at Western Catholic. One night at the big midwinter sports dinner at the Buffalo Hilton, he sat with his hockey coach and watched a boxer, Rocky Graziano, tell the crowd, "My friend Joe says, 'Get here,' I show." Seated alongside Graziano was Joe Louis. Graziano now waved out to the audience. "Hey, Joe." Joe DeCarlo, who ran crime in Buffalo, waved back.

At DeCarlo's table was a priest from Youngstown, Ohio, who

was having a wonderful time, and was still being treated with great deference by the mobsters at the table.

Instantly, Napolitano fell in love with the notion of being a priest, and doing something good for people, and also having the delicious fun of being around the mob. He couldn't join, but he could be close.

A week later, scrambling behind the net in a game against Canisius at the Buffalo Auditorium, he felt his left knee buckle, followed by bones snapping in his right foot. When he took his skates off, he had a sock full of pretzels and was through.

Instead of a dream of playing professional hockey, he went to the seminary. When he came out, proud and happy, his bed was covered with congratulatory mail. One card was from his Dellacava cousin, who said everybody in her family was delighted to hear that her favorite cousin was a priest. "You are her dream. Her first child a priest. She thinks you're hers."

His first parish was St. Barbara of the Cataracts in Niagara Falls. He took his first Sunday sermon down to the *Herald Express* and found the schoolboy sports editor, who, in addition to his sports writing, was the religion page editor for the Sunday paper. Father Phil's sermon was narrow, about adoration, and meant to please the hierarchy. The paper printed it in advance of its being delivered at the twelve o'clock mass. The bosses of the diocese immediately had to soothe other priests whose words didn't make the roundup of sermons. Two weeks later, Father Phil's sermon was up from notes to the column headline. Father Phil now was making an open campaign for advancement.

Father Phil wanted to become an archbishop, a meaningful politician, or — the one he secretly wanted most of all — the Boss.

Father Phil took over the post made famous and familiar in old movies: the priest from a hoodlum neighborhood who knew everything and understood that sin was relative. He was practically the chaplain for his brother's taxicab mob.

While the idea of a Mafia priest seems dramatic, they actually cause the commotion of a feather in the religion. There must be a couple of hundred of them among Naples, Calabria, and Sicily, and the Vatican hardly notices. The Catholics first formed into a religion when there were tigers and lions loose in the arenas and today the religion is virtually unchanged and German and Belgian sightseers climb around in the ruined coliseums, the tigers much preferred.

There are maybe a billion Catholics, sixty million of them in the United States, and people can say they have left the faith, and yet let there be one chest pain and they return fast. As there is no such thing as a major religion that does not own cemeteries, the Catholics are supreme. If your aunt dies, who buries her — some preacher on television or the pastor who not only sends her to St. John's Cemetery, but blesses the grave?

The Catholic Church in Rome always was ambiguous about the Mafia, with no concentrated opposition ever coming from the Church hierarchy. All through the religious organization, the clergy looked up at new steeples built with money from the parish don, but never at the don himself, who begins a rapist and ends up a revered murderer.

Father Phil's dream of becoming archbishop went out with a roar of tons of water exploding on towering sheets of rock. The sound dissolved but the spray blew through the light from the streetlights and soaked the lawns in front of St. Barbara of the Cataracts, in Niagara Falls, and the streets around it. This was the first home parish of Father Phil. That night in Niagara Falls, while cars had their windshield wipers on against the mist, he made his vigorous pursuit of this first great ambition, to become archbishop. He walked through the mist with somebody he hoped was a dear companion, Auxiliary Bishop Joseph Gilchrist, the papal supervisor for the Northeast. The mist did not stop. Their hair, Gilchrist's sparse red and Father Phil's black, had turned wet and curly. Gilchrist pulled the collar of his black jacket up.

Gilchrist was on his second visit to Father Phil and Niagara Falls. The first time, Father Phil said that on work and ability he thought he should try to become a monsignor, which is the foothills of the Catholic hierarchy. He said this while reaching inside his tunic for a folded five hundred, which he had placed there earlier and which Gilchrist now took while looking straight at Father Phil through round tight wire-frame glasses, acting as if the money did not exist.

"Phil, that would be a great job for you," Gilchrist said. "We'll be in touch on this."

Father Phil couldn't get the man on the phone for nine months, at which point the list of those elevated to monsignor was released. His name was noticeably absent. Father Phil finally got Gilchrist on the phone. Who said, "I never lied to you. You didn't listen to what I told you. I said that monsignor would be a good job for you. I never said you were going to get it."

Father Phil decided that the man was so duplicitous that only the Devil could have placed him here on earth.

"Do your people in Rome know about you?" he said. "I wonder if they know in Rome that you are nothing more than an extortionist? You must rob every priest in the east."

Gilchrist said, "You don't understand."

"The trouble is, I do," Father Phil said. "The people in Rome should know, too. You're lucky I'm not talking to them right now."

This disturbed Gilchrist, who, having lived in Rome, sometimes lapsed into confusion between the Italian treachery and his own Irish, who are responsible for placing the word *informer* into the English language.

In Rome, he saw many Italians going to confession, but he did not understand that they confessed only what they felt like, and if pressed by a priest they would commit perjury before their God. On the other hand, he knew the Irish, once out of their teens, were so afraid of hell that they confessed almost the entire truth of their lives, and then threw in the sins of the near neighbors just to round it out. The more he thought of this, the more he feared Father Phil's testifying against him.

He called three times, with increasing nervousness in his tone and words. The last time, he told Father Phil, "I did try, you know. But I must talk to you about why I could not get it done."

Immediately, he made a date to come to Niagara Falls. Father Phil knew he was coming out of fear that he would be reported.

This is how stupid the Irish are, Father Phil thought. Just because they are stool pigeons at birth that doesn't mean that Italians don't stand up. He would never understand that.

Gilchrist arrived. He had the usual combination of fear and arrogance. Immediately, he wanted to take a walk by the river.

"We'll get sopping wet in the mist," Father Phil said.

"Fine. That's what I want," Gilchrist said.

Suddenly, Father Phil's suspicion arose. "He would love to see me go into the water. That would knock out a witness. He'd tell everybody I slipped."

The two walked to the river that ran straight and fast and foaming right into the falls. Gilchrist began to talk of the wonders of the Irish in the American Church. Father Phil noticed Gilchrist's size. Big broad back and large, heavy hands.

"Where do you think we'd be without the Irish, Father Phil?"

"I'd be a monsignor. I got jobbed by you people."

Gilchrist shook his head. "You know why as well as I do."

"What do I know?"

"That it had to take a lot more than you came up with," Gilchrist said. "Italians. Why are you people so cheap? Why don't you get me a thousand for myself and then another thousand so I can give it to somebody to get them past your mob name, and then we see what happens?"

Gilchrist now took a half step toward Father Phil. He could have been going around a wet stone, or actually going into Father Phil. Father Phil pushed Gilchrist, out of reaction to the sudden movement. Perhaps it was combined in his mind with the open insult. Or perhaps he just pushed out of meanness. However he did it, he did it as if he was moving a piano, with his arms straight . . . Gilchrist barely had time to feel the cold water of the river before he sailed straight over the falls like a piece of shredded wheat. His tight, prissy wire-framed eyeglasses were pressed to his nose.

In one story, the local paper reported excitedly, "Man Goes over the Falls with Glasses On."

Later, when asked, Father Phil said, "The poor man had problems we didn't even know about."

Father Phil reasoned to himself, "I deny that my push put him into the water. Let's look at it. There are three requirements for a mortal sin. Grievous matter, sufficient reflection, and full consent of the will. Grievous matter, a shove over the falls is grievous. But it was because of his language indicating deep hostility and then his advance toward me that could have been construed as being menacing. He also was destroying his own ability to balance. I'll tell you the truth, I thought a lot of bad things about this man, and for very good reason, but I never figured on a thing like this happening. So I say the grievous matter is not on my hands. Next, sufficient reflection. What could I reflect on? Full consent of the will? How could I have that if I didn't have sufficient reflection? A clear not guilty on all counts. He floats, I walk.

"Besides, God would never put any temptation in front of me that I could not overcome. If the Irish abuse me and take my career from me, in fact take my chance to serve God better, then I must defend myself and my faith."

15 "Frances Dellacava?"

"Here."

Right away the name and the sound of the voice caused Concetta to pick up her head. She is in high school in Yonkers and she thinks she is hearing things. The voice is Fausti's voice coming out of a young woman. When she looks over the room, she sees the girl. It is Fausti's sister.

She and this girl were sitting in the homeroom class at Roosevelt High School in Yonkers. When the period ended, she went right over to the girl.

"Are you from downtown Manhattan?"

"No. I'm from Yonkers."

"Do you have anybody living in downtown Manhattan?"

"No," Frances Dellacava said. She left.

Con saw her in the homeroom for one term, and as they were only in the room for a couple of minutes she never spoke to her. Then Frances would slip out quickly and become lost in the crowded hall. During the many months in that school, from one term to another, Con would see her only sporadically: in a hall or leaving school or coming to school, but the girl never looked at her or spoke to her.

Finally, walking down the hall one day she heard the girl laugh. Or, rather, she heard Fausti and his sisters laugh. It started with a razzberry and broke into a full "ho-ho, ho-ho, ho-ho."

Con stepped through other students and stood directly in front of Frances.

"Which Dellacava are you?"

"Frances."

"From where?"

"I told you, Yonkers."

"You must have somebody from downtown. You look like the Dellacavas I know downtown. You sure you don't know Fausti?"

Her answer was a shake of her head as she walked off.

At the end, on graduation night, Con came down the aisle to the music and glistening eyes of her father, who was sitting near the center aisle. He rose with his camera to his eye. She presented him with a face of joy. Afterward, she saw a man over in the side aisle also holding a camera and looking anxiously at the graduates coming down his aisle. He saw the graduate he had been waiting for. And Con and her father It is usual at these moments for people to wave excitedly and happily to each other. But the problem here was that Larry Dellacava, Fausti's father, was present for a secret daughter. The Fist and a lot of the others had started living brazenly, in the open, with two or more families. Not Larry. If he had been ready for people to know this, he would have brought the daughter home in excitement and triumph to Sullivan Street. Instead, he was being ambushed in Yonkers. He fled. Larry Dellacava was fast all right. He got out of that row and went sideways up the aisle, paused for an instant, snapped a picture of Frances, who was a shower of light, and then was up the aisle and to the back of the auditorium. He had a decision to make when he hit the doors, but it was not much of a one. Realizing he was caught dead, he turned around, leaned against the wall and proudly watched his daughter graduate. Afterward, when Con mentioned it to her father, he said, "I knew Larry was here. I spoke to him."

The next day she came home from school for the last time, holding her high school yearbook. In the D's was Frances Dellacava. Con had not seen Fausti in over a year but she found herself wondering only how Fausti was going to accept the secret sister.

After graduation, Con packed up and took whatever she had and went to live with her brother back on Thompson Street. "I packed my clothes and I'm here," she told the brother. "All I got is in my purse. Confirmation money. I got $2,500. That's all I got between me and the streets."

"I'm working," Pat said. Pat worked church fairs and outdoor feasts. He spun wheels, sold cashew nuts, called out the prizes to be won shooting baskets. Once, he tried out-of-town work at the State Fair at Syracuse, but one night he stood on North Salinas Street, where there were supposed to be some wise guys who would make him feel at home. He saw nothing but closed stores and empty sidewalks and he nearly went crazy. When a cop car came along he quit. He went home where he belonged, to the noise and dirt of downtown.

"When there's no feasts for you to work, I better have my confirmation money," she said.

16

That year, and all the years to follow, the smell of creosote on the boardwalk told him it was summer and he was young. Even when it was winter cold, the creosote on a telephone pole caused him to stand on the streetcorner and imagine, no, almost believe that he was on the beach of a day in the middle of summer.

This started when he took the City Parks Department lifeguard course during the winter at a pool on West 59th Street. Most from Sullivan Street go to Jersey, to Long Branch or Bradley Beach, for a couple of weeks in the summer. The lifeguard jobs were in the city. He began the summer on Memorial Day a couple of blocks away at the Carmine Street pool. The first weeks were delightful. He was getting paid to watch a pool of sunny water with kids splashing and the familiar smell of hot cement right on the other side of the fence. He understood that he had to keep looking at the pool bottom as if pressed to a microscope. The fear is one of the neighbors' children going unnoticed on the bottom as everybody's feet walked past or on them. On baking hot days when the pool was filled from 9 A.M. until nightfall, it was harder to see as the day went on and the urine from all these children clouded the water at the shallow end.

In mid-August the pool needed a new filter and the Parks Department promptly shut the pool down. Fausti was given a slip directing him to work all the way out at Rockaway Beach, on Beach 84th Street.

Rockaway is a glorious peninsula of wide white beaches and an Atlantic Ocean that sometimes comes thumping in with enough waves to make it a favorite surfing place. At one end, in the 140s, wealthy people live on the oceanfront and the blocks running up to it. At 126th Street, a boardwalk begins that is crowded and popular. But Rockaway goes until Beach 1st Street. It starts running down in the 90s where the streets turn into junkyards and the houses are three-story wood summer houses now turned into packed rooming houses.

In the middle of this desolation is Beach 84th Street, with enough parking for a convention. They drive from all over to get here, for the beach is splendid.

Fausti was in time for two big August days. The first was when it was officially declared that there was a Cure in the water. This was a decree from some Catholic priests, Irish of course, that anybody entering the ocean with an illness would emerge with the disease dripping from the body like ocean drops. This time the people congregated at Beach 116th, where they stopped in Devaney's and the women had a late breakfast of Bloody Marys and the men and priest had big cold beers. Fausti was one of the extra lifeguards assigned. Matilda Kearney, sixty-five, had her two brothers push and carry her wheelchair right smack into the ocean in the center of the beach. One of the chair wheels sank a foot deep into the sand. She was in danger of tipping. A wave accomplished this. Fausti and a couple of others were in the water and reclaimed the chair and sputtering Matilda, who had the brothers carry and wheel her right up to Devaney's on 116th Street. She said she would find her own cure.

The other important day of the summer was the annual Mafia Day mass that was said at St. Michael's and St. Edward's church on Navy Street in downtown Brooklyn. It was the church where Al Capone was baptized; he had a godmother, but the parish book shows that there was no godfather. The annual mass was being said here out of respect for excellence. As Fausti's uncle and father were not attending, he was designated worshiper. He arranged with his beach patrol supervisor to come in two hours late.

In church, the three in the front row, three big guys who looked like they were evil, and looked exactly that way on account of they certainly were evil, were standing respectfully while a strange priest, Father Phil, was about to read the Gospel and deliver a sermon from the pulpit at this annual Mafia Day mass.

Nobody ever had seen the priest before this morning. Just before the mass, Fausti was introduced to him and the priest smothered Fausti. "My favorite cousin!" he bellowed. He noticed the thick cord around Fausti's neck and pulled it up. His lifeguard whistle dangled from it. "What's this for, to call the cops?" the priest said. When Fausti said he was going to work as a lifeguard, the priest said he always had walked the shore of Lake Erie until they had begun using it to deposit so many bodies. He was certain Rockaway wasn't a seaview mortuary. Sometime today he would be at Fausti's post to walk the ocean shore.

Fausti knew that his mother was something like a fiftieth cousin to the priest. If at all. His mother never had seen the priest until last night. He was from Buffalo, living in the snow, who knew from what he was. But the guys in Buffalo loved him, and Baldy Dom, who had been up there, said he was the greatest. When Father Licavoli of St. Rocco's in Bensonhurst, who always said the Mafia Day mass, came up good and sick, and a couple of retainers were leery of saying the mass this year, what with all the federals, Baldy Dom brought down "a real cousin" from Buffalo.

So here was the priest, Father Phil, forty, fresh, up there on the pulpit in his first New York appearance. Fausti sat in the middle. His black hair was brushed straight back and stood up like a crewcut. He had full lips and sleepy brown eyes. He sat without fidgeting. You always can tell when they went to Catholic grammar school.

The church is silent as Father Phil reads the Gospel, which is the Passion of Jesus Christ, according to Matthew. In all other parts of Catholicism, this Gospel is read on Palm Sunday. The Mafia feels close to this Gospel and thus the priest read it on this day and with full emotion.

The prayer book for the mass was in the form of a play, with parts for a narrator and the ones speaking. Father Phil read all the parts.

Father Phil read the narrator's part: "One of the twelve, who was called Judas Iscariot, went to the chief priests and said —"

Now he became the voice of Judas.

"What are you willing to give me if I hand him over to you?"

Father Phil switched his voice back to that of narrator. "They paid him thirty pieces of silver and from that time on, he looked for an opportunity to hand him over."

As narrator, Father Phil continued: "When it was evening, he reclined at table with the twelve. And while they were eating he said —"

Now he read Jesus' part.

"Amen I say to you, one of you will betray me."

Now as narrator again he said, "Deeply distressed, they began to say to him one after another:

" 'Surely, it is not I, Lord.' "

Father Phil tore off his glasses and ruffled his black hair in agitation. He hated Judas.

"And he said in reply —"

He was Jesus again. "He who has dipped his hand into the dish with me is the one who will betray me. The Son of Man indeed goes, as it is written of him, but woe to that man by whom the Son of God is betrayed. It would be better for that man if he had never been born."

Father Phil paused. "You see, we all should have paid close attention to our faith over the years. For many of our thoughts and the things we still say, things we think, are horrible, are suddenly placed in context when we read the words of the Lord himself.

"How often have all of us said about some informer, 'He should have died in his mother's womb'?"

The three in front grunted loudly. Around the church, all the guys nodded. One was Joe Dente from the Pork Store, whose face now was wreathed in agreement. It was good for him that he showed up. He was all the trouble there was in the world. In fact, so much so that he was never to get home from church because of the sewer on the way home.

"Of course that's how we talk. Well, here we read of the Passion of Christ, and there never was a stand-up man like this. He died for us. He didn't even have to do it. He could have walked out from under the crown of thorns. He could have made the nails pop into the air. We are able to stand here today because he took the worst beating and torture and hideous suffering you ever heard of and did it for us.

"And look what he is saying about Judas. He is saying the same thing we say. That Judas should have died in his mother's womb."

Father Phil's voice rose. "Not by abortion! I say abortions kill more than the Mafia!

"But an informer is different. If we could find out that the fetus definitely is a future informer, a threat to us all, then we could consider the danger of allowing the baby to be born.

"Now, one other thing we must learn from the Passion. We

learn from Christ how many people know what it is to stand up. Peter said he'd be with him all the way. Jesus said Peter would deny him three times before the cock crowed. That's exactly what happened. Do you know that a servant woman said to him that she had seen him with Jesus and he cursed and said no. Saint Peter. Our rock! Because this made Peter look weak, we would have figured him to rat. We would have done something. And we would have been wrong. We must give people the benefit of a little doubt. We shouldn't be too quick to whack some guy."

Father Phil had black hair and a Mediterranean face. The brown eyes always are fixed on anybody who spoke to him. He loved being a priest, he crowed at a ceremony celebrating his fifteen years as a priest. He thought it was a sin punishable by torture and horrible death for anyone fortunate enough to be a priest who did not arise at any hour and tend to the sick and broken and grieving.

Never once did he say what he kept in a hidden chamber of his mind: "Why are these nice people here and all these rats are out there with nothing happening to them? Couldn't we pray so hard that our people get up, and the rats fall over dead?"

He had his own views on other issues, particularly on the celibacy of priests. "I believe in adoration of God and preaching his word," he said to everybody who questioned his ways. "I don't believe in a cold life. They spread a rumor that I had a girlfriend in my last parish. That was a lie. I fell in love five times in that parish." He found great support in the library, where several histories noted that the celibacy rule was based on land. Priests were married and raised families all over the earth until 1074, when the Vatican suddenly ruled that priests could no longer consort with women. One pope after another said there would be horrible suffering in the hereafter for all who defied this rule.

Love or fear of God had about as much to do with it as yesterday's air temperature. The new law was a lance thrust at these monks who owned huge estates and were about to start families who would inherit the lands. They were the target. The Vatican ruled out marriages and soon, on the Church's idea of rapidly passing time, generations of monks were dying without heirs, and all land reverted to Rome. Popes were so ravenous over new free land that they could eat it with a knife and fork.

There was one aspect to celibacy that Father Phil liked. "No pope can jam his son into the job," Father Phil said. "I think all regular politicians should live the same way. They leave us their sons. How can we thank them enough? The father is a bindlestiff and a stumblebum and he asks you to turn over the world to the son."

He also thought that papal succession should be handled by a rule, and priests everywhere else allowed to live normal married lives. Father Phil's rule would be simple: If any pope tries to maneuver his son into St. Peter's, the Vatican must murder the son immediately.

Now, at his Mafia Day mass, Father Phil closed the service by saying, "We do know that there are some people who are only sent onto the earth to inflict harm. They have no other purpose in life. They go into a court and invent a story that will put an innocent person in jail.

"God did not send people to lie on the witness stand. That is not God's way. God hates people who bear false witness. Wasn't his own son, Jesus, the victim of an informer? Can you imagine from what we have just read what happened to this Judas when he died? He committed suicide. That was just the start, dear friends. So know this: These liars come from the other person! They are from the Devil. They are his disciples on earth. The only way to handle them is to make them go away. They have no immortal souls. It is a killing for Christ."

Fausti became dizzy. He was not going to kill anybody. He slid out of the pew and walked to the door as silently as a pallbearer. But he knew that he had to stay for the entire mass. He could hear them going back to Sullivan Street and telling his father and uncle, "It was beautiful. What happened to the kid? He walks out like he don't like it. That's not respectful." He stood in the back.

When the mass ended, he was right out the front door in plenty of time to get away and here was the priest coming out of the side door.

"When do you work?" he asked Fausti.

"Now."

"The place is Rockaway?"

"Yop."

"What part?"

"Beach Eighty-four."

"Why don't I go with you now?"

"Because I don't get off till six o'clock."

Fausti could sense and see that he was necessary to the priest's ambitions. He didn't have to think long to realize what the ambition was: get close to The Fist. Why? It is enough for somebody in the mob, chaplain or delivery boy or soldier, to stand close to the Boss.

"You know what I'll do? I'll pick you up when you're through and drive you back to the city."

Fausti left for the subway, a couple of blocks away.

17

Fausti caught the A train from Hoyt Street. It was a beautiful ride in the morning, even under a threatening sky, coming high over Jamaica Bay and down to the beach. He walked in the creosote smell and wet sand in a green wool tank suit with black band across the middle, the whistle around his neck and Noxzema on his nose. The beach was between two wood jetties that were covered at high tide. The sand was an assembly hall of Catholic schoolgirls. He was the Prince up on the chair, even though he didn't know how to talk to them.

Suddenly, a powerful wind came out of a dark sky and the ocean was an opponent. When the tide started running out at

3 P.M., there were swimmers in trouble all along the beach. Fausti was in and out twice. Nothing, but needed. The lieutenant came along the boardwalk in a truck, calling down to the lifeguards to close the beach. Fausti and the guy with him, Larry Goldstone, blew whistles to get everybody out of the water. They put up red flags that meant no swimming.

Soon, it grew dark and chilly and the place emptied.

Then Goldstone said he was going to take a chance and go home. On the next beach, Bernie Mulhearn walked. Going to McGlone's, a mile away.

Fausti was thinking of changing in the lifeguard shack, doing it casually, as if he was just putting on something warmer, and sliding right out for the A train.

As he stood on his beach, 84th Street, and thought about this, Fausti suddenly imagined or saw the black hair of a person going under a wave over on the next beach, which was Bernie Mulhearn's, far out, where the tide was causing swollen water to rise higher and break with a thunderclap. There was another wave and he didn't know whether it was a head or the dark water under the foam. With nobody on the next beach to stop him, whoever it was could have just walked right in. Fausti started walking. There was nothing here, he was sure of that, but still he walked, now trotted and, the hell with it, ran as fast as he could across the wet sand.

He went under the first wave and as he came up he saw a hand out of the water. Whoever it was couldn't lift a full arm. He swam for it, but then a wave covered it. Then there was something in the middle of a wave. He swam right for the spot, and was sure he saw it somewhere else. He went under and down to the bottom and raked a hand over sand in darkness. He felt nothing. Up he started, into a crash of water as heavy as cement, pinning him to the sand, forcing him to hold his breath and outwait the bottom of the wave before putting a foot on the sand and rising. Still nothing when he got on the top. Now he decided, or the waves helped him do it, that the head was a hideous fantasy. He came out of the water and waited for a man to suddenly walk out of the water. The beach was empty.

There was a blue blanket on the white sand near the boardwalk. Nothing else. Two young girls strolled along the beach toward the blanket. They were the only other people on the beach. They had their backs to Fausti as they picked up belongings, folding something. They walked away with white towels and beach jackets over their arms. The blue blanket was still empty on the white sand.

At six o'clock, when he was supposed to quit, and the beach officially closed, he gathered up the blue blanket. Sunglasses, Salem cigarettes, a *Beaver* magazine and, under the towel, a billfold and program from Aqueduct racetrack. He took a last look at the ocean.

The stationhouse on 98th Street had a municipal smell and walls of chipped green paint. Sitting at the high desk was a short, chubby sergeant with his light hair in a crewcut. The sergeant rubbed a hand across his face. He took the blanket and wallet.

"Why don't you sit down over there?" he said, pointing to a bench.

The sergeant took the missing guy's identification card from the wallet and made a call. Then he told two cops, "The woman says he went to the beach after the racetrack today."

Fausti was at the door. "Where are you going?" he called out.

"Make a call."

"Make it here."

Two cops drove him to the man's house, which was in Ozone Park. When they got to the new ranch house on a dirt road, Desarc Road, the cop driving said to Fausti, "Go ahead in. It's your job to tell them. If the lifeguard loses the person, the police have to drive the lifeguard to the family. But he has to tell them. That's union rules."

Fausti walked up and rang the bell. A woman came to the door with a young guy of about eighteen, wearing a blue tank top. The son. Fausti didn't know what to tell her. He excused himself and walked halfway back to the police car.

"What should I say?"

"That you were the lifeguard on the beach where her husband left everything on his blanket — hasn't returned. You don't know if he drowned. She ought to check us and the hospital later. See if she thinks he commited suicide."

He could be heard by the woman in the doorway, who suddenly was in a heap on the floor. A young girl fell on her.

The son in the tank top came through the door and detonated.

"What happened? You let my father drown? My father? I'll kill you."

"No, you won't." Fausti said it by reflex.

"Who are you, you fuck, you're the lifeguard. My father drowned."

"We don't know that," Fausti said.

The voice rose into a shriek and there was foam on his lips.

"You're gonna get hit in the head!"

Fausti didn't know who the kid was, but he knew by the phrasing what he wanted to be.

When he got back to the precinct, he found Father Phil talking loudly to a lieutenant in the low light at the desk. Seeing Fausti, he said, "Here he is. If I didn't happen to pass by there going to the bridge I still wouldn't know where he was. You had no right to take him to the family. That was your job. He's done nothing wrong. How could you do this to him?"

It was almost 8:30 when they walked in the beginning of dusk at Fausti's beach. Fausti showed where he had started.

A trail of footprints was still on the wet sand. All alone, with nothing near them. At first, they were outlines. But then footprints were breaking the sand wide and deep. A person running. All the way from Fausti's station on the 84th Street Beach and onto 83rd, which was supposed to be guarded by somebody else. The last sharp footprint was a step from water.

"That's the boy's footprints," Father Phil said. "Nobody else ran across this sand but this boy trying to find out if somebody drowned on a beach that wasn't his post."

The lieutenant nodded. "The Parks Department supervisor told us they never authorized anybody to go home before six o'clock."

Father Phil held out his hands. "What do you want from him,

then?" He clapped Fausti on the shoulder. "Come on, let's get you home."

In the middle of the street in front of the precinct two patrol cars were parked, blocking a black Oldsmobile. Up on the hood was the son in the blue tank top. Pointing at cops, yelling, snarling, and when he saw Fausti leaving the precinct, a shout came from the pit of his stomach.

"Kill YOU!"

"Act like he's not even there," Father Phil said, opening the car door for Fausti.

At this, the blue tank top dived from the car hood. One cop's arm stopped him and others came onto him and formed a cage. Through a tangle of arms could be seen a twisted mouth dripping spit. A face from a zoo cage.

"I wonder who he is," Father Phil said on the way home.

Fausti shrugged.

They rode in silence for some time. Then at a red light on Woodhaven Boulevard the priest looked at Fausti.

"I hope you don't have to kill him."

Fausti was unable to speak.

They drove on in silence. Coming out of the Midtown Tunnel, Father Phil said, "I've only seen a few in that much rage. I'm afraid it's that simple. He wanted to kill you. You might have to."

There was nobody in the club at this hour.

"I have to go back to Buffalo," the priest said.

"What time you get there?"

"After midnight. I'll be back soon. I wish you luck."

"Thanks."

He looked solemnly at Fausti. "I hope you don't have to kill this kid."

With that, he was off to Buffalo and Fausti went up to his house.

18 In the morning, Fausti got a phone call from the lifeguard supervisor, who told him not to come in. "Do you know how lousy these people are here? Do you know what one guy says this morning? He says, 'Gangsters can't swim.' "

Two days later, the *Daily News* newspaper death notices read:

"PICCOLO, STEVEN. Beloved husband of Louise. Devoted father of Diane and James. At Stephen Romanelli Funeral Home, 89-01 Rockaway Boulevard, Ozone Park. Viewing 2–5 P.M., 7–9 P.M."

He went into the Children's Aid Society gym and hit the puck into this straight-backed net. He stood in the center of the floor and shot, then shot again, then again, and every once in a while he stopped, his brain cold with fear, then thawing, then jagged. Now he saw this other kid for what he was. Shrieking himself purple. He decided that the son was around some outfit, too.

He knew that he only had to walk across the street and see his uncle. That was easier than telling his father. His father would jump into a car and go looking for the kid. With the uncle, he would tell the story three and four and maybe five times. That would do it. But then you might as well just join the army and pull guard duty with all the other guys in front of the club. The Fist couldn't tell you stay away when you're using his troops to whack somebody. And the father would squall but it was too late; the moment Fausti finished telling his story and asked for something to be done, he not only was in, but he had no choice anymore. He was in and he couldn't leave.

"Fuck it."

He walked across the street toward the club, but was stopped by the sight of a man on his hands and knees scrubbing the sidewalk with a toothbrush. Stefano Geraci appeared at the top of the steps from the clubhouse.

"How's he doin'?" his uncle's voice called from inside the club.

"Slow," Geraci said. He walked out and kicked the guy hard.

"He owes," Fausti said to himself.

He knew that it had to be over not paying a $5,000 shylock loan, which was the line between trouble calling for a slap in the face or, more, a good beating. The terms for a $5,000 street loan were payment of $150 a week until you got the entire $5,000 together and erased the loan. If you never got the principal together, you paid that $150 a week forever. Not to come around and pay the interest, the vig, left you with a toothbrush in your hand and at the least sore ribs from being kicked a lot.

Fausti turned and went home. At four o'clock he put on his one dark blue suit and a checked sports shirt, but decided to change to a white shirt and tie. He took his wallet and change from the dresser. He looked at the identification in the wallet. He was mad at himself for looking at it. But he did.

He walked along Bleecker Street to Sixth Avenue and was about to turn to go to the subway when he crossed Sixth and went to Miraculous Medal, which had a couple of old women saying the rosary through the empty late afternoon. Fausti knelt in the last pew. He said the entrance money of three Our Fathers and three Hail Marys, then started talking directly to the cross over the altar.

"Listen to me, will you, please. If you could just help this other kid, his name is James Piccolo, at least that's what the paper says, if you could just help him see that I had nothing to do with this. If his father was there, then his father would be here now because I wouldn't miss. You could put it in the kid's mind that maybe this was a true accident, that I was not around because I wasn't supposed to be around. Please listen to me. You do this for me, then I'll step out and do something really good for a complete stranger."

He walked to the subway entrance at West 3rd and took the A train for Queens. The riders started out white and then at the first Brooklyn stop, High Street, the whites were gone and it became all black, all through Brooklyn, and when it came out of the ground and climbed spindly el tracks into two-story Queens, Fausti was the only one in the subway car as it ran along Liberty

Avenue in Ozone Park. He got off at 90th Street. At the foot of the staircase, two guys were standing in front of a club with windows of brick. One of them had little fires all over his front and hands set by his jewelry in the light from the streetlight. The other was as wide as a doorway. He was dressed in his best black suit for funerals.

The two walked ahead, talking. Diamonds said, "We just stay enough to get marked present. Nice guy, Steve, shylocks at the track, goes to the beach. But I don't want to be chief mourner."

The heavyset guy said, "I don't know what's going on. A made man got killed. That's not supposed to happen without permission."

Diamonds said, "They think somebody got him out in the water and drowned him."

Fausti walked down the short block, past attached two-story brick houses with small lawns. At the corner there was a low brick wall of a Catholic church. He sat on it and thought. The two guys, the one with diamonds the standout, were over the front of the funeral parlor, kissing hello.

Fausti thought about what to say. "Do you go in and say to the kid, 'Could I see you for a second?' Maybe I go to one of them and tell them who I am and that I am really sorry and could he get the kid over so I could tell it to him?" Fausti dreamed of some guy with an open face who is one of the big guys and would say, "Sure, kid, come on, I'll do it." Of course it was hope that could not exist. But Fausti existed. Right now, existed alone. He walked across the street with his arms swinging straight out and his stride becoming brisker as he walked right up to the funeral parlor and into the lion's mouth.

The kid sat in the front on a couch talking to the mother. They had no casket in front of them because they had no body.

Fausti walked down the aisle to them.

There was a stillness greater than all rages.

He held out his hand to the mother. And he held her reddened large brown eyes, surprised and smoldering eyes, to his.

Alongside her, the son sat with his lips compressed and face quivering. From out of him came the sound of a high insane whine.

Fausti looked and spoke only to the mother. "Mrs. Piccolo, I'm Fausti Dellacava. I'm the lifeguard who tried to find your husband. I want to say that I'm sorry. I'm really sorry. For your husband. But I had nothing to do with it. It didn't happen on the beach where I was working. I tried to look. I never saw your husband in my life and I'm sorry but I didn't know who he was. I'm really sorry. You have my prayers. It's all I can do."

The woman stared. There were others seated on the couch with her, a sister maybe, a bald man who perhaps was her father. He never looked at them long enough to know what they really looked like. His eyes were riveted on the woman and she was studying his, not in any anger now, but in some sad hope that maybe some of the pain, some of the anger, could be taken away by something this young guy with eyes so piercing could say to her.

Slowly, stiffly, her right hand came up and touched Fausti's.

Right away, he said to her son, James, "I want you to know that I'm sorry. I'm very sorry. And that I know how you must feel, but you have to know that I had nothing to do with it. He was on another beach. I didn't even know where he was. Please take care of your mother. You have a big job."

Before there could be any reaction outside of stiff shock, he walked out, arms swinging, palms down, head up, eyes looking right through everybody, and he stopped to sign the book then went through the vestibule and out into the warm night.

The guy with the diamonds came up to him.

"I'm Ralph Gurino."

"Pleasure."

"I have to axt you, did you go on record before you came here?"

"I put it on the record," Fausti said.

"Nobody calls us. Who did you go on record with?"

"With everybody. I signed the book."

"What are you saying to me. You're from Sullivan Street, right?"

"Around there."

"I saw what you signed. I don't care who you are. You had to have somebody call for you and go on the record you was coming."

"I spoke to the mother and the son," Fausti said. "It's over."

"That don't end it with that kid," Diamonds said. He turned and went back into the funeral home.

Bus exhaust drifted through the light from the streetlight. An Ozone Park station wagon, a tow truck, performed the rare act of stopping for a red light.

Fausti walked to the el station, went upstairs, and sat on the empty platform for five minutes, waiting for the train. He still had not considered one moment of that funeral parlor. When the train came, he sat, put his head against the window and thought he would think about it, but instead he simply passed out. When he woke up, the train was at Fulton Street, downtown Manhattan, his face and hair wet with sweat from the heavy sleep.

19

"I told you," Rabbit the Music Teacher said. He was called Rabbit because he had good ears for music.

"It's that bad?" Buster Greco said.

"I told you a trumpet can turn on you," Rabbit said.

"This fucking thing."

"This fucking thing says it needs hard work."

"Should I get another trumpet?" Buster said.

"What are you saying? Do you know this is the fifth new horn you brought here. How long have we been at this?"

"Year."

"Five horns in a year. Louis Armstrong had five lives and one horn." Rabbit sighed. "You have to do scales every day."

"I do."

"What am I, a cabbage? I got ears. You haven't touched this instrument in, I'll bet you, two weeks."

"Yes I have."

"Is this how you lie in court? It's a wonder they don't bury you in jail. Music isn't something you put in a box like a loaf of bread. In music, you either are going ahead or going behind. There is no standing still. You don't practice for two weeks. You sound like you never played."

Buster was disconsolate. "It's my muscle tissue in the lips," he said sadly. "I guess I got no lip flexibility."

"Somebody told you that," Rabbit said. "I'll tell you what's wrong. You got no ass power. You're supposed to do scales at least an hour a day."

Buster Greco packed his horn and went into his pocket and handed Rabbit a hundred and fifty dollars.

"I won't be able to take this from you much longer," Rabbit said. "You'll go play somewhere and people will say I'm robbing you and you'll come back here to kill me."

"You got to keep me," Buster said. "This is the only honest thing I ever tried to do in almost my whole life."

As he was leaving the studio, Buster said, "What should I do most of?"

"Scales. At least an hour a day. C-major arpeggio."

Rabbit sounded, up and down, "Ba ba ba ba ba bahhhh."

"You got it," Buster said.

Buster is practicing one day, as he practices every day now, and that "Ba ba ba ba ba bahhhh" went through the air, time after time. That was the first day the woman across the street came to his house in the Bronx to complain.

"I'll stop," Buster said. "When I got no more to practice, I'll quit."

He began practicing at night, too. This led to more complaints, and a summons to Civil Court. Buster never gave it a thought. He went to court with his lawyer, Klein the Lawyer, who was making a free speech case when the judge stopped him. "Does Mr. Greco have a mute?"

Buster thought. "I must have a hundred of them. I got all music."

"Then use one of them and none of us will hear you," the judge said.

Buster went home. Klein the Lawyer went to the Yankee Tavern on 161st Street, yards up from Yankee Stadium, and he had two good golden scotch-and-water drinks and he saw Marvin Mahlman passing by outside and Klein let out such a holler that Mahlman came in. He was coming from a murder arraignment and here was Klein from a domestic dispute at best and they laughed about this and had another drink and Klein asked him about the Yankee baseball team, of which Klein knew nothing, and Mahlman expounded, succinctly and brilliantly, and when he was through Klein said he now knew all about baseball and ordered a drink on that and finally Mahlman said he had to go downtown. An hour later, he was in the hallway in the Supreme Court building in Manhattan and he told the story about Klein and Buster Greco's trumpet and mute to Lee Richman, who had Tony Pistols with him on some kind of case. Richman said that it was a good thing that Buster was taking trumpet lessons and not singing lessons and when they stopped laughing at that, Tony Pistols said:

"What lessons does he take?"

"Trumpet lessons. You ought to see him," Klein said. "He got a gold horn worth a fortune."

Tony Pistols grunted. That night, while playing cards in the club with The Fist, he happened to mention that Buster Greco had to be crazy, that he was taking up musical lessons at his age.

"What kind of lessons?" The Fist said.

"The lawyer says he takes trumpet. He says he got a big gold trumpet."

Now Buster is walking one day toward the junkyard office on the night that he is asked to be there for a special matter and he is whistling nice and walking nonchalant when his tense changed from present to past, which means that he was whistling when he got shot and then hit with an ax, after which he got put in a big orange drum. As this was a rush assignment, the two who killed him had not arranged for a machine that would make Buster part of a car fender. They took him for a ride along the Belt Parkway in Brooklyn, pulled into the old army terminal, and rolled the barrel off a pier and into the waters of the harbor. The barrel went down and disappeared into a strong outgoing tide.

Among debris bobbing in the waters of the harbor of the City of New York was a large orange oil drum, just the top third showing, but moving in and out with the tide, which runs at a knot and a half over a harbor that is mostly thirty-five feet deep. The barrel bobbed in the tide under the Verrazano Narrows Bridge, out past Sandy Hook, and often was sent to the east, until the ocean pushed it back, sometimes toward Jersey, and other times into an incoming tide that took it right back into the harbor, from which, six hours later, it moved right back into the open ocean. It was around for seven months and neither sank nor disappeared. This is not a first-person report, for inside the drum Buster's body was chopped up like stew meat. Nor were there any eyewitnesses, until those observers at journey's end. But there are charts of the tidal movements in New York Harbor to which this particular oil drum had to adhere. The currents dictated when and where it was, but machinery always was eligible to take over.

During this time, James Piccolo, the son, walked from his job in the junkyard to the Bergin Hunt and Fish Club, two storefronts whose fronts had been bricked up and were the headquarters of John Gotti.

"He tole you," a guy who looked like Dracula said. He was standing in the entranceway.

"He tole me nothin'. I didn't see him," Piccolo said.

"He tole you the last time for good. He tole you, 'No.' He tole you, 'No fuckin' way.'"

A voice boomed from inside.

"What's the fuckin' problem?"

"He wants to see you again."

"Fuck him! Who is it?"

"Piccolo's kid."

Suddenly Gotti was in the doorway. "I ought to make you suck my prick right on the sidewalk. I tole you. Fuck, we went with you as far as we want to. We're not goin' into some fuckin' war over you, we don't even know who the fuck you are. We know or knew or whatever the fuck your father. You can't even prove what happened to him. And you want to hit The Fist's kid."

"It ain't his kid. It's his nephew," Piccolo said.

"Good. Guys die over a fuckin' nephew. Leave me ast you somethin'. Didn't that kid come to the funeral parlor, come right face-to-face with you?"

"I want to go to his wake and tell his mother I'm sorry he had to die."

"Beautiful. I tell you what. You go and fuck yourself. Don't come here no more. You're on your fuckin' own around here."

20 Father Phil came down from Buffalo for a weekend, staying with people he knew in Brooklyn. He came around on Saturday night to see the club. The Fist knew him by now, and thought he was all right, but he still was a priest and The Fist advised him to stay out, that it don't look good. "I'll take off the collar," the priest said.

"Don't you dare do that thing," The Fist said.

Father Phil was embarrassed that The Fist just wouldn't let him in like they were supposed to. He tried to make it look all right by saying that he couldn't stay long because he had important business as a priest in Niagara. Which he did. It involved another side of his personality. It was as far away from the mob as possible. But perhaps he could get reassigned closer.

One gloomy afternoon in May, a bill called Defense of Gender was coming up for a vote in the City Council. The bill was to guarantee rights for gays and lesbians. Father Phil received letters from the archdiocese office saying that the heirarchy wanted the bill opposed by all Catholics.

Walking in out of a heavy rain, a Buffalo priest came into Father Phil's office and said, "You must oppose this bill. It is necessary to our salvation."

"How?" Father Phil said.

"They will steal children and turn them into homosexuals," the priest said. "They will come into the classrooms and steal our children."

Father Phil gave him the usual double body action, to imply agreement. The priest was certain that he had convinced Father Phil to oppose homosexuals. The Buffalo priest sent a note relaying such good news to the archdiocese office.

A few mornings later, he sat in his car in front of City Hall and wrote in longhand a press release stating:

Father Phillip Napolitano will make a significant announcement concerning the infamous Gender Bill that will be debated and voted on. Father Napolitano will make a "Definitive Statement" on the bill. He has tried to stay out of it, in order to demonstrate the separation between church and state, but his Church has pushed him to make this statement.

He loved it. The moment it was passed around City Hall, gays in the lobby snarled. The newspaper said Father Phil was following Church directions and would oppose the gay bill.

The following day Father Phil stood on the City Hall steps with his statement.

He read:

"I am troubled as a Catholic and as a priest because some elements of my church have created confusion about this bill. I am also upset because through propaganda they have encouraged a kind of bigotry and irrational fear toward gay people. I am shocked by the repulsive language and uncharitable attitudes expressed to me in letters that have swamped my office.

"This bill, my fellow citizens, simply recognizes that there are human rights common to all people. There should be no fear to recognizing homosexuals as people; they are human; they too have human rights. With the immense pressures that have kept millions of gay people in the closet, only a very few courageous people have proclaimed their sexual orientation to comfort the lonely homosexual, who is filled with guilt because society tells him that he is sick and unfit as a human being.

"My conscience tells me I must support this bill."

There came a morning when Father Phil sat on a folding chair in Lockfield Prison, his presence meant to influence people to get a parole for K.O. Lucas, serving five to ten for manslaughter reduced to assault. It should have been mass murder.

Barbara Timoney, the trim forty-five-year-old parole commissioner, was first to arrive in the bare hearing room. She had a container of coffee on the table and was going through thick files of letters begging for clemency for K.O.

Father Phil spoke the last words to K.O.

"Remember, you are so sorry that you can't sleep."

"Sorry for what?"

"For having to defend yourself when he pulled that gun on you."

"Sorry? I fuckin' cheer every time I think about it."

The case was weak, the sentence stiff but not astronomical. And at this time, Father Phil was trying to bring K.O. back to civilization.

"I care that you've made the best presentation," he told K.O. "We did an awful lot of work. Look at all those letters."

"Don't you worry. Watch me shine."

Lucas called out to Barbara Timoney.

"I'd like to fuck you," he said.

"Who are you?" Barbara Timoney said. She looked for a guard, but the one in the room had a hearing aid and could hear an explosion but little else.

"Isn't that pretty foolish of you?" she said calmly. "You want parole and you start with outrageous abuse."

"No, it's a very smart move. I knew it would get you very mad. But I say the truth. I'd like to fuck you. You know I'm not lying. From now on you know that anything I say is the truth."

"What is your name?"

"Harold."

"Harold what?"

"Harold."

"I meant your last name"

"I don't need no other name."

"Maybe you don't, but I do. Are you the Harold in these letters?"

"Ast anybody. Just say Harold. Watch them get scared. It's fucking beautiful."

Father Phil stood. "Ma'am, I am Father Phil Napolitano and I am the spiritual counselor of this fine person, Mr. Lucas. This is an excitable person. He comes here from behind bars and he understands that this is a chance to regain his liberty. He is beside himself with anxiety and anticipation. Could you see it in your heart to have compassion for this man?"

K.O. said, "You could let me out. I won't do anything wrong. I'll do four and that's it."

"What does that mean?" she said.

"That I'll only do four."

"Four what?"

"Murders."

When there was no reaction he became restless.

"You let me out, I give you a word that I'll do the four and no more. You'll never hear from me again. You'll never know I'm around. Just four."

Later that day, The Fist asked Father Phil, "How did he do?"

"Good. They had him back to the prison general population in time for his lunch."

21

A few days later, Fausti saw Con standing in the door of her house on Thompson. She held dresses on hangers to her chest and tried to lift a duffel bag with a free hand. Fausti held out a hand, but she looked straight through him and went upstairs, body lopsided with the duffel bag.

Fausti walked on and didn't dare reveal himself by looking at the doorway.

Seven times that day, Fausti walked down Thompson Street, past her house, turned the corner, went around the block, and came down Thompson again. Five times she wasn't there. Once, she was talking to a woman he didn't know. Con didn't look at him and he didn't look at her.

On the seventh trip, what was going to be the last, her brother Pat was standing with her.

Fausti waited until he was almost abreast of Pat, only two feet away, and he shouted, "Hey, Pat!"

Pat said hello warmly. "You remember Concetta."

"Are you crazy? Of course."

"She's moving back with me," Pat said.

Fausti asked her if she wanted to go for a drink, or coffee, and she said no, that she had to be up early to look for a job. Pat invited Fausti up to the apartment with them. Con seemed reluctant, but Fausti got alongside Pat and could be turned back only by the collapse of the staircase. The apartment was on the third floor. A small dining room and kitchen, a living room that had two windows looking onto the street, and one small bedroom and a second so small that it was best used as a closet. The brother had been living there alone, but now he gave Con the bedroom and slept on the couch. Over coffee, they sat in the living room and looked through the collection of books and pictures that Con had brought down with her.

She took out the Roosevelt High, Yonkers, N.Y., yearbook and put it down on the table alongside Fausti.

"Do you want to see how pretty all the girls in my class are?" she said. He went through it and found her picture, stared at it for a long time, all the while saying how beautiful she was, and she said, "Go and see the rest." There was the face of his family looking out at him with the name Frances Dellacava.

"Who is this?" he asked.

"She says that her father is your father."

Fausti had nothing to say for a long embarrassed moment.

"I think he is," she said.

"Why?"

"Your father was at graduation. When your father saw my father, he ducked out of his seat and went way in the back. We saw him. Then he even talked to my father."

"That doesn't make him her father."

"Ask her. She'll tell you. Better yet, go ask your father."

He retreated into silence again.

"Are you working for them now?"

"How could you ask me that?"

"Because. When I was down here last, I took a walk and saw you."

She walked out of the room. A call did not bring her out. Fausti got up and left. Walking home, he tried to figure out what she had seen that could upset her this much.

The first to know was the Old Ladies Network, whose messages are carried on winged words. An aunt, which is a proper name and needs no more, was walking home with a cart from Grand Union when Maria, who was inspecting the air from her second-floor window, called down.

"Your niece thinks Fausti is in with the men."

"She's crazy. Who did she tell that to?" the aunt said.

"Barbara Broncaccio," Maria said.

"She didn't tell me. Nobody told me," the aunt said.

"Concetta seen him in the club or something. He had some hat on or something. I heard her saying that to her brother by the shoemaker's. But then I heard from Baldy Dom that the other fellow yells at Fausti for trying to look like he was in."

"Does Concetta know that?" the aunt said.

"Oh, I don't know," Maria said.

"Why don't you tell her?"

"Oh, we're not supposed a mention the other fellow."

"That's complete fuckin' nonsense," the aunt said.

"No, it isn't. If I tell her, then I get two people in trouble. Baldy Dom for saying to me and me for telling Concetta. You're not supposed to talk."

"You just told me!" the aunt said.

"I was just thinking out loud. I didn't come down and tell you on the record."

The aunt stormed into Con's apartment and scolded her. "This time, you happen to be wrong, too."

Later, Fausti came around and told her, "Do you think I'm capable of being in? Killing somebody? How could you think that?"

"It's all I've ever been told." she said. "They kill guys in the street and their families at home. Look in my own classroom. Secret families. Does Frances's mother know that your father has two families? Does your mother know?"

"Then you might as well marry me right here, because I am going to marry once and that's it. Forever. For all time," Fausti said.

The Old Ladies Network agreed. They had decided that Fausti and Con were to be married. If it wasn't an arranged marriage, then they would make it as close to one as they could.

"You take one look you know," Old Teresa said.

"You could see," Rosa said.

"Pretty soon, we're the only ones here not married."

"At least we were," Rose said.

"Both guys dropped dead because they were livin' with us," Aunt Cammie said.

This was while observing the first time they went out together. Fausti came around with tickets to the Rangers' hockey game that his brother had given him. From the corner, he could see Con, in a short black coat, her hair in careful curls, standing in front of her doorway.

She watched with a smile as Fausti walked down the block.

They got on the subway at West 3rd and rode the six minutes up to Madison Square Garden, at 34th.

The game was between the New York Rangers and the Detroit Red Wings. They had good side loge seats, and when the teams came on the ice to warm up, the speed of their skating and the jersey colors whirling in the lights dazzled Con. Then Nick Fotiu, of the Rangers, threw hockey pucks into the stands. He threw four before every game and the last one this time, wobbling through the air, came in Fausti's general location. Right away, one hand out, shoving people with the other, he tried to catch it and could not, despite a fine shove of some guy alongside him in a blue sweater.

"I'm sorry. I was trying to get it for you," he said to Con.

"You could have got closer," she said.

"How? The other people were like a fence. What do you want me to do, punch them out?"

"Sure."

Fotiu came from Staten Island and was called the Rangers' "Enforcer."

Fausti remembered his father saying, "Why do they make him an 'Enforcer,' just because he's Italian? He's a nice kid, he has barbecues for everybody where he lives. These papers give Italians a bad name."

"You know him?" Fausti asked his father excitedly.

"No. He don't live in our territory. Besides somebody hears. Oh, here, this is Larry Dellacava and his brother the Fist man, they are good new friends of Fotiu's. Do you know what people would do? Dial 911."

Now, when the game began, Fotiu swung down the ice like an avenger, black hair flying; he was one of the last players in the National Hockey League to play without a helmet.

He knocked down a Red Wings player. Con yelped. Fotiu of the Rangers sunk a knee into somebody else's belly.

"Wooo-oww!" Con said.

"You like that?" Fausti asked her.

"I want him to do it some more," she said.

Again in her life, she heard a high loud aria soaring from a stage, rising to the banks of lights so high above — as the figures on ice rushed after each other with murder the intent at all times. She squirmed with glee each time there was any unnecessary roughness. There were two goals. The goals were all right, but not as much fun as the violence.

"You act like you belong in the club," Fausti said.

"No, I don't. I don't go for two families and that's all they do. And I don't want anything to do with jail. If the man goes to jail even for a week, the woman should be gone. I know I'd be."

"One week?"

"That's for other women. Me? I'm gone first day by noon. I'm not staying in jail in the kitchen."

Malocchio had lasted thirteen years and then one day a black came down Sullivan Street and Malocchio couldn't even get up on his haunches.

"If he can't try to bite one of them fuckin' animals comes this close to him, then it's time he went for a good long fuckin' ride," The Fist said.

Then Malocchio began to whimper and one eye closed on him and he began to cry continually. Fausti asked if they could take him to a veterinarian. They took him up to the Animal Hospital on the East Side and left him there for two days for tests. The vet came into the waiting room and said that an artery had given up in Malocchio's brain. An aneurysm, actually. It had burst and blood, so toxic on the brain, had seeped all over. It was too late even for animal neurosurgery. They took Malocchio home. He was listless and still whimpered in pain. "He gets the ride," The Fist said.

Soon, a big black limousine from Royal Ride, a Staten Island private car company, came to the club. Baldy Dom was in hit clothes, a black cap, black leather jacket, and somewhere on him, there legally, a gun. Permit issued by The Fist. He took old Malocchio out to the car, which was being driven by Ritchie of Royal Ride.

"Wait a minute."

The Fist walked out and ruffled Malocchio's fur.

"Get a good rest," he said. "I'll be thinking of you. I got to be in court."

Baldy Dom put Malocchio into the backseat, and got in front with Ritchie of Royal Ride. Malocchio had his head hanging out the window. The car started down Sullivan Street and suddenly Malocchio bayed and barked at Fausti, who was standing on the corner with Con and a crowd of others. "Take us with you," Fausti called.

"I don't want them to come with us," Baldy Dom said.

The driver already had stopped the car and Fausti and Con came racing up to it and climbed in back with Malocchio, who tried to show pleasure, but with one eye shut and his head in pain, he could only move his tail slightly.

Baldy Dom asked Fausti and Con if they shouldn't be home. They said, no. He said they were taking a long ride. They said, great!

Baldy Dom had Ritchie of Royal Ride take them across the Verrazano Bridge to Staten Island, after that up to a dirt road ending at a brick cottage with a field behind it. A sign on the front of the house said:

"Last Pet"

Buster, Prop.

Buster was a small man with sparse gray hair. He wore a gray work shirt with red stitching on the front advertising "Burn Brite Oil." He took bills from Baldy Dom and stuffed them into his pocket.

"You do it yourself, you know," Buster said. "We don't do the puttin' to sleep. If you want me to do it, it costs."

"We know," Baldy Dom said.

"No shotguns," Buster said. "Guy shoots both barrels they could hear it down the bar the cops drink."

"We don't do it noisy," Baldy Dom said.

"What do you do, you strangle them?" Buster said.

"Just a pistol," Baldy Dom said.

Buster shrugged. "You just give the dog a last pet and do what you got to do."

"We got to do this personal," Baldy Dom said. Buster the owner went inside with his cemetery payment. Dom helped Malocchio out of the car and started walking him along the path to the field in back. But Malocchio couldn't make it, and Baldy Dom had to reach under him and try to carry him. The dog was too unwieldy. Fausti ran from the car and hooked an arm under Malocchio, and the two carried him up into the darkness in the field. With each step, Fausti realized what was occurring. They came to a small fresh ditch lined with white tarpaulin in a field marked with wood crosses.

Baldy Dom stopped at the tarpaulin. "He fills this up later."

Baldy Dom bent down and eased Malocchio into the ditch.

From behind them, they heard Con call, "What are you doing?"

"He can't take any more pain, Con."

Baldy Dom said, "Why don't you go back with her? You can see what's going to happen here. Go by the car."

"I want to see," Con said, walking up to them. She knew what this was.

Fausti bent over and patted Malocchio. The dog was quivering with pain.

"Nice fellow."

Con ran her fingers over Malocchio's neck.

"I love you, poor dog."

"All right, now youse go," Baldy Dom said.

His leather jacket squeaked as he brought out a pistol. There was something about the sound and the motion of taking it out, a wallet when it was time to pay, that was too businesslike.

The pistol had a long cylinder, a silencer, growing out of the muzzle.

"I want to do it," Fausti said.

"What are you, crazy?"

"No. He's mine. His name is Malocchio. End his pain with a bullet."

"That's what I'm going to do. Blow him away."

"No. Stop his pain. I don't like how you say it. You don't care about him."

"What am I, out here for the air, I don't care about him?" Baldy Dom said.

"I still want to do it. He's mine."

Baldy Dom handed Fausti the gun. "You keep both hands on it."

"Con, you go away," Fausti said. She backed off.

"Con, you get out of here," he said firmly. She turned and walked back toward the car.

Fausti looked down at Malocchio and saw the eye closed and the dog whimpering in the steady pain. Now he put the pistol down with one hand, aimed it right at the head, where he thought the pain was coming from right behind it and tears filled his eyes and he aimed carefully and pulled the trigger.

And missed by a good foot.

"What do you mean, just like me?" The Fist growled when Baldy Dom gave his report on the missed shot from close range.

"I mean he had your style. Took right over."

Baldy Dom reminded himself, one more of these mistakes and I will be a memory.

Fausti's father got Malocchio II from the same guy in the Bronx who stole the original Malocchio. Not once did the dog go after a man in uniform on Sullivan Street. He only tried to bite blacks. One turned out to be a law student walking down to NYU. It was nice. The kid got a graduation present of five thousand dollars as a settlement.

22 They were on the other side of the street from Con's house, with a couple of others walking a few yards up, when Con said, "Maybe I ought to go over and see if my aunt wants anything."

They looked for an opening between parked cars in the middle of the block so they could cross. Traffic always limped here and even when it was clear everything still moved slowly and people crossing the street went around cars as if they were puddles.

"All she ever wants," Fausti said.

"Is a pack of cigarettes," Con said.

"So she can keep coughing."

"You can't get her to stop."

"Who could do that? Just go to the store and bring her back," Con said.

They stepped between parked cars.

"Then why are we even goin' ove —"

A rush of air, a small rattle.

Fausti pushed off his feet and fell backward, yanking Con's hand.

The car rushed by, missing them by the length of a finger.

They were in frightened silence against the fender of a parked car. Fausti held her arm tightly.

The car raced furiously to the corner of Bleecker Street, paused, and raced onto the next block of Sullivan, going up to the park.

"The freakin' bastard," Con said.

"You all right, Con?" he said, finally.

Fausti had the back of the driver's head in his eyes. He didn't even know the make of the car. He knew the driver's head.

This time, they waited until the street was completely empty before going over to Con's house.

He left her at her door.

"We're not getting cigarettes for my aunt?"

He didn't answer.

"She'll go out herself midnight."

He didn't answer.

"He sure came close," she said.

"Go on up. You must be shaky."

He watched her hair shining in the vestibule light. Imagine this. She could have been mangled by now. That fuck.

If it was just some driver, he thought, walking up to the club, and he stopped thinking about that because the idea of being killed by chance was impossible for him to get a purchase on. Then he saw the driver's head. That was him, wasn't it? Inching along, following us, pick a spot and come running up and stop and get out and shoot. Except for the people there behind us. So shoot from the car, run us over, whatever. He knew we'd be there sometime. Fausti wondered if he could be right.

"Is that Buster?" the woman was saying to a couple of them in the club doorway the next day.

"Who?"

"Buster in the barrel," she said.

"What?"

"We want to know. He got an aunt wants to know. What is she supposed to do, run a memorial or a regular mass? She wants to know about her Buster."

"Who told you to come here?"

"The bulls say Buster in the barrel."

"When was this?"

"Last night."

"Who told you?"

"Missing Persons bulls come to the house."

"Missing Persons?"

"Sure! Buster's missing. What is he, sittin' on the couch front of the TV? We reported him missing. Missing Persons comes around last night. There was dredging or something and they said up comes the barrel off of the bottom. They think maybe Buster. But they can't get no fingerprints. Buster got no more fingers. They went out to Queens and told his family anyway. Anything to cause trouble."

"What are you telling this to us for?"

"The cops say maybe you know. You should tell. Buster's aunt misses him terrible."

They knew that if she ever got in and spoke to The Fist they would be sentenced to death.

Which is exactly what she was going to do. "I'm going in and tell him."

Fausti's father held up his hand. "You go in there and tell him, you're dead."

She said, "Why shouldn't I ask him? He's the Boss in charge of everything. The bulls said that if it isn't Buster then maybe it's some guy from the beach last summer. Missing. They was going down to see the family after they left me last night."

Later, Fausti's father put his arm on Fausti's shoulder.

"You can't tell nobody nothing."

"He just tried to run me over. I go —"

"You tell nobody. Listen to me. Don't fuck around."

"This guy tried to fucking kill me. Kill Con too. Somebody got to tell him it ain't his father they found."

"I just told you. Don't you fucking breathe this."

"I'm supposed to keep my mouth shut and get fucking killed?"

The father said, "If they hear Buster's in that barrel, then they all over us. A murder case, they do anything. You don't know what they try on you. A murder they do anything."

"Where do I come in?"

"With your mouth shut."

"You're crazy. I'm going in and ask him."

The father's finger began poking Fausti's chest hard. "If you go in there and say anything, one fucking word, you're talking about a murder with him and he got to protect himself. You know how? By fuckin' shooting you."

The thought of an enormity like this left Fausti frozen.

"Besides, that other fuckin' kid won't be here long," Larry said.

"What are you saying to me?" Fausti shrieked.

"I told you not for long. In the meantime, you can't say noth —"

"If he thinks that's his fath —"

"He is going to be no more. Do you understand what I am telling you? He is going to be no fucking more."

Since his father was chained to whatever the mob decided, Fausti wanted a contrast to this violence that would comfort him. He knew that at his age he was too young to be in the shock of murder, that he would carry in him the rest of his life, and that was going to be long years.

He called Father Phil.

23 Father Phil was elated. He could do God's work. He could save somebody from being whacked. "That's a corporal work of mercy," he said to himself. And if he couldn't prevent the killing, then at least he could keep the blood localized, lure the kid to some quiet place where nobody except the shooters had to watch the thing. And at the same time he could show his proficiency as a magistrate of mobsters and The Fist himself would love him for saving everybody from so much dangerous exposure of a hit.

"The Missing Persons ministry," he told Piccolo's wife when he came to her house on Desarc Road in Ozone Park.

"How come we don't have a thing like that in our parish?"

"That's why we were asked to come here. Ours is so successful in Buffalo that I have been asked by both dioceses to start one here."

He noticed the mailbox was full. "Let me bring this in for you."

That was always his move. Perform a little domestic thing and they love you.

"Thank you," the wife said.

She walked into the living room and put the mail alongside a stack of others.

"I only open mine, you know," she said. "I never touch his. I keep thinking that maybe he comes back. You know, we had a service for him in the funeral parlor like he was dead."

"I heard that," the priest said.

"I never should of done it, you know. You never know, you know. Then the cop comes last night and says they found somebody. In a drum someplace. They say they don't know who it is. But they were asking about my James, if I had any idea his father went with somebody or something. My son, James, says he knows it's his father. Father got murdered, he says."

The son would never know me in the collar, the priest said to himself. I had on a rain jacket when I saw him. I'm not sure he even saw me, he was so crazy. Besides, nobody around here touches a priest. The collar is stronger than an armored battalion.

"Is your son around?"

"No, he goes to work every day."

"Where is that?"

"Francisco's junkyard. Right on Rockaway Boulevard. There every day. He's a good boy."

"It's just down the street from here?"

"So close he don't even need a car. But you know young guys, they drive fifty yards."

"A lot of people from around here work there, I guess," the priest said.

"Nope. He goes down there alone and comes back six, seven at night alone."

"Tell me, where does a boy his age go when they finish work?"

"He comes right home. Takes a shower he's so messy. Then he goes out. Oh, boy. Goes to someplace Bubbles Howard Beach. Who knows where else?"

"Louise! Who's that talking?"

"The priest, Mother."

"What priest? What's he here for? Why didn't you tell me a priest was coming? You have to tell me these things before you do them."

Father Phil smiled.

"She's been living with us," the wife said.

"How long?"

"Twenty-one years."

The mother came into the kitchen. She was in a black dress and had her hair tied in a bun.

Even in Buffalo we don't do that anymore, the priest said to himself.

"It's a terrible thing, my daughter loses a husband," the mother said.

"We have no proof that he's gone," the priest said. "He could have hit his head and be wandering around not knowing who he is."

Father Phil was wondering why he even let them entertain the notion that the guy could be alive. He went into the ocean forever. Why am I giving them false hope in the bargain? I'm only here to get an idea of how dangerous her kid can be.

"He knew who he was every day of his life," the mother said. "He knew he wanted anything that didn't belong to him."

The wife sighed. "I still miss him so mu —"

"My husband died. I miss him every day all day long. It's too hard without him. I should've died before him. I wish I'd die right now."

The mother's voice rose and her hands clutched the front of her dress.

"When did the poor man die?" the priest said.

"Nineteen fifty-two."

He looked at the wife and said, softly, "Do you remember what you were talking about the last time you saw him?"

"I remem —"

"He said to me what he always said to me," her mother said. "Nothin'. Absolutely nothin'. And that's just what he was good for."

"I was wondering what he said to you," the priest said to the wife.

"He tol —"

"I never had six words with him," her mother said. "Every night after supper he went right out the door, off with these hoodlums."

"So he said nothing you can remember from the last time you saw him," he said to the wife.

"Nothin'," her mother answered.

Father Phil was fingering the stack of mail. Not for anything, just doing something with his hand. Then as the mother was talking on he happened to look through the stack of mail for Steven Piccolo.

There was a sales announcement from Brief Interlude, the clothes shop used by the mobsters, a fund-raising letter from the Nativity Church, a letter from somebody in Allenwood Penitentiary, a statement from Columbia Savings and Loan on Jamaica Avenue, a letter from the Pennsylvania Motor Vehicle Bureau, a magazine subscription letter.

He went back to the Motor Vehicle letter.

"You don't open this?" he said to the wife.

"I like to leave it for him in case, you know, what if he ever comes?"

The priest shrugged. He tried to speak about the son in the junkyard, the missing husband, and the barrel the police reported finding, but he got nowhere what with the mother butting in on the syllable. He took his leave.

He was in the car when guilt got a claw on his stomach. He had spent all the time starting to find out the son's habits and hadn't done anything to comfort the woman for a half hour like he should. He went back to the house and went straight to the mail.

"Why don't we open just this one?"

"All right, I guess. I have to tell you." She looked around to make sure her mother was absent. "I have to tell you, the last thing my husband says to me that day, he says, 'I can' take that' — excuse me, Father, but he said—'I can't take this effin' mother of yours no more. She got me insane.'"

Father Phil held the Pennsylvania Motor Vehicle letter. Father Phil ripped the letter open. It was a notice of late payment of a traffic ticket for making an illegal turn at Clancy Avenue in Scranton, Pennsylvania, on November 24.

The fool must have shown them something that made them send his court records to his Queens address.

"What day did your husband become missing?" the priest asked.

He remembered. He wanted to make sure.

"August 23," the wife said.

A week later, they entered Scranton on an underpass under the railroad tracks and came to a main street that had been turned into a mall. A block away was an Italian restaurant, "Piccolo John's."

He never thought he could get this far without the kid in the backseat, and Fausti, next to him, erupting. But one thing calmed. The notion that the guy faked a drowning and ran off the beach forever. Nobody could conceive of him doing that. Simultaneously, they knew that the man had to be here.

The priest let wife and son and Fausti get out, and he went to park. Deception doesn't do it, he thought. You're supposed to use a disguise that people more or less can see through and yet accept. That's the agreement. Not pretending to die.

In the late afternoon deadness, a woman and two little girls were in a booth along the far wall. The owner suddenly came out from the kitchen.

Mrs. Piccolo gasped. The son tried to dive over the table to get at the father.

Who kept absolute composure as he turned and walked into another room in the restaurant.

"He doesn't know us!" the wife said. "Oh, dear Lord, the poor man. He's in a coma."

At this moment, one of the children at the table got up and ran after Piccolo.

"Daddy."

Now Mrs. Piccolo drew in a breath. "Daddy?"

Mrs. Piccolo came through the veil of love and into the chill daylight of fury.

"Daddy!" the little girl called again, running after Daddy Piccolo, who was in full egress. He was making quick steps that would have put him out on the sidewalk and off and running away when Mrs. Piccolo picked up this thick shaker of red pepper and threw it at him. By weight alone, even a glancing blow was critical. This time, it was a full hit. Piccolo went down and watched the floor spin.

"You hit my husband," the other woman yelled.

"Husband? He's a pimp fuck."

"Maybe he is. That's why he divorced you. Because you're a whore."

"Divorce? There's no divorce, you dopey bitch."

"I had these children with him!" the other one screamed. "Are you saying they are illegitimate?"

"Fuck you and your children," she said.

James Piccolo, standing over his father, trying to make up his mind whether to kick him or not, glanced up at Fausti. He made a face that meant he was sorry, ending the adventure that at one point had been death-defying.

As a reward, Father Phil represented The Fist at a sit-down to settle a dangerous beef between Sal Rastelli of the Bonnano mob and Vic Arena, who thinks he is the official acting boss of the Colombos. The girl, Gina Rastelli, is twenty-three, and Vic comes up sixty-five. How had he arrived at this notion, that a guy sixty-five can run with a twenty-three-year-old? By not giving it any thought. But Sal Rastelli, the young woman's father, put in a superseding charge that Vic Arena was married, which was against the most important rule that a married member cannot take up with any wife, daughter, or sister of another member. This makes it difficult for a mobster who needs another wife.

Father Phil, a priest, was met with enthusiasm by both sides.

He ran the sit-down in the rear of Riverview Bakery on Twelfth Avenue. The priest was wedged between a worktable and a large threatening oven.

The participants stood at the other side of the worktable. This was a stand-up sit-down. Both sides agreed that the illicit affair began at a swell graduation party for Sal's daughter, Gina. She had just graduated from Dealers School in Las Vegas.

Vic announced that night that it was also his birthday. "It is my birthday and George Washington's birthday. Seventeen seventy-six. God Bless America and Vic Arena."

At night's end, she let Vic drive her home in his black Mercedes.

They arrived at her house three days later. Her boyfriend, Teddy, who works in the Lightning Auto Parts store on Cross Bay Boulevard, was in the doorway with Gina's mother, who was crying.

The mother asked Gina where she had been. Boyfriend Teddy also wanted to know. "Out with a real man," she told them. The next thing, she's home looking at blueprints for her new house — her and Vic's, she says.

Now at the stand-up sit-down, Vic said the rules didn't apply to him. He believed that a married member going out with another member's wife, or anybody else in the personal family, called for severe punishment. But he was out of it.

Vic Arena said that he was not married to his first wife, his official wife, anymore.

He sat back, smugly. "What helps me is that I know what I'm talkin' about when it comes to rules," he said.

"You are divorced?" Father Phil said.

"I'm not with my wife no more."

"No, we realize that. But do you have a New York State divorce?"

"Not official New York. But I got in my mind I'm divorced. I just don't want to get a divorce until I'm married again, like your Boss, and double up on wives, all that there."

Father Phil spread his hands. "I give Sal Rastelli the right. You're not divorced. You are doing a wrong thing."

"What do I have to do?" Vic Arena said.

"Get a divorce."

As a sit-down fee, Father Phil said he wanted $1,500. They squawked, but he was representing The Fist and they had to pay. Father Phil decided this was a good job. He had the number one job in the Mafia. Running a sit-down was the same as being on the Supreme Court.

24 Just when it was supposed to get good, the atmosphere around Fausti was ominous. Nobody said anything, or went into a cellar to hide, but the faces around the clubhouse were coated with anxiety. For the first time, lawyers were around on a frequent basis. There were a thousand wiretap court orders for them to fight.

"Get a job out of them before it's gone," Sloane the lawyer told Fausti on the street.

"Should I quit college to look to go to jail? I don't want to go to jail," Fausti said.

"I'm not talking about jail jobs. I mean a safety-first job. A good Mafia no-show job. Ask your uncle."

Fausti regarded that as an illusion. The thing that was real was the urgent need for luck. "Something has to happen," he told himself.

"There must be some way," Nini was saying in his candy store.

"To do what?" Fausti asked.

"To pay the rent without going to jail."

"Sure there is," Fausti said.

"How? They wouldn't let me in the thing on account of I'm from the neighborhood. They say, look what you got. What have I got? I got a penny business and I need dollars."

He swung his arm, upsetting a stack of bubble gum cards on the counter. Many of them dropped to the floor.

"I don't know why I have them. They're no fucking use," he said.

"Kids like them," Fausti said.

"You tell me if I can make money with these things," Nini said.

Fausti looked at the first pack. The featured picture was a listless face in color as vague as a watercolor of Stanley Musial of the St. Louis Cardinals.

"You tell me who the fuck he is," Nini said.

"He was a big player," Fausti said.

"What did he play?"

"I don't know," Fausti said.

"Neither do I," Nini said. "And for sure nobody knows his name, they're under twenty-five."

Fausti was putting the packs back. The last featured a full-length of pitcher Warren Spahn of the Braves.

"I know who he is," Fausti said.

"Ten other people do," Nini said.

"But you learn by having the card of an old guy," Fausti said.

"I can't make money on a fucking museum," Nini said.

Fausti happened to glance at *Godfather* tapes on a shelf behind the counter. Nini plays the *Godfather* movies in the store for six hours every Thursday. At 7 A.M., Nini puts on a tape of two *Godfather* movies and plays them for six hours, and has been doing it for nineteen years.

Most people don't watch anymore. A lot of times, Nini turns off the sound and just watches the movie's sets, which he loves.

The sounds in the store come from the busy furniture store — Haute Decor — opening up for a day of customers who read *Architectural Digest*.

But at 12:35 P.M. every Thursday, by habit as unchanging as a man delivering bread, Nini looks up to watch Hyman Roth come through the airport from Cuba, Hyman Roth being Meyer Lansky, and one of the guys jumps out and Hyman Roth gets his but good.

In real life, Little Frederico, who once had the contract to blow this John Gotti away, came in every Thursday for weeks and stared at the Hyman Roth murder.

The Fist heard about it and approved. If that's what Frederico needs to give him heart. Good.

"What do you call those," Fausti said, pointing to the tapes. "These are old. Everybody knows the names. Sonny. Who don't know Sonny from *The Godfather*?"

"Movies are different," Nini said. "They got power. Fucking baseball players got zero."

"Why not get gangster picture cards?" Fausti said.

It was just something Fausti spouted out. The two of them laughed. "Can't you see a kid buying gum and taking out a picture card of your uncle?" Nini said. It was such a ludicrous idea that they didn't bring it up for two whole weeks. Then Nini said, "I know we don't like John Gotti, but we could make some money off the bum selling his card."

Fausti now was openly wary of taking what seemed like a random remark into an open insult to Gotti.

"That's because you don't have to pay the fuckin' rent," Nini said.

"Why does it have to be Gotti?" Fausti said. "Why not like an Albert Anastasia?"

Nini listened attentively, since it suddenly was a thought worth encouraging. Besides, Nini found mobsters so much more interesting than baseball players and he was sure a lot of others did, too. . . .

"What cards would you put out? We could use *Godfather* cards?" Nini said.

"No, real people cards."

"Like who?"

"Like I said, put Albert Anastasia. The whole world knows him." Fausti's eyes went wide with excitement. Suddenly, he could see Anastasia on a gum card. The picture of Anastasia they had back in the club. Big dark guy.

"We call it 'Mob Stars,'" Fausti said, without thinking.

Fausti loved chasing an idea through the air so much that suddenly he could see even Gotti cards. The next day, he took the one picture of Albert Anastasia out of the Concerned Lutherans Club. Anastasia was in a lineup with The Fist and several others, with the tile wall of a precinct as background. This time, Nini became apprehensive. "Are we going to get in trouble around here? We're going to be using pictures and names and all that."

"Of dead guys," Fausti said. "Nobody cares. Anybody else can't wait to see their names anywhere, in the *Daily News*. They'll go to my uncle, 'Jeez, you're right. The fuckin' newspaper runs your name, your picture without even talking to you. Look what they done to me, should I bite their fuckin' throat?' Then he goes out and buys twenty-five copies. Charge five dollars for the paper, they'll still buy you out."

There was no question that they should start with Anastasia. He was dead and you could tell the truth on him, that he slaughtered hundreds. "Nobody will say he didn't do it," Fausti said.

Three days later, Nini looked up to see the artist from West Broadway, Hansen, at the curb, picking up candy wrappers. He was an impossible person for most people to figure out. What they didn't know was that he had been born in Ozone Park, with his father's crane in the driveway. The boom stood high over the house. Each day, therefore, Hansen was born hating manual labor. He much preferred the worst days of an artist. Once, when the Ferris wheel at the Feast of St. Anthony's was stuck, he tried ignoring it. Then he took a look at what the mechanics were doing, then cursed and yanked tools from them and set about fixing it himself. Shortly, he had the machine working. But mostly, all anybody saw him do was pick up cigarette butts and candy wrappers. He made collages out of them. The rumor was that he had sold one of them for some money. He said he was working on a much better one now, a collage featuring the silver "H" of a Hershey wrapper. When Nini offered Hansen a clean fresh Hershey bar with wrapper, he shook his head. "I got to have it ripped by somebody," he said. "I don't want to disturb the purity of ripped paper."

Nini gave him a pack of Marlboros, then showed him the picture of Albert A. and told him what it was for.

"Print this on plain dark cardboard?" Hansen said.

"I don't know the first thing," Nini said.

"I do," Hansen said. "You'll need four over one color and coated on one side."

"So?"

"It'll cost. Not me. I'll color the photo just for you. It costs after that."

"Like what?"

"A printer costs thousands."

"That's the end of that."

"Don't say that. It makes me crazy when somebody drops an idea in the face of money. Burn all money. Firebomb the banks! What we'll do, I'll color this picture and see what it looks like. We can't just do it with one. We need, I don't know, fifty faces for a print run."

"The fucking money," Nini said.

"I can't stand that talk."

"We can't do the work," Fausti said. "We got to do the write-up on the back of the card."

"I'll do this one here, this Anastasia, and then we'll talk about the printer. Look for a guy who could think ahead. But you'll still need fifty different faces."

"We can't do it," Fausti said. "We got to have a biography on the back of them," Fausti said. "I don't know how long it'll take me to do a back of one card. Fifty is out of the question. I never wrote anything before."

"Let's just do the one," Hansen said. "I'll do the picture and then we'll go over the life story on the back."

Fausti went to the Jefferson Library on Sixth Avenue and read of Anastasia in *Murder, Inc.* He also took out *They Called Him Trigger,* and the central character in the book, Trigger Stein, said of Anastasia: "He was a sweetheart of a guy. I don't know why they got down on him so much. For a few lousy bastards, they make him a mass murderer. Besides, anybody he hit was long overdue."

Denise was the first to see the biography notes for Albert Anastasia's card. She worked in the doctor's office on Prince Street, and worked in the candy store as a lunch-hour volunteer. She would have typed up the notes gladly, but she was confused by the number of murders Fausti printed, a thousand in one place and then only 118. A week later, when Al Hansen came around with the painted picture, he read the biography and snorted. "More yet!" He scrawled all over it, catching the murder error, and made Fausti take it back to Denise, in the doctor's office.

Al Hansen's "Mob Stars" mockup card had Albert A.'s picture on front and his record on back, much as they put lifetime batting statistics of a shortstop for the Chicago Cubs on baseball cards.

UMBERTO ANASTASIA.
ALSO KNOWN AS ALBERT ANASTASIA.
BORN: Naples, Italy, 1903.
NICKNAME: "The Executioner."
RANK: Founder and Boss of Murder, Inc. A reputed killer.
MADE: 1927, Brooklyn.
GROUP WORK: Slaughtered hundreds. Top hit crew with
    Lucky Luciano, Caesar De Francisi, Bugsy Siegel, and the
    great Joe Adonis.
LIABILITIES: Unfortunate temper.
ASSETS: Steady gun hand.
DEATH: 1957.
CAUSE OF DEATH: Barber chair.

Nini asked his best distributor, A & R Candy and Amusements,
if they could help. The distributor asked the Big Chew bubble
gum people if they could perform a personal favor and put a
couple of Mob Stars cards onto their print run. This wasn't quite
as warm and informal as it appeared. In making the request, A & R
Candy and Amusements said exactly what their salesman believed,
that they had been specifically asked by the De Francisi crime family, The Fist Dellacava, field marshal.

Fausti thought it was necessary to have a nice card made of The
Fist so he wouldn't get mad at the whole project. To show respect,
they made up a card with a great family wedding picture of The
Fist, who had a flower in his lapel.

Al Hansen again did the final writing.

UNDERWORLD HERO
BORN: West 3rd Street, 1929.
MADE: Self-made.

Underworld Hero found fruit stand owner had no change at all, things were that bad. Underworld Hero paid $500 for the fruit and walked off. He said, "I can pay whatever I want for fruit."

No drugs on his streets. Paid for many people in college. Underworld Hero spits at John Gotti. "He is made of paper."

Nini and Fausti agreed that this was a card that would interest about four people, all of whom were in The Fist's personal family. They decided to make this one to be shown only to The Fist, and then send out an improved Mob Stars card on The Fist.

The first two cards, Anastasia and The Fist, diluted, were printed and inserted into some of the gum packs, and a stack of the cards was delivered straight to Nini.

People called the distributor right away about the Anastasia card. The first callers were from Anastasia's descendants, who said, "We're good people, what are you doing to us?" However, several candy stores and newsstands complained that people who had been told about the Anastasia Mob Stars card were angered when they bought gum and found no such card. The reaction convinced the company that the Mob Stars cards, rather than printed as a favor to the mob, could turn into a magic receipt box. They sent a statement showing that earnings thus far of $4.50 were applied to a $3,500 print bill. Someday in the future, there might be earnings enough to produce commissions to Nini and partner.

The card with the timid description of The Fist wound up by mistake in a few scattered distributions. One did reach Our Family candy store at 100–10 101st Avenue, Ozone Park, Queens. The gum and cards sat on the Our Family candy rack like overheated nitroglycerine; two doors away was the bricked-up front of the Bergin Hunt and Fish Club — John Gotti, executive.

Two people from the club chewed bubble gum, Dukie off of Liberty Avenue, and Anthony Rampino, also known as Dracula because he looked like Dracula. Each bought packs of Big Chew.

When he made his entrance each day at the Bergin Hunt and Fish Club, John Gotti paused in midswagger to look at the newspapers spread over the table where the others, including Dukie and Dracula, drank espresso. If Gotti didn't see his name in a headline or his picture in print, he stamped on the floor and went back into his office, where he sat in a barber chair and screamed bloody murder, which coming from him was too real.

This time, Gotti stopped at the table and saw this gum card with The Fist's picture. Anthony Rampino chewed steadily.

"What do you call this? " Gotti said with a snarl.

"I seen it already," Anthony said. "I was just going to go out and throw it in the sewer."

"What is it?"

"They give him a write-up on the back," Rampino said.

"Yeah, and?"

Anthony picked up the card. Among things he couldn't do was read. He looked at all these unfamiliar letters.

"It says he's a cocksucker."

"Good for the fuck. What else does it say?"

"That he dresses like a fuckin' pig."

"Lemme see." Gotti looked at the back.

"'. . . spits at John Gotti. "He is made of paper."'"

He got both those big hands under that table and tried to throw it through the ceiling.

Rampino fled.

"He is goin' to fuckin' die!" Gotti yelled.

The next couple of cards were historic in nature and did good.

A must was a Mob Stars card of Ernesto Basile Brady, who retired himself after The Fist's near miss.

ERNESTO BASILE BRADY

BORN: Casenza, Calabria, Italy, 1893.

MADE: By himself. Succeeded Lucky Luciano. One of the founders of what was to become the De Francisi Family.

RANK: Boss of the De Francisi Family until sudden retirement in 1958.

ASSETS: Good manners. "The Prime Minister of the Underworld." Ran national gambling syndicate. In 1948, barside, Gallagher's Steak House, Manhattan, booked two-hundred-dollar bet for Truman on himself to win election. Brady paid.

LIABILITIES: Did not shoot many people. Became too well known. Tried clinging when Caesar De Francisi challenged him.

DIED: 1973, on his own in Monarch Apartments, 115 Central Park West, New York City.

The Fist was in a rare setting late that night. He was dining out in the Moondance diner on Sixth Avenue, with his crew. Brother Larry showed him his personal Mob Stars card and the Brady card. He looked at his "Underworld Hero" card and shrugged. It was all right, he guessed. He turned over the Brady card and when he didn't see his name, he threw the card away. Nobody brought up the cards again because they knew that The Fist had seen the one on him, so there was nothing to growl about.

"Gotti'll love it," one of them said.

"Gotti could eat it," The Fist said.

They now made up a real true Dellacava card, which the gum company and distributor felt confident enough to mix into a press run with Omar Bradley "The GI's General," Stan (The Man) Musial, St. Louis Cards, Jolly Cholly Grimm, Cubs' manager, Roger Maris, Yankees, Nick Etten, "Lou Gehrig's Replacement."

FAUSTI (THE FIST) DELLACAVA

MADE: By Caesar De Francisi, 1945.

RANK: Boss of All Bosses

CAREER HIGHS: Twenty-five professional fights. He shot Ernesto Basile Brady, but he is a human guy and only winged him on purpose and got him to retire.

ASSETS: Most revered Boss. Helps a million people. Never talks or uses phone.

LIABILITIES: None.

Al Hansen thought up good lines for the cards — "Well liked in Bensonhurst." He thought the best was "Has ice in his hands and a smoking gun in his pocket."

— Should it be "hands of ice" instead? Or would it be better to say, "He walked out of the place with ice in his veins and a smoking gun in his pocket."

He rolled this through his mind. He also wrote out for his Mob Stars cards, "Good to the last shot."

Fausti had the luxury and satisfaction of passing judgment on others that were put into print. Say the guy was a murderer and the card makes it so. As so many were dead or about to be, or in prison or about to be, his causing affliction to anybody appeared to be no issue. Then beyond this, Al Hansen told him one day, "Do you know why I do this work for nothing for you? Because this idea is going to go. Money! Legitimate money! Money from an idea!"

This brought such a thrill to Fausti, and in turn to Nini in the candy store, that they felt no inhibitions and searched the sidewalks for a Mob Star who could sell gum.

Suddenly it developed that Al Hansen came from the same street, 101st Avenue, as Gotti. He felt so familiar with the subject that he worked up what became their hottest card.

> ## JOHN GOTTI
> BORN: 1940. Still alive, for now.
> MADE: September 1968 by Carlo Gambino.
> NICKNAME: None. A homicidal maniac.
> ASSETS: None that anybody knows.
> LIABILITIES: His clothes. He dresses for police cameras.
>
> ---
>
> *Dreams of being the Big Boss. Home club: Bergin Hunt and Fish Club, 101st Avenue in Ozone Park, Queens. Also in Ravenite Club, Mulberry Street, Manhattan. Home: Howard Beach.*

It happens that these two cards, for The Fist and Gotti, made Mob Stars a commodity and created excitement for people of all ages. The gum company had to go into a second printing. Never had there been a rivalry in crime like this one. Big guys want to kill each other! That these two Dellacava picture cards, the first one, the one that was otherwise nominal, calling Gotti a piece of paper and the second card, much more real, noting that his personal assets were nil, poured a five-gallon drum of gasoline onto a fire at its beginning, went unnoticed. But John Gotti had a huge meeting in his clubhouse during which he hissed that Dellacava was to be killed.

He made a million death threats every week, John Gotti did, but this one came from his bones that seethed with hatred for The Fist.

Learning of this, The Fist sat at his card table and said, only once, "John Gotti gets whacked."

Regional requests also came in. Montalbano's candy store, South Passyunk Avenue, South Philadelphia, called the gum company and asked if there were any cards coming out on a neighborhood favorite, Tony Bananas. Montalbano said he had a huge number of requests for Tony Bananas. What he had was Tony Bananas ripping up all the gum packs while angrily trying to find his picture.

Fausti went through a pile of papers and old nightclub photos in his father's storefront and came out with Tony Bananas, a large swarthy guy, standing with his arms hanging over a boxing ring's ropes. Fausti regarded staring at library files as far more interesting than college. He took the date on the back of the Bananas picture and went to the files of the *Philadelphia Inquirer* and *Newark Star-Ledger* for that date and found stories about Bananas, fight manager, watching his boy Joey Giardello warming up.

ANTHONY CAPONIGRO aka TONY BANANAS

BORN: Newark, 1913.

FAMILY: Angelo Bruno.

MADE: By Angelo Bruno himself.

ASSETS: He is a very handsome guy. Unafraid of anything. Boxing TV announcer Stan Ellman beat him for $4,500 on a car loan. Ellman had one clubfoot. Tony Bananas broke the other foot and got paid.

LIABILITIES: Too many people know the story. But is still well liked. Has many fans in South Philly.

"How do you like it?" Tony Bananas said in the candy store. His eyes skipped right over everything except the praise.

"I'm a very handsome guy."

"Yes, you are, Tony," one of his hangers-on said.

"I'm well liked in South Philly."

"You got no idea, Tony."

"I got fans in South Philly."

"I told you that, didn't I always tell you that you got a following?"

"Somebody got to go!" Tony Bananas said.

At this time, Tony Bananas decided to ask New York for permission to kill Angelo Bruno, Boss of Philadelphia, so he could be the Boss. He could not wait to ask Natale Grassi, The Fist's director of New Jersey and Philadelphia, for permission to unseat Bruno. Grassi said he would get back to Bananas.

Grassi failed to mention that he felt compelled to tell Nicky Scarfo from the Philadelphia mob. Grassi told Scarfo because

Scarfo was his best friend from prison, and also because he was the chief money producer, the rainmaker, for Atlantic City concrete money that went to The Fist.

Beyond all this, it happened that Nicky Scarfo wanted to be the one in charge in Philadelphia.

Now Grassi went back to Bananas. "Do what you want to do." Bananas asked, "The Fist knows?" Grassi said, "He knows."

Dellacava was the Robert's Rules of Order of the Mafia. The rules for murdering members were strict, and breaking them was punishable by death. No made man could be killed without the boss of that family's permission. No man from one family could kill one from another family without permission of both bosses. Nobody could shoot a boss of a family without permission of all the bosses of the families in the city.

This was the great rule. No boss would vote for the death of another. They could be next. Therefore, the bosses should have been able to live until contracting liver disease.

Tony Bananas, who was going to shoot a boss, thought he had immunity from the rule. So one night in Philadelphia, Boss Angelo Bruno's driver brought Angelo to his house at 10 P.M. The driver lowered the window on Bruno's side. This was good because it made it easy for a guy to put a shotgun through the window and blow Bruno away.

Tony Bananas told all the guys that he was going up to New York to get confirmed as Boss and would return as head of a new kingdom.

He stopped off at the diamond center on West 47th Street and tried on a nine-carat pinky ring. Tony Bananas kissed the ring. "All guys in Philly kiss the ring like I'm a bishop."

Two of The Fist's people came by supposedly to take Tony Bananas downtown to see The Fist. It happens that The Fist never had given permission for the Bruno murder. His men drove in the opposite direction. They went to the Bronx, to DuPont Street, a one-block stretch of abandoned factories and empty lots that ended in weeds and oily water. Both shot and stabbed Tony Bananas. They stuffed his mouth and ears with twenty-dollar bills, as a poster for greed.

In the candy store, Nini asked Fausti, "Do you think we had something to do with it?"

"Nobody told me that," Fausti said.

Once, he had heard out on the street that somebody had a poison pen and was making the neighborhood sick. Upon hearing this, Al Hansen shrugged. "Pens tickle. Evil kills."

On a December evening in 1985, Paul Castellano, head of the Gambino Family, which was named after his uncle, was shot dead in his car on East 46th Street in the most crowded part of the rush hour. Television camera trucks were like flies trying to get through screens. They were unneeded. News like this is carried through air and down streets on its own strength. The story is telling itself in the air as you breathe.

The only thing that Gotti missed in publicizing his role was to appear on David Letterman's show down the street. The Fist, however, knew nothing about the murder in advance. The act, then, was treasonous.

"We did not contact him because we knew he was close to Paul, and he also had rules he stayed with," Sammy (The Bull) Gravano, Gotti's second, admitted.

Nobody asked him about Castellano. The Fist would have voted for Castellano and against this Gotti. If Gotti could kill Castellano, then Gotti could be expected to do only one thing: try to kill The Fist next.

At the end of an afternoon, two FBI agents walked into Larry Dellacava's storefront. One of the agents told him, "Somebody has been planning to kill The Fist and his personal families."

"Get the fuck outta here!" Larry yelled.

One of the agents said, "The people talking about whacking The Fist say that they don't care if women and children go, too. Sounds like a bomb to us."

Hearing this later, The Fist sat in silence in the club for a long time. He grunted. Nothing else.

There was a rule that the Mafia couldn't use bombs. A long

time ago in Youngstown, Ohio, a Dellacava possession, one Guy Cavallo and his son got in the family Cadillac at their house and it blew up from dynamite. While Guy was long overdue, it was a shame about the kid because he never did anything bad that anybody knew about. As the Mafia always was against child abuse, a commission rule was passed banning bombs, particularly in cars where juveniles rode.

But now, in a cellar in North Bergen, just across the river in Jersey, Louis (Fuse) Biscardi put together a nice remote control bomb. It was sanctioned by The Fist.

Biscardi needed a servo, which is the silver engine on a model plane. He had the four sticks of dynamite that were going to blow this slob Gotti into the sky. Biscardi went down to the craft shop on Bergenline Avenue and bought two model plane sets to get the servos. He put one into his bomb and saved the second for some other bastard.

This first one was a remote-control bomb and it was put into a car owned by Frank DiCicco. He was supposed to show up on a Sunday afternoon at a club on Eighteenth Avenue in Brooklyn with John Gotti.

The information was only half right. DiCicco came out alone. Otherwise, everything was on schedule. Two blocks away, one Tony Nap clicked the clicker and the bomb in the car blew upward, in a cone shape. DiCicco was part of the shape. A mounted policeman a block away was blown off his horse. Pieces of the car punctured light poles as far as a block away.

When Gotti saw it later, he was shaken. "He bombs us. We bomb his wife and kids," he said. "Get anybody. Get the fuckin' nephew."

Fuse Biscardi's second servo was going to be part of the bomb put in Gotti's own car when he left it at a car wash a few blocks from his house in Howard Beach. Then suddenly, the law seemed everywhere and nobody could put a bomb in Gotti's car like it was supposed to.

25 Rita Klimova, the new Czech ambassador to Washington, addressed a packed meeting of the Czech mission to the United Nations on Madison Avenue.

"What is it that you all do?" she called out.

"We spy!" many voices answered.

"Spies!"

"Don't you read newspapers?" she called out. "Don't you see television? We don't have spies anymore."

"Then what do we do?"

"Pack your belongings and go home to Prague and get a job!"

FBI agents from the counterintelligence and counterespionage special squads secretly videotaped the weeping Czechs leaving the meeting. Bulgarians sent their spies home to hovels in Sofia. Soon, the FBI agents feared, the Russians would leave. And they did.

Rita Klimova unintentionally was uprooting the lives of many people she knew nothing of, and who were unaware that she even existed. Besides sending Czechs off to work, she was responsible for a loss of excitement in America. She helped cause the unthinkable, the probable elimination of the Mafia on the streets.

For so long, there was a belief that the Mafia represented the best chance for attaining the zenith in public order, better crooks and better cops.

The Mafia was almost openly admired by millions because they were dark and exciting and everybody else was boring.

The Mafia thrived on books and movies. The public believed in the Mafia and the Mafia believed in the books and movies.

The first movie ever made about the Mafia was the one that put it into the culture forever. In 1930, they brought out a new actor, Edward G. Robinson, and told him he was Al Capone and to go out on camera and be Al Capone. He did. He made the combination to bust the game open, a Jewish actor playing an Italian mobster. This was the first Mafia movie, *Little Caesar,* and its closing line was to last at least for the rest of the century.

Robinson's character, Capone, with the film name of Rico, was shot up all over the place by the cops, and gave as his dying moan:

"Mother of God, is this the end of Rico?"

Before the movie came out, Catholic organizations in some cities protested, so the last line was reshot with Rico saying:

"Mother of Mercy, is this the end of Rico?"

Hollywood found there was nothing better than a tough-looking Jew playing an Italian gangster.

Gone were cowboy pictures with mumbling stars of such male sweetness that you gagged. Paul Muni now appeared in another Capone movie, *Scarface.* Muni was a huge success. He delightedly held a Tommy gun, with the round cylinder, as if it were an Oscar that can hurt people. Another first-time face, George Raft, became famous for flipping a coin.

After this, Muni decided gangster movies were beneath him and he refused to play in the next gangster movie he was offered, *High Sierra.* Raft immediately imitated him. Although he started working for a West Side killer named Owney Madden, Raft announced, "I don't want to be known as a cheap Mafia tough guy. Get me a good dramatic part." He wouldn't appear even in non–Mafia crime movies *High Sierra* and *Double Indemnity* and *The Maltese Falcon.* He became a dramatic actor highly eligible for home relief.

Year after year, gunfire and knifing, came some 417 American films about the Mafia, the stars predominantly Jewish.

The Godfather was the only movie The Fist ever saw. It was at the Mayfair Theater on Sixth Avenue. Usherette Paula reported in the *SoHo Press* that in an afternoon showing of the guys blowing away a fresh Las Vegas casino guy on the rubbing table, The Fist said, "It's too bad he had to die so quick."

Otherwise, he was offended by the glamour and walked off in his zipper jacket and came back no more ever. The neighborhood kids remember Fausti's father taking them to *The Sound of Music.*

26 The Light Brigade of the FBI charged through the trenches and took so many prisoners that suddenly everybody feared a shortage of gangsters. In FBI headquarters at 26 Federal Plaza in downtown Manhattan, a supervisor held up a Mob Stars bubble gum card of Fist Dellacava.

"Who is that?" he asked.

"His name is college tuition," he said.

And at the FBI headquarters on Queens Boulevard, a supervisor held up a Mob Stars card of gangster John Gotti.

"Who is this?" he called out.

"Mortgage payment," everybody answered.

On one trip downtown from East Harlem, Pepe Sabato, as Fat Tony Salerno's chauffeur, stood on the curb and talked to Fausti and a couple of others. He told them of Un Occhio, who twice was the Boss of all Bosses and now stayed in a candy store on Pleasant Avenue. He had a white wolf with him behind the counter. When Pepe came around again, he said, "Oh, I can't talk to you about him. He's a secret."

"You already told me last time," Fausti said.

"Yeah, but I didn't tell you nothing really."

"How did he get his name?"

"Oh, he bombed a bakery over on the East Side and the glass come flying out and he loses his left eye. That's how he got his name. One Eye. Un Occhio."

Following which Pepe told Fausti everything about Un Occhio that you wanted to know for a great big smashing successful Mob Stars card:

UN OCCHIO or "ONE EYE"

BORN: Near Lercara Friddi, Sicily, 1908.
Could be still alive. People afraid to ask.
MADE: 1927 By Ralph Capone, Boss of 10th Street.
ASSETS: Does not forget or stop. Lost left eye in bombing of a
bakery on Rivington Street. Came back two months later
to strangle bakery owner.
LIABILITIES: Kept a wolf in headquarters, Pleasant Avenue.
Hard for people to meet with him. Is known to feed ene-
mies to wolf.

A couple of people said they didn't believe there was such a guy. "I'll prove it to you," Pepe said. He returned with a picture of Un Occhio in the doorway of a particularly shabby candy store. Alongside him was a white wolf with a head as big as a school bus. The picture of the wolf did it. The card sold out everywhere. A guy called from Mayfield Road in Cleveland, where the Mafia too long had been quiet, called and begged for a rush delivery of Un Occhio.

The cards also told everything about the Mafia. If they were reduced to picture cards in a candy store, they were through.

There would be about three years of investigations that would end the game.

Which was the last thing anybody thought of when they saw the cards around. First off, The Fist was on a card. If he let them put his picture on a card, then it was a good thing.

There now came a card for the crowd-pleasing Anthony (Fat Tony) Salerno. Four days a week, Fat Tony left his horse farm at Red Hook, New York, and drove down to business in Manhattan. He always first looks at the magazines in the candy store on East 115th Street. Then *Business Week* magazine put his picture on the cover. He had a cigar in one side of his mouth and a scowl on the other. The big headline said Fat Tony had $500 million and was the Boss. The Fist was Boss and you better fuckin' know it. Fat Tony looked at the magazine.

"Good pitcher!" Fat Tony said.

He developed a proprietary feeling for *Business Week*'s cover. He thought he should be on the cover every week. "Except if they put The Fist on like he belongs," he said. The magazine's next issue came out with a big cover picture of Robert Allen, head of AT&T. Fat Tony took it personal. He looked at Allen's cover picture. "I slap you in the face."

FAT TONY SALERNO

BORN: Bronx, March 13, 1911.

MADE: By Ciro Terranova, aka "The Artichoke King."

Youngest made in history of crime. At age twelve, truck driver for Dutch Schultz. Liked to take off tires and run over guys with rims. Regarded dead guys as business and not some juvenile delinquency.

ASSETS: He makes friends for crime. The Tip O'Neill of the underworld. Newspaper columnists love him. Big story teller.

LIABILITIES: Sits in nightclubs throwing $50 bills in air. Bums fly around him like gnats. Too much attention.

It was the toughest writing job because Fausti told Al Hansen so much. The federal agents would have liked more. Fat Tony was by far their most popular figure. Already his income tax return had them at once angered and amused. It was the shortest return in the nation, probably.

> GROSS INCOME: One million. $1,000,000.
> SOURCE OF INCOME: Gambling. I won.
> TAXABLE INCOME: One million. $1,000,000.
> PAYMENT OWED IRS: Half the score. Your end, $500,000. Enclosed bank check, $500,000. Use it for the soliders in the army.

The card and the return made Tony so enormously popular in law enforcement that one day he walked up to one of the many agents in disguise, in this case a mailman who gave himself away by not knowing addresses, and said, "As long as youse goin' be with me all day like this, why don't you breathe for me?"

For a veteran crook, he made an amateur's mistake. Whenever you taunt the law they have years to get even. This time, they put two extra IRS accountants on Tony's file.

The next card was made after Joey Young, a truck driver who delivered soda for Top Soda and cocaine for a ring in Miami, begged everyone he knew to get him on a card. After many conversations, it was scheduled.

He had a picture of himself standing next to the height measure in the reception room of Greenhaven State Correctional Facility. Hanging from his neck like a civic medal was the license plate with his convict number, B-832965746.

"Make a card out of this," he told Fausti.

"What are we supposed to say? Who are you?"

"Put in about me. Like you did in the one for Lucky Luciano."

"Yeah, but still — who are you?"

"Put down, Joey Young, the rising star. I'll be made soon. I'm well liked by Sonny Francese. You could ask him. How much does it cost? Here I'll give you a dime. Make me a card."

He went into his pocket for a roll of bills that a delivery driver shouldn't have. Then he ran off and Nini stood in the doorway with the picture and the money.

"A thousand dollars for a picture," Nini said, wondering.

"Wrong," Fausti said. "About six hundred for you. What do you think my end should be, nothing?"

"We get a few more like this, we'd be all right," Nini said.

"We don't break any law," Fausti said.

"Isn't that something?" Nini said, handing Fausti the four hundred and putting the rest in his pocket.

It was as if he knew about the money, which he didn't, that Al Hansen did not show up for two days and a woman from the studio came around and announced: "He hurt his hand. The doctor says to rub it with money."

Fausti came up with two hundred and Nini with two hundred.

Joe Young's card was the only one of a guy wearing his license plate and number that would be part of the first press runs of Mob Stars.

JOEY YOUNG
BORN: Brooklyn, 1968.
MADE: That's coming soon. His goombarda, John (Sonny) Francese.
ASSETS: Ambitious and speedy. The world's swiftest shylock runner.
DUELS: None.
CAREER HIGHS: We've only just begun.
LIABILITIES: Is he trying to move too fast?

The last line said it all. The day the card appeared as part of stacks of Mob Stars wrapped with Big Chew gum, Joey Young leaped from the Top Soda delivery truck and grabbed an armful of them. That night, he went into a pizza stand on South 2nd Street in Williamsburg and sat down across from Biff, who pushed plenty of drugs. He threw the Mob Stars card on the table. "I'm going to get straightened out soon." He gave a look he was sure was menacing. "From now on, I take twenty points off you."

"Why, certainly," Biff said. He picked up a nice big heavy pizza tray and bounced it off Joey Young's head five or six times. Bounced it hard. Yet despite the stitches, Joey believed his card was a license to be in a secret society.

Then The Fist went out and caused everybody to go on a crash investigative program.

Walking on Madison Avenue, a street of gold, in a cap and zipper jacket and old loose pants and white socks and old lace-up black shoes that were caved in.

His first wife and family still were in Briarcliff Manor. He never went back there. The town house had an elevator; on Mulberry, where they came from, there were flights of steps to climb. The town house was about seventy-five yards up 68th Street between

Madison and Fifth avenues. The street is tree-lined, with town houses that rate great at the bank.

The Fist's mother, Rose, in her eighties, refused to enter the triplex. Nor would she let the priest go there. It was one thing to have a woman friend. But to have children with her! There was nothing in the upbringing in her church that would suggest that love can be the reason for these matters. Mama was the first to say her son was crazy.

Never before at this hour of 12:30 A.M. had there been more than a few people at this spot. The Fist had just finished looking at a brass plaque on the entrance to one of the Madison Avenue shops: Mundener Safe International. "Elegant bank-quality residential safes."

"Fuckin' Germans, hah?" Baldy Dom said.

"I got better safes than that," The Fist said with a grunt.

The woman had her left shoulder jammed into the outdoor phone booth on the southwest corner of Madison Avenue and 69th Street.

The woman screaming had an indescribably ugly face.

One of her costly shoes, and they were costly, you only had to flick the eyes on them once, tapped impatiently.

"I can't give you a number," she shrieked. "Do you know why I can't give you a number? Because I have no number. I am fucking homeless. I told you that on Monday and you didn't believe me. Homeless! This sonofabitch is inside seeing some princess. He stole my duplex and sold it. That leaves me right where I am, homeless. Where am I going to sleep tonight? Pick a doorway. Why don't you send a photographer and get me in the doorway? Call? Call who? All right, when I get in a doorway I'll call your photo desk. Who do I ask for? Good."

She hung up, but kept that shoulder screwed into the phone booth. She had on a cloth coat that was deep, rich, and lustrous in the light from the streetlight. The dress underneath it was silvery. Out came another coin. She never looked to see if somebody was waiting.

The Fist always used this outdoor phone at 68th Street as his late-night office.

Here on his corner pay phone, the woman was shrieking: "He's at a party with his fucking wife and I don't have a roof over my head. . . . Oh, you sonofabitch! Here they come out now. . . . Oh, you should be here with a camera."

She brushed past The Fist and raced up to the moat of photographers encircling a convention of anorexics in formal wear.

"You fucking thief!

"You stole my house, you stole my money!"

This was the significant moment of a night that was to explode into New York's social history.

Upon hearing the mention of his favorite topic of all, stolen money, The Fist shuffled to the fringes of the spectacle.

The woman from the phone booth was screaming at a light-haired man in tails who was trying to assist his wife, who was so skinny she swayed like a tall weed. Then, removed from them, there was a scrimmage that was uncontrollable between a pack of cameramen with greasy hair and black leather jackets and two men in dark blue suits, apparently bodyguards. They fought on street and curb, with the other photographers trying to get past the ones fighting and reach a light-haired woman with an apparently famous face who had come out of the hotel and was trapped and seemed terrified. A limousine was at the curb and there was a black Mercedes sedan, an escort car, with it. But she was afraid to run across the sidewalk, and the driver and bodyguards couldn't get to her.

Her only strength seemed to be the two dark blue suits, who had The Fist fascinated. They were pudgy and pugnacious and he was sure that if they fought on Sullivan Street they would get killed. A blue suit punched in classic style, dropping in a short right hand that came from many hours of being professionally tutored.

He missed his punch by about a half foot.

A skinny derelict with a six-thousand-dollar Nikon F-5, a dirty greasy wretch, brought a cell phone swinging from high and wide and smashed the suit on the side of the head. He bent over, groping for the ground.

The other blue suit was frantically grabbing leather jackets. The blond woman edged her way along the wall and now went into the doorway of a bridal designer. Alone in the light in the window was a white satin and pearl dress with a tiny card, a card you had to bend over and squint to see, listing the price as $15,000.

Now a heavyset doorman came slamming and slapping through people and making his way to the blonde's side. He was the night man with whom Dom Dom, while waiting for The Fist, had smoked a thousand cigarettes. Dom Dom, partially motivated by his friend the doorman, but mainly responding to his total inability to stay out of trouble, came from the corner and kicked off, as in a major gridiron game. His boot went into a photographer's groin. The photographer went down on his face with the loudest groan on the avenue. In front of Dom Dom now was a turned back. What was Dom Dom supposed to do, wait for the guy to turn around so they could have a fight on the square? He hit him with some rabbit punch. Whoever it was went down. Then Dom Dom swaggered right up to the woman huddled against the wall.

A photographer got past the suit and was racing up to the woman, his camera up, when Dom Dom swung a foot back and brought it forward with all his might. The cameraman howled as the kick caught him in the shins. Dom Dom pulled that leg back to kick him again but he saw police bursting out of a car.

The officers escorted the woman to the limousine. Now more police officers came, and they shoved Dom Dom out of the way, but the blond woman held up her hands to make them stop and she reached out through the police and shook hands with Dom Dom. They exchanged words and Dom Dom turned and pointed to The Fist.

Now this woman gave a great wave.

And then, smiling across the limousine roof, she blew The Fist a kiss.

Now the three Doms all were around The Fist, who shuffled to the phone booth. Baldy Dom dialed one phone. "We here," he said. The Fist took the phone and whistled softly. As the limousine now emerged from the crowded gutter in front of the hotel and started uptown, cameramen were running after the car, bulbs flashing, lights blinking. The car rushed past The Fist at his outdoor office.

A photographer stopping his chase of the car suddenly recognized the famous gangster.

"Der Mafioso!" he yelped in German.

He ran at The Fist with his camera up and others hanging from his neck. The streetlight fell on his leather jacket with the yellow foreign press card of some sort pinned to his jacket.

"Wow!" he yelled in German.

He got the picture, turned, and ran off. The picture would run in *Bilt* and of course *Paris Match.* Then the *News of the World* in London. Money. Money. Money. He was beside himself; he must get more of this man.

Dom Dom put The Fist into the car. The photographer stopped.

They drove up Madison to 69th, turned onto Fifth, then down to 68th Street and went slowly up to number 13, home of the triplex. Dom the Driver stayed in the car. The rest went into the town house. It was an unusual night. Father Phil was making a rare visit to the town house.

It was not unusual for The Fist and party to walk into the house and come right back out. And now, almost immediately, the door reopened right onto the sidewalk. Nobody even had a foot out before the camera exploded in The Fist's face.

The photographer meant to run away. Father Phil looked up at the night sky. "O Lord, please understand that we see this as more than a trespass. This was an assault with a camera. A direct attack on our very being. O Lord, you must understand that we must defend ourselves!"

All went dark for the photographer, who became the first German missing persons poster since the war.

But the next morning, exploding from the front page of the *Daily News* newspaper and the *Post,* was a large picture of The Fist, eyes glaring from under the cap, present front and center at a wonderful fracas involving all these rich riffraff. The German was missing; but apparently not the camera.

The front page picture went on the wall in federal cop offices. You put that together with these Mob Stars cards on everybody's desk and there becomes what is known as a constant reminder.

27

A thick gray cold rain that emptied the street and blew in gusts forced Fausti to step back into the doorway of the Laundromat. A car at the corner made a splashing noise and then stopped. A blue car that had gone by the corner had stopped and rolled back, was starting to turn onto Sullivan Street, realized it was the wrong way, and drove off in the rain. Fausti ran across the street and under the archway of the six-story building at number 251. It had been built for successful bohemians and had a couple of artists living there now. The archway leads to Europe: There is a large courtyard with an ailanthus tree rising several stories and brushing the windows of the apartments facing the courtyard. In the center of the courtyard, a large fieldstone pool of warm water was smoking in the cold rain. Wind came through the courtyard and lifted the steam to show a school of large goldfish. The wind went away and the steam covered the face of the pool and the fish. Two turtles on a board stretched their necks. The pool was heated by the boiler for the building, which was directly under the fish pond. Fausti stared through the steam to the street outside.

The blue car pulled up directly in front of the Laundromat. The two men sat in it for some time. The one on the passenger side got out, eyes squinting in the rain, and looked in the direction of the club. The driver was looking down, writing something.

They were gone in twenty minutes. Fausti went quickly up to the club and walked in.

"They weren't local," Fausti said.

"How do you know?" The Fist said.

"They were in a car looked like a rental. It didn't have a dent."

He told The Fist that because they didn't know the street at first, and then like brazen amateurs had parked right in front of the

Laundromat and acted like they didn't see the club across the street, they had to be new on the job.

A deer hearing the first faint baying of the hounds. There was a great pack of them out there somewhere, and so far they didn't even know how The Fist maneuvered each day. But that first bit in prison came out of a thing like this, an investigation from nowhere, and over nothing, a couple of strange lawmen investigating smoke in the air and they put him away for four and a half years.

The coffee man, Jerry the Jeweler, handed The Fist a small fresh hot espresso. He ran his tongue around the rim of the cup, licking the foam. Suddenly, there was a sensation that ran from the tip of his tongue and to the single, solitary memory that he could not banish. He had taken that last sip of black coffee on the morning he went away. Usually, a noise reminds The Fist of something. This was a soundless attack. The taste of espresso from the past.

That was something like thirty years ago. The whole thing threw a shadow into his mind. Here he was in 1997 and suddenly coffee makes a suppressed memory come unwound.

That morning years ago, he swallowed that coffee and was driven the few blocks to court, where a judge sent him away.

He isn't in the place a month and it's going all right, say hello to this guy, say hello to that guy, all connected, and then on this one day The Fist goes out into the big yard, the biggest, Lewisburg has got to have the biggest prison yard in the world. So The Fist is out there and he starts throwing a couple of punches to loosen up. Bing, bang, pow! Just like he's supposed to, finish a combination with the left hand. So he starts throwing his punches and now he is ending it with the left hook. Suddenly, The Fist sees the wall for the first time. Sees it, not looks at it. Rising high into an ominous sky. The Fist's left hand freezes in midair. He sees only that big gray cement wall that runs to the sky and along the ground into infinity. The wall starts moving in on him, moving, moving, moving, growing closer and higher until he sees nothing but Wall, sky and ground blotted out, and he stands there as Wall changes the formation of his brain.

He never knew when he left the yard and went to his cell that day. The Fist Dellacava sat in that prison with mind of gray, the sameness of the color never changing, noon sun or sunset, the color always one, the color is gray, neither light gray nor charcoal gray nor battleship gray, just gray gray that did not go away; that kept yesterday and tomorrow out of his mind and left him only with today, and today is gray. He tried to change. In his cell he got up on his toes and held his arms out like a plane and whirled in a full circle, whirled furiously, faster than his body could spin because he kept falling off his toes, but he got right back up and whirled until he brought on vertigo. Through the nausea, he could see only gray. He flopped on his back, placing his palms backward and on the floor at his head, raising himself and putting the top of his head on the floor, with all weight on it. He stayed there until his neck felt wronged and said so by the throb. He picked himself up to a gray wall that started in the back of his eyes and made dead anything that caught his glance. Somewhere in here, it appeared The Fist started a fifteen-round fight with reality.

This time, here, this rainy afternoon, he sensed it was different. He could smell the law like it was a disease. Even before the law knew they were to gather forces and attack The Fist, he knew they were coming. The averages told him he was overdue, even if the law didn't know it yet. The changes in the people on the streets around him were a cold knife cutting deep. In silence, The Fist got up, walked to the clothes hooks, and removed his windbreaker, shirt, and pants. On went the light blue pajamas. An arm punched through the sleeve of the blue bathrobe. He paused for a moment. Outside, the darkness and rain fell. He had lived a makeshift life and through perseverance and boldness had been able to put together the only substantial crime business outside of those on film. With his money, he held two personal families together and professed love for both and received love in return. He was the Boss because he could see ahead and envision trouble. Now he prepared for it.

Until now, The Fist was the supreme criminal. He made money with the speed of a camera shutter. In Brady's life, the last five thousand went into clothes. "I pay rent," he said of the apartment he supposedly owned. If The Fist snatched a hundred dollars out of the streets, he put the hundred away. If he snatched a million out of concrete for the Atlantic City casinos, then he put the million away. He spent money once a week for a haircut.

He did not participate in anything else. He wouldn't attend a union pension fund meeting or walk the piers or front with a concrete or garbage truck. He sat in his club and had men he knew for most of his life running things. Jersey docks and trucks were under maybe his oldest friend, Natale Grassi. In uptown Manhattan, there was the Army of the North, under Fat Tony Salerno. Then there was a Bronx crew and a Queens and Brooklyn outfit, each under a Boss who had been with The Fist for decades. The Fist almost never went near them. They ran their areas and came down to Sullivan Street to report. If they had trouble, Sullivan Street wheeled out a field artillery battery.

The Fist loved anything by Elvis Presley and his favorite single had always been Fats Domino's "Blueberry Hill." But then his favorite song became "My Boy Lollipop." His friend Stanley Sunshine, who owned the record company, was listed as a coauthor of the song, and received huge royalties for it. His contribution to the writing was a pistol in the ears of the performer and two legitimate authors. Sunshine first told The Fist that he was one of the writers. The Fist, who understood royalties, thought it was great. Then Sunshine said, to hell with it, and he turned over the whole file to The Fist — record profits, sheet music sales, everything. Worth millions. Immediately, The Fist learned the words to his new all-time favorite song, "My Boy Lollipop."

The Fist sat here and also recited the words to another great hit of his, "Splish Splash."

"Splishsplashwuztakin'abathlongaboutSaturdaynight."

He still sees Stanley Sunshine walk into the Concerned Lutherans club and start singing this song to him one night.

"Splish Splash. I was takin' a bath . . ."

"Get the fuck out of here," The Fist said.

"For this one you're going to put up a statue for me," Sunshine said.

Stanley Sunshine had some kid, Robert Walden, singing his

own composition in a studio upstairs from Patsy's Restaurant on West 56th Street. Walden was from the Bronx, singing under the name of Bobby Darin. He grew up with a mother who told him she was his sister. Then it gets worse. He is some fucked-up kid. His song that he sings is called "Splish Splash."

Stanley Sunshine tells him, "I want to put it out big. You know why? Because I'm the coauthor with my partner, you know who my partner is, my partner is The Fist, he's a very nice guy."

Walden knew. He says, go ahead, long as you don't break my arm. The Fist wanted his name on nothing. Names lead to prison numbers. That day, a disc jockey named Murray Kaufman — Murray the K — was in Stanley Sunshine's office with his mother. So Sunshine points to her, nice lady, and says, "She wrote the song."

Right away, Murray the K's mother says, "I can't wait to tell my sister in Brooklyn. This is all I want. The thrill."

The Fist and Stanley own the song, the rights, the record, the sheet music, the whole fucking world. Here comes Stanley Sunshine down to Sullivan Street one night in a limousine that he couldn't see out the windows because the money bags are piled so high around him. The song has to make thirty million. The Fist just puts his end away. Morris gives Walden, now known as Bobby Darin, lunch money. Darin chose life and said nothing.

Stanley claimed Murray Kaufman's mother demanded royalties for writing the song and said that she would go to eleven district attorneys. Sunshine told her see The Fist, that he couldn't wait to give her money. So she comes to the club. She walks down the stairs, and as she stepped inside, she got a look that caused her to stutter. She was glad to run away broke.

The most prominent larceny was committed against Frankie Lymon, who came out of Harlem with the body of a jockey and a voice birds tried to imitate. The only question was how such a small frame could handle so much heroin. The song that he wrote and performed and danced into fame was "Why Do Fools Fall in Love?"

"I'm not going to give this fuckin' junkie any money," Stanley Sunshine said.

He did not. He took it all, an end going to The Fist. The song was famous and would last for decades. Frankie lived and died broke. His widow sued Stanley Sunshine. Stanley had three women testify that they were Frankie Lymon's ex-wives.

They made a movie of Frankie's life and portrayed Stanley as a crafty show business guy. Not a hint of muscle. It happens that Stanley was out of a Bronx orphanage and worked as a bouncer with The Fist and once punched a guy's eye out. He didn't cheat Frankie Lymon. He just took the money from him.

The Fist had crime at his fingertips, just as the cards on the table.

"He's been the Boss forever," Fat Tony said in a conversation overheard by a bug. "He tells this guy, go act like you're the Boss. Then he tells Benny Squint. Then he tells me. That's so if they want a big name for the papers and the law, I'm fuckin' it. All the time he stays in the back and figures, let them take the heat. I'm up on him. He's a fuckin' user. You go away, he plays cards. He lets you know who you are. You can't reason with him. I don't know what to say. I swear I don't. You wanna, you wanna say, 'I took care of this all by myself. Youse wanted two hundred seventy-five t'ousand collected, I'll go out and get it. You know what he said? 'Give me all the money now.'"

He always had others out front. There was a big trial over the cement business. The Fist wasn't a defendant. Then there was the big Mafia commission trial. He had been seeing that the names of new bosses he kept having would get in the newspapers. The government didn't even come near him. Easily, he was the biggest, richest man in American crime history.

And now he stood and watched the rain beat down on Sullivan Street and muttered, "How could you believe this fuckin' thing, some picture cards with gum turn into tigers come down the street bite your fuckin' head right off. Agents got the cards. Candy stores got the cards. Fuck." He would not allow himself to think of the picture from Madison Avenue. What was I doing around a fight involving the Queen of England or whatever she was, that there broad? There was nobody to blame but himself. With the cards, the agents buy them all up, come lookin' to fuck around with me. He remembered throwing the one card down in the diner and paid no more attention. He wanted to kick himself for that.

You could blame fucking Westchester, too. At The Fist's first Christmas in Briarcliff Manor, Carmella Dellacava, in charge of the household, gave the police chief a Christmas envelope for himself, and envelopes for the town's five policemen she saw in her area. The head of the town's bank did this, too, and Carmella thought she was doing the right thing.

Doesn't the mayor of the town start yelling, "Gangsters bribing our cops!"

The Fist and Carmella were indicted for bribery and lugged out of the house in handcuffs and arraigned in the county court. She was a suburban woman raising children who never had been near any of this. Getting arrested was her husband's business.

On bail, the wife went home. The case against The Fist was so minor and senseless that it was just the sort that puts people in jail. His doctor, Dr. Leonard Warren, took The Fist to St. Raphael's Psychiatric Hospital in Yonkers. The Fist didn't know what good it was going to do, but in he went. Besides, he clearly could stand a rest.

All medical assistance came from Leonard Warren, M.D., who had a nervous system that caused him to hate legitimate people. In search of a practice of known murderers, he found his way to Antonio's restaurant on Grand Street in Manhattan, which was a mess hall for criminals.

One night he was asked to come to The Fist's clubhouse on an emergency call. The Fist was sick from overeating. He had sauce Genoese and two pounds of number 10 macaroni. The Doc reached into his pocket for the same antacid tablets he used for himself when he blew a month's income at a crap game.

Within an hour, The Fist had a nice strong espresso and a couple of cigarettes. "You're the family doctor from now on," The Fist said. The De Francisi family.

With Warren, The Fist learned to live on one word: Thorazine.

"I don't think we use Thorazine anymore," the young staff doctor at St. Raphael's said.

"Thorazine," Warren said.

"I feel he should take it," Father Phil said.

Thorazine turned The Fist into a tree stump, but that was the price. He trusted the doctor.

Thorazine is out of the long-ago of mental treatment, when dazed patients walked in the Thorazine Shuffle. The Thorazine displaces the chemical dopamine in the brain, without which you take on the trembles of Parkinson's disease.

Twenty-five milligrams given as a shot is sure to knock out a raging crack addict.

In that first hospital, The Fist took a shot, after which he had his hand out for the first 25-milligram tablet of Thorazine. The Fist rattled like an old taxicab as he took pills all day.

The county judge in Westchester had one look at The Fist, unshaven, lethargic, shaking, mumbling. He preferred not to touch the case. What if the guy dies on him in the courtroom? He ruled The Fist incompetent to be tried.

The Fist never went back to the house in Briarcliff Manor. "Fuck Westchester," he said. The wife and family remained there. He moved into the dim ground-floor apartment on West 3rd Street.

His uniform became a robe and pajamas. His armaments were Thorazine, which he took right now, and a shelf of drugs that were similar and did the same thing, the better to testify that Thorazine was only one indication of his problem —

A wheelchair was turned to face the opponent, the government of the United States.

The other arm starting into the sleeve of the robe was an announcement that life as he had crafted it had ended. Any future he ever had thought of had to be postponed. It was helpful that at this moment he yearned for no sensation, no sight, only for liberty to be enjoyed by walking across the street.

He tied the robe in front, slapped his cap back on, and, forming spittle on his lips, sat down.

A wolf chewing off the paw caught in a trap, he never gave in. He thought that he knew the magnitude of the move. He had just surrendered his liberty, as surely as if he had entered a prison cell on his own volition. He thought that as his needs were simple to begin with, maybe he wouldn't miss many things. He threw his life into a closet and only took it out to look at it a couple of times in all the months that turned into years.

He now was dedicating his life to staying out of prison by having no life at all. He began on that first night in the club with silence. When somebody tried to talk to him, he answered with a vacant look. After that, he pulled his head to the right, as if hearing something.

Then he started mumbling.

"What are you saying?" California, aka Frankie Condo, said to him.

The Fist did not answer. He just kept mumbling at a rapid speed with no breaks.

"What is the matter?" Jimmy from Greenpoint said when he walked in.

"He got stroked," California said.

This rainy day it was the first round of the long winter battle — The Fist would go into the psychiatric hospital twenty-two times, and six times into other hospitals for heart trouble, including open heart surgery twice. He was taking benzodiazepine, digitalis, Tenormin, Restoril, Pamelor, Dalmane, Valium. Trying to stay out of prison with an overcrowded medicine cabinet. With a face covered by ragged hair growth, a body that barely moved, he mumbled rapidly for months that became years. The Fist was a prisoner of his own defense. During any attempt to walk, the feet barely come off the floor, and the person is best dropped into a wheelchair. Thorazine weighs. The head droops in sleep, the mouth drools, the speech becomes a babble. He was either shaking and shuffling with Thorazine or off it for a while and walking around as if he was still in its clutches. He had no shame over what he was doing and his family forcefully said he was crazy. If The Fist wanted to be humiliated instead of in jail, then humiliate him.

At first, the public relations firm handling Montrose (Monty) Martin IV, chief of his hugely successful fund, copied words from the sports pages, describing Martin as "hard-nosed, mentally tough, hard-charging powerhouse."

A young account man saw The Fist on television. He was leaning on Father Phil's arm and half shuffling, half stumbling along the street.

He had Montrose put on a robe and cap and walk down empty Wall Street for both still and video cameras. He had Montrose scheduled for covers of *Forbes, U.S. News and World Report, Barron's,* and *Business Week.*

Al Munro Elias, the oldest man in the PR company, looked at the picture of Montrose in robe and pajamas and said quietly, "I don't like it."

"It's beautiful, Why don't you like it?"

"Because I am a great fan of never arousing sleeping dogs."

"What sleeping dog?"

"A big bad one," Al Munro Elias said.

The next week, the magazine *Money* came out with a great cover of the Wall Street terror, Montrose (Monty) Martin IV, in the middle of an empty Wall Street. In bathrobe and cap. The cover line read, "Most Feared Man on Wall Street."

Montrose knew nothing of this, that Fat Tony would make sure The Fist saw the clever publicity. This occurred when The Fist would enter and reenter the psychiatric hospital, at all times having a stream of his men coming in to keep him informed in complete detail.

Once, seeing one of Martin's ads, he was irritated to the point of near action. Upon leaving the hospital one Saturday morning, he told the chauffeur, Baldy Dom, to take a side road.

Montrose was on his course, Deep Pond CC, in a sweater that looked like spun gold. His swing was made with broken hinges.

"Great!" his accountant, in the foursome, said.

"You belong on the tour," his lawyer said.

Montrose cocked his head to watch the ball roll. "Good golf shot," he said. He never said, "Good shot." Always, he said, "Good golf shot" to make him sound like an insider.

It was a fine warm, spring day and Montrose walked rather than drove a cart. He was about halfway to the ball, talking to himself about himself every step of the way, when he saw this apparition step out onto the edge of the fairway.

The Fist whistled softly. He had the dark blue robe that he pulled around him. The pantlegs of pale blue hospital pajamas showed at the hem of The Fist. The Fist had on white socks and old lace-up black shoes that were caved in. The Fist reached down and picked up Montrose's ball and put it in his robe pocket.

His black eyes stared at Montrose, who involuntarily went back, his right foot going onto a drainage plate, and he fell backward, twisting the ankle. The Fist disappeared. Montrose limped home. He no longer would appear in robe or cap.

28

He mostly lived alone in an apartment on West 3rd Street that had no windows. Once, his brother Larry came in to check on him and found The Fist asleep and twenty-one dead mice in traps.

One remained alive. Black little eyes stared from under a chair at The Fist, who now sat in his bathrobe at the kitchen table. He was eating a veal parmigiana alone. He remembered grumpily that he was 303 pounds when he was trying to beat an attempted murder charge by losing so much weight that no witnesses would recognize him. Now he was a nice 284 and eating veal parmigiana.

By living a Thorazine life, he would lose weight to the bones. But when he was not taking huge doses of it, and the haze lightened, he kept chewing food flavored with conscience pangs.

He took a small piece of the roll, with tomato sauce on it, and threw it toward the mouse. The mouse did not move.

"Fuck ya," The Fist said. He went back to his sandwich. When he looked up, the morsel was gone.

"I told you take it," The Fist said.

The next day, when The Fist got up at four thirty in the afternoon and began eating a breakfast of baked ziti and bread with a hot thick crust, he saw the mouse looking at him from under the same chair.

"What do you want?" The Fist said.

The mouse stared. The Fist threw a piece of bread at him and again the mouse did not move. The Fist told him to go fuck himself, turned his head, then turned back to find the crust gone.

The next night, the mouse came out from under the chair and right up to The Fist's bare feet. The Fist dropped the bread right on his bare toes. The mouse crept up onto The Fist's toes and nibbled up the bread.

"Fuck, you tickle my toes," The Fist told the mouse.

That's how it started. Now whether this was at the point where The Fist's outward insanity became reality inside his head is impossible to know. Or if this occurrence is straight out of Thorazine, the effects of which can linger sometimes forever. At 2 A.M. one night, he and the mouse couldn't sleep. He picked up the mouse and put him into the bathrobe pocket and walked across to take his place in the card game. Little squeals sounded in his robe. "Gimme," The Fist said, taking a fistful of potato chips from Jerry the Jeweler and stuffing them into the robe pocket.

"Gin!" The Fist said, to the sound of chips crunching

It was only a few days later when The Fist looked around the apartment in the late afternoon and saw what looked like a dozen mice. He took a big piece of cheese out of the refrigerator — the only food in there — and put chunks of it in all the traps. He started to put the traps out when he thought of his own mouse. He didn't even have a name for him yet, but he didn't want him to die of a fucking broken neck. When Jerry the Jeweler came over from the club and delivered his daily sandwich, he dropped another piece on his toes and the mouse came out from under the chair and scrambled atop The Fist's toes.

He picked up the mouse and put him into the robe pocket. This time he flaked off bread crust for the mouse in the pocket. Then he set the traps.

"There goes your gang," The Fist told the mouse as they left the house.

After this he took the mouse over to the club.

The new Malocchio's nostrils never picked up anything strange. Besides, by now he knew enough never to inquire of The Fist. A sniff gets you a broken snout.

There were two live mice in the house when The Fist arose the next afternoon. His mouse was in his normal spot, under the chair. The other, the only survivor of the traps, scurried for the kitchen.

The Fist was nearly lucid, but spoke aloud out of habit to the empty apartment. "— I'll have to hit him, I can't have him here account of he'll only get my friend here killed. Somebody comes in and sets the trap and who the hell knows who dies in it, I lose my friend here, so let me fix this other guy.

"Kill the cocksucker," he said loudly.

The Fist went under the couch and came out with one of his blackjacks. He banged the kitchen floor once and the mouse went up a drainpipe and paused on the sinktop. The Fist took him out in one.

The Fist's personal mouse became part of his daily routine, and was around crime enough to need a lawyer.

Sally Briguglio came out of Benito II restaurant on Mulberry Street and a car stopped dead and two guys ran at him. They were in disbelief. They had orders to kidnap him so he could be killed far away, and here he was right in their arms. Or at least they thought so. He gave some jump up in the air, did Sally Briguglio. He whirled, shouted, wailed, and one of the kidnappers, Frankie Obtaz, for Crazy, sanctioned by The Fist to have a gun for this detail, said the hell with this and shot Briguglio in the chest five times. Briguglio fell backward through the restaurant's open cellar doors like a sack of onions.

Next on the docket was Joe Cuz, an ambitious dimwit, charged with telling many bar owners that the "The Fist" wanted him to install gambling slot machines or "The Fist" would have them busted to bits. Learning of this, a dispatch from the card table went out: "Find him and don't bring him back."

With great anxiety, Joe Cuz went to his friend Al D'Amico, who was highly ranked in another gang, the Lucchese outfit. He also was smart enough to hang out in Milady's Bar on Thompson Street, so he could be in high favor with all the Dellacava mob.

"Why did you use his name?" D'Amico asked Cuz.

"Because when you say it, people get ascared."

D'Amico told him to hide in his mother's house. He found Baldy Dom parked at the corner of Thompson and Prince in a blue Cadillac coupe.

"Joe Cuz is a friend of mine. He never used anybody's name in his life," D'Amico said.

"Why didn't he tell us you was his friend?" Baldy Dom said.

"Because he doesn't use anybody's name," D'Amico said. "If he doesn't say me, how's he going to be using that other fellow's name?"

The next day, D'Amico came back with Joe Cuz. Dom got out of the blue Cadillac and hugged Cuz. "Why didn't you tell me you was Al's friend —"

"— He don't mention names," Al D'Amico said.

"I'll take care of it. Don't worry," Baldy Dom said.

And Cuz said aloud, so all the street would know whom he knew, "I shot a lot of guys for him. I did a lot of work. I still should thank The Fist for giving me the okay to go earn with poker machines like he should. He's all right, The Fist. He's my personal Godfather."

This was precisely what Baldy Dom reported to The Fist. Sitting in his robe, putting cheese doodles into the mouse pocket, The Fist had the story told for him five times. Then he walked out, which meant the matter was being held in abeyance. He was halfway across the street, deep in conversation with himself, when he heard the mouse speak from his pocket:

"Kill the cocksucker."

He is driving to Sheepshead Bay for a great shore dinner, is Joe Cuz, and he thinks he recognizes the fellas in the car alongside. He does. Why, one of them even waves good-bye to him. Into Joe Cuz's car, and into Joe Cuz himself, come thirty-one shots. The papers say it is "a suspected gangland shooting."

29 Once, the Mafia calendar was in five-year intervals. That was the usual sentence given to a Mafia guy, part of the overhead, the store needs redecorating. They returned to the street as if nothing had happened.

Suddenly, the government indicted Vic Arena, who wanted to run the Colombo Family, on one thousand offenses. "You have a case that they couldn't win in China," the lawyer told him. Vic was so sure of winning that when his girlfriend, Gina, came to visit him while he was in detention awaiting trial, he told her to take his entire wardrobe to the tailor. "I lose a few pounds here and I want the suits to fit nice for the trial. Then right afterwards we go straight to Europe." Girlfriend Gina took care of the suits. Vic Arena's wife, Mrs. Vic Arena, lived on the next street from the girlfriend. Mrs. Vic Arena brought him new made-to-order shirts because he had lost weight in his whole head, which included the neck.

The Fist's interest in the case was that the judge, Judge W., usually got mob cases, such as The Fist's, if one came up and it sure looked as if it would.

When the jury came in, Vic Arena told his lawyers, "I could tell by their look. Vic Arena lives."

The juror announced, "No!"

Judge W. now handled his part of the matter. He gave Vic Arena two life sentences without parole and an eighty-year sentence on another charge, just to make sure.

"Which sentence do I do first, one of the lifes without parole or the eighty years?" Vic Arena said.

"Whichever one you want," Judge W. said.

"Put me down for the eighty years first. At least it got a number I could count."

30

It drove The Fist to the basics. He kept the robe wrapped around him and made a last visit to his money before the cops made a caravan out of every trip. The Fist's driver was Frankie Condo, who was approaching seventy-five and in need of sleep. He was grateful when The Fist sent him into a bodega for chips for the mouse in his pocket, then told him to go home. Of course as Boss he should have had a couple of gorillas a half block behind him, but he wanted to be alone on this trip. He also happened to be afraid of nobody, daylight or dark.

The Fist walked in the night mist, up a block, made a left turn, always checking the sidewalk and street for cars or men, then down the block and made another left turn, and at the end of that street made a third left. That brought him back to where he had started. The three left turns let you pick up anybody tailing you. The sign, under the lone streetlight, read "Cartier Street."

At the end of the block was a red brick church. St. Martin's.

The church and rectory were the last buildings before the corner, which was taken up by an old white cinder-block garage and auto shop. Walking up to the church, The Fist was carrying a white plastic garbage bag in one hand and a wrapped package, a big one, in the other.

For years, The Fist had supported this church in order to have the basement. The various priests had caused other gangsters, and the police, to scream that the priest hid guns and dead bodies in the church. Which never happened. A fortune of money next door was another story.

Once, when there was factory work in cities, this was a twenty-four-hour street of Irish workmen, with night workers coming home just as longshoremen and sandhogs left their houses and walked out into the darkness to start the day. Now, the neighborhood spoke Spanish, and at night, it was a dark cave.

Walking out of the darkness from his room around the corner was the old man who cleaned the plaza. He handed The Fist a ring of keys and then went to sit in the night in the plaza.

In a space between the rectory and the garage there were cracked stone steps to a basement door whose ugly metal fit to withstand a naval shelling. It had recently been painted green, with the black iron banister streaked with the green. A crowded key ring came out. There were three locks. After this, there was a second door, equally thick, also with new green paint, also with three locks.

When he stepped into the basement, The Fist turned on a lone light. The second metal door needed keys or a device stronger than a Halligan Tool to pull it open.

Suddenly, The Fist felt something brush his leg. Here was a big old tomcat, a South Bronx rat fighter, a dog fighter, a bird chewer, pushing against The Fist. The Fist gave the cat a kick that sent him whining into the air. He landed and disappeared into the darkness on his cat feet. Then The Fist remembered that he had the mouse with him. No wonder the fucking cat showed up. I should of strangled him, The Fist said to himself. He put another chip in the mouse's pocket.

The Fist was extraordinarily careful as he opened the second metal door. As the door was pushed in, going from your left to the right, a good strong wire cord attached to a hook atop the door tightened considerably around the trigger of a Mossberg 12-gauge shotgun that was in a brace off to the right. The shotgun had a bear shot of nine-millimeter bullets. When the cord pulled the trigger, the person coming through the door became no more.

The Fist opened the door enough to get a hand in, then reached up and took the cord off the hook. It became completely slack and The Fist stepped in.

A few steps inside was a gleaming standard bank vault, with a wheel for a doorknob and a combination. The Fist muttered at the difficulty opening it. There were duffel bags piled along the walls, leaving only a narrow space for someone to step through.

The Fist opened one of the duffel bags. He stuck a hand in and crunched the money at the top of the bag. Crisp lettuce, no wonder that's what they call it. Ripping open the package of money he had with him, he tried to stuff the bills into the duffel bag. There was barely room for tipping money. He opened another duffel bag, which had room, although he would have preferred it filled.

After that, The Fist didn't touch any more bags. Who knows what it comes to, you add it up someday. It doesn't seem real.

What was it, back at the start of the '80s, he wanted to pool his fortune with the mob treasury of Paul Castellano and buy the World Trade Center towers. He often stood in one of the World Trade Center lobbies and pretended he owned the place. He was going to name the buildings "Dellacava I" and "Dellacava II." His plans were altered somewhat when Castellano got murdered. Over several years, however, he had been buying the old, empty factory buildings along the bottom of the West Side, sometimes buying an entire block or, in two cases, a square block. The buildings looked gloomy, dull, and unexciting at best, with their old deserted loading platforms, but they were actually the delivery room for the largest exchange of money for real estate in the history of the city.

The Fist's Village was changing; anybody walking in the past trips on the present, and the legs go out from under him.

As leader, The Fist felt it his duty to save his neighborhood as an Italian colony. He went out shopping with real estate agent Pancetta. The sun splashed brightest on the bricks of number 116 Sullivan. Carved wood on the sides of the doorway was made to look like curtains drawn through rings. A polished brass plaque alongside the door said this building was erected in 1832 by General Al Sullivan. Over one hundred fifty years later, another general, General Fist Dellacava, stands and inspects the property.

"Buy it," he tells Pancetta.

"They don't want to sell," Pancetta said.

"I'll see them myself," The Fist said.

Making the call, The Fist came with his brother Larry. A sallow man in a silk robe with satin lapels answered.

"He wants to talk to the owner," Larry said.

"Oh, he is not here."

"When does he come back?"

"I really have no idea. I only maintain the house for him. He is in Europe for some time. Directing pictures."

"Do you speak to him?"

"No, not I. His manager has an assistant who calls once in a while. Beyond that, I have no contact."

"Well, he must be coming back sometime," Larry said.

"Sir, he is a director. He returns when he returns."

The Fist then tried to buy a square block of houses south of Houston Street, but by now it was SoHo. Pancetta reported back that all would not sell.

"Which of these fuckin' people won't sell to me?" The Fist said. When the real estate agent told him there were twenty different owners, he turned and walked off the street. You frighten the first owner, the other nineteen go to the law. He concentrated on the empty buildings along the North River.

The Fist could loan shark by himself a million at interest of twenty thousand a week, or two million at forty thousand a week, or three million at sixty thousand a week, if somebody was desperate enough. The weekly interest ends when the entire million is paid back at one time. If they miss any payment, somebody dies. People tend to pay him back.

The Fist hated doing it, but he and the mob of the East Side downtown under Carlo Gambino every month paid $100,000 each to the police department headquarters and the Democratic party boss of the moment, whose job was to pass it on to City Hall. The figure comes from the underworld and not the authorities because they took the money and would like to deny every dollar of it. The money was for illegal things in the Manhattan South district only, from 14th Street down to the Battery, East to West.

These citywide payments ended with investigations and commissions, but for long afterward families of inspectors and up could tell of colleges their kids attended and vacations and second homes and boats and travels to Asia.

Which sounds warm and thoroughly understandable, but most of the money went to the nights, to girlfriends. As the cops weren't under the leadership of The Fist, they didn't have two families. They had girlfriends that cost money.

The bribe money was carried by Al Kelly, who, as a first-grade homicide detective from the First Precinct, could roam anywhere, see anybody, and explain nothing.

"It is good to have a job nobody watches you," Al Kelly said.

When he was on regular duty for the public of his city, Al carried a rubber chicken in his pocket that he slapped on the bar or some suspect's kitchen table, causing laughter first and answers to questions next.

Other times, he carried his packages first to police headquarters, where top commanders sent out an assistant, also a first-grade detective, thereby fit to do business as an equal.

Always, the police regarded being gay as a crime. If gays on Christopher Street in Greenwich Village walked along three abreast, they were arrested and beaten for not having a parade permit. Gay bars were raided and smashed, except those owned by Dellacava, who paid his money to the cops. If any cop bothered The Fist's gay bars, or dared touch his street loan sharks or bookmakers, the cops involved were called in for an official sit-down.

Once, squads were shuffled and a new group of ten plainclothesmen closed The Fist's places. By appointment, Sergeant Edward J. Brennan then stood in a doorway on MacDougal Street with The Fist.

"We made our payroll here," The Fist said.

"Nobody come saw us," Brennan recalled saying.

"We paid first of the month," The Fist said.

"We get here the second," Brennan said.

"Get it off of them," The Fist said.

"How? They got transferred and run with the money."

"You got guns," The Fist growled.

Smith carried the second stack of tens of thousands under his arm like a newspaper to the Democratic headquarters in the Westminster Hotel at Madison Avenue and 44th Street. He handed the money personally to an assistant to the county leader, who sat in a back office and tried to appear busy and innocent. The leader wore dark glasses because his eyes were sensitive to light and smoke. Visitors always were asked not to smoke. Fuck that. Al Kelly came into the place humming "Smoke Gets in Your Eyes" and puffing a cigar until he turned the place into a forest fire. "Look at this fuck wince," he enthused. The leader gave most of the money to City Hall. Of course it was all for campaign contributions. The day one mayor, Williams, left the job, then paying about $50,000 before taxes, he rolled up in front of the "21" Club in a Silver Cloud Rolls-Royce.

There were some days when Al Kelly had to get money to politicians in City Hall who were so critically ill that they were unable to arrive on payoff day. There was no such thing as leaving the money with somebody. "You're safer off giving the money to a pickpocket to hold than to a politician," The Fist told Kelly. When City Councilman Kahn of Rosedale, in Queens, became so ill with flu that he couldn't come around for his money, Al Kelly first went to Kahn's primary residence, and official family, at the end of Queens. A woman and three kids. He gave her one envelope. After which he traveled to one of Kahn's alternate homes in Maspeth, in Queens, which is one thousand miles away. A woman and two children. She got an envelope. Al Kelly could not figure how Kahn makes the run back and forth. Finally, Al went to an apartment on West 67th Street in Manhattan and gave a third envelope to a third wife, who also had children.

"If he has one more family, I'm going to make him move to Utah," Kelly said.

The air in the money vault was old. The Fist had to take two breaths for every one out in the street. The place looked like a post office loading platform, with all these bags piled up. To The Fist, it was a lovely garden. Somewhere, what sounded like a church organ started to play a hymn. It was the money playing. He sat intoxicated as the money played a concert for him. The music was classical, moving, inspiring. It was only a brass quartet playing here, but just outside, in the basement hall, a great orchestra struck up. He never listened to such music until he came here. Money doesn't talk, it sings, he said to himself.

He felt a rustle in the robe and the mouse crept out of the pocket and chewed the crumbs on The Fist's lap.

The Fist still was half asleep when suddenly he saw in the air a vision of a young woman with long dark hair who kept looking back over her shoulder, and who was holding a knife big enough to use in a war. She had a large shopping bag, and for a moment looked like she was going to stuff it with money. Noticing The Fist, she looked straight at him and smiled. The knife was gone from her hand, as was the shopping bag.

Suddenly, The Fist noticed that her face was small and the nose narrow and pleasant looking.

She was the mouse.

He held the pack of chips out and she smiled and stepped through the money and took a couple of them. She walked out of his sight with a smile.

The Fist liked her. She wouldn't do anything to harm him. Once he had that thought, he never let go of it for an instant. You could tell him it was caused by Thorazine, and he would not listen. She wouldn't do anything to harm him.

Pushing the mouse into the pocket, he prepared to leave the treasury. First, he reset the Mossberg 12-gauge. Leaving the basement, he felt the cat rush past his ankles on the way into the night outside.

"Go on, you fuck!"

He gave that cat some kick in the ass to get him going far and faster.

The Fist walked next door into the church as an obligatory stop. The door was left open for the night, which is unusual in churches. But people in this parish sense that trying to steal anything from the church would be insanity.

The Fist slipped into the confessional. He was going to make his confession. That was good. He always did that. That there was never a priest in the confessional was crucial. He could answer himself, which is how he liked things. The Fist didn't want anybody hearing a word of his life or getting between him and God when he took up his problems. A priest would only get mad at him for what he was saying.

"Bless me, Father," The Fist said.

"I got a thing I don't understand," The Fist said.

"I got a guy I don't know. I don't talk to people. But I got this guy doing some major work for us. And he, he got a son, who is in.

"I don't let no sons of mine in under any circumstances. I want you to know that. Only the nephew could try. Which he don't.

"Anyway, he got this son in. What does the kid do right away, he deals drugs. In my business you deal drugs you — you know, you go, you get hit in the head. That is a killing in self-defense on account of the drug peddler will give it to your kids and that is a real murder.

"This kid is not only doin' drugs. He also got told by the boss of his crew to go out to California and kill a guy. California got a death penalty. Now his own father is in the same crew with him. The father tells his own son, you gotta do it. His own father. He wants his son go out there commit a murder. If he gets caught they execute him.

"That's what the father is like. It gets worse. The father introduced a guy to us who run up a big bill. A very big bill and we ask him for vigorish and he laughs at us.

"I got to do something to the guy owes us. But the kid could go out to California and get grabbed. Being that he is a execution case he could talk and put us all in the can.

"That is an important thing. We got to stop the kid from doin' that. How do we do that, I ask myself. I say first we got to get the money off this fat slob that took us for it —"

He was talking in a raised voice right now.

"Then we got to drop the kid in California into the water at Los Angeles. Then we drop the kid's father and the fat guy into the Atlantic. A sea-to-sea warning. Now does this mean that I get blamed for it? Getting rid of the kid, the father, and the fat pig steals off us, that saves thirty lives minimum. Ain't that a good bargain?"

The cat's paw was on the hem of the robe, which was so thick that The Fist never felt it. The cat had nice position for his next move. Which was to get his head up there even with the robe's pocket and get a paw in there and his snout in there and then the paw pushed the mouse into his mouth and the cat wheeled and was gone just before The Fist's hand slammed down.

"F—" The Fist hissed, cutting the word off because he was in church.

He went down the near aisle to the door. He could hear the mouse screaming but he didn't know where the sound was coming from.

No longer could he hear the mouse screaming.

He heard the cat give what sounded like a quite triumphant and loud meow, and he went for what he thought was the sound, over on the far side of the church, and when he got there he thought he saw a form hurtling under a pew. He stooped and tried to see, but he couldn't. It was dark and it was unfair. The cat could see in the dark and he couldn't.

"I'll strangle this . . ." The Fist hissed.

He never did. The Fist prowled that church for an hour without finding the cat.

Once, he looked at a statue of St. Anthony and muttered, "Give me a hand."

Then he thought the better of it. "No, do what you're doing."

At first light, he was out of the church, in order to prevent the priest from walking into the church in usual great reverence and finding Fist trying to massacre a cat. He told the old guy in the park, who was out picking up papers and putting them into his sack already, about the cat and the mouse. The guy was too afraid of The Fist to laugh about the mouse. "Find the cat for me and you got a score." He handed him a fifty-dollar bill to start. Then he had a thought. "Get some schoolkids and see if they could help. Surround the fucking cat. But don't kill him. Just bring him down to me."

Onto Sullivan Street late that afternoon came a procession. The old guy walked first, holding his sack. After him came three grammar school kids, their arms folded over cats. A fat tan face looked out from one set of arms, then a jet-black face, and a gray with black stripes.

At four thirty he emerged from his apartment and found the cat lineup.

"One of yez is going to fuckin' die," he told the cats. "Lemme see yez."

The kids knelt on the sidewalk and held the cats. The Fist's eyes narrowed.

He asked himself three questions:

"Did somebody bite my mouse to death in the church in the Bronx?"

"Yes," he answered.

Hearing this question, the old man from the park jumped forward with his sack. He held it open. Down at the bottom, his feet in the air as stiff as toothpicks, was the mouse, now well deceased.

"I didn't even have time to give him a name," The Fist said.

Now he asked himself a second question: "If I figure one of these cats did it, will the cat die?"

"Of fucking course."

"Which cat done it?"

Those black eyes of The Fist's relentlessly and fiercely scrutinized the three cats. He bent down to intensify the rays from his eyes. All had their stubby little ears sticking straight up. "I don't know one from the fucking other," he said, in bewilderment that was something fierce. He wanted to kill somebody.

He realized he didn't know what he was looking for. There was no memory of what the cat who ate the mouse looked like.

He did think of the dog lineup for Malocchio that was such a success and now here was the same form, a three-cat lineup, and it was no fucking good.

This time, he was the fool trying to make an identity.

"I'll bet you," he said to himself, "that this is like a warning. Where we done good in the past, we catch a beating. Now."

He sat in the empty room and happened to glance under the table. The mouse sure was not there. But he had left The Fist with the only pleasant, positive feeling he had had in a long time.

The next day, a cat dozed in the doorway of Coogie's Bar. When the porter opened the door, another cat slipped out.

"We only got them yesterday," the porter said. "Got them off a kid. You ought to see them go after mice. Should have had them here for years."

The Fist wanted to go over and strangle the cats and maybe the porter, too, but he didn't and he didn't know why he didn't.

31

Inside, Nini Scalfaro was behind the counter of his candy store with his eyes closed and his hand supporting his chin. He had started at 6 A.M. with the same three hours' sleep he got every night. He hated his wife, and when he closed the store at 10 P.M., he drank vodka until he decided his wife was asleep. The small hours during which he slept were like diamonds on the clock. Three hours at most. Half-closed eyes greeted the cheese store guy from next door who came in to make a five-dollar lottery play. The machine made a grinding noise. The customer took the ticket. Nini put the five right into his pocket. "I'm going to be careful with the money from the machine this week," he said.

Fausti was there because he again cut an afternoon macroeconomics class at St. Leo's College. He couldn't wait to get over to the guys in front of the store.

Soon, he stopped going to another class. Finally, he just stopped going to school.

"What are you doing home?" his father said to him on the street one day.

"I stopped going to school," Fausti said, glumly.

The father slapped him, weakly.

Fausti went to the candy store.

Larry Dellacava was plagued by another of these colds that sometimes sent him to bed for a couple of days.

Purportedly, he was living on Cornelia Street, although he had a home and second family, Fausti's half sister, Frances, in Yonkers. He stood listlessly on the street. In the club one day he watched Magic Johnson on CNN in the late afternoon, announcing that he was leaving the Los Angeles Lakers because he was HIV positive.

"Poor bastard, he'll be dead," Larry Dellacava said.

"People can live a long time with that," Fausti said.

"What do you know?" Larry said. "I told you he's a dead man."

Fausti said to himself, "Look at this. He's an expert on everything."

A couple of months later, Larry was in bed and Fausti asked him, "What's the matter?"

"Nothin'." He went to no doctor. He blamed a common flu. "If I can't beat this, I don't fuckin' deserve to live anyway."

Two weeks later, he was back in bed.

32

At Fausti's school, St. Leo's College in downtown Brooklyn, jobs that might interest night students were posted in a dean's office. Salary was $250. Fausti assured himself that he would continue in school at night, but of course it was an empty promise.

One job was at D. J. Bushell, Investments, 72 Maiden Lane, financial district. Fausti got the job. But the general unease of suddenly being a working man and no longer a student caused him to be overly eager to hold Con's hand.

"I want you to promise me," he said.

"What?"

"That we won't go out with anybody but each other."

"No," she said.

He asked her this three times in the following week.

"Stop hounding me."

She had been going out with a boy named Joe in Yonkers for four years and he came down several times and begged her to come back to Yonkers with him. She said, no, but she felt sorry for him.

"You can't talk to him anymore," Fausti said.

"Oh, no?"

"I said so."

Her brother, Pat, watching television, said, "I have to agree with Fausti. You shouldn't have anything to do with this Joe, anyway."

They were in the front room of the apartment, with two windows onto the street.

She got up and punched the glass and shattered the first window.

She picked up a chair and put it through the second.

St. Valentine's Day was a Saturday. She called on Friday night and told him, "I'm going up to Joe's parents' house for the weekend. Look in the paper tomorrow."

In "the paper," which was the *Daily News,* there was a page of Valentine's greetings. Fausti scanned them in the candy store.

> Fausti —
> Our first Valentine's Day together.
> Con

She returned on Monday, and right after work, she followed her heart through the streets until she found Fausti. Of course she had missed him so much she had almost died. They went for a drink on West Broadway. She pledged a life of love to him. And he to her.

"Want to go to a club Saturday night?" Fausti asked her.

"Sure."

"Good."

"Which one?"

"Heartbreaks. Where else would we go?"

"I may not want to go there," she said.

"Where else would you go? I'm taking you."

"I have to go where you want to go?"

"Of course."

"Be a boss in charge of everything like your family." She went into her house.

Saturday night, she went where she wanted to go, with girl-friends to the 4D on East 53rd Street.

A week later, she asked for his car so she could go out to a relative's house in Mastic, on Long Island. Fausti had a used IROC convertible, a good and souped-up Ford, which he gladly gave her. Why not? This is about boy and girl, and there are no rules that make sense. She left without asking him to come along. Fausti borrowed his sister's Buick Regal, and paid her $50 for the weekend. He filled it with gas and lasted one day in the rain on the Jersey shore. He came home and left twenty more in the glove compartment, went up to Penn Station early on Sunday and took the Long Island Rail-road out to Mastic. He was staring out the window as the train went between Rockville Centre and Baldwin, and right below him, driving along the wet highway alongside the rail tracks, heading to the city, was Con, her hair flying as she drove his convertible. He got off at the next stop, Baldwin, and waited for a train back to New York. By rushing, he got to Thompson Street by noon, just in time to miss her by five minutes. "She goes out to the movies," the brother said.

On Monday, he changed his beeper. A real guy making a stand. Never would he give her the beeper number. He saw her on Wednesday for moments, time enough to give her the new number. In the next year, he changed the beeper eight times. Once, he kept it a secret for two weeks. He was driving to the Jersey shore when he turned around and came all the way back to Thompson Street to leave the new number under her door — "In case you got an emergency and I'll come right away. You know how I can do that." Usually, he just saw her on the street and gave it to her the day after he got the new number. Still, he was in turmoil over her.

"You've got to understand," his brother said. "You listen to Father Phil."

"I'm telling you the only thing you ever have to know about women," Father Phil said.

"What?" Fausti said.

"They crazy," his brother said.

"There is no question about that," Father Phil said.

He held the page with Con's ad.

"Do you have to know anything more than this? She don't know whether she's with you or an eskimo. You can only do one thing," Father Phil said.

"What's that?"

"Establish limits in your mind. Obviously this is a beautiful girl and you like each other very much. Good. She puts in the paper for the whole world to see that she loves you. Then she says, I don't love you for the rest of the day, I'm going to see my old boyfriend and you could get lost. She goes off with some bum in Yonkers. All right. That's her. She'll be back. One day she won't go anywhere except with you. But just in case, make sure this is the furthest anybody goes with you. You take me, I'm very careful with women. Around the church, around here, wherever I go. I don't have any nuts around me. They can be dangerous."

"Pay attention to him," his brother said. "Father Phil knows."

As Fausti had not as yet nailed the priest with a girlfriend, he didn't understand how he became such an expert.

The first thing Con did when she looked for a job was to speak to nobody. A foundation wall of the Mafia was that it often operated as a political clubhouse, where the loyal got assistance for the most common family problem, a relative in need. In the Dellacava organization, Cathy from Williamsburg needed a job. She came from good people, her father was a bookmaker. Cathy's job came through Fritzie, who went to Ciro in Howard Beach, who went to Sal at the airport and Sal had the young woman hired as an office worker for a freight-forwarding company, a block outside the main airport trucking entrance.

She started on the first Monday in March. She talked on the phone and left for lunch. She came back at four because she had left her housekey in the desk.

"What do you call this?" the office manager said.

"My job," she said.

In putting the men on jobs, sometimes three and four men were placed on the same construction job, as laborers, which they sure didn't want to do. They sat and watched the work.

Con, who asked nobody, did it her own way. She picked up the newspaper classified section one Sunday and found, under a heading, "Fashion," a listing for an office assistant. There was a phone number and name. At 9:01 on Monday morning, she called the number. "I saw your ad. I am young and just out of school. But I am smart and very honest. I'm known everywhere for my honesty. I don't know how you would rate me for fashion. But I really try to look good."

"Where did you go school?" the guy asked.

"Garfield High in Yonkers."

"I thought you were just out of college."

"Would college have made me any more honest?"

"Why don't you come down?"

The company was Calvin Klein, the designer. She did office work and noticed that the glamour she saw on billboards and magazine photos was not present in the office. It was a business.

33

Going down the long hall to the personnel office at Bushell, all Fausti could remember was high school, at the Capuchin Academy on Second Avenue, when he saw his two friends Vincent Gilmartin and James Principe, standing in front of the principal's office with worried faces.

"We're getting thrown out," Gilmartin said. "They busted us for Black Beauties."

"What were you doing, taking them?" Fausti asked.

"We were selling."

"How could you do that? When you're friends with me? I'll bet you —"

"Oh, no, we already said, right away, that you weren't in."

"Why did you even have to say that?"

"Because it was the first question we got asked."

He should have realized that this was the way it would be for most of his life, as it was right now, as he came into the personnel office and sat at the table.

"What is your name?" the security man giving the polygraph at his job asked.

"Fausti Dellacava."

The guy showed great eagerness now.

"Where do you live?"

"Two thirty-five Bleecker Street."

"What is your mother's name?"

"Laura."

"What is your father's name?"

"Larry Dellacava."

The polygraph guy was stunned. His machine had no reaction to this true statement. The man's face was flushed. How could this be? Larry? Everybody had told him that this was The Fist's son, Fist Junior.

When Fausti applied for the job, he put down his name and didn't think anything of it and neither did the woman in personnel. That her name was Joan Catalano might have had something to do with it. She had light hair, but a round chubby face and dark brown eyes backed up her name.

He told himself that he would learn this business as thoroughly as he knew the sports of the day. His body tingled with thoughts of shouting and waving in a crazed trading pit. In his mind, he was succeeding on his own, the name just a string of letters.

A bit more than that when the papers came up with nice strong headlines and The Fist's picture about how the federals were closing in on the feared Fist Dellacava for a major indictment. He went over big on the television, too.

Here was Fausti at the job he loved being questioned as a common thief. The first lie detector questions were supposed to set the reaction boundaries.

"Have you ever taken anything with value of over fifty dollars?"

"No."

"Have you ever helped somebody steal something valued at over fifty dollars?"

"No."

"Have you ever been asked if you had anything to do with objects missing with a value of over fifty dollars?"

"No."

"Did you lie when asked this?"

"No."

"Have you ever stolen from a store?"

"No."

"Ever steal from a previous employer?"

"No."

"Have you ever been in the presence of somebody stealing?"

"No."

He answered with confidence.

Suddenly, all Fausti could think of was his father's rage if he found out that Fausti was sitting here as submissive as a prisoner. "I'll take that polygraph and shove it down your fuckin' throat, you rat cocksu—"

When Fausti was finished, the security guy took off the sensors and told Fausti that he could go.

"How'd I do?" Fausti asked.

"You should know how you did if you told the truth."

"Who tells me?"

"Somebody will talk to you," the guy said.

The second test was five days later.

"Am I the only one you've brought in twice like this?" Fausti asked.

"I don't know," the personnel woman said. "I was asked to notify you of the test."

Fausti was angry. If there was a thief fuck somewhere in the place. But they probably didn't want to hear another name from anybody. Dellacava was enough.

"What is your name?"

"Fausti Dellacava."

Five days later, he was asked to come in for another test. When he finished, he glanced back to see two of the partners coming in through another door. They want to see the test personally, Fausti thought.

At four thirty in the afternoon, the personnel woman came by. She stood nervously with an envelope in her hands.

"This is three weeks' severance pay," she said. "I'm afraid you'll have to leave now. We'll mail you the papers on medical benefits. You can pick up your coverage yourself."

"I passed the polygraph."

"Yes, you did."

"They know I passed?"

"Yep."

"Can you tell me one thing I did here besides work?" he asked her.

She closed her eyes. "They were almost going to fire me over this. Nobody realized who you were."

"Who am I? I'm an American citizen."

"They think you're associated with criminals."

"Why? Because I'm Italian?"

"No. Because your name is Fausti Dellacava. They think you have some way of cheating a polygraph. You have anything personal in the desk, take it out now while I'm here. I'm sorry."

Later, an overwhelming depression came over Fausti as he looked out over this street with its tenements and fire escapes and women walking slowly in the late afternoon shadows. He was on the block where he was born and raised in the comfort of a father and uncle he thought were tremendously popular, and even loved, on the streets where he lived. Through all those early years he never knew that people were at least scared to death of his whole family.

"You tried so hard," Con said. She came straight from work and stood outside with him, with part of their fine dream in pieces at their feet.

"Is this what it's going to be?" Fausti said.

"Don't be silly. It's one stupid place."

"Nobody helped me get the job."

"I know."

"I stopped going to school because of it."

"Maybe you shouldn't have. Maybe you ought to go back and finish."

"I sit in school all day. What do I bring home, I bring home a schoolbook."

"I'm working."

"You're going to support me?"

"Just while you're in school, I'll pitch in."

"You're the woman and you're going to support me?"

"Just until —"

"— I get in an argument on the street, you're going to come down and do my fighting?"

"Don't be silly."

"No woman supports me. I starve until I get a job."

"What's that supposed to mean to me?"

He said nothing.

"I know I have the church for the wedding."

He was stunned. "It's a surprise wedding," she said. "I'm through waiting."

He walked into the candy store. She walked away. Great sorrow for him had turned into anger. Nini didn't even ask for help. He walked to the back of the store and flopped into a blue beach chair. Fausti got behind the counter.

Staring out the window of the old store, watching women who seemed ancient walking slowly past the church across the street, Fausti had the hours running backward into days and turning into months or years, ice on the sidewalk, sun on the sidewalk, walking down the street with bare legs.

Right away, a tall black woman, the same one who was around day after day, a woman with defeated eyes, stepped into the store. Short hair had not been brushed in so long that it looked matted forever. She wore a brown top and long skirt and under her right arm she had a large old handbag, bulging with cracks running through it like veins.

"You got a cigarette?" she asked Fausti.

At the sound of her voice, Nini jumped up in the back as if answering a fire call.

"Nothin'. Get out of here. Do I have to chase you every day?"

"Yep," she said, leaving.

Hope suddenly appeared in the dreariness. First, the distributor came in with a check for $263.84 as royalties for Mob Stars. He also had packs of Mob Stars cards without gum. "Yez sell them like art pictures," he said. They would give Nini and Fausti a larger percentage. "Maybe I can keep up with the lottery receipts," Nini said.

One thing atop another, there now came from nowhere a known personage, Tony Café of the Bonnano mob.

"Put my picture on a card. I'm good people."

Tony was called Tony Café because he was always in cafés.

The picture showed Tony Café at a table with a drink.

When the card came out a month later, he was ecstatic. "Beautiful!" he told Fausti.

VINCENT RAMPARTS aka TONY CAFE

He is called Tony Café because he is always out at nightclubs.

BORN: Brooklyn, New York, 1950.

FAMILY: Bonnano.

MADE: By Joe Bonnano himself.

ASSETS: Terrific personality. Great night guy. Really loves
  Regine's.

LIABILITIES: Wife Lisa screams she paid $20,000 for union
  book, Tony gets no jobs. All lies. Tony don't want a job
  you work at. They robbed his wife.

He ripped up several packs of gum and looked at the cards inside. Generals and movie stars and a ballplayer and a mob guy. He saw the straight packs of Mob Stars cards, with Joey Young's atop one pack.

"This guy is a complete lunatic," he said.

"We know that," Nini said.

"But he's lucky bastard," Tony Café said. "You play cards, he always wins. Go to Atlantic City, the fuckin' guy comes out with money. Anything this little prick touches turns into a diamond."

He went through the other cards and compared them to his. "It's a nice card. I'll be the only to see it," he said with sadness. He was wrong. His was the first card that had a direct reaction from a personal family. Tony Café's first wife, Mrs. Tony Café of Greenpoint, went into Manfredi's candy store up the corner on Lorimer Street. The men were looking at the mob pictures. They held up her husband's card. "Look," they said. Look, she did.

The neighborhood women saw her drop her packages and shriek. They thought she had just been told someone near and dear, undoubtedly her husband, had died.

It was way worse than that. It was a second woman.

So it was that some nights later, here was a sidewalk altercation at 2 A.M. in front of Regine's on Park Avenue.

It featured Mrs. Tony Café, age forty-seven, mother of two.

And Tony Café's wife without license, Ms. Marianna, age twenty-seven.

"Tony, she's got a gun!" Ms. Marianna said as she stood frozen outside Regine's.

"Not a gun," Mrs. Tony Café said.

And now Mrs. Tony Café said, "No, no gun. This is one of Tony's best tools." She took out a hammer that was big enough to be used breaking cement.

Mr. Tony Café stood wide-eyed behind Ms. Marianna. He knew he should be in front of her and he seemed to be trying to do this, but not so much. If Ms. Marianna gets hurt because of him not being in front of her, then I guess she gets hurt.

Tony put both hands over his head but they could not stop a swinging hammer. The blunt instrument came through his hands and hit him right on the top of the head. Down went Tony Café on the back of his head.

"Tony, are you dead?"

He groaned and moved slightly.

"What a fucking shame," Mrs. Tony Café lamented.

34

"They don't want me to live," Fausti said. "I'll try with another name, hah?"

"Tell your father," his cousin Romulo, overhearing him, said.

"He's home sick."

"So go tell him." Romulo had a job setting up conventions at the Javits Center.

"I can't. I told you he's sick."

"With what?"

"He's got a bad cold."

"Didn't he just have one?"

"Now he got another one," Fausti said. "He can hardly get out of bed."

"So, you could talk to him with a cold."

"He can't even talk."

"Then go across the street, tell him what you want," Romulo said.

"I don't want to ask anybody for anything," Fausti said.

The cousin shrugged. "I'll say you need a job and I'll tell him the last name twice."

"I had enough of that," Fausti said.

"If you want a job, I got to tell them who you are."

That was on a Monday. The next day, the cousin told him, "They say, don't even think about your name. They're glad to have you. They'll bury you somewhere nice. Nobody'll ever notice."

He told this to Fausti at night. The idea of another name had passed through Fausti's mind like a Broadway local. Stopping for a moment, the doors open, calling you inside, showing you Langdon or Lansing or Louisell, then quickly pulling out, leaving you still on the platform, and another local on the way. He did nothing, and carried the old name into a new job. The Javits Convention Center sat on the West Side like an old felon. It was a building of smoked glass that took up five square blocks across a wide expressway from the Hudson River. The politicians and builders did not extend it to the river and let the road go under it. Nor did they build a convention hall worth the name. They put up a series of glass boxes and convention spaces not quite large enough for something like a political convention. But they charged the taxpayers enough money to buy France. Enormous money was made by those involved in the building. The citizens of the city were not given the courtesy of being told to hold up their hands as they were being robbed.

When Fausti walked into the Javits Center, a man in a shirt and tie darted through the circles of men in sweatshirts and tank tops and came up to him and said:

"You're Fausti Dellacava? Am I glad to see you! I'm Philly Mancini. I'm the shop steward."

"I got what they told me to bring," Fausti said. On a carpenter's belt he had a hammer, pliers, tape roll, screwdriver, and handsaw. He had never handled any of these tools because there are no garages or basement workshops on Thompson Street.

"Yeah, that's good," Mancini said. "We carpenters union. But you got something we need more than tools."

"Like what?"

"We got these fuckin' Irish here, they're Westies mob, you don't believe it, they actually come around try to put the bull on us. I tell them, I'm going to take this to somebody, you know what they say? 'Fuck him and fuck you.' How do you like it? How do you like these rat bastards?"

"What do I do about it?" Fausti asked.

"Get good and fucking rough with them."

"How do I do that?" Fausti asked.

"Issue beatings," Mancini said. He paused. Fausti did not react. "Break fuckin' heads."

"I don't do those things."

"All right then. Whack them out. Torture them. I bet you like doing that. You ever cut anybody's head off?"

"You're nuts," Fausti said.

"What do you do? Carpenter?" he said sarcastically.

"What I do is go home right now."

He turned and walked through the crowd waiting to go to work. Laughing, smoking, boasting, Georgetown and Chicago Bulls T-shirts, everybody in Nike sneakers, all with that unmistakable confidence of a man with a job. You can tell if a man is working just by looking at him.

And Fausti with his crackling new work belt, and pliers glistening, walked through these people knowing he was an outsider, who would earn no money today. He went out onto the street with the empty day ahead of him.

At week's end, Larry Dellacava was in front of his club, blowing his nose.

"How do you feel?" Fausti said.

"Forget about me. How's the job?"

"No job. They wanted me to bust up people. They thought that was a good job for me."

The next day, the father rang the doorbell and called up for Fausti.

"You didn't ask for nothin', am I right or am I wrong?"

"Not a thing."

"Go back over there today and see that stupid fuckin' Mancini. Walk right in. If he even says gorilla, I don't hear that you get mad. I hear that you told him off. I want to hear you smacked him in the fuckin' mouth."

This also was the last time anybody saw Larry Dellacava walking the streets. Fausti asked him, "What's the matter?"

"Nothin'."

Two weeks later, Larry was back in bed.

"Why are you so sick all the time?"

"Nothin'."

"Will you tell me?" Fausti shouted.

Larry never answered. He went back to Yonkers.

Then on Christmas Eve, Fausti and his brother stood on the corner; they had just come from seeing the father, who was in Yonkers with his second wife and daughter, Fausti's half sister, Frances.

Fausti and his brother said very little, but when they got outside, Fausti grabbed the brother's arms and said, "Tell me what's he got? Tell me."

"Nothing," the brother said.

"Tell me!"

"AIDS."

Larry was in New York University Hospital, with Fausti sleeping on a cot next to him, and he was in bed in his house in Yonkers with Fausti holding his hand. When Larry Dellacava died, he left cash to two families, and it wasn't all that much cash because he had worked across the street from the Lutheran in both location and violence and therefore made no huge scores. Killers make the money in the Mafia. His legacy was this young guy with bristled hair and big eyes that riveted on you when he said, "My father died of AIDS."

At the Javits Center, Fausti worked on the car show, with the Toyota exhibit in one block-long section. The Toyota display was a double-decker with a curved staircase going up to the car, which had been put up there by forklift. It was done three days before the show began, and with exhibitors bringing around their own security, there soon would be a melding of square badges that would shut down stealing.

Fausti was working overtime, one of the great blessings of a working life, when four of the workers climbed all over the Toyota exhibit.

One guy, Eddie Hartman, got in the car. The other three were around the forklift.

"Hey, where they put the keys?" the one in a Georgetown shirt asked.

"What for?"

"Wha? We takin' this right out of here now."

"Drive it right through the aisle, out the door," the guy in the car said.

"You don't see nothin', all right," Hartman said.

"Wrong. I got to work here. If I get asked, what am I going to say, that I never saw a whole red Toyota taken right from in front of me?"

"Why not?"

"On account of I want my job."

"You could still have the job. Just say you saw nothin'."

"How much is the car worth?" Fausti said.

"Thirty-two!"

"You can't make thirty-two here?" Fausti said. "All of us make what, seventy-five thousand. At the least."

"Yeah," Hartman said.

"Then what's the matter with you?" Fausti said. "Don't you like your jobs?"

"No. I like stealing better."

"I hate to tell you, if you put me in the middle I'll have to tell."

"You can't be a stool pigeon. You'll get whacked."

"If you think I would ever tell the cop or somebody in here, you're crazy. I'm going to tell the Other Fellow and we'll see what's what."

They left and Fausti worked his overtime on the Toyota double-decker. Soon, he became the best in the house at looking at plans for a convention floor, glancing at the vast empty place and then moving quickly around and marking aisles and exhibition spaces. As he had two things on his mind, work and a marriage in a short while, and both things showed on the jobs he did, he was soon in demand all over the hall. Large trade shows grew complicated and intense. To the exhibitors, a show opening caused the nervousness of a stage show's opening curtain.

"A half hour till the doors open!" a voice came over the loud-speaker.

"Oh, oh," everybody on the floor cried.

Fausti would be in full run by now. Tacking up curtains on a booth, moving something in. He found his job had a dimension to it that so few others anywhere had: it was exciting.

"Fifteen minutes till the doors open."

"Oh, oh."

More rushing.

"Five minutes."

"Oh, oh."

Doors swung and people flooded in and for the three days the aisles would be jammed. Suddenly, the show closed and the workers rushed about even more, breaking the thing down. The biggest closing night always was for the plant show. Union workers from all over the city came to the Javits Center's back doors as the exhibitors had their plants and trees put out on the curb for refuse. There was no way to ship them back to Vienna, Virginia, and have them in any condition. The steamfitters, iron workers, and their families grabbed plants and brought them home to Brooklyn apartments that became ads for *Better Homes and Gardens*. It was all legal. The same as the overtime Fausti was making for breaking down the show, taking a breath and starting to mark up a new one.

Every Thursday at lunch he went to the bank to cash his paycheck, and also the one for the foreman, Mancini. After which he went into a bodega and bought a week's supply of lottery tickets. His daily bet was $10 straight and a dollar box on number 2667. It came to $77 a week.

35

"Your girl should have this," the jewelry guy said.

"How much?" Fausti stared at the ring.

"Twenty thousand."

Twenty thousand is a step away from a million.

The dazzling light disappeared as Fausti snapped the box shut.

"I love the ring but I can't. This is not me."

The jewelry guy had been a friend of his father's. He said he would be back with another ring. He came, all right, showing a ring that was almost as dazzling. Fausti loved it.

"It's only fifteen," the guy said.

"Oh, but it's so beautiful," the young woman standing with them said. She was Marie Meli, who was there with her father, Sal Meli.

Fausti took a breath. Fifteen thousand dollars was a figure as high as the sky. He saved money and talked to Con about marriage. It was wondrous, but the ring on her finger depends on what the guy tugs out of his pocket. He was about to say no again when Sal Meli looked at it and said, "You got yourself a real beauty."

"Will she love you," daughter Marie said.

Fausti was too embarrassed to say no.

"That's fifteen," he said dully.

"Fifteen."

"That's the same as we're paying for the watch here," Sal said. His daughter held a Rolex watch in a box. "She's giving it to her boyfriend for a present. They're going to get married, too."

"Congratulations," Fausti said.

"Thank you," she said.

"I don't know why she's marrying him," Sal Meli said.

"Daddy."

"Moron. Irish, would you believe that?"

"Oh, Daddy. Will you stop."

"Tell that to him. He pulls on my arm. 'Get me in.' I tell him he's Irish, the only thing he gets in is a barroom."

"He's good. He works very hard."

"Cars," Sal said.

"What's wrong with that, Daddy?"

"Because he's an imbecile going to get caught a hundred times. Fausti, you want to buy a car, Fausti, this boyfriend will get you one this afternoon. He's liable to take it off this fuckin' block. He'll take a cop car if it's the only one around."

Meli had a sheaf of new bills and he counted some out and handed them to the jeweler.

Fausti told the jeweler, "I'll be around with the money in a couple of days."

"Take your time."

Fausti said to himself, "The time it takes to get a loan."

He knew all he could get was a secure loan, putting up the fifteen thousand, all that he had saved, as collateral.

That way the ring would cost $1,800 in interest in two years. Like all street logic, it was insanely expensive.

He took Con to a party at his aunt's house in Briarcliff Manor, during which they went outside and stood on the lawn and he took her hand and put the ring on it. The lights from the house made the ring send off flashes each time she moved her finger.

"I want to thank you," he said.

"For what?"

"For saying you'll marry me."

She cried.

36

124. On March 11, 1990, at 11:29 P.M., Fausti Dellacava and Dominick Raguso arrived at 16 East 68th Street, in Raguso's car. Both men walked to the front door. Raguso jimmied open the door. Dellacava was carrying a manila envelope. After a brief discussion, Dellacava entered the building and Raguso left. At 11:33 P.M., Dellacava was observed in the dining room where he was greeted by Carmella Bella. He then entered the kitchen, but returned to the dining room where he conversed with Carmella Bella. Dellacava then walked to the bookcase/desk, picked up a handful of United States currency, and gave 2 or 3 bills to Carmella Bella. Thereafter, he replaced the money and departed to the bedroom. At 2:15 A.M., (March 12, 1990), Angelo Dante was observed operating a vehicle in the vicinity. At 2:30 A.M., Dante arrived at and entered the residence. There he met Dellacava and Carmella Bella in the dining room, where all three sat down and engaged in a conversation, each contributing to the dis-

cussion. At 3:05 A.M., Dellacava and Dante rose and walked to the elevator. Both men talked and motioned to Carmella Bella, who responded. Dellacava put on a black hat and coat over his robe and picked up a small unidentified object from the table. Dante went into the kitchen and returned with a white plastic bag. At 3:12 A.M., they departed from view toward the front of the building. At 3:14 A.M., Dellacava and Dante, each carrying a white bag, left the residence. The car went to 250 Sullivan Street, where Dellacava exited the car and entered 250. At 6:10 A.M., agents of the Federal Bureau of Investigation arrested Dellacava at 250 Sullivan Street.

UNITED STATES OF AMERICA
DEPARTMENT OF JUSTICE

CR NO. 93–068
(T. 18, U.S.C., 1962 (c) and (d). 1959 (a) (10 and 5), 1951, 371, 2 and 3551 et seq.; T. 29, U.S.C. 186)

UNITED STATES OF AMERICA AGAINST FAUSTI DELLACAVA, ALSO KNOWN AS "THE FIST"

THE GRAND JURY CHARGES:
INTRODUCTION TO ALL COUNTS

At all times relevant to the indictment, unless otherwise indicated, The Enterprise.

1. The members and associated of the De Francisi Organized Crime Family of La Cosa Nostra (the "De Francisi Crime Family") constituted an "enterprise," as that term is defined in Title 18, United States Code, Sections 1961(4) and 1959(b)(2) that is, a group of individuals associated in fact. The De Francisi Organized Crime Family was an organized group that operated in the Eastern District of New York and other parts of the United States. It engaged in, and its activities

included, interstate commerce. The De Francisi Crime Family was referred to by its members in various ways, including as a "borgata," a "family," a "cosa nostra" and "this thing of ours."

2. The De Francisi Crime Family operated through groups of individuals headed by "captains," who were also referred to as "skippers," "caporegimes" and "capodecinas." These groups, which were referred to as "crews," "regimes," and "decinas," consisted of made members of the De Francisi Crime Family, who were also referred to as "soldiers," "friends of ours," "good fellows," and "buttons" and associates of the De Francisi Crime Family.

3. Each captain was responsible for supervising the criminal activities of his crew, and provided crew members and associates with support and protection.

37

Into the Javits Center came this stubby little guy with sleepy eyes who padded around the building saying nothing and after that went into his office and dozed. The guys on the floor laughed at him.

On payday, the union's three hundred men were told to pick up their checks at the cashier. There, each man had to hold his check against his chest and have his picture taken.

Forty checks were left at the end of the day. They were for no-shows and nobody would dare pick them up in the camera's eye.

Fausti saw the story in the middle of the night. His friend Whitey from Thompson Street called him. "The *Daily News*. You're it." Fausti got up and met him in the diner on Sixth Avenue. The *News* headline said: "Javits Center is Fausti Dellacava Social Club." The story said, "The Special Attorney General for Organized Crime has started a massive probe of the racket-infested Javits Center.

Records turned over to the prosecutor show that the nephew of mob boss Fausti (The Fist) Dellacava was paid $150,000 last year as a carpenter."

"They lied," Fausti said. He had his W-2 in his wallet. It was not there by accident. The form proves he works. "I got eighty-three thousand two hundred and thirty-three dollars and I worked every hour for it."

"You think anybody cares?" Whitey said.

"Nope. They care that my name is Fausti Dellacava and anything you do after you say that is all right."

On television, the state crime man said, "I'm not satisfied with a state government that allows itself to be bullied by Mafia gangsters who force us to pay as much as one hundred and fifty thousand a year to some mobster's grasping relative. I want to know why mob boss Fausti Dellacava has a nephew making that much in the Javits Center."

One day, an assistant supervisor from the Javits Center told Fausti to make a floor plan by the morning. He was to make an aisle and mark a large piece of space at one end. He had to do it quickly because there was a lot of fancy food coming during the night, he was told.

"What is the space for?"

"Nothing," he was told.

For marking the space this time, he was specifically told to use chalk. Usually, he used shoe polish because it lasts for a couple of days. For this time, they wanted lines easily scuffed away and the event forgotten in a hurry.

"There you go," Fausti said to the assistant director. It was five A.M. and the caterers were carrying boxes into the large space.

"It looks good to me," the assistant said.

"What's it for?" Fausti said.

"Press conference."

Fausti was home asleep when the state guy stood in a well-marked place and announced that all of the three hundred men working the Javits Center were being fired because of gangster influences and outrageous raiding of the public treasury by such as

Fausti Dellacava, the nephew of mob boss, who earned one hundred and fifty thou—

Fausti had his W-2 for the year 1996, showing the $83,233. He had a packet of paystubs that showed he had earned so far this year, halfway through 1997, $40,000.

They put the two together. Then they added on another thirty to make it a hundred fifty.

Then they all copy each other. The *Post* came out with the same figure of hundred fifty and so did the *Times* and *Newsweek* magazine. The *Economist* of London did a long article on the "Two hundred thousand pound gangland carpenter, Fausti Dellacava."

The assistant director called Fausti at home.

"Don't worry, you'll be back."

"I do worry and I won't be back."

"They're doing everything from the ground up. Come in and fill out an application and then when it gets up to us, you're in. Understand me? In."

"I won't fill out an application."

"Why?"

"Because by now if I have to tell people what I can do and how fast I do it, then I never should of been here to begin with."

"You're right. But, ah, don—"

"The other thing is, I'm not going to have an application in there so all those guys can look at it and laugh."

On Friday morning, the assistant called again. "They're meeting all day and night on hiring people. They'll notify them by FedEx. If I were you, I'd stick around all weekend. I think you'll get one."

Fausti started the weekend by not going to the store for the papers on Saturday. He was afraid he'd be gone when the delivery arrived. Con and her sister waited with him at his house. They saw nothing but taxis. On Sunday, he missed mass while he waited outside the front door. It went like that all day long. When he woke up on Monday, his head was heavy. Instantly, he knew why. He was out of a job. This is some name I got.

38 He headed straight up Houston Street for the courthouse to change his name. Right now, he told himself. Before it truly fucking kills you. All he had been hearing was the federal agents clamoring at the gates as they put together an indictment against his uncle. The name would live forever in New York's criminal histories and there would come a time when the real Fausti, also known as The Fist, would be gone and the legends and darkness would fall onto nephew Fausti. Of course his name is that of an old mobster. While it might be an act of high disloyalty to change his name at a time like this, with the father who named him recently dead and the uncle whose name he bore seemingly in great distress, Fausti felt that with the years he deserved in front of him and without being able to envision a decent day in them, he was called on to lash his life to a pier before it sailed away.

"Change of name?" the clerk said. He was behind a long counter in the civil courthouse basement on Centre Street.

"I want to see what it looks like on the books."

"What books?"

"They told me you have books here of people changed their names."

"Why do you want them?"

"I might change my name."

"Oh, you've got to go up to room 315 for that."

"I just went there. They told me if I wanted to see the book with the name changes I should come here."

"Is it a book with name changes you want?"

"Yeah. That's what I want."

"Down the end of the counter on the rack," the clerk said.

"Thank you."

The clerk said, "My name was changed. Flaherty. They dropped the O when they got off the boat."

At the end of the counter were large, heavy, dusty bound ledger books that had the name changes for the last 150 years entered in pen and ink in neat columns. The vast majority of name changes occurred at the piers when immigration inspectors gave new short names to anybody coming in with many syllables from Kiev. "Your name is Max Stern!"

The first page he turned to showed the name Charles O'Garry changed to Count Pardee Bentley. Right away, Fausti started dreaming. A royal name. Count Bentley. Count Collins.

Patricia O'Gara and Barbara O'Gara, changing to Patricia Cessa and Jean Cessa. They're beating somebody, Fausti thought.

There was Jack George, changed to Marvella Winslow Lucille. In the middle of the next page, Edward Halloran to Juanita Kay.

One Al Sweeney switched to George Ryan and that was obviously done to double bank some bill collectors, while retaining the beloved Irish in his name.

Fausti went back to the third floor where two clerks handed him seven pages of instructions. To change his name, Fausti had to have a legal notice published in the *Law Journal,* a paper he never heard of. "I can change my name to anything I want?" he asked the clerk.

"You can't use nobility anymore," he said.

"Who says so? Did you tell that to Count Basie?"

"I don't know if his name was real," the clerk said. "I just know that there is a rule that you can't use nobility."

"Stop Duke Ellington?"

The clerk shrugged. "Maybe his name wasn't legal."

"He made it legal every night. I'm thinking of becoming Count Collins."

He also had to assemble and bring in a lot of things he didn't like: Proof of present name. If born in NEW YORK STATE annex certified copy of birth certificate.

The first time Fausti filled in the blank for his new name, he printed in big letters, MALAPROP WHITNEY.

"Can I say something?" the clerk said. He was the one with a mustache and thick black hair. Good Italian guy.

"This name will only make people laugh at first. Then they'll think you're a jerk. Don't take me wrong. You can have it. You be Malaprop the rest of your life. I'm just saying."

Fausti filled in another name.

STYLES BITCHLEY.

"You know where I heard this name? And you'll hear it from a lot of people. Rodney Dangerfield's CD. He give the piano player that name. That's why you think of it now. You heard it before. What else have you got there?"

Fausti printed out, "BREADALBANE."

"I never heard of anything like that. Where is it from?"

"The *Daily Racing Form*. I spent four dollars on it to get the horse names."

The fourth name was BLANFORT G. MELTON. The clerk nodded. That was more like it. The clerk took the money for the legal ad and went back into an office.

Immediately, swinging out of the office was a new face. This guy is no city clerk, Fausti told himself. He had his jacket on and he had short light hair and big aviator glasses. Who is he kidding?

"Just one question for the forms," he said. "Is there a reason for changing your name?"

Fausti said nothing.

"By that I mean, from your name, the name you want to change. . . ."

Fausti stared at a spot off the guy's right shoulder.

It took four days before the legal notice showed up in the paper. Nobody on Sullivan Street saw it because the legal notice ran only in the *New York Law Journal,* which interests only those in the shadow of a courthouse. He had complained about this, why not place it in the *Daily News,* let somebody see it? He asked the clerk in courtroom 315, the name change room in the courthouse. The clerk said that the publisher of the *Law Journal* runs the judge's names in the paper so all the legal notices go there.

Three times he went to the *Law Journal* offices on Broadway because he couldn't find the paper anywhere on a newsstand. Each time, his notice wasn't in. On the fourth day, today, along the bottom of a column of agate type, he found:

CHANGE OF NAME

Know this by all present that FAUSTI DELLACAVA of 235 Bleecker Street, Manhattan County files application with this court, Part 3, New York County, Alice M. Schlein, justice of Supreme Court, that henceforth he shall be known in all personal and official proceedings as BLAN-FORT G. MELTON. Notice has been filed with Part 3, State Supreme Court. The duration of waiting time is six weeks, after which no objections shall be heard.

With his new name in print for the first time — Blanfort G. Melton — Fausti came up to the candy store and somebody said, "Here comes Fausti now."

Fausti said to himself, "Wrong. The next time they'll say, 'Here comes Blanfort.'"

39

It was Thursday morning and Nini had *The Godfather* on, but as Fausti would be in court for his uncle's trial when the part about Hyman Roth getting hit came on, he was disinterested in watching the show.

Fausti leaned against the outdoor pay phone alongside the open doorway and called Con.

"Good morn . . . what's that music you got on?" she said.

It was *The Godfather* theme coming out of the candy store.

"Do you have to listen to this all day?" Con said. "Oh, I forgot. No music in the courtroom. You're going to be there all day for your uncle."

"Wouldn't you be there for your uncle?"

"My uncle Felix? He went to work at United Parcel in the morning. W-O-R-K. And I'm going to my job."

"I'm sorry, I have to show support for my uncle."

"Great. How much do you get paid?"

"I . . . never . . . touched a dollar from them. I don't want nothing ever. My father would kill me for even thinking about it. You know that."

"Do I? You're wrong. I say they make you too much the heir."

"Con, it's my uncle."

He said it with a sigh. He knew what was coming. The date on the papers on the newsstand read July 18, 1998. They were supposed to have been married for thirteen months by now, since June 23, 1997. Then the uncle was arrested. Fausti writhed over the wedding date. He mentioned this to his grandmother. The Fist sat in a chair in the living room. The grandmother rocked her head back and forth and said it would be up to The Fist. Whose answer was a wolf's growl. Fausti put the wedding off until September 23, 1997. Con agreed, reluctantly. In late August 1997, the family was looking for a defense lawyer. Fausti had nothing to do with that, but he wondered about whirling around a dance floor while The Fist was trying to concentrate on finding a lawyer who could keep him out of jail. Fausti went to the grandmother's apartment and again wondered about a marriage at this time. The Fist was there. Fausti was silent.

The date was changed to five months later, December 26, 1997, definite, no way it will not be. Con made all the arrangements. Suddenly, The Fist had a misunderstanding with the new attorney, John Bartolomeo. The Fist thought he was paying the lawyer to get a good long postponement; an FBI guy retires, a witness drops dead, the judge gets sick, you can walk right out of the thing.

Lawyer Bartolomeo, however, thought the judge was in charge when he set a March 1998 date for the first hearing. After that, a full trial.

Con and Fausti lost two hundred fifty dollars on table favors for the postponed December 26, 1997, wedding. She then picked August 23, 1998, which she felt was plenty of time for the family to get over the March trial, no matter which way it went. She told Fausti that if that date was called off, there would not be another one. There would be another man.

Now over the phone outside the candy store in the morning Con said, "I've been pretty loyal. I was happy to put the wedding off last year. After that, I never could get a straight answer from you. You said, oh, don't worry. Just until, un . . . when? We had so many dates."

"Con, what would it have looked like if we had a big celebration?"

"Like I got married."

"He was preparing for court. He had to put himself in the hospital."

"All I can say is we put down August twenty-third and that left plenty of time for everybody to get over a trial."

"Yeah, but I didn't know the judge would set a new date."

"It's only July. The trial has to be over in plenty of time to get married. We postponed this three times and that's it. Now or never."

"It isn't because of me. It's my family."

"You're around them so much, you act like you're getting into the thing."

"But I mean, what could I tell you, it's my family."

"I was only going to be your wife."

"If you loved me, you'd — you sound like you don't love me," he said.

"If I don't love you, if I don't love you. What am I supposed to do if he loses, wait until he gets out?"

She hung up in his ear. Right away something heavy fell in his stomach. He had less than five weeks if he wanted to cancel the wedding, like he wanted to.

His guilt didn't allow him to see what he and she both knew, that later, after this call, she would be dreaming of being married in her bridal dress, the time and place immaterial. Maybe the same sentiment about the guy, too. Get another one, Fausti thought, gloomily.

40

Rose Dellacava spoke Italian and only a little English. Her Italian passed on to The Fist and Larry, but after that only one granddaughter spoke the language. It was this way in all the Italian households up and down the streets and stairs, as the old flavor of the city lessened. A greengrocer on Bleecker Street, Fortunio, brought the first broccoli to America. He was famous and revered on the old streets. Then all these new people came in and didn't have the least idea of what the guy had done.

In all the changes, the most significant was the one represented by Heidi Wasserman, age twenty, at least a half century younger than the old Italian women in the building at number 250 Sullivan. As she walked into her apartment, 3C, the Mafia suffered its first missed breath. For some reason, The Fist did not own the building and had no control over the tenants. Heidi Wasserman was a film production worker who moved into this tiny one-bedroom apartment that had been rented for the last seventy years by Anna Guccione. At the time of Anna's death, at age ninety-one, she was paying $41.40 a month and hated the landlord.

"Your grandchildren will be born with no arms."

Anna was replaced by Heidi Wasserman, rent of $1,100. Millie from 237 Sullivan, across the street, sixty-six steps to climb to her apartment, right away saw her as a deadly invader. The street had survived, and even welcomed, anybody who cast a wicked spell on the street through all the years. But nothing ever was this dangerous. "They pay a thousand dollars a month for a matchbox and they come home with their food in their hands. They watch TV and go to sleep. They get up in the morning early and go to work. They don't know about the men on the block — unless they seen movies. A few more of these people and we won't have nothin' left in the neighborhood."

There is no way for a decent Mafia outfit to survive when the only Italians in the neighborhood are involved in high fashion. Or in Wall Street. Sometime soon, the neighborhood would tilt from Italian to boutique, and that would end the Mafia in the Village, quicker than federal arrests.

Upstairs, on the fourth floor of Stefano Geraci's De Francisi Family storefront at 17 Thompson Street, was a new tenant, Bill Dutton, rent at $1,300, studying for the New York Bar Exam. He was from the University of Michigan, where for twelve years he had lived in a house that adjoined the parking lot for the university's 100,000-seat football stadium. From August through December, the school marching band, 358 strong, stepped with great life and pounding noise around the parking lot. There were 40 clarinets, 44 trombones, 16 tubas, 64 trumpets, 12 tenor saxes, 32 alto saxes, 12 French horns, 16 tubas, 28 percussionists, 12 euphoniums, and even more, all in Dutton's ear at once. They rehearsed the university march, "Victors," for hours and played it as loud as horns can make sound. The band was on television every Saturday and wanted sound and style perfection.

After twelve straight years of "Victors" exploding from the parking lot outside his windows, Dutton had diminished hearing in his left ear. After 385 instruments, he now had one mobster's voice.

Leaving the house one day, Dutton passed Stefani Geraci, who said, affably, "What's doin', pal?"

Dutton never heard him and walked on.

"This fuck," Geraci said.

Geraci paid $200 a month for his ground-floor clubhouse. He assumed the landlord, Glauberman, was satisfied. Which Glauberman was. He was satisfied that some day, one day, any day, the law would catch up with Geraci and the clubhouse would be empty and ready to rent to some scarecrow woman designer from Milan for thousands. If it took time, Glauberman said, then it would take time. But there would be a day in the future, when either he, Glauberman, or his children would get a handsome — no, an exorbitant — rent from this store now occupied by Geraci and hoodlums.

Each morning, Glauberman grabbed the *Daily News* and was

thrilled to see a headline about any Mafia arrests. Next, he would sink into despair when Geraci was not even mentioned in the story.

Then came the day when Geraci was busted on, the paper said, a huge federal case. Glauberman folded and threw his paper away and in hours he had that Geraci's clubhouse rented as a shop for dresses from Milan to a woman who was so thin she looked as if she never ate a slice of bread in her life. She stood at a small shining new wood counter in an elegant shop whose only sound came from the step of a customer. Her rent was nice: thirty-five hundred.

Simultaneously, Baldy Dom was in federal demand because of larceny in the installation of new windows in New York City housing projects. The beginnings of his problem was that federal funds were in the windows program. Also, there was a lapse of self-control on the part of Baldy Dom when he walked into the AAA All American window warehouse on Avenue D in Brooklyn, whose owner had not paid his ten percent tax to the guys Baldy Dom arrived as a collection notice. He had three men with him, unneeded when Baldy Dom, seeing all this clear, glistening glass, and realizing he was owed money, grabbed the machine gun and shot the stacks of thousands of windows. A shower of glass went whizzing through the warehouse and rained on all walls. The more Baldy Dom fired, the more delirious with joy he became. Only when he felt his legs stinging with flying glass nicking him did he stop firing.

"What do they say they have, they have bullshit," Baldy Dom said to Shaw the lawyer in the detention pen in Brooklyn federal court.

"That you used a machine gun in restraint of free trade. That's federal. They have an eyewitness."

"Who?"

"A night watchman."

"What is he?"

"A citizen."

"When?"

"He says he saw the act."

"Where?"

"From a balcony. He's supposed to watch the whole thing. He made your picture."

"Let me think," Baldy Dom said. This he did. Then he said, "He has to come in on a hearing, right? We'll make him then. Unless you could get a picture of him so I can give it to somebody and they shoot him in the fucking head now."

At his arraignment outside, Baldy Dom made his lawyer press so hard for an immediate hearing involving the eyewitness, a hearing right now, this afternoon, that the magistrate became suspicious of a murder nearby and soon and held Baldy Dom on twelve-million-dollar bail.

With a gargle, Baldy Dom dropped; his head went right into the judge's high desk. It hurt like hell when his head hit, but what was he going to do, break the fall with his hands for all to see the fake that he was? He crumpled to the floor. The judge, deeply suspicious, but more terrified of a man dying on him, squalled for medical help.

At first, when the marshals took him by ambulance from court to Beekman–Downtown Hospital, just over the bridge in Manhattan, Baldy Dom was allowed only short vists by his legally married wife. She kissed him lightly and spoke nervously about his diet, which could have clogged the insides of a rhino.

They called the second wife, Marie Pandolpho, remember, living in Westchester now, and let her know where he was. He then drew up a schedule with the United States marshal assigned to him. There were no visiting restrictions for the weekend, which was fine if you had a completely legitimate life. In Baldy Dom's case, however, he had to build a seawall to prevent his entire life from pouring into the room at once. He and the guard made a list of people and times for visiting Baldy Dom.

For Saturday and Sunday, Baldy Dom listed his legal wife, the former Angelina Rocco, for visiting from 11 until 1:30. At which time, he was supposedly scheduled for complete rest until 3 P.M. At that time, the second wife, Marie Pandolpho, the one from Canada, now in Westchester, was to arrive. She was to leave at 5 P.M., the stated reason was medical exams and monitoring.

At 6 P.M., his girl friend, Pam Principe, twenty years younger than the wives, would be up for some laughter and television and, Baldy Dom was sure, a trip outside to Ballato's on East Houston Street.

On the first day, Saturday, the schedule worked wonderfully well. The two wives were in and out on time and each left saying they loved him, just saying it. There was pain in seeing him wired and with an oxygen tube to his nose. There even was more pain remembering every lousy thing he had done to them.

At 8 P.M., Baldy Dom had that clip off his nose, the lovely Pam Principe on his arm, and the marshal driving to Ballato's for a fine dinner of pasta and lamb.

Then came Sunday. First, his official wife, Angelina Rocco Cataldo, stopped by and said she had left their children at an aunt's house on Sullivan Street. She'd return with them later. This confused Baldy Dom right away. The second wife, Marie Pandolpho, now walked in with their two children, against rules. The kids pounced on Dom and this didn't seem to bother him at all. They watched television and rushed around the room with Baldy Dom's IV pole. Baldy Dom liked this, because they were breaking the rules.

At 4 P.M., the official Mrs. Baldy Dom was with the two children in front of Miraculous Medal. She saw Con and Fausti talking in front of the candy store across the street and went over to them. She said that the children wanted to see their father and bring something to him. But the rules said that only one child at a time was allowed in the stuffy room. Con and Fausti said they would go over to the hospital with her and take care of a child at a time down in the lobby. Baldy Dom's official wife took an order for green salad and steamed vegetables from SpaghettiOs, across from the church, to bring to the father.

There was nobody at the reception desk of the hospital. Rather than stay in the gloomy lobby with one kid at a time, they all went upstairs. Right away, the two childtren bolted from the mother and raced to the sound of the voice of their father.

Who was loudly admonishing his two children by Marie Pandolpho to be good to their mother.

Marie Pandolpho was on the left side of the bed as you entered. Mrs. Baldy Dom walked in with Con, who was carrying the food from SpaghettiOs. She and the child took positions on the right side of the bed.

In the middle, Baldy Dom's breathing became erratic.

The two women had known each other, or of each other, for a few years, all the while each pretending that the other did not exist. They gave each other death stares, over Baldy Dom's suddenly laboring body. Both indicated by rolling eyes and nodding head that because of the children there was to be no warfare.

Baldy Dom's eyes were in the top of his head, à la coma. Had he known that this could happen, had he known at the start when he faked a heart attack in court, that it would end up with two wives and children right in the same room, he would have pled guilty in court and ended it there.

Doesn't Baldy Dom's chest give a kick and immediately a high whine ran through it, from one armpit to the other. His breath was short. He had turned a cheap courtroom complaint into a dangerous reality.

He picked out a spot on the ceiling and concentrated on it. Once he had seen on television that if you did this, you could forget everything else.

Con and Fausti were able to get the four children out into the hall. They were talking about going downstairs to the candy machines in the lobby. The marshal made the great mistake of standing with them.

Inside, the official Mrs. Baldy Dom said, without being asked, "I got these clothes Segal's."

"I don't go there," the second wife said.

"Why wouldn't you go to Segal's? Everybody goes there. I buy Mighty Mites there."

"I go by Kids 'R' Us," the second Mrs. Baldy Dom said.

"Why would you go there?"

"Because it's better than Segal's."

"How could you say that?"

"Because it is."

"It is not."

"Segal's got rats."

The offical Mrs. Baldy Dom leaned across the bed and hissed at Marie Pandolpho:

"Putan!"

Marie Pandolpho leaned across from her side of the bed and said in a low, searing voice:

"Bitcha."

Baldy Dom rattled like a gourd.

Suddenly, Ms. Pam Principe, party of the third part, girlfriend twenty years younger than the wives, now breezed past everybody in the hall, including the marshal, and went into the crowded room.

"Who are you?" Mrs. Baldy Dom said.

"Who are you?" Ms. Marie Pandolpho said.

"I am Baldy Dom's girlfriend. And you two must be his aunts."

Baldy Dom sucked in air.

The marshal now was in charge of nothing.

The noise brought Fausti back in a hurry. Fausti came back and did beautifully. He got in a position at the end of the bed where he could block everybody.

"Yow!"

"Dominick!"

Baldy Dom's eyes rolled like they were in a marble tournament.

His breathing through the mouth stopped. Stopped dead, if you wanted to get technical. The marshal was out the door and hollering for a nurse and doctors.

"Mouth-to-mouth," the official Mrs. Baldy Dom said.

"Give it," second wife Ms. Marie Pandolpho said.

"Youse do it. Youse is married to him," Ms. Pam, occupation girlfriend, said.

"Am I?" Mrs. Baldy Dom said.

"Yes, you are," the other two shrieked.

"I hate this man," Mrs. Baldy Dom said.

"Still!"

"What about you?" Mrs. Baldy Dom said to the second wife, from Canada now in Westchester.

"Me? I wouldn't touch this filthy man."

Doctors, nurses and emergency people rushed into the moment and pushed the three women out of the way.

To the sounds of wives and children gasping, he gave one good good-bye rattle, Baldy Dom did. Baldy Dom had done the job; he had followed The Fist's extra family policy, only now he had created an orphanage.

41 All through the bleak months at the start of motions, lawyer changes, and postponements, between indictment and the upcoming trial, The Fist tried for incompetency, either physical, that he would die in the courtroom, or mental, examinations that would show that he was at least disoriented from the onset of Alzheimer's.

They began with his heart. He shuffled into the doctor's office like an accident victim at 6:15 A.M., talking to himself at the speed of running water. Father Phil and Fausti pushed him in. For an outing like this, The Fist got out of his bathrobe and wore a black cap pulled over his eyes, a short-sleeved shirt and baggy trousers and black work shoes and white socks.

He kept murmuring.

"The poor man is completely disoriented," the priest said.

"That is a different problem," the doctor said. "This is cardiac." The doctor, Wilfred Chace, was at the top of the list of doctors who advised federal court judges on the true condition of defendants who claimed that if they were put on trial, they would drop dead right on the witness stand.

The Fist's doctor, Warren, and priest agreed enthusiastically. This man has a bright pain coming out of the chest. He is at the lip of death with the slightest jolt, the smallest excitement.

The priest said, "Can't you see he is a very sick man?"

Wilfred Chace had a face that had taught itself for years to show only a smooth morning shave.

"He could die now," the priest said. "He could drop like a vase off the shelf."

The Fist had the face of a homeless man. Black hair was matted. The face was gaunt and steel gray. Man doesn't shave in two weeks. His full lips were pursed but immobile. Then the neck led to the chest of an old middleweight. Once, muscles had been packed flat under the nipples, with mean power running from them into the leverage points in his arms. Now the chest was a lumpy mattress. But the outline of a fighter was there. He had been undefeated in twenty-five professional fights. He did fight the same guy five times. The name was Steve Winslow. But then he was over-matched against Jimmy Roxborough, a true light heavyweight with punch. Dellacava's arms were short and he couldn't get the leverage needed to be a big puncher. Still, he never beat himself; you had to beat him. Only Roxborough did. He opened an enor-mous cut over Dellacava's right eye. The fight was stopped in the sixth round. He took one look at the eye in a mirror in the dressing room. The Fist knew exactly what to do. That was it for fighting. The only time he ever seemed to get angry over stories about him was when the *New York Post* made fun of him for fighting the same guy five times.

Doctor Chace now ran an EKG tape through his hands like a fishing line and stopped. The Fist's doctor, Warren, said, "There is your trouble."

Chace said the irregularity on the tape was old, and it was un-changed from the first cardiogram tape, taken ten years before.

"He's a sick man," the priest said.

Chace said that the only thing the man shouldn't do is work high steel.

Warren brought out a sheaf of papers and licked the tops of the pages as if they were ice cream cones. They formed the record of a halter monitor The Fist had worn for a week and recorded all indi-cations of heart deficiencies. The Fist's halter monitor recorded heart rhythms that looked like tracings of tree branches waving wildly in a high wind. Nobody lives long like this, Chace said to himself. Suddenly the wild undulations became a flat line that stretched across the paper like a sidewalk.

The monitor ran out right there, Warren said affably.

"No, whoever was actually wearing the monitor did," Chace said. "Whoever it was, he is dead and buried."

The priest put his face nearly into the doctor's.

"Doctor, do you want to put this man through a trial? With the government bringing out these, these federal rats! They want to kill this man. They want to send him to prison to die. Look at him. He's so beautiful."

The Fist's eyes remained closed. His full lips and jaw beneath did not so much as twitch once. "He'll die in the courtroom," Father Phil said. He was in complete denial.

Chace said to The Fist, "We are just going to place three more of these sensors on your chest. It will be nothing." The test was an echo cardiogram. Showing the great vessels of the heart and the chambers and valves on a screen, rather than as lines on paper spewing from a recording drum.

The Fist did not move.

Chace stood over a video terminal as a technician slipped in and sat tapping keys, pausing, tapping more. Splashing onto the screen was the topography of the heart. Tap key. New view. Tap key. New view.

Chace watched each with noncommittal eyes. Now he saw one more splash on the screen. He said in a quiet and firm voice, "That is a perfect aorta."

There was a loud ping as the first sensor thrown by The Fist hit the wall. His eyes were two dark smoking wood fires. He ripped off the other two sensors. Bandy old middleweight's legs swung off the table. The Fist hit the floor in a fury that started in his bare toes and ran up those bandy middleweight legs and seized the rest of his body. He grabbed his cap and pulled it over his ears. He ripped his pants off the coat hook.

"A fongool!"

He held out the shirt and punched his right arm through the sleeve, causing a wind.

He went to the town house. Part of his bail arrangement was that he would live there with family that could care for him. They bought a brand-new maroon bathrobe for The Fist. The old blue one was left hanging on a hook in Concerned Lutherans.

42

After this, they went mental. How could he not be incompetent? There were times, right here during the day in the courthouse, that the Thorazine had The Fist pretty much helpless. It took three and four in his family to get him out of the wheelchair and up to the urinal and open his pants. "If he can't piss by himself, what do you call that?" one of the lawyers said.

The Fist ran directly into a pillbox. She was Sabrina Kalish, M.D., Kings County Psychiatric, appointed by the judge to see if The Fist was in or out of it.

The first famous patient she had interviewed was David Berkowitz, aka the Son of Sam. He was in his bare feet because they were afraid if he had shoes he would kick somebody to death. He was as lumpy as biscuit dough, but Sabrina knew that somewhere inside was a plunger for dynamite that an insane mind could slam down, and do so at any moment. When it did, a month later, he injured eleven guards in a hallway.

She remembers asking Berkowitz, "Are you heterosexual or gay?"

"I don't know," he said.

"I guess that's the answer," she said.

Sabrina now was standing in the doorway of the emergency psychiatric room at Brooklyn State, her arms folded.

Sabrina Kalish, M.D., didn't even look at the priest as Fausti wheeled the man past her and into her headquarters in the psychiatric emergency room. She was looking at the two uniformed federal cops who now were right behind this entourage. She identified her life as "Manwatch!" At the tenth anniversary of her medical school class, she was the only one who wasn't married. If she was going to cure any condition in the world, first it was going to be this one: manlessness. One of the cops was old, the other, holding a file folder, had a good face, but the chin of an owl in a barn. A good gym could cure that.

"Any guns?" she said, automatically.

The owl patted his side lovingly.

"Out at the desk," she said. "You know you can't bring a gun in here."

"We're not staying anyway," the cop said, handing her the folder. "He's all yours."

The lawyer, Sloane, a thin dark-haired man in a gray chalk-striped suit with yellow kerchief and tie, came up to her, holding a large stuffed folder.

He indicated The Fist, who sat slumped in the wheelchair, his head hanging over the side as if he was about to tip the chair.

"My client has schizophrenia complete with hallucinations and delusions. It is my conten—"

"He is not well," Father Phil said.

"Why don't you let me do the examining?" Sabrina said. "First of all, tell me who you are."

"I'm Lawrence Sloane. I'm the lawyer for Mr. Dellacava."

"And he is?"

"The Boss."

"I see. And what business is he the boss of?"

"Everywhere all over the world. You never heard of him?"

"I'm afraid I haven't."

"You never heard of The Fist?"

She wasn't being sarcastic about The Fist. She didn't know the first thing about what was going on in the world except in her own professional work.

On the morning of her graduation from medical school, she received a phone call from the secretary of state of New York, who was congratulating her because she had gone through school on a state scholarship. He tried being coy by giving his name, an Italian name, and he said, "I work in the state government."

She said, "Oh, how nice." Then she put down the phone. "Some big fucking Italian state trooper. I want more than that right now."

Five years later, she still didn't know the name of the governor. But she would take the state trooper or his cousin.

Now, she said to Father Phil, "And who are you?"

"I'm his priest. I'm here to take care of him."

"Oh. If you're his priest, you can wait right outside here."

"I should come inside."

"I'm sure you can find a seat outside."

She looked at Fausti.

"I'm Mister Dellacava's nephew," he said. "I push. I don't do anything else. I don't know anything else."

"You can wait outside, if you don't mind."

"I'll tell you the truth, I do mind. I'm the only one I trust today to push him so he don't have to feel even a bump."

"He's not going to be moving," she said.

"You're sure?" Fausti said.

"I am."

"Swear on God."

"I can't do that."

"Swear on your children."

"I don't have any."

"All right, then. Go back to swear on God."

"Come on. Please leave." The gaze was firm, the voice sharp.

"Let me ask you one thing first. You ever testify in court, you've had to testify, right?"

"Certainly."

"Did you raise your right hand for a Bible and swear on God? Right, didn't you?"

She cut him off. "Please leave here now."

He understood he couldn't win on her home court. He started for the door. "You sound like my girlfriend."

"I hope your girlfriend remains that way," she said.

He had been content and satisfied just with the plan to marry Con. That she had to make him set a date caused anxiety and frustration. He looked at the uncle slumped in the wheelchair. How was he going to have a wedding with his uncle like this?"

He left the room.

She looked at the folder. It was filled with papers from a court case. The papers prominently mentioned thirteen murders.

"Why are you here?" she asked The Fist.

"They think I'm crazy. I got a voice I hear."

"Whose voice?"

"God."

"Are you sure it's God?"

"Positively."

"How do you know?"

"He tells me so."

"Does he speak louder in one ear?" she asked.

He paused.

"Why are you stopping to think? If you were insane and incompetent you would just keep talking. But you are stopping to think."

She leaned closer. "Do you hear more than one voice that says more than one thing?"

"No, I only hear God."

"Does the voice frighten you?"

"No, God does. I'm afraid he gets mad account of they bug him."

"How do they do that?"

"The FBI put a bug in my ear that hears everything inside my head where God talks to me."

"Why you? Why does God choose you? Why does the FBI put a bug in you?"

He paused.

"There you stop again so you can think. If you were crazy you would have something on the tip of your tongue, about a dog telling you what to do. You paused to think. That is all you ever do. You are certainly not incompetent. Go to trial!"

The lawyer, very nervous, came in. "He had a 55 IQ when they tested him at the last hospital."

"Then he undershot. If he had a 55 IQ he wouldn't be able to go to the bathroom by himself."

Immediately, The Fist peed right in his wheelchair. It ran onto the floor.

"Is that enough?" the lawyer said.

"I'm sure we've seen this before," Sabrina said.

She looked out the door and called to the security man. He was a square, good-looking black. One day he had walked up and asked her out for lunch. She turned him down — and the stupid bastard thought it was because of his color. Doesn't he know that it's a fucking insult to me, after medical school and a residency, to be asked out by somebody who didn't even pass the New York City police test?

She called to him, "Would you please get a maintenance man to clean up for us? This man decided to pretend he was crazy."

In the waiting room, Father Phil jumped up. "What do you mean 'pretend'? You're in with the FBI. You're a federal spy."

The lawyer said softly to the priest. "Please, Father. This woman has more power than Stalin."

Sabrina was more interested in Mordecai, who was the only resident on duty. And there he was! Looking down at his watch without raising his wrist. Sneaky fuck! Checking the time because he knows Mary is coming over any minute now from hematology. The moment I turn my back right here, the two of them will be on the way to Long Island. I pay the most for the summer house and when I got to the house last Friday night, where were they? They left me a note that said they were at a movie. But I know what it really said: Fuck you and your money.

Mordecai doesn't even pay and he makes a triangle.

And Mary and I are fighting over a fucking gay.

Sabrina was leaving the room when she glanced at Father Phil. He had a great gait, she thought. She only knew one thing about priests. They were single. Most of them aren't gay, either. And some of them even leave the Church.

43

The Fist had only the toe of his left foot on the floor under the defense table. Then he started dancing on that toe, making the whole of his leg jiggle under the table.

Q. Agent Lyons, were there any other streets on which you observed Mr. Dellacava?

A. Houston Street.

Q. Will you tell us what you saw?

A. He was crossing Houston Street from the uptown side to the downtown side. He was on Sullivan Street. Two individuals with him held him up. He had on a bathrobe and pajamas. His head was on his chest. He kind of shuffled, he did not walk. The two individuals kept holding him up. They got halfway across when the light changed. That is a busy street and traffic came right away. A bus was coming. Mr. Dellacava pulled away from the two individuals holding him and ran to the other side of the street.

Q. How quickly did Mr. Dellacava run?

A. Like in a track meet.

Q. When Mister Dellacava reached the other side of Houston Street, what happened?

A. He goes right back to drooping his head. He waited until the two individuals reached him. They took him by the arms and they go down Sullivan Street.

The Fist's leg acted as if he was working with a jackhammer. That's all he got to do, The Fist said to himself, watch me cross the street. He don't even know why we were there. We were coming from Gerasi's club. This guy Artie Cavallo told Frankie Condo when they was standing over on West Broadway that my lady, Carmella, the second Carmella, she lives on the East Side, the first Carmella, who is my wife, lives in Westchester, and Condo says that Covallo called my Carmella a vampire. She's a mother. You don't talk like that about anybody's mother. That's my children that she's the mother of. That means you're insultin' me and my family. Fuckin' die. So we're down by Gerasi's club and this guy Covallo is begging. He says he never said nothin' like that. Frankie says I heard you. Covallo says to me, "That's why you call him Frankie Obatz. He's crazy."

I says, we'll let you know. While we're going back up to my club I says to Frankie Condo, who was holding me up, I says, give that Covallo a good fuckin' beating like he deserves. Let him live. Just break his motherfuckin' legs. The both of them. A couple of weeks later Covallo runs in a parking lot and they got him good there. He didn't walk for a long time. And he didn't do much talkin', believe me.

He kept jiggling that left leg. The jury could see the leg jiggling, as could the judge. Look at this Fist shake. Of course he's nuts. He had wasted so many years in hospital rooms and psychiatric wards, while living in squalor at home and in a bathrobe on the street, that he looked crazy and maybe by now he actually was crazy. He had to be far beyond that, however. If he wanted to roll out a free man he had to be incompetent, unable to assist in his own defense.

The Fist had on a navy blue blazer, but only because the judge said The Fist better not show up looking like he's homeless. The Fist had wanted to wear his robe into court, but the judge said he'd revoke the million-dollar bail and put him in jail if he did.

A white polo shirt and the top of a white undershirt showed at the neck, the two together under the overhead lights becoming blinding. So much light came from The Fist that he appeared holy. Father Phil, who sat in the front row with his Roman collar on, did not catch nearly as much light.

Q. Did you observe Mr. Dellacava on any other occasion?

A. Yes. He was walking on Sullivan Street and I think he noticed one of us. He stopped and knelt down in the middle of the street and prayed.

This made The Fist mad. You bet I prayed, he said to himself. I prayed against this rat agent. I can't let Father Phil know that sometimes I pray against people. But that's what I do. I sure prayed against these fucks.

At day's end, there was an immediate quarrel between The Fist's lawyers and the prosecutors over a picture card that one prosecutor, Steinmetz, was looking at.

"What's that?" one of The Fist's new lawyers, Buscemi, said.

"A bubble gum card," the prosecutor said.

"That's no ballplayer on it," the lawyer Steinmetz said. "What is this, a game? That's a mob guy."

"I thought you told the jury there is no such thing as the mob?" the prosecutor said.

That ended it. Lawyer Steinmetz didn't like the card, or know exactly what it meant, nor was there anything he could do about it.

44

Sweat ran off the helper's face and his green jumpsuit was dark and wet. He was hanging on the outside of the green carting truck, his hands clutching the passenger door through the open window. The driver, Lopez, was a dark Puerto Rican with immense black arms coming out of a cut-off green T-shirt. A red and white gypsy bandanna wrapped around his head and a large earring gave him the look he sought, that of a Pirate.

Thick leather weight lifting belts were tight around their waists.

It was two in the morning and the two were off the truck again, walking to this line of black plastic garbage bags. One in each hand, they swung them into the hopper.

When Fausti got out and tried to help, the driver waved him away. "I'm supposed to learn the business," Fausti said, defensively.

"Not a fuckin' thing to know," Lopez said. "You give to the driver the list of stops. He drive, you go home."

They shot forward to the next pile. The noise shook the silent streets. Picking up waste in front of restaurants with small lights on and at the sides of darkened movie houses. Moving crosstown, to dim streets on the sides of department stores, where the sidewalks were lined with Dumpsters that brought heaves and grunts from Lopez and his helper. They were connected to the compactor, which lifted and tilted them and the waste tumbled in.

Four A.M., the hour of bread began in the city. There were scarred delivery vans from small bakeries in Queens Village and Long Island City, and gleaming trucks from the big bread companies. Wonder Bread, Thomas's English Muffins, Pepperidge Farm grain and white. The city of starch. Also here were the pretzels and potato chip deliveries. They were parked one after the other in front of supermarkets and coffee shops while drivers carried in bread, cellophane glistening in the light, and the pretzels, chips, and doodles that form such a major part of the American diet. The streets looked like billboards for Frito-Lay. Looking into the supermarket, there were rows of cheese doodles and pretzels two and three high for as far as shelves went.

The starch drivers looked like they ate their own wares. The muscle in the night belonged to the garbage trucks.

The stops were close together at first, and the driver and the helper, Thomas, worked as fast as their arms could move. On 56th Street and Park, there was a large office building that Lopez said would take fifteen minutes. After that, they were going directly across Park Avenue to a restaurant called "L." Lopez said, "You should see that place. Fuckin' rich people."

Fausti had seen the name of the restaurant in gossip columns. The canopy went out to the curb, and in its shadows two porters in night workers' rags tugged at garbage bags. They regarded him for a moment, but when he told them he was waiting for the truck, they resumed tugging the bags.

Fausti walked through the open glass doors and down the entrance hallway and into an explosion of Latin music that rolled into him with enough power to push furniture. Three steps called for a sweep, a pirouette, a haughty entrance to a restaurant trying to sleep under starched linen. A boom box the size of a stove was set up on a bar famous for being muted, elegant, European. The porter wailed with the Latin music as he polished the mirrors.

Fausti picked up a large brandy glass and tapped his nail against it. In the din of the box music, he still could hear this small beautiful glass note.

He thought of Con.

By 4:30 A.M., the truck was at the side of a closed supermarket on the corner of Water Street in Manhattan. At the corner down the street, there was a bodega with the same red and yellow metal awning that virtually all the hundreds of bodegas have around the city. Sweat dripping like rain from their chins, they started on a long row of garbage bags at the supermarket. Fausti walked down to the bodega. The least he could do was buy them soda. The owner had a small old misty television set on a stool under the awning. He sat riveted to the picture in the night. He was built like a John Deere reverse hoe. His chest was bursting out of a red T-shirt proclaiming "Junior" and "Chihuahua" in yellow letters. He might have been the fattest Mexican now in North America. A black beard grew from around a mouth curled in great dislike at what he watched on the small outdoor television: a thin dour man on a screen the size of an air mail stamp that had ribbons of stock market quotations running over and under it. There was no way to hear what the man was saying because Junior in the red shirt was making a pronouncement:

"Jerkoff," Junior said, loudly.

"Double jerkoff."

He pointed at the screen and said to Fausti, "See this guy here do you know what I do to this guy I make a

                mother-

                    fucking

                      girl!!

                        out of him

"He is giving stock market advice this motherfucker he is up, what time is it now, it is four thirty in the motherfucking morning and he is up telling you what is going on in the stocks if this motherfucker knew, do you think he would be up on the television at four thirty in the morning? This motherfucker would be home in bed with some woman sucks his prick who is up at four thirty? Motherfucker look at this fucking thief."

"This guy rob you?" Fausti said.

"No, not this guy but all motherfuckers like him they all the same."

He leaned forward and spat at the television. "Too! You motherfucker."

"I got to get soda," Fausti said.

"Get it by yourself. Inside in the case."

Fausti came out with four cans of Pepsi cradled against his chest.

"Five even," Junior said, getting up to collect from Fausti.

The next stop was a couple of blocks down, where Wall Street sat awaiting the end of the moist night and the start of another day of novenas to money. Lopez drove to the last slumbering building on the street, at 120 Wall, directly across the street from the East River. Little red and green beacons showed on a tugboat moving steadily along the polished onyx river surface. The stop took some time because of the many Dumpsters. Two superintendents, in white shirts and ties, stood at the service entrance on the side of the building.

"You need two guys watch me?" Lopez said.

"No, I watch him," one of them, with short sandy hair, said, nudging the other. Pens were fastened to the shirt pocket.

Arriving home in the early hot morning, he dropped his clothes out in the hallway and fell into bed until noon.

"You know I'm not well," his mother said to him. "Why are you leaving clothes on the floor like that?"

"Because I was out on the garbage truck," Fausti answered.

"You're going into that?" she said.

"Maybe."

45

"Make more room, I don't want to touch any-thing here, ooh, what a pigsty, How did I let you talk me into this? I got to be crazy," Con said.

She sat on Fausti's lap in the front of the truck. She had her arms tight against her so that she wouldn't touch anything in the cab. She looked at Lopez's sweaty arms and the torn dirty cab and grimaced.

"I'm going back to bed."

The assistant's hands came like claws over the door, causing her to turn a shoulder as the truck boomed into the hot night.

"I'll never be out on a truck like this," he said.

"Then what do you have me out here now? Yick. I hate this."

"Just to see what happens when they go around."

"I see. What happens if the driver calls you up sick, two in the morning."

Lopez the driver gave a great laugh. "You doan have to pick out what clothes to wear. You yust make sure you come here with your two arms."

At Sardi's, Fausti started to get out of the cab, but she stopped him.

"I'm not going to touch anything getting in and out," she said.

"Sardi's. Don't you want to see Sardi's?" he said.

"I want to see my house. I still got work nine o'clock. Work like human beings. Not like you got here. Coal mining for garbage."

When they got to the Park Avenue office building, Fausti tugged Con right out of the cab. "Don't yell. I really want you to see this." He led her across Park Avenue to the awning at the "L."

The same two porters were pulling refuse bags to the curb.

"You here again," one of them said.

"We're going in, get a big drink," Fausti said.

"Yust say I tell you have two."

Con lagged in the doorway until Fausti led her down the hall. This time instead of music that put tremors into the earth, there was a high sweet trumpet. When she stood at the top of the three steps, Con's lips parted.

"Who comes here?"

"Rich people. People who rob money without the cops knowing about it. Stock market, banks I bet."

"It's beautiful," she said.

She asked him, "Your father ever come here?"

"I never heard him say."

"Would the people know who your uncle is?"

"Are you crazy? That's the beauty of him. He don't want to be known by anybody. He just wants the money for collecting the garbage from here."

"They won't play Spanish music like this, I'll bet," she said.

"The box goes out with the guy when he finishes cleaning. He doesn't belong here. He's not rich like you."

He walked to a table and pulled out a chair and used one of the words he knew from hearing the waiters at Catanzaro:

"Una sedia?"

Slapping one hand to his stomach, he bowed and held a chair for her.

She laughed.

"Una sedia!"

"Thank you. This is a very good table you're giving me." She slipped in.

"Vino bianco? Vino rosso?"

Behind him was the maître d's table with a stack of heavy leather menus.

"Here is our wine list."

She looked over the list, holding her chin high and imperious.

"What's this? 'Cristal Roederer.' It's got to be a joke, waiter."

"No, no, this is a real list."

"Who pays a hundred eighty dollars for wine, champagne, whatever?"

"A rich woman like you."

"I forgot."

"You got a husband owns gold mines."

"Great."

"It's almost as good as having garbage trucks."

"I'm sticking to my gold mines."

She tapped the wine list. "They've got two Cristals listed here. Give me the one cost two hundred."

"Certainly, miss," Fausti said.

"You don't say miss anymore," she said.

"Oh, *senora*, Mrs. I forgot."

"That's wrong, too. I'm not married."

"Of course you are. Here's your rich husband coming in right now. He owns the world. He got forty guys working overtime keeping track of his money. That's just for today."

The two porters came in from the street in their night rags and walked past the bar and to the kitchen door.

"They out there?" Fausti called.

"Not yust yet. It take us five minutes more. We got yust a few more to take out."

The porter polishing the bar called out, "Serena!" and began singing with the music, which was still these high, thrilling trumpets. A woman sang. "Serena!" the porter called out again as Con left the table. She stopped. Her head rocked back and came forward with her body catching the music.

"I want to stay and dance."

"You're letting make-believe carry you away. We got to go."

"Come on. We're here. When are you going to be here again?"

"I tell you what. When we get married, I'll take you here."

"We'll see."

She held out her hands. "Let's pretend we are. Come on," she said to Fausti. She put an arm around his neck and they stood on the floor and swayed. They danced slowly and they looked into each other's eyes.

"I never danced with a rich woman before," Fausti said.

"My husband is as good as gold," she said.

"You going to have kids with your rich husband?"

"Yop. I want babies."

The trumpet sounded beautifully in the dim sumptous room. They danced slowly, bodies obeying each other.

"Look at us," she said. "Right off a garbage truck."

"I fall in love with you anywhere. You really are beautiful."

"Thank you."

She kissed his cheek. "This is how you start one of these families. Two hundred years from now there'll be a whole town looks like us."

"Too simple," Fausti said.

"You had a half sister in Yonkers you didn't even know she was alive and she looks like you, sounds just like you. There'll be people all over the earth looking like us. For a good reason. We started them off. My aunt Rosie has four cousins in Jersey. Every one of them looks exactly like her. Two of them got the same walk even."

"My family," Fausti said. "I know the one side, my grandmother's family. Nothing before that. The other side probably was on a garbage wagon in Italy."

"Then they came off and started stealing," she said.

"Never," he said.

"I don't believe that. I believe in you. That's why I love you. We're going to have an honorable family two hundred years."

"How do we start it off? How many kids are we going to have?" Fausti asked.

"Two. A boy and a girl."

"What if they're two boys? That's all right. That's all you need, anyway."

"Who wants two boys? They go out on the street, all they meet is tough guy bullshit artists. I got to be chasin' the other bums out all day long. I'll never have two boys."

"How do you know?"

"Because I'm in charge of havin' babies."

"What if you had two girls?"

"Then I stop. That's perfect. I'll never have more."

"All right. I'll settle for that. I'll walk them to school."

"School where?"

"Miraculous Medal."

"No. I told you the nun pulled my hair. My children aren't going to Miraculous Medal."

"Where else? That's where we're going to live."

"They might not live there. Do you know why? Because we're not even married and you're starting to boss me. You'll boss yourself right out of your girlfriend."

"You're more than a girlfriend."

"Really? I don't feel it."

"You don't feel love for me?"

"I'd like to have a wedding date on the calendar. That would make me feel love all day."

Fausti stopped her and kissed her on the neck and then the cheek and then her eyes.

"I'll get it definite," he murmured.

"Only because I told you." She smiled.

Now one of the ragamuffin porters called, "They there outside!"

The music changed into Latin shrieking and the porter behind the bar was yelling out lyrics and Con pushed the hair from her forehead and twisted to the rhythm.

"We got to go," Fausti said.

"Not me. I had enough. I'm catching a cab."

"You've got to come."

"Never. I've had it. You want me to leave here and get back in that truck? You're crazy."

"The two of them'll think I'm made out of paper, I don't come."

"Then you go."

She took a last look from the top of the steps. "I want to come back here."

"I'll bring you in here forever. You'll thank me. You'll be so tired from two kids of yours running you down."

Suddenly, she buried her face in his neck.

"Three."

They walked outside laughing and he started to beg her to come with him and just like that, she shrugged and got on his lap again in the truck.

"Nothing romantic here, I'll tell you that," she said. "I hate it."

"Yeah, but there's nothing wrong as long as I'm involved."

"I hope so. I believe you. I just don't trust the rest of this."

"What rest?"

She waved out the window. "Anything to do with the street."

An hour later, Junior in the bodega was in the same red shirt and watching the talking head on the financial news station.

"I win seven thousand from my own lottery machine ten fucking years —

"Oh, I apologize miss. I do not know you well enough to say in front of you yust what this motherfuck —"

"You get the soda," Fausti told her. "Five cans. You won't have to listen."

"— Not just a regular motherfucker, he is the worst motherfucker ever to be alive I play this machine I win seven thousand the motherfucker they tell me, 'Junior, take the money to Merrill Lynch.' I say, 'Let me see some motherfucking action with my money.' They tell me, 'Junior, you got Altimeter and ATT, one is a little bit of a chance. ATT is good for your grandchildren, all right?' I look it up. I am a half and then the other goes down a number two and I call up Merrill Lynch and I say to the guy, 'You told me ATT is good forever what is this bullshit?' You know what he say to me. 'Oh, you don't have that anymore don't you look at the slips we send you' I say no, they say they send me about my new stock Budget something that fuck go down like a motherfucking plane crash. I give them seven thousand, right? I say, 'Fuck this, give me five thousand of my motherfucking money back.' They send me forty-five hundred dollars I say where is the other five hundred? This *maricon* tells me, 'Junior, you look at the slips we sent you the trades you pay for each trade you wanted action Junior we give you action you trade a lot you pay a lot and now you broke'

你you

rob me

I make

a girl

out of you!"

In his chair Junior held his arm straight out at the television and his hand clutched a big black pistol that worked when he pulled the trigger.

The explosion and flash and glass storm caused Con, inside, to bolt from the soda case to the wall at the back of the store. Fausti, standing under the canopy, ducked behind the fruit display.

"Fuck him two times," Junior yelled at the black smoking shattered set. He stuffed the gun back in his pants pocket.

With shaking hands, Con was paying for the soda.

"What do we have here?" It was the sandy-haired guy with the pens in the breast pocket. Fausti did not place him as the super at Wall Street.

"The set blow all up," Lopez said.

"I can see that."

"I am mad that the fuck was not really there inside the set when it blows up. I yust wanted to kill this fuck."

"You can't do that."

"You can't stop me. What are you, federal bank or something? You federal, I know that. You federal. Kill this fuck is no federal crime."

"Yes, it is."

"You sure?"

"I'm sure. I should know."

Con had started for the truck and didn't hear this. Fausti walked quickly to catch up and left the conversation behind. He had stopped paying attention when Lopez mentioned the federal bank, this high gloomy gray granite that was just up the block. He assumed the guy worked nights in the bank.

They sat in the truck drinking soda. Lopez threw his can out the window. "Give them work."

"Look at this," Fausti said when they got to Wall Street. "Look what I got into. Fucking law."

The two guys in shirts were at the side door, holding coffee containers.

"They're some building supers," Con said, sarcastically.

Fausti opened the door on the passenger's side and they slipped out and walked, heads bowed, until they hit the building across the street and were out of any camera range. They sat down, out of sight under the highway for the riverbank and sat down behind a highway pillar.

She pointed far down to the right. The fish market was ablaze with light.

"You could get in trouble there. Or you could get in trouble here. You don't have to go far."

He was silent.

"On your name alone."

He stared at the river.

"You better remember," she said. "I love you."

The next time he saw Tortorello, Fausti was asked: "How did you like it?"

"Not so good."

"Why, they told me you even had your girl with you."

"I don't want the life," Fausti said.

"What life?"

"Jail."

"You're crazy."

"Yeah. Well, you better ask them about the two agents at the building on Wall Street. I told them to tell you."

"I guess I was too busy for them to get me."

"You better get them," Fausti said.

Tortorello grinned. How could he worry? Who could believe anything could happen to his whole world? A world he now thought of as legitimate?

46

He had two ways to go with this name. He could change it and go live someplace where nobody would know it wasn't his real name and he could have a life as this other person. Taking a great troublesome weight from him. What was a name anyway, he wondered. A few stick lines and loops signed on paper.

That doesn't say what you're like or who you really are. A woman changes her name when she gets married; most of the time they can't wait to sign their new name, while the old family name, they've had it all their lives, means nothing to them. The old guys in the mob used to take Irish names to try and fool people and also break the fucking cops' backs. Tommy Eboli was Tommy Ryan. Willie Moretti was Willie Moore. They wound up believing that the Irish names were theirs from birth.

Or, he thought, he could keep the name and go where it could do him the most good.

I lose two jobs. What do they want from me? He had a craving for normalcy, for work, which he recognized as the most important part of his life. This had been swiped away from him. So long as he was being penalized for having a gangster name, why not go with the name and see where it takes you? Let everybody else worry about the name. Of course these were sudden thoughts that he never had held for more than instants. Always, he banished them in fear of his father.

But now Larry Dellacava, this hauser across a deck awash, was gone. He walked each day on footing begging for a misstep. Anger bred carelessness. He was interested in any whim. He stood in a candy store and watched the sun climb high over the high church and then plunge, spilling shadows onto the street, and wondered why he shouldn't get a chance to work for a living. If they don't want to give me a chance, what do they expect me to do?

Sal Meli came out of the club at 250 and ran his hands over the sides of his hair, the better to appear.

"How do you like this?" he said.

"What?" Fausti said.

"My daughter's marriage is off, you heard that."

"I don't know anything about it," Fausti said.

"So now you know. I told her he was no fuckin' good. The bum doesn't even come up with a ring. So now she knows."

"I never even seen the guy, so what do I know?" Fausti said.

"You were there I got the Rolex."

"And he tries to keep it," Fausti said.

"She asked him for it back. You know what he says to her? He says to her, 'If I give you the watch, I don't have one. If I keep the watch then you'll go get another one and the both of us will have watches.' How do you like it? How do you like what he says? You know what I say, don't you? 'Give me the fuckin' watch or you die.' I just said that inside. That I'll axt first, then do what I got to do. I went on record."

He went out to a blue Cadillac.

"Take a ride."

"Where to?"

"Up the West Side."

"I don't know."

"Come on, it's good you come. Shake them up."

Usually, Sal Meli would know enough never to speak to Fausti like this, except he was out on the sidewalk in midafternoon and he thought that Fausti, like anybody else not at a job at this hour, was open to any proposition. And while he said he was "on the record," meaning The Fist had given him an OK, there was no Fist inside; The Fist was a defendant with a dubious future and Meli just used him. Fausti didn't bother to look inside to see if his uncle was there.

"How shake them up?" he said.

"Just by being there. They hear The Fist got a nephew outside, they shake up."

"What good is that?"

"So you could see how even these fuckin' insane-asylum Irish guys act when they see who you are. You never know. What's it cost you, ten minutes? I can't wait to see this guy's face. A total fuckin' coward. His son steals a watch off us and the father don't even try to make him make good. What does he think, he's stormproof?"

"It's only one watch," Fausti said.

"What's the matter with you, you know it's more than that."

"I don't."

"You must of heard. The kid's father borrows a hundred thousand fix up a restaurant. He don't pay."

"Who give him the money?" Fausti asked.

"Who? Your uncle, who."

"And the father don't pay."

"The father don't pay."

He shrugged. "We make him give us five hundred a week plus. I'm here for the money. I'm here for the watch. I'm United Parcel, yeah?"

He drummed his fingers on the seat. "Take a ride."

When Fausti made a face, he said, "You got an end. Don't worry."

He did not want the money. But at the same time he was standing on the street all day without earning a dollar. I'm supposed to stand here and go broke? It just came to him that way for the moment, a devil tugging at his arm again, and of course it was insane and he would have nothing to do with it. Fausti got in the car. Sal Meli drove along Bleecker Street to the river and came up Tenth Avenue.

He was listening to a loud crash of music on the radio and slapping a hand on the steering wheel.

"Where do you have to go?" Fausti asked.

"White House where they hang out."

What there was to see of the White House, a bar whose grimness was almost obscured by parked trucks on the corner of Tenth Avenue and 49th Street, was a front door partly open because it had been smashed almost off its hinges. Through the space, the inside appeared as a dungeon. Next door was a tire-fixing shop, after which were the painted-over windows of a storefront that rented jukeboxes to saloons. This was the old West Side of the dock Irish, with a treeless avenue of five-story walkups. Crossing the avenue, 49th Street went two blocks to the river and the old dripping docks where once three and four ocean liners could be found moored on many days. The piers would be covered with men moving like noisy spiders. One liner, the *Queen Mary,* had a rule that even in port, people entering the grand lounge had to whisper when carrying supplies.

The neighborhood was a frontier existence, with men walking down to the docks each morning in uncertainty and standing in a circle around some psychotic hiring boss who tantalized them until either picking them or sending them away. One hiring boss,

Danny St. James, some mornings would pick only men wearing glasses. The losers walked back up the block and into the saloon to open up for a day of drinking on credit until drunk. As the hours went on, they became great recruits for West Side crime, which was the Irish way, spontaneous, on the whim of an instant, and violent, consisting mainly of armed car holdups, payroll heists, or unplanned shootings based on rage and Irish bitterness.

Those who had been hired came back up the block at night feeling they deserved a drink for all the good work they had done. They went right into the bars and spread bills like rags onto the wet bar. The wives of either group, the nonworkers or the ones hired, had the same life at home: a husband coming in late, drunk, and at least abusive and without enough money for the kitchen table.

Now, with only one liner left on the seas, and with the freighters off in the Port of Newark, there was no work at all and the bars that were left, like the White House, were chaotic.

Sal Meli pulled up alongside a seafood truck that was double-parked. He left Fausti sitting in a car that now was triple-parked and had half the avenue blocked. A mobster's first ambition is to break every rule of every day.

Sitting in the car, Fausti heard only a word or two of the arguing in the bar.

Suddenly, a young guy with uncombed hair falling onto his forehead, walked past the car. He had a yellow Hawaiian lei around his neck and wore a short-sleeve Hawaiian shirt that was out of place in the late spring chill.

He walked with a hand motioning to Fausti to come along.

Fausti did not move.

The young guy reached the middle of the street, then he turned and called, impatiently, "Come on."

"What?" Fausti said.

"You Fausti, right?"

"Yeah."

"You supposed a come up and get a watch. Once I get upstairs I'm not fuckin' comin' down."

Of course the familiarity must come from knowing me, Fausti

thought. Yet he couldn't recall ever seeing the guy. Although who knows, they're in and out of the club on Sullivan Street.

Fausti followed him without noticing the guy who came out of the bar and walked behind them. Fausti went through traffic to the door to a walkup entrance between a storefront financing taxi medallions and an empty spot.

"I'm Eddie," the guy with the lei said.

"Fausti."

"I know. I know who you are," the guy said.

They went into a narrow hallway with initials carved into the walls. A staircase began a few steps into the dimness. The guy started up.

"Third floor," he said.

The sound of the guy following them into the hallway should have disturbed Fausti.

They went up one flight, then a second, and at the top, the third floor, another young guy, wearing a Rangers hockey team jacket, stood at an open door. He looked about twenty-five and had sad eyes in a long face.

"How are you?" Fausti said.

The sad eyes said nothing.

Inside was linoleum and a couch with plastic covering on it and a stamped tin ceiling, and now the gun was pressed hard to Fausti's neck. It was in the hand of the first guy, Eddie, in the Hawaiian shirt and lei.

The gun pushed Fausti through the living room and into a bedroom that had a bare mattress with clothes thrown on it and a stain at the top and pillows without pillowcases and with large and ancient two-tone stains. This is where people die. The terror of the thought washed his mind blank.

He heard the Rangers shirt say, "I got the mattress cover put him in."

They are going to kill me, Fausti thought.

He didn't know which way to twist or kick to save himself. The gun pressed hard into his neck.

This Eddie shoved him to the window, looking out on the street. Now he switched the gun to the side of Fausti's head.

"Don't you fuckin' move," he said.

Rangers shirt was on the phone in the next room. For the first time, Fausti saw a third guy, older, in a red sweater. He had light hair, a protruding forehead, and cheeks washed with alcohol. He tipped back on his heels. Drunk.

"Yeah," the one in the Rangers shirt said into the phone. "I said, yeah. Put the greaser on. Put that Sal on."

He paused. Then he said, "Look out the fucking window. Look up at the third floor across the street from you. Do you see what you see? Do you see? Look, you cocksucker."

This Eddie kept his arm extended and the gun pressing harder into Fausti's temple. Eddie was breathing quickly and madly.

Fausti heard a rustle. His eyes flicked once. The Rangers shirt was standing with the phone in one hand and a plastic mattress cover clutched in the other.

I'm going to die, Fausti thought.

"All right," the Rangers shirt said into the phone. "You could see. Put five thousand on the bar or we'll blow his brains out right here. You could watch. Right fucking now!"

In the window with the gun to his head, Fausti could not see anything across the street in the bar.

Where Sal Meli was at the pay phone directly alongside the door. The place was filled with smoke and guys walking back and forth nervously and they had something in the back that they were arguing about and he looked through the crack in the doorway and with a clear line between trucks parked at the curb he saw Fausti at the third-floor window across the street with the guy holding the pistol to Fausti's temple.

Sal had five thousand from collections in his inside jacket pocket. They could have caught me with only half the money. What the fuck then. The money was unfolded and held together with rubber bands. He let the phone dangle and put the money on the bar.

"You can't shoot him now," Sal said.

"Shut the fuck up," somebody said.

"There'll be a come-off!" Sal said.

"Who's to tell?"

Now he froze. All these angry voices in the place. Irish. "They'll kill any fucking body," he said to himself.

One of them at the bar picked up the phone.

"He paid," the guy said into the phone. "Tell them to send the fuckin' guy down."

The guy became excited.

"— What?"

He looked around. "They want to whack him right there."

"They crazy."

"Yeah but they want to do it."

"Tell them no fuckin' way. We need him."

"Don't even think of it. No fuckin' way!"

Fausti heard the guy in the Rangers shirt say, "They got it." Fausti felt the pistol being removed from his head. Suddenly, he sensed nobody was there. The Hawaiian lei was gone. He didn't feel the Rangers shirt.

Fausti was numb. He started to walk softly toward the door. He was afraid of the next step taking him into gunfire.

He heard the two arguing just outside in the hallway.

"And let him go and fuckin' tell?" the Rangers shirts snarled.

"They say they need him yet."

"Shoot this fuckin' guy right in his fuckin' shoes."

"You mean it?"

"Yeah, let's go.

Fausti heard the rustle of the mattress cover.

He saw the edge of the staircase with its banister painted maroon. The two were two steps, not much more, to the left of the doorway. Fausti took a flying step to the maroon banister, slapped a hand on it, and vaulted. He landed and raced down one, two, three steps and leaped with both feet and landed with a crash on the platform at the bottom. He heard feet pounding behind him. He scrambled and scurried down these worn cracked marble stairs and took another long broad jump and when he landed he wheeled onto the next stairs. The pounding behind him was louder. These worn cracked marble steps flew under his feet and with one last leap he was in the hallway and flying down it to the door. His back froze because he heard a noise. Hunched over, he came out the door and onto the sidewalk.

He ran toward the car and threw one look back and saw the Rangers shirt emerge from the building. He was out there on the sidewalk like anybody else. To look at him, he's just a guy on the sidewalk.

Now Fausti saw the difference between life and death. About six steps.

As Fausti got out by the candy store, Sal exhaled loudly. "He finds out you went with me — I'm gone."

"It never happened," Fausti said.

Sal nodded.

"What's that thing?" Sal said.

"Like what?"

"The nose for a nose. Or fuckin' ear or something like that."

"An eye for an eye," Fausti said.

"That there is it. That's what's going to happen."

"They took your money, I didn't. I want to forget we even were there."

"They're dead people already," Sal said.

He held up a hand. "I didn't even get the watch. What a shame. My daughter is going to be good and mad."

47 She never saw him for the first week, when he stayed home and said he had a flu and sat troubled in front of daytime television. Then when he went out to a movie with Con she asked him why he seemed quiet. Fausti blamed unemployment.

He was pasting up cards of the famous old gunmen, with most of their deaths occurring in cars, when he thought of it. "Cars," Fausti said. "Nobody should get in a car." He had a picture from the club of Tommy Ryan, in a white trainer's sweater, under the ring lights, assaulting a referee. In the background, swinging a barrel of a body through the ropes, was the young Fist. Ryan's fighter, Rocky Castellani, had just been flattened by Ernie Durando, in a fight that was supposed to be fixed. The rest of the photo showed police on the move. Right away, Fausti thought of Tommy Ryan's last ride. He told Nini, "They think of the driver as a second stringer, but he really is a big important guy. The drivers determine who lives or dies."

It took him a week before one of Tommy Ryan's old girl friends gave him a picture of Joe Sternfeld, who drove Ryan to appointments, including the biggest appointment of all.

JOE STERNFELD

BORN: March 5, 1927.

NICKNAME: Joe the Driver.

MADE: Disqualified. Mother and father real Germans.

ASSETS: Has never lost a passenger except when he's supposed to. When he sets a guy up, he does it for good.

LIABILITIES: May not be on your side. Drove Tommy Ryan to girlfriend's house on Lefferts Avenue in Brooklyn. Parked car directly under streetlight. Light lit Ryan like a sparkler. Many, many shots from the shadows killed him. Joe the Driver left for Sullivan Street.

"What's this?" Father Phil said, looking at the card. Fausti said that nearly all Mafia guys die in cars, except for the few who get hit in restaurants. Also, all Mafia guys get their cars tailed. "You might as well put a billboard on the roof."

"How do they get around to make drops?" the priest said, with the least sarcasm. "Walk?"

"Subway," Fausti said. "You have all your meets riding the subway. That way nobody can hear you. You get a subway schedule and you ride a train and the guy gets on at a certain stop and you do all your business on the ride. The agents never can keep up with you. Not in this city."

Oh, he could feel them right behind him, Father Phil could, faceless people trying to blend in with shoppers. Of course The Fist's trial stopped nothing. They had squads for each Mafia family and also an Assets Recovery Unit for The Fist. The priest was a suspect for controlling the money, so they picked him up wherever he went. At the corner of West 3rd and Sixth Avenue, where the black playground bests from around the city come to play, Father Phil's eye caught one of the agents standing in front of a torn poster. Father Phil was carrying a large white plastic garbage bag. Father Phil went down a flight of stairs to the toll booth and put his token in. He got a glimpse of the agent looking around frantically. The agent had no token and there was a line of about twelve people waiting at the booth. He went to the turnstile and held up his badge and put one leg over the turnstile.

"Yo!!!" the toll clerk yelled.

"FBI!"

The toll clerk beckoned. "Only city police can do that."

Father Phil was on the train and looking out the window as it pulled out, and the agent had not even reached the platform. He went up as far as Penn Station on the D train, walked through the crowds to the N train going downtown to Canal Street, where nobody can be traced through all the wet tunnels. That was it for the day. He threw the white plastic bag full of cut-up newspapers into the trash can. He now knew that these Wichita farmers can't make it in New York no matter what badge they have.

The next time, one of the two agents following him had a token. The second one was lost in the crowd by the token booth. Father Phil sat on the train with the two big white plastic trash bags about which he knew nothing. He had not asked or looked. He wanted to be able to say without lying that he didn't know what was in there. That wouldn't get him off but it would soften the charge. The train was white starting into Brooklyn. At Atlantic Avenue, the riders changed color and it was all dark, with the one pale federal agent in the corner. Father Phil went to a Number 3 across the platform. The agent was good and game and hard to discourage. Father Phil was through the doors from one car to another. It was only natural for the agent, in from Duluth, to think that every eye was on him. It slowed him up. Two cars up, Father Phil stood at the doors and at the last moment threw the bags to the platform at a stop called Rutland Road. Frank Bono grabbed the bags and was gone into the Brooklyn he knew. The train now climbed onto old el tracks to the last stop. Father Phil went down the stairs and onto the carnage of New Lots Avenue. The agent took a look down from the platform and saw there was nothing there for him. Walking off, Father Phil announced to himself, "I can show these people what to do."

48 His confidence rose at a moment when the Ozone Park organization of John Gotti held a meeting to get a leader. Gotti was buried in an underground prison in Illinois. He sent orders home with visitors that all corned beef wholesalers should be lined up so they could gouge the fuckin' Irish on St. Patrick's Day. When the guys heard that the joint government task force investigating them was taking March 17 off for a huge corned beef and cabbage dinner, they dropped the idea. Gotti exploded in prison: "Fuck the task force! Do what I say." That was it. The guys met secretly to name a new family Boss, Zu Zu from Canarsie.

Now, Ignatzio, the ancient keeper of records and oaths, walked over to Zu Zu from Canarsie and gave a ceremonial kiss that confirmed him as temporary successor to John Gotti. Ignatzio is a famous gangster story from Prohibition. Boss Lupo the Wolf had Ignatzio wear an armor suit, like the Crusaders, and drive a speedboat with whiskey through Coast Guard gunfire in Jamaica Bay. Ignatzio wasn't hit, but the boat was. Down it went. Ignatzio was gone for sure, except the water was so shallow that he hit bottom and still had his nose a couple of inches above the water.

Zu Zu was so ecstatic he forgot everything else, which wasn't hard for him because he did not have all that much to think with.

Father Phil, appearing on behalf of The Fist, congratulated Zu Zu at his installation at the Ravenite Club on Mulberry Street. "At least one family has a Boss. The Fist can't supervise all five," the priest said.

Right off, Zu Zu gets a guy to drive him to Florida. He had never worked a single solitary day in his life but he needed a vacation.

Zu Zu is walking along Miami Beach, no, he is strutting like a penguin along Miami Beach, because he is the big Boss now, and he loves it, you got to shoot a lot of guys to get this big, and now he could wave a finger and pick the guy who does the shooting of the guy he doesn't like.

These three young men in business suits and street shoes walk through the sand toward him.

"You fellas hot in those suits?" Zu Zu said.

"Not at all," one of the men said. "We have to dress this way. We're agents."

"Yeah, so?" Zu Zu said.

"So United States of America versus Zu Zu."

Zu Zu had been the Boss of the gang for seven days. They put him in the iron house, from which he was not expected to emerge, nor did he.

The seven days of Boss for Zu Zu gave him the shortest term in the history of the Mafia. Even in Palermo, where it is a tremendous thing to live past breakfast, the memory was not long enough to find a bust that occurred this quickly.

At this time, the Mafia had so many men in prison that such places as Howard Beach, which once had an overcrowding of gangsters, now was a widow's walk. Always at Christmas, people came from all over the city to see the decorations. On one lawn, on 86th Street, a floodlit sentry box's doors flew open and a four-foot-high British soldier in his bearskin hat emerged and marched across the lawn, turned smartly, and went back to the box. High over three rooftops, brilliant in the spotlight, was Santa Claus in a sleigh, pulled by soaring reindeer.

Neighbor Mrs. Marie complained, "What is this, you put up Santa Claus in my face, I got a husband away for fifty years? We got no Santa Claus in my house my husband's away fifty years."

Santa Claus came down.

After many secret meetings and whispers, the Gambino crew and survivors from other families decided to risk another meeting in order to replace at least short-term Zu Zu.

In the days before this meeting, The Fist told everybody to put out the word that the new Boss of the mob was Benny (Squint) Sinagra. His people were to tell this as a great secret to the loudest mouths they could find, thus assuring Benny Squint's becoming the newspaper Boss. Nobody told Benny, who was retired in Delray, Florida. Benny woke up one morning with federal agents in cars outside his house. Benny had some health problems, but the real cause of a death that occurred soon after was parked cars.

When Funzi Tomasetti, next, heard of his ascension to the new newspaper Boss, he said he was very sick. They said he was just afraid. He said that all this pressure was going to make him die, and it did.

Barney Beltrone was next. At forty, he was young enough to handle anything, The Fist thought. Barney was at a lunch counter one afternoon and eleven agents walked in and carted him off. Everybody knew at the start that he was good for a sentence of ten years, which was what he got.

The meeting was in the Northeastern Hotel, an understated hotel, but still a very good hotel, which sat unnoticed on East 50th Street in the middle of the block between Lexington and Third Avenues in Manhattan.

The twenty-two captains were scheduled to check into single rooms on staggered timing, so as not to attract attention. The twenty-two single rooms were booked to thwart any possible federals. Twenty-two outside lines and twenty-two room-to-room lines meant that they would have to get forty-four separate wiretap orders.

"Title Three," the guys said to each other. This meant federal Title III on wiretap provisions. The agents must show the judge a reason for tapping forty-four lines. The meeting would be over a week before they even figured out the aliases on the room registry.

Everybody was supposed to show at 4 A.M. in the big suite on the ninth floor. You come a different way. You're on the tenth, you walk down to the ninth. You're on the seventh, you go on the elevator to the lobby, then you come up on the elevator to the eighth floor and walk up to the ninth. The meeting must be late at night because the room service ends at midnight and no waiters would be outside the door and overhear them while pushing carts to some other room.

At 3:30 A.M., the first captains drifted into a ninth-floor meeting room that was usually used for a company meeting of insurance agents. One room of the suite was set up as a meeting place, with folding chairs. The second room had a buffet of hot and cold food for the captains.

The Fist was represented at this Northeastern Hotel meeting by Father Phil, who gave sort of a Benediction.

"Then let us all hope that the next time we meet, I will not be here. That The Fist will be back and be the Boss in charge of everything like he is supposed to be. He has been a merciful Boss, and we hope that he receives mercy in return. You think of it, what does it mean to the jury if they say he is not guilty? What is guilty anyway? Guilty of a specific act that never bothered anybody except those deserved to get bothered? Put this against a life of selflessly helping people. So they could let him go on this case now in court. Who could get hurt? The cops that investigated it? Some young evil rat prosecutor who wants to step on The Fist's body to get a big job in a law company?

"Please. We ask of you. Free Dellacava. Free The Fist!"

The twenty-two captains sat at a large conference table. Chairs were placed along the side wall for the Bosses of two Secret Gangs that they always had in the Mafia. One was the Irish gang from the West Side of Manhattan but mostly from Keansburg, New Jersey, which is a place where people live in summer bungalows in the winter. They had nobody who wasn't in jail out and thus were not represented.

The other Secret Gang leader, Moishe Wolfe of the last of the Jew killers, showed up early. He ran the window washing for all of New York and New Jersey. He kept his customers for life. When a store owner wanted to use a less costly window washer, Moishe said to the customer, "What happens to your windows somebody breaks them?" Wolfe also sold large amounts of drugs out of a hamburger stand on Seventh Avenue in Harlem.

At the head of the big table were five empty chairs for the New York Bosses, who were absent. They were absent for the following reasons:

Junior, Boss of the Colombo gang, was in federal prison, Lompoc, California. He had 165 years to do. He wrote a note to his brother that the brother showed to everybody.

"Irregardless of what you here, I don't give up my special license plate number." He meant his title as Boss. "I read the medical stories in the library. I got 104 before I meet the parole board. Maybe they got a way for me to live 104 more years. Maybe I got a shot. No vote for somebody else from me."

John Gotti, Boss of the Gambino mob, was doing pushups in the middle of the earth, which was the location of his cell in the below-ground federal prison in Merion, Illinois. He doesn't write. He reads his appeals. He had five of them. The sixth was done by a big law professor from Harvard and it read beautiful. The judge's clerk hit it with a big stamp. "Return to Sender." John is doing three lifes without parole. He refuses to vote in this election because he still regards himself as the Boss.

The Fist. On trial.

At the next empty chair, somebody had placed a Mob Stars card on the table.

ANTHONY CORALLO aka TONY DUCKS

BORN: 1913.

Boss of Lucchese Mob.

MADE: By Tommy Lucchese himself.

Received the name "Ducks" because he extorted Long Island duck farms. Ran all private carting in two counties of Long Island.

ASSETS: So loyal he moved into Malba neighborhood of Queens where Tommy Lucchese lived. If Tommy said he didn't like somebody, Ducks hit them in the head. He is such a man he whacked Vito Guzzo himself.

LIABILITIES: Had no respect for past. Said Tommy Lucchese was too conservative. "I'm going to open up." Feds closed him up. Had talked in car because he said they couldn't bug his car. They played tapes for eleven hours in court.

His proxy was confiscated by a warden. Tony's sentences add up to 137 years.

The Mob Stars card was put like a place card at Ducks's seat. Cards also were put at the four other places. This was such a cute idea that each replacement in the place of a missing Boss wanted to kill and maim.

Angelo Schileppi of Ducks's mob growled at the card.

"Who put this here here?"

There was no answer.

"Don't worry about it," Father Phil said.

"You say. This got to be everywhere. They put Lou Guzzo here. Lou Guzzo got three brothers, they kill Tony."

"Tony is away forever," Father Phil said.

"So they kill me while they're waiting," Schileppi said.

"Let's look ahead," the priest said.

"Why you say that? They put this out right here now."

Suddenly, Joe Sabatino from the Bonnano mob snatched the card for old Boss Joe Catania at new Boss Mikey Malario's place.

"How could they do this to Joey? He's a nice guy. He'll break their fucking heads."

There was a snarl from one corner of the room and three people were looking at a card and then somebody else slammed his hand down. At this, Father Phil stood up and counseled them, "These are cards with words on them. Remember, sticks and stones can break your bones, but names —"

"— can get you fuckin' locked up!" Buster from Staten Island yelled.

"We got to get the guy making these cards," somebody from the Colombo family said.

"I heard it's a guy got a baseball card thing, too," somebody said.

"Yeah, we find him."

"And fuckin' whack him."

Father Phil lowered his voice so that they had to strain to hear him, the effort causing them to curtail waving cards around. He spoke of peace and the need to calm tempers and complete business in this room. "We will talk about these cards and how they get here afterward," he said. He got the room to agree.

To replace Zu Zu as Boss of the Gambino family, "a anonymous vote" was required, meaning one dissent blocks a candidacy. The Mafia's clerk, Ignatzio, sat in a corner and held a small notebook with instructions in Italian for the swearing in of a new Boss. He had this old greasy copybook. The book had a short paragraph, which was both oath and greeting and dire warning. It was in Italian, which he recited from memory. He heard it first when a man called the Sulphur Devil was Boss. He used to bury people in the mine outside his town of Lercara Friddi in Sicily.

The part of the oath Ignatizo loved was "The dog should not be cursed and killed as will the man who does not live up to this oath. He should be cut so that blood pours from every part of his body. After that he should be dropped down the center of the volcano. Dropped into the fire of the earth. His family should be killed to the second cousin."

There were no volcanoes in Brooklyn, but Ignatzio knew that there were many chimneys with huge incinerators that were a thousand degrees hot.

At this point, Little Mickey Roma was supposed to be replacing Zu Zu as new Boss of the John Gotti crew from Ozone Park.

"I want no part of it," Mickey said, pointing to Big John's chair.

"No part of what?" one of the captains said.

"Of being here. Or being a Boss. Or anything."

"What do you want?"

"I want to be busted down to below soldier where nobody sees me, knows who the fuck I am."

Now Little Mickey stood up. He pointed dramatically to the five empty chairs.

"Where do you think they all are, fucking Acapulco?"

He stepped behind Big John's chair. "I can't wait to jump into this chair so the government can lift me out of it and you never fucking see me again. Like John Gotti. This is some man, isn't he? What a stand-up guy. Don't nod. Give the man a hand."

They all clapped and yelled, "Johnny Boy!"

"Thank you," Mickey said. "You hear that, John? What's that? You can't fuckin' hear? Why can't you hear? Oh. Because they got you in a cell five motherfucking stories under the top of the ground? You can't see nothin', you can't hear nothin'. You're in six years already and you only got a hundred and eleven to go before you meet the parole board. You might as well die right now."

"Johnny, I love you. But I pass."

In all the years of the Mafia nobody ever had refused a presidential nomination. This had a stunning effect on the room. For the first time, their private fears were being discussed in a formal setting. When somebody growled that Little Mickey was yellow, he cut them off and pointed out that it was his belief that if the federal police sensed that a man was frightened, they did not hound him to death. In fact, they became so lax that there was a chance that the man could slip away. He would be a dog, but at least a live dog. If, on the other hand, the man opposed them, scowling and vain, the whole government would fall on him and when seen for the next and last time, his head would be dipping as he entered an FBI car.

Mickey announced:

"I says, 'Do I want to go to jail or not?' I decided, 'I don't want to go to jail.'"

Somebody said, "Not for nothin', but where does this leave us? We lose. Next, we lose The Fist, right?"

At this, Father Phil was on his feet. "How can you talk that way? The Fist's trial is only a few days old. The lawyers think they have a good shot. A good shot. Let me tell you, any talk about his losing his case will be regarded as an attack by you on The Fist and will result in instant retaliation. I want to hear what you have to say about his trial now."

Fat Andy, a Gambino from the Ozone Park brigade, got up.

"The Fist walks . . .

"He never done it."

Now the whole room chanted:

"The Fist walks . . .

"He never done it."

They went back to the meeting that ended with nothing. This caused a postponement, and it also showed that the Mafia was nothing more than a three-legged fox.

Before they left, the only thing some of them had on their minds was the Mob Stars cards.

"You will have to let me take care of it myself," Father Phil said, firmly.

Father Phil studied the guys as they left. Most of The Fist's family was shredded and those remaining were wary. At least they still could go out and collect money. The other mobs didn't know the time if they stood under a clock. He could recognize immediately the smartness of the strategy that Fausti brought up. Simultaneously, he wondered about what this meant. The subway idea was terrific. Could this kid try to take over by saying he was smarter? Right away, Father Phil assured himself, who says that I wouldn't have come up with this by myself?

49

"This is pretty good," Father Phil said.

"You could have it," Pepe said, looking around the 116th Street subway station in East Harlem. Pepe was a bookend for Fat Tony Salerno, in charge of East Harlem, the Army of the North, for The Fist.

"You must remember that there are no wiretaps or bugs in the subway," Father Phil said.

"No bugs," Pepe said, staring at the black crusted trackbed. "I'll tell you what they do have."

He stood up and pointed down. "Mother-

fucking

rats!"

Atop the third rail, crouched on the wood covering, was a dirty rat. He crept forward a few inches, then stopped to pose in the dirt. The bright lights of the platform made the rails shine in the dirt and grease but the rat did not reflect or soak in the light. The rat stayed in perpetual dusk. Feet came from under his fat middle and reached down to clutch the third rail. The body dropped and started creeping along the third rail. Its tail was a tow rope pulling unseen freight.

In the middle of the platform, by the turnstiles, a woman carrying a yellow shopping bag suddenly pointed at the tracks.

"Ratan!" she said in Spanish. She did not yell; the rat was a familiar sight, like a neighbor's cat.

A little boy with her leaned over the edge of the tracks.

"Ratan! Ratan!"

"Big one," the woman said. "You need a gun to shoot him."

That was all for Pepe. "If you think that I'm staying here," he said.

He and Father Phil went upstairs to the Delightful Coffee Shop on First Avenue and 116th.

Pepe started to talk.

Father Phil had a finger to his lips.

"Why?" Pepe said.

He wanted to talk about a guy who owned three bars and owed $3,000 a week from the restaurant he bought with money from the East Harlem Branch. He does not pay. You let ten others like him get away with it and what do you have? Father Phil got up and whispered into Pepe's ear. "Believe me, the subway was safe. You know this place. A thousand bugs. How could you talk here? This place turns into a jail cell."

Father Phil next used only the subway for a pickup and delivery system of cash money, and it worked beautiful. A guy, Buster from the Bronx, rode the Number 6 train from 177th Street at the Parkchester apartments down to 86th Street and Lexington Avenue in Manhattan. He did five trial runs until he could figure out an appointment time. He made it at 4:03 in the afternoon. He had a good package of money for downtown and he had a kid drive him to 177th. At this point, the Number 6 subway line is an el right up there in the air. A few stops down it plunges into the ground and runs under the city for miles. The agents following him laughed when they saw Buster go up the el staircase; he'll come down the staircase on the other side of the street and think he is a genius.

Buster got on the Number 6, right on his schedule, and rode it down to Lexington and 86th.

On that platform, Buster stepped off the train and here was Blastoff, in his blue sweatsuit and big white sneakers. He handed Blastoff the big good package of money.

"Great!" Blastoff said, taking it from him.

"Beauty!" Buster cried.

Blastoff went upstairs and Buster went downstairs and onto the other side and rode the train back to the Parkchester stop.

Every Tuesday, Buster was to bring the money down to 86th Street. It was wonderful on the first two Tuesdays.

On the third Tuesday, Buster overslept.

Blastoff waited for four trains. Blastoff in a fury kicked the fourth train as it was leaving. He was wearing those good yuppie health club sneakers and his toes screamed in pain.

50 Father Phil had wanted to tell The Fist about the subway system, but he knew he couldn't ask the guy to think of anything except beating this hideous case. By now, Father Phil had an entire network of people meeting each other on the subways and not once were they disturbed.

Foolproof Falcone made a difficult three-way handoff from the underground Bay Parkway stop in Bensonhurst, where he started with his own pack of loan shark receipts, to the Smith–Ninth Street stop, which is high in the air over South Brooklyn, and where a guy, Larry, waited with more money. Foolproof didn't even have to get off the train; he took the package through the open door and rode right to Manhattan. The next day, sauntering to the turnstile, he noticed a door that said NO ADMITTANCE. Inspiration was born. "Why am I paying a dollar fifty to these bastards?"

Foolproof went through the door like he was supposed to, causing the token clerk to reach for a special emergency phone.

At first, police made no fuss about Foolproof's arrest. He said he never had been arrested before this. He didn't think they'd check his life just because of a fare beat arrest. They did. His past arrests took six pages on the return fax.

"You should tell the truth as much as possible," Father Phil said when he showed up in court to post bail for Foolproof.

51

Will you look at this slob, Fausti said to himself when court started that day, right at 9:30, and agents wheeled in Louis Carlino, a prosecution witness. He was still getting over being shot. How could anybody listen to this guy? He had not been enough of a personality to make a Mob Stars card.

Carlino looked like he ate furniture. He was striking in a black turtleneck. He had black hair and large eyeglasses. His face had no expression because he didn't have enough in him to show anything. Carlino, a fat deranged killer, was the avoirdupois champion of serial murderers, weighing in at 500 and change. The FBI witnesses said that after shooting Jim Garrity, an Irish union leader who deserved to die with all the other Irish, Carlino then sat down on Garrity's chest and yanked off all the jewelry. Who buries a guy with a good watch? He took the money from Garrity's pocket. "They could use it as evidence."

Suddenly, Garrity moaned. "Please shoot me and get me out of pain."

"We already done that," Carlino said.

In court now, Carlino spoke dully.

Q. Mr. Carlino, was there ever an attempt on your life?

A. Why do you think I'm in a wheelchair?

Q. Who ordered the attack on you?

A. That could only come when The Fist says.

Q. How do you know that?

A. Because he bought murder from the dictionary book. He owns it. I disregarded him being the Boss and killed two guys without his permission. I thought he never hears about it, but he did.

Q. Can you tell us about it?

A. What's to say. You pull a trigger, the gun goes off.

Fausti felt the priest nudging him. "Nothing," he whispered. You couldn't get a more tenuous connection to a crime than Carlino. Hearsay, at best.

Judge, jurors, and lawyers put on yellow headphones to hear a transcript of Fat Tony Salerno of the Army of the North who was speaking in his clubhouse on East 115th Street. The club was called the Parma Boy Club. There was no "s" in Boy, because there was no "s."

What the prosecutors were doing was using hearsay from Carlino and making it seem like something much more definitive by using tapes of Fat Tony talking.

FISH: So I go down there yesterday.

FAT TONY: Yeah.

FISH: The Fist has me sittin' there like it's the dentist.

FAT TONY: What do you want? He's the king. He makes everybody else the queen who got to shut up.

FISH: He lets you know who you are. You can't reason with him. I don't know what to say, I swear I don't. You wanna, you wanna say, "I took care of this all by myself. Youse wanted two hundred seventy-five t'ousand collected, I'll go out and get it." You know what he said? "Give me all the money now."

FAT TONY: You can't reason with him. I go over and talk to him like, like the first time, the argument I had with him in the barbershop that day so he says, "Fat Tony . . ." Like I'm a fuckin' joke. I want something and I have to run downtown to see him when I want somethin' done.

FISH: You can't have the . . . the guy treat you like . . ."

SALERNO: Fuck that shit. I won't take orders from the guy. Anyways, I'll retire. I don't need this.

FISH: I know you'll retire, I know you'll retire.

SALERNO: It's a shame.

FISH: An awful fuckin' terrible shame. When you retire, I have to take over everything up here.

Upon hearing of this new order about subway riding, Fat Tony growled, "I took the subway to see Louis box Schmeling. I never set foot in a fuckin' thing since."

Yet when Fat Tony had to go downtown, he sulked up to the subway at 116th and Lexington Avenue.

He tried to give the clerk a fifty-dollar bill, but the clerk pointed to the sign saying that no bills over twenty were allowed.

"What do I do?" he asked the clerk.

"You need a token, but I can't break a bill that big to sell you one."

"A token?" Fat Tony said. He saw this coin on the cement at his feet. "What do they look like?"

"Brass."

Picking it up, he said, "How's this?"

"That's good."

Fat Tony exulted. "Now what do I do, I put it in the slot there?"

"Yep."

"And I beat the fuckin' city!"

He rode the train down to 51st Street. He was supposed to go many more stops, to downtown, but he had no idea of where he was, and then suddenly he saw a sign saying 51st Street and he knew that was where the Waldorf-Astoria was, and he knew that's where he belonged. A big bar and good big drinks.

Fat Tony got into the bar on the ground floor and he led with the fifty to the bartender.

"Start you off. Don't go away," he said. "I want a highball."

The bartender never left him. Later, Fat Tony came out of the bar with a big highball in his hand and he walked hazily to a subway kiosk and this time he had two dollars ready for a token. He then pushed two more dollars through the slot.

"What this?" the clerk asked.

"That's yours. It's a tip."

Fat Tony got on the subway and drank his drink and put his head down and nodded away.

He woke up with a start.

"Can I help you?" a train conductor said. "Last stop. Jamaica Center. You in Queens."

"Give us a highball," Fat Tony said, holding his glass out.

"You got the wrong place," the trainman said.

"You got the wrong fuckin' guy," Fat Tony said.

"What are you talkin' like that to me for?"

"Give us a highball and shut the fuck up. You're playing with the big guys now. You're playin' with the commission. You could get your head blown off right now."

The transit police made this arrest. It wasn't much of an arrest, but what it did, it speeded them up in the United States Attorney's Office. And that put Fat Tony up there for one of those record sentences that helped knock out the outfit. That, and the changes in the neighborhoods that they never noticed.

52

Father Phil looked at the jury, five black women, four black men and one Hispanic, with the last two seats owned by whites. In his new parish in Brooklyn, he had seen the beginnings of color finally determining jury verdicts. He was looking for one juror here to show the same thing.

The one in Brooklyn involved a woman, Ramona Perez, beaten often and with great facial damage by a husband, Santiago, a drunk. She called the rectory shrieking for help one day. Father Phil, carrying his favorite baseball bat, a 32-ounce Louisville Slugger, Joe Pepitone model, got to the apartment with his assistant, Big Mario, found Ramona Perez in her apartment standing over her husband, who had this big carving knife as deep into his belly as it would go.

"What did you do that for?" Father Phil yelled. "We were going to take care of this for you."

Her jury was eleven Hispanics, eight of them women, and a white gay. When the judge conferred with lawyers at one side of the bench, Father Phil said softly in Spanish to the jurors, "Hello, ladies. Father Phil, ladies. I'm here for Ramona. She tried to save his life, ladies. But he stabbed himself before she could save his life. Believe me, I know. He wanted to commit suicide like Donald Manes. Remember him in Queens? *La polica irlanza sucio* here are trying to crucify her. Believe me, I know, ladies."

The jury took thirteen minutes and told Ramona to go home. Father Phil knew that this would occur again as surely as a season changing. He looked for a way to have The Fist's name identified with the aspirations and anger of nonwhites. The only question now was at which point jurors would sit smoldering as a white lawyer aims his commuter-train words at them. They will toss them off like rain on a window. Oh, this sounds like a generality, but I don't think it is, the priest told himself. Someday, maybe soon, a lawyer will get a civil court jury to award a million dollars for a broken toe. In the criminal courts, if they have any guts, they'll give the white police and prosecutors hung juries and acquittals. His only question was, how could The Fist benefit?

He saw the news about young blacks who had raped and left for dead a woman jogger in Central Park. First, and you have to give him this, he was pierced by the sight of the mother of the youngest one, Richard Caverts, fifteen, climbing heavily out of a livery cab at the 20th Precinct with pajamas for her son, who was going to be held somewhere for the night. Father Phil then saw Billman, the lawyer for the youth Caverts, leaving the precinct. He called the lawyer up. "The boy doesn't belong in jail. He belongs home with his family. I don't want him to go unpunished if he is guilty. But until that can be determined, he belongs home. I want to post bail for him."

Bail was twenty-five thousand dollars, and Father Phil's hand was on the boy's shoulder as he walked him past the long desk in the lobby of the Spofford Youth House. Everything had been signed, doors opened, inmate coming out. Handing in the twenty-five-thousand-dollar check at the front desk was the only detail left.

"Good evening, dear," Father Phil said to the woman supervisor.

"Father," she said. She was afraid to say anything else. She pushed the buzzer that opened the locked front door.

Father Phil and the boy breezed out the door, with the twenty-five-thousand-dollar check warming the priest's heart. Who are these people to try and hold my money? The boy already was in the car when another supervisor, his dinner coming back up into his mouth, came running out the front door.

"You didn't post the bail."

"What bail?" Father Phil asked.

"Twenty-five thousand."

Father Phil waved the papers. "This paper says he is released on bond. I had to sign it. See? My word is my bond."

"Yeah, but the money."

"You must be nuts, you want twenty-five thousand from me. You have my signature. It's worth millions."

"Then he's got to come back in. He belongs to us."

"What are you talking about? He belongs to his mother."

"But you didn't post bond."

"I am dealing with liberty for a boy and you want to put a price on it. What kind of a human being are you? You let the boy out and he's out. Don't you try and shake me down for money."

"Yeah, but you see, Fath—"

"Tell this to a judge. He'll hear the case by the end of next summer. If you're still around."

Father Phil drove off with the boy and his mother and aunts. Soon, black women were on television and in the newspapers praising the family of The Fist.

His act outraged so many whites. Father Phil could not care less. All he needed was one black on The Fist's jury to know about this.

53 In court that left leg was pumping up and down good, causing the rest of him to vibrate somewhat. He doubled the tempo and that left foot made him shake like he was seated on a third rail. He had spent so much time telling himself that he was crazy that now he heard fast cars running along the hallway outside the courtroom door. But his lawyers had to convince the judge that he was more than nuts. They must make him incompetent. This poor man can't understand a phrase in his own defense. That's the winner; that's what gets you off.

The Fist kept mumbling at a rapid speed with no breaks. He was reciting the start of his all-time favorite song.

My boy Lollipop,
You make my heart go giddy-op . . .
My boy Lollipop

You make my heart go giddy-op . . .
"Myboylollipopyoumakemyheartgogiddyop."

When he tired of mumbling his song titles together in court, The Fist said the Hail Mary. If there is one recitation that lasts forever in Catholic kids it is the Hail Mary. It is short and once learned never goes away because it is said so often. Saying the rosary or at any service, the Hail Mary is repeated over and over and over again and somebody like The Fist still can recite it a thousand times, never pausing, never missing. It is misused by sports people, who call a long desperate-appearing pass a "Hail Mary." That is in terrible taste because it is calling for intercession in a cheap game for boys. The Fist used it in deep human trouble. Besides, somewhere in there he might have had some legitimate faith powering the words. By endlessly mumbling the prayer he could make it appear that he was carrying on a raging discussion with his favorite ghost.

The Fist sits in this sixth-floor federal courtroom in Brooklyn as the last of the demons who ran organized crime, the only Boss left on free soil.

There was a conference on this morning about a juror's sick child. The judge was absorbed with this.

What the fuck does a kid have to do with this? The Fist said to himself. My life is on the line and they talk about a kid.

This woman juror's kid has chicken pox. The judge says he don't like a kid being sick without the mother around.

The Fist said to himself, What about me? I'm good and sick. My mother wants to take care of me.

He says he got a limousine waiting at her house, but he won't bring her in. She stays where she belongs, with her kid. The judge said he worries that chicken pox is a disease could spread to the whole jury.

So we get a alternate. I don't know what it means except that they believe chicken pox from some fuckin' kid and they don't believe me that I'm crazy and incompetent. Kid with chicken pox is out in the street playin' three, four days. I could get a hundred years.

Maybe the new juror's the one going to be with me, The Fist thought. I only need one. Eleven to one, I win the game. Ten to two, I win. I win everything up to twelve nothing, an anonymous decision. Tie Score Joe Joe. I need him. I told everybody don't you show up in the court, make it look like all wise guys. I shouldn't have told Joe Joe not come. I never lose with him.

The Fist dipped into another one of his visions of life as he daydreamed it should be.

I guess I close up the joint now. He is in the ticket booth in this movie house in Chicago. The Biograph. He is counting the ticket stubs and making sure the money evened out and then out the door comes Father Phil. Father Phil looks around and comes up to the ticket booth and stands there, like he's waiting for The Fist to finish.

"I don't like these people I see all over the neighborhood," the priest says.

The Fist makes believe he is not looking but he is looking. Will you look at these fucking people? One by the corner, three down at the end of the movie house. Look at that big Packard out there. Fuckin' four them sittin' there. Bet me they got machine guns. The Fist says to Father Phil, go in and tell him, and the priest says he already did but the guy don't want to know from nothing.

The movie is breaking and all over the street you got these fucking guys appearing with guns and Johnny Dillinger comes out the front door with this broad all in red. She's the one done him in. She had a immigration beef and she trades him for citizen papers.

The Fist opens the ticket booth and hisses to Johnny Dillinger: "The law's all over the place. Johnny, the broad with you brings them here."

Right away the broad starts to run away. Johnny shoots the broad right by the ticket booth. Then he walks straight ahead and this pudgy little guy, John Edgar Hoover, runs up to him and starts screaming, "G-Man!"

Look at what Johnny Dillinger does to him. G-Man, fuck you, G-Man. He puts four into that pigeon-chested bum and leaves him flat dead under the marquee. His legs are up in the air like a fuckin' turkey. The whole rest of them don't know what to do.

They all could go and fuck themselves. Johnny Dillinger walks right out into the night.

On other times when he turned his head to stare, he thought he heard voices that he didn't start. Was it because he claimed he heard them, or did he really hear them? By now, he had done this for so long, and had taken on a boxcar of Thorazine, that he wasn't sure of right or left. He told the doctors that it was God talking. He was afraid to tell that to himself. The only one talking in the courtroom now was the FBI agent on the witness stand.

54

Right here in this courtroom there was a row of people in from the FBI's Assets Recovery Unit. At every break in court, the Assets Recovery group went into an office down the hall and talked of the honors and pay raises if they found The Fist's cash.

Agent Fitzsimmons mentioned Fausti. "He's only a nephew," somebody said. "Wouldn't his own kids be closer?" Agent Fitzsimmons said that The Fist's kids were not allowed within a thousand miles of the business. Through the whole family, there wasn't an outstanding traffic ticket. They needed no cars; they all had every kind of car made anywhere in the universe. However cash reached them, there was no way to investigate. Somebody said that a new face — his name is Richard and he's forty now, living in Red Bud, Illinois — suddenly appeared in court for the last week. Agent Fitzsimmons said, "He told the family in the diner that he has a $50,000 pool table ordered for his house. He wants the family to come up with the money. I say in the end the ones who'll know what's going on are the priest and the nephew Fausti."

"Fausti don't mean nothing," an agent said.

Agent Fitzsimmons thought the best way to get The Fist's money was by plea-bargaining. "He's looking at a thousand years.

If he gives up all the money, we'll get him a nothing sentence. Spitting on the sidewalk. Two years or something."

"For all his money?"

"All of it. His money or his life."

Outside, The Fist was wheeled right past the door. If The Fist had known of the conversation inside, he would have bitten the doorknob off.

Before his life turned into testimony, The Fist had taken one last tour of his riches.

Two blocks away, two men from the FBI's Assets Recovery Unit watched from the shadows. The Fist had his west flank secured by purchasing abandoned factory buildings on these gloomy streets on the far West Side of the Village. Ownership was in the names of so many front companies that the best researcher for government could not find any proof that The Fist owned a building.

He started by tapping the side of a building with a loading platform. Then he went across the street and put a hand on a dark seven-story empty factory. You count money and touch real restate to prove it's there, he told himself. His tour took some time and he touched so many buildings that it was apparent that he owned almost every building in the new searing-hot neighborhood called Tribeca. The first white eyes showed on the dark faces of nearly empty buildings.

When The Fist took a step, they took one. They did not crisscross the street. They each took a side. At every spot where The Fist had tapped the stone, one of them chiseled an X. Someday, they knew, they would have to come back here with a full team and probably use jackhammers to burrow into the stone and find the money they were certain The Fist had buried in there.

Walking ahead of them slowly, The Fist muttered, "The two guys are agents. I can't do nothin' but hope they die."

55

The Fist was shaking like an aftershock from over-medication. The priest was in the hallway trying to convince the reporters that The Fist was a hopeless, helpless, but dear incompetent. After that, he tried to take it to the mental health community.

Father Phil started the morning on East 65th Street, at the medical offices of the famous psychiatrist Joshua Gold. He supposedly was the leading expert on incompetency in the English-speaking world, and was going to testify and assist the defense for the usual ton of money. The psychiatrist Gold rubbed sleep from his eyes. "I shall place the full weight of my name and knowledge on this woman at Brooklyn State," he promised. "When medical persons have these government sinecures, they enter a state of grandiosity. They make snap judgments and feel there are no consequences because it is their decision and they cannot be wrong." He stood up. "Can we go out for some coffee? I didn't have anything home today. I haven't had anything at all home since my wife left me. Walked right out. She left her lawyer's office as a forwarding address. The lawyer? That reptile. He and my wife crawl looking for money. Crawl. Slither. My wife and that lawyer have left me almost naked. One more court order and I will be walking around with my penis in the air. Look at this. We're out in the rain with no umbrella. How shortsighted." He led Father Phil from the office and down the street. "I hope we won't get too wet. I can't stand the smell of wet wool. I get into fights because of it. That wife certainly turned on me. Do you know a good hit man?" They were entering the Vendome coffee shop on 65th and Madison Avenue, a block up from his office.

"I guess I didn't think for a moment there. I must have made you terribly nervous asking for a hit man. That was unfair of me to say to you. Do you have one? A real hit man? I need a murderer. I can gladly see my wife dead. I just don't want to go to jail. Sure, there must be somebody you know who doesn't care whether he is in or out of jail, and could do me a marvelous service, for which he would receive the last of my financial fortune. All he has to do is kill a hideous woman who deserves to die."

Afterward, at the cashier's, Gold looked at the rain outside. After that, at an umbrella that was leaning against the counter only inches from its owner, a tall man in a raincoat who was waiting for an order. Gold casually took the umbrella and went out the door. The tall guy never noticed a thing. Outside, Gold opened the umbrella right in the coffee shop window. It was a red and white striped umbrella of the size seen in wet weather at major golf matches.

He walked with Father Phil under the umbrella, turned the corner quickly, and waved for a cab as if nothing had happened. Father Phil rubbed his eyes. How am I going to bring this fruitcake around to the hospital with me? That doctor'll put a net over the two of us.

On appointment, he and Doctor Gold were delivering a large package of medical records to Sabrina Kalish that revealed that The Fist was going to die very soon. They also wanted to put The Fist through a new battery of tests in order to show conclusively that Alzheimer's was beginning to own his brain, thus making him incompetent. One test, the PET scan, was new and it arrived to great applause in the psychiatric testing community.

But in court, the judge already had ordered that all tests be ceased and The Fist's medication be unchanged. "I don't want to be called on to deal with further test results every morning," he said. "We are not going to proceed by ambush of medical records. Please do not schedule him for any tests I don't know about. When I say please, it is an order."

All searching for any relief had to begin with Sabrina Kalish, monitor for the court. She had seemed hasty to the point of being unprofessional on their first encounter with her when even The Fist's urine was regarded as common. But now they had to go back up that mean hill and hope that she would agree to anything that they could get on paper and wave around in court. These new tests and examination results by doctors hired by the lawyers were advanced science, everybody agreed, and required detailed examination. Maybe one result could even put an element of doubt in the discussion of The Fist's condition. Arriving at the hospital to see her, Gold remarked to Father Phil, "Perfection is elusive." He placed his purloined umbrella against the reception room wall and sat down with a newspaper.

Inside the emergency psychiatric room was a semicircular Plexiglas booth where hospital people in white were working on looseleaf files.

Sabrina Kalish, M.D., directoress, stood in the booth and held up a large cardboard sign.

"Arm restraints!"

The room rattled and clinked with chains. Suddenly, a guy darted from a bench and swung the manacled hands at the Plexiglas like a hammer. The glass could withstand an artillery hit.

"I'll kill you!"

He could be heard in the waiting room.

She now held up a sign. "Leg restraints, too!"

Then, seeing the priest, she motioned familiarly with her hand. The sight of Gold made her frown. When she came into the reception room, she seemed noticeably warm to Father Phil even with her professional manner. Gold she clearly hated.

Father Phil handed her the manila envelope full of papers about possible new testing that the lawyers had given him.

Right away, Gold said, "I'd like to explain the urgency of this test —"

"— I will hear from you when I absolutely have to," she snapped. Gold sat down.

Father Phil said, "You must forgive me, when the appointment was made to bring these files to you, I'm sure the lawyers didn't fully understand how busy you are."

"Thank you. I'll be sure to go over them."

"The material about Alzheimer's," he said.

"I'll read everything, and confer with the judge over what can or cannot be done. I am only an observer. He makes the decisions, as you might have discovered."

"Not for anything, but you are a beautiful woman."

"Thank you. I hope you don't think I'll give an opinion to suit you."

"Of course not. That's why I'm here. I know you're tough and truthful."

"The only way to get me to change my mind is to marry me."

"I'd be delighted to marry you. Tell me when and I'll perform the ceremony."

"You don't understand. Only if you marry me."

He did not know if she was trying to be amusing or if she was crazy or —

"I just put it down," Gold yelped.

Gold was spinning around, obviously looking for his umbrella.

He shouted at the receptionist, "You didn't see anybody taking my umbrella, did you?"

She shook her head.

He said to her, "You didn't take it, did you?"

"I am sorry but I resent that."

"What do you mean, you resent? What about me? I resent not having my umbrella."

Gold now wheeled around the room, looking under the one bench, pressing his face against a window in the door to see if it was outside in the hall.

"This bitch stole my umbrella," indicating the receptionist.

"You are free to leave right now!" Sabrina said.

"I go nowhere until the person who stole my umbrella returns it. And you know who stole it and so does she!"

"You're free to leave," Sabrina said in a flat voice.

"This bitch."

His face was suddenly red. He had instant foam in the corners of his mouth.

Father Phil said softly, "Come on. I was with you when you got it, remember?"

He reached out to touch Gold.

Who jumped up in the air and snarled.

"Security!" Sabrina called.

"Security!" the receptionist called.

They came through both doors, from the emergency room and the hall. Two stocky guys who clearly couldn't wait to destroy Gold.

"Restraints!" Kalish shouted.

The guards had Gold by the arms, and he was struggling wildly. His legs came off the floor as they lifted him. He kicked the air wildly. They had a straitjacket ready to wrap him in.

"Please," Father Phil said. "Just get him out to the street and I'll see that he goes away."

"Take him out of the building," Sabrina said.

Out Gold went, kicking and screaming. "My umbrella!"

Father Phil said to Sabrina, "I am deeply apologetic. Why don't you let me take you to dinner — someplace close, I mean, if you ever have a chance?"

"Maybe. I'll go only if it's Mafia food."

"I don't eat any other kind."

"A mob meal! Oh, I can't turn that down."

She patted her midsection, which was a trifle large.

Outside, in the driveway in front of the entrance to the psychiatric wing, Gold was brushing himself off and gesturing wildly. "The umbrella," he said.

Father Phil threw him into a cab.

"We'll see her in court," Gold yelled.

56

She walked across the red brick plaza in front of the church. Now he doesn't have to look for me to take me to dinner, she told herself. Women were standing around him in the late afternoon. As each spoke, he took an arm and walked with the woman off into an empty part of the plaza, where they talked with only the sky listening. Obviously, it was about the filthy men they were living with.

A short, wide woman in a summer dress and sandals stood near Sabrina.

"You wait for him?" she said.

Sabrina nodded.

The woman stepped over, holding out a card.

"See? Famous."

She had a Mob Stars card.

"You want it?"

"Do you have another?"

"All the stores have them. Everybody has one. Father Phil!"

On the front of the card was a beautiful picture of Father Phil, his face radiating concern, the collar turned around. The back said:

THE REV. PHILLIP NAPOLITANO
Mafia chaplain.

BORN: March 10, 1931, Buffalo, relocated to New York.

NICKNAME: Just "Father Phil."

MADE: Official induction unnecessary.

CAREER HIGHS: Helps everybody. Champion of gays. Put roofs over people's heads. Prayed for Carmine Galante when shot at lunch. Runs funerals for those denied last rites of church.

LIABILITIES: The church keeps him busy. Mob needs him all the time.

ASSETS: Absolutely fearless of anything, even legitimate. Smartest of De Francisi family and all other Mafia families by 45 points on IQ. People truly like him. People who don't have great difficulty.

Certainly, she knew all about the Mafia; she had seen one of *The Godfather* movies. It was unthinkable to traffic with them, even for a cup of coffee. The first thing in her life, her very first thing, was to consider her career. That, she could never harm. She had invested all of her adult years in her profession and thus far it was a success. She would never risk it on a man. It would take an extraordinary man for her to do such a thing. Sometimes, a man can be extraordinary just by being there at a particular moment, standing in a certain light in a room or on a street or in a car or anyplace in the whole freaking world. Now if he was just some crumby gangster strangling people like these louts in *The Godfather* . . . yick! . . . greasy bums. But if he was a big shot in the mob, walking around with senators and the like. Who knows? The chaplain of the Mafia. Is that just something they say, or is it real? He could be a big shot if it was real. She put the card away as he walked up. Looking at her more than closely. He said, "Not for anything, but you are very beautiful."

"Thank you. Do you say this to all the women in your church here?"

"Not all."

"Oh, but you do to some."

"I've not been here very long. The people are wonderful and outrageous. Look at them. They seem so sweet. They live on gossip about sex. Do you know what they say about me? That I had a girlfriend in my last parish."

"They shouldn't slander you like that."

"I agree. It was a filthy lie. Saying I had one girlfriend. One girlfriend. I fell in love five times in Buffalo.

"Do you think I took a vow against love? I believe in adoration of God and preaching His word. I don't believe in a cold life. How can love be wrong? I praise God and preach His word. I can't wait to get up in the morning to do that. But I never said I'd turn my back on the only decent human emotion. Love.

"I want you to see something."

He led her into the rectory, which was noisy with women in the office, and up creaking stairs to the second-floor sitting room. On the wall were three framed pictures and a painting of The Fist.

"Look at him," Father Phil said. "Isn't he beautiful? You saw him under the worst of circumstances. The poor man is sick now. Look at him when he wasn't."

One picture was of The Fist at a wedding, a carnation in his lapel. Two others had The Fist in a family group picture, probably at weddings. The painting was a large head and shoulders of a serious Fist, but not so serious as to be threatening.

Father Phil said softly, "Isn't he a beautiful man?"

Sabrina nodded.

"Tell me the truth. Does he look like he could kill somebody?"

She looked steadily at the painting.

"How could anybody think he could kill somebody? How could they?"

Sabrina said nothing.

"Do you think this beautiful man could kill somebody?"

Softly he said, "He is a beautiful man."

"He looks pleasant in the painting," she said.

They drove downtown and were part of the early crowd in Catanzaro, which is around the corner from Sullivan Street but is a universe away, so elegant and expensive.

Now, she had no idea who might be inside. If there were a lot of these people of his, she would have to leave before even sitting down. On the sidewalk, her face full of skepticism, she took out the card.

"And what is this?" she said.

"Chaplain."

"It says Mafia," Sabrina said.

"What do you care?"

"Because it makes me feel stupid. I believed you when you told me that you only eat in Mafia restaurants. I thought that was great. Then I believed you when you told me there is no Mafia. Now I see this. Not only is there a Mafia, but you lead them in prayers."

"How can you talk like that? There's no Mafia. I'm a priest. A priest can't be in the Mafia. That is something from the movies."

She held the card up. "This isn't a movie."

"Then why don't you eat the card for dinner?"

He made a motion to leave, which was terribly unfair of him because it struck fear in her. How could he leave her at the gate to a restaurant like this?

"No, I want to eat. I'm so hungry right now. I just want you to know I'm not stupid. You want me to stand here like a dope and believe you."

"Dellacava's not in the Mafia because there isn't any Mafia and I'm not in the Mafia either."

"I've decided on something," she said. "You can't make up your mind about the Mafia because you don't know whether you are in it or not, if you are proud or ashamed of it. It's your problem. How's that?"

"I can live with that."

"But I can't go without dinner," she said.

The owner and headwaiter remembered to bow when Father Phil came in and introduced them to Sabrina. They sat at a table next to a large round crowded table which had Bill Cosby and his family.

Sabrina only glanced at him. As long as there wasn't some obvious mobster next to her, she was totally unconcerned.

"This is a lovely place. I know where we are now. I buy shoes around here. Then there's a dress shop I like. Larese."

"That used to be Stefano's club!"

"Who?"

"A lovely, wonderful guy. Stefano."

"What kind of a club did he have?"

"A place for men to meet. They played cards. They had conversations. A club for men."

"Where did he move to?"

"Why do you want to know that?"

"Because I'm interested in everything. Where is he now?"

"He's not here."

"Did he just disappear?"

"Almost."

"Where did the people from his club go to?"

"With him."

A tourist at a table next to Cosby's asked politely if he could take a picture of Cosby and his family and Cosby said, sure, and Cosby and his family smiled and the tourist stood up with his camera. Two waiters immediately dived at Father Phil's table. One landed beautifully. His elbow hit the table and did not go into the spaghetti. Both waiters now spread their arms and hovered over Father Phil. There was no way to take his picture. They regarded the tourist as an agent taking a picture of Father Phil. It never occurred to them that anybody would take a picture of Bill Cosby ahead of him.

Leaving the restaurant, Sabrina said, "Now I don't have to ask you questions about yourself anymore."

"You have to believe me. I told you the truth."

"Just one thing. What do gangsters pray for?"

He ignored this. They turned the corner and walked on Sullivan Street. He paused and looked at the club, which had a big silver padlock on the door. He fingered the lock for an instant.

"You'd like to open that place, wouldn't you?" she said.

"Never!" he said.

Looking up at the buildings, and at teeming Bleecker Street at the corner, she could imagine quite easily how people used to be drawn to a street with this life.

Suddenly, she became very bold. "This weekend do you want to come to the beach? I have a lovely house in Southampton."

He thought. "I could never leave until Saturday afternoon."

She had to weigh what she liked best, walking onto the beach in the morning, with the ocean clean and foamy, or this man.

At a little after four that Saturday afternoon, they were driving on the Belt Parkway. She had told Mordecai, "Stay the fuck away from the beach this weekend." She didn't have to tell Mary from hematology because she was away. Now they were driving past Aqueduct racetrack.

"There you are," Father Phil said.

"Oh, I know this place," she said. "I come to the flea market here. I bought this." She showed the big gold pin with a bird decoration that was on the lapel of her white jacket. "I never was inside for the races. I'll bet it's fun."

"It sure is. I know a man who lost a spaghetti factory in there."

Even at this time, when the attendance was down because of the Off-Track Betting, the place was exciting. Through the fence you could see horses being walked toward the grandstands and a race, and at the stable entrance grooms were lounging and right behind them were horses with steam rising from their coats being walked to cool out.

"I'll have to take you here," he said.

"That would be fun."

"Do you like sports?"

"I don't know much about them."

"Friends of mine have a house right in here," he said. "On one of these streets right behind the stables. They watch the horses work out every morning."

He started the drive to Southampton by turning on the all-news station.

"Who is that?" she asked.

"Reno."

"Oh, Nevada."

"Reno is the attorney general."

"Oh. I don't think I know her."

He turned the station off.

As they came into Southampton, with its big old Long Island trees shading a road filled with Manhattan whites, there was no question about it in Father Phil's mind. He was ready to fall in love. And alongside him, Sabrina saw her name in the *New York Times* Sunday wedding page.

Sabrina Kalish, M.D.

She could not decide whether next line should say, "Phillip Napolitano, Former Priest," or "Phillip Napolitano, Builder."

The late afternoon sun fell on the green lawns of South-ampton on a slant. The road to Sabrina's house was empty. There was a reason for that. There were many cars parked at the field they used for softball or whatever. Father Phil slowed as he passed the cars.

From the field came a shout.

"Phil!"

There on second base, in the middle of a softball game, holding his hands up, was Freddy Hand, the priest from St. Raymond's on the East Side.

His call caused others to turn. One after another they shouted for Father Phil.

He stopped the car and walked over to the game, which was the Brooklyn Diocese priests against the New York Archdiocese. About thirty priests were at the field, with hot dogs on a grill and a ton of beer in ice buckets.

"We're having a big barbecue tonight," one of the priests,

Reilly from Blessed Sacrament in Manhattan, said. "You've got to come."

"We're just out to visit," Father Phil said.

"You've got to come," Reilly said.

Now somebody got a hit and from second base, his middle heaving, running on stubby legs, home came Freddy Hand. He made Father Phil and Sabrina have a can of beer with him to celebrate.

The barbecue was all right. Sabrina hated it. Her house was out. They got home to New York by ten. Father Phil said he'd take her to the races to make up for it.

57

Fausti pushed his uncle up to the triplex on East 68th. It opened and he got the wheelchair inside and then he turned and went out to the curb. He'd wait in case they needed him. He had never been inside the house, and for a good reason. He had never been asked, and he had no business being there.

Fausti was around again today because he wanted to show some loyalty to his uncle, and that is true, he felt for the uncle because he had grown up with him. He also had another good reason, which was that he had no job. He could thank his fucking name for that.

Stepping out of the morning pedestrians and traffic on Madison Avenue came Sabrina Kalish. She walked with the authoritative stride of a patrol sergeant. She had an attaché case that in her hands suggested immediate confinement.

"Good morning," she said. "This is the house, I take it."

"Yes," Fausti said.

"Good. I've got a minute." She went into her shoulder bag and took out a pack of cigarettes.

"Leave me ask you something," Fausti said.

"Of course."

"How can you be a doctor and smoke?"

"Because I know."

"Everything on television has doctors telling you not to smoke. They scared me to death out of smoking. You're saying they're all wrong?"

"No, I'm saying that I know all about smoking. You die a horrible death."

She stood with a long filtered cigarette conspicuous in her right hand. The people walking in the morning on the street were predominantly women walking briskly with attaché cases and without cigarettes. The men rushed out of doorways and into limousines. There was no sign of them smoking. That Sabrina had the cigarette made her a notable exception to the new custom that as you ascend in importance of work and money, smoking decreases. Two doors up from Sabrina, a maintenance man in a khaki uniform was smoking in the doorway. Across the street, wearing dirty blue coveralls, an oil truck driver with a cigarette hanging from his mouth watched the dials at the back of his tank truck. In front of an embassy residence, a guy in a dark blue uniform with gold braid leaned against the building and followed his exhaled smoke into the air. People breathe by income levels.

"Let me ask you something else," Fausti said. "What are you coming to the man's house for?"

"The judge."

"You don't wait until court?"

"Because his lawyer is having the tests here."

"And you have to be here?"

"Absolutely."

To say something between drags, she said, "How is your girl-friend?"

"Mad at me."

"Oh, come on. Why?"

"We're supposed to get married and we can't because of this freaking trial."

"That's no problem. You can take a day off for that."

"Not with my family. I have to wait right to the end."

"Who says a thing like that?"

"Everybody."

"They're all going to stop their lives?"

"No, they're going to stand there until something tells them they can start again."

"Really, is that what your family is like?"

"It's what I'm like and what this family is like."

"That's very loyal. The trial could take a year, how do we know. What does your fiancée say?"

"Good-bye."

"No way."

"Yes, she did."

"Then you have to marry her right away."

"I can't."

"Of course you can. How long have you been engaged?"

"All my life. I told you. We were in carriages next to each other."

"Then come on. The two of you just have to assert yourselves, you've been together for so long."

He shook his head. "I've been in one place longer. The family."

She listened as she bent over the curb to drop the cigarette. She spoke with a shrug and went inside.

It was at least unorthodox and a cause for suspicion to give psychological tests to a man in his own house, and then offer the results as evidence. But it required so many people to move The Fist around that the notion of testing him in his own house seemed the easiest.

"Ball . . . Flag . . . Tree."

The doctor giving the test said, "Now, just repeat them."

"Ball."

"Good answer!" one of the guys said.

He was told to shut up; The Fist was supposed to be wrong, what do you want, him so smart they put him in the fucking electric chair?

"Tree."

Now The Fist was silent.

"Was there one other?" the doctor said.

The Fist had a pained expression. "I think so. I don't know what it was."

The doctor said slowly, "Ball . . . Flag . . . Tree."

The Fist thought. "Ball."

"Flag."

Silence.

"You missed one. But you'll get it. That's fine. We'll do it again," the doctor said.

The Fist got all three on the fifth try, but no matter. He failed the Immediate Recall part of the test, the Mini-Mental State Exam. He got 12 out of 30, with 23 the cutoff for dementia.

The test was being given to The Fist in the first-floor room of his triplex. Around him were three of his family and two of the guys from the club. Administering the test was a doctor named Bateman from Memorial Sloan-Kettering Cancer Center. He was an expert witness and acting as defense assistant. Although it was at the bottom of bad taste, his presence was legal. The doctor, Bateman, had been recommended to The Fist's lawyers because he dealt every day with people whose minds were under extraordinarily savage attack.

Father Phil, however, had been immediately disheartened when he first met Bateman in a seventeenth-floor room at Sloan-Kettering. Bateman was interviewing a woman who was hollow with disease.

"Are you depressed?" he asked her.

"Yes."

"Do you find yourself crying and asking, 'Why me?'"

"Yes."

"Do you have any thoughts joined to that?"

"Yes. Why not him?"

A sparrow on the woman's windowsill would have known enough not to ask the question. Father Phil knew it wouldn't matter to the lawyers. They were buying the name of Memorial

Sloan–Kettering Cancer Center. Everybody is so afraid of the word *cancer* that maybe they wouldn't challenge the doctor.

Test results would be a defense exhibit, nothing more. The court-appointed monitor, Sabrina Kalish, M.D., watched in silence. She was present to observe that the tests were given and not made up. She and Father Phil nodded to each other, but otherwise showed nothing.

Near the end of a battery of tests, The Fist was given an animal-naming test to determine verbal fluency. Asked to tell of animals he knew, The Fist said right away, "Sammy the Bull" and "Tony the Lynx" and "Lupo the Wolf."

The Fist showed an IQ of 55, and a verbal IQ of 53. An old Minnesota Multiphasic test showed that he didn't have such a good personality, either.

"At these numbers he could not have any ability to have a strong relationship with a woman or children," the doctor, Bateman, said.

"None at all," a voice agreed.

"We have nothing more than a zombie here."

Hearing this, a dark-haired young woman on the side of the room showed distress on her face. Obviously, she was a daughter.

The lawyers, psychiatrists, and psychological people talked in front of The Fist as if he were a couch.

"Minimal body functions."

"Then minimal brain functions."

"It leaves him without the ability to feel anything about somebody else."

"What if somebody kissed him?"

"He wouldn't even notice it."

"Somebody in the family, too?"

"He wouldn't know if he kissed a cow."

The daughter brushed her right fist against her eye. Quickly, she brushed the eye again. She bit her bottom lip.

The hell with this, Sabrina thought.

She stepped over to the daughter.

"Give your father a kiss."

The daughter stood uncertainly.

Sabrina poked her back. "Go ahead."

This caused The Fist to look at Sabrina with these coal black eyes. Now at Sabrina's poke, the daughter stepped over to her father and kissed him on the cheek.

The Fist's mouth softened.

"No," one of them called, a lawyer probably, on guard against something like a sudden kiss that would cause an involuntary reaction that would make The Fist seem aware.

"She did that on purpose!" somebody said, pointing to Sabrina.

Who immediately was walking out.

"You'll testify you saw this."

"Saw what? A daughter kissing her father?"

She went out onto the sidewalk.

It was obvious what it was about. They were getting him ready to be catatonic during the trial. Knowing what she knew, it was impossible to carry this out. Therefore, she could seem offended by their suspicion. She was not going to do anything to them. They already had done that to themselves. And it happened that she meant it with the daughter's kiss.

The door opened behind her and the daughter came out.

"I wanted to thank you."

"For what?"

"For being nice."

"And that's nice of you. But you must know that I have a job to do. This was a little departure from it."

"We won't forget you."

"Then don't," Sabrina said with a laugh.

58 In court, in an effort to make The Fist officially incompetent, a doctor named Burnside came on as confident and tremendously excited about his new science, the PET scan, which does neurological imaging of the brain. The Fist couldn't have an MRI because of his pacemaker. The other test, a CAT scan beam, is stopped by a dense skull. The PET scan is done with glucose and radio isotopes, and was given in a soundproof chamber, with The Fist's head encased in a mold that didn't permit him to move. The PET scanner picks up slices of the brain less than a half-inch thick. A collection of dots colored blue on the large monitor mounted in front of the courtroom screen might indicate the temporal onset of Alzheimer's.

Doctor Burnside, consumed by his topic, concluded by stating, "I was at a scientific meeting in San Diego at the time of the testing. My staff gave the test."

Still, Judge W. found it fascinating. "You are on the cutting edge of modern science."

Now everybody was high in the sky of hope. He then said, "It is attractive pictorially, but not as satisfactory as I would have hoped. It is fascinating, but not persuasive. It is for the future. It is like DNA was years ago. There is no comparison base. We don't have enough information. To get it, you must follow the patient through to autopsy. However, this is a daily trial. The defendant is required to be alive. We can't wait for autopsies."

The judge said that one of Freud's contemporaries, Theodore Meynert, searching the brain for the roots of violence, chopped up ten thousand brains in Vienna and found tuberculosis and syphilis. Other than those two, the brains gave him nothing about murder and maiming. Meynert asked permission to chop up the brains of a whole prison and was denied. That ended his experiments.

"What difference does it make whether his IQ is 101 or 71?" the judge asked. "He still has enough to be part of a gang. At 90, a person can be a raving maniac. Then a lot of people have a high intellect and you wouldn't send them across the street to buy a cigar."

He looked out into the courtroom air and saw a great truth: "You don't have to be so neurologically sound to be a judge."

The judge now said, "I have no alternative but to deny the motion and go forward with trial. I rule him competent to stand trial. I don't care if he malingers. He can come or not. I don't care. The case goes on."

Sabrina, sure that she wouldn't be a witness at any stage, walked out in a debate over where she was going with all this free time. It was Tuesday and she didn't have to go back to work until the following Monday.

"There she goes," the priest said by the elevators. He was with two of the lawyers.

Hearing him, Sabrina said, "I'm not an evil woman. I do have a job. If you don't respect that, then don't talk to me."

"If you say so," he said reluctantly.

"That's all right," one of the lawyers said.

On the elevator, the lawyer said, "I'll stop off at the house and go over a few things the sons wanted to know. You coming?"

"No, not this time," Father Phil said. "They're too depressed to have me remind them of a Hell. What I'll do is get them a ticket on the lottery. You get them thinking they are going to win. Anything but reality." Sabrina smiled.

Father Phil went into his pocket. "Here. Look at this." He held out Joe Young's Mob Stars card. "This nitwit came around and handed them out. He told me to play his number. He is so crazy, this kid, I'm going to play it for The Fist. Maybe we'll put some luck in motion. Wins the lottery, win an acquittal, too. Here, you take the card here so they'll know what number The Fist is playing."

"Can you imagine," the lawyer said. "If he won, he wouldn't even know about it."

"No, I can't," Father Phil said.

The lawyer offered a ride, but he was going up to the East Side. Sabrina Kalish, M.D., and Father Phil walked through the park toward the subway.

"Now let me go out and do some shopping tomorrow," she said, mostly to herself. "I want to buy shoes. But the place I want is in your neighborhood."

"Where?"

"On Thompson Street."

"So what?"

"I don't think I ought to be seen there for a while. In case anybody ever notices me. I'm so popular."

"How can you say that? There are so many people shopping there that I get lost in the crowd. They don't know who I am. It's their neighborhood now. They don't know we used to own it."

"I guess I'm paranoid."

"You go there, then go around to Miraculous Medal Church. Right across, there's a candy store. His name is Scalfaro. Nini, we call him. He's about the only one left who I know. Just tell him I told you. They'll know if I'm around."

59

Fausti was on the pay phone outside, talking to Con. Actually, he was mostly listening to Con. He didn't have to say the name once. Even distracted by the pain in her feet from shopping, Sabrina could see from her last stop, Depression Modern, that this was another girl-boy argument.

Fausti was saying, "Do you want to go —"

It was obvious that she cut in.

He said, "You don't trust me for any —"

She stopped him again.

He said, "It's my family and —"

Sabrina knew exactly what the girl was now saying to him. "You and your family could go and . . ."

Oh, she said something like that. You could see it on Fausti's face. Of course Con hung up on him. He was in a trance at that pay phone.

Finally, he noticed her.

"How are you?"

"My feet hurt."

Inside, Nini had his glasses up on the top of his hair and spoke intensely into the phone. He tried to talk low, but he was so tense that his volume kept rising. "Broke."

Fausti walked over to the magazine rack and began arranging new magazines.

The same tall black woman in rags suddenly was at the door and Nini was abusing her.

"Get out of here. Didn't you die yet?"

"No."

"Well you should've."

Father Phil stepped around the woman. "You shouldn't be talking like that to any—"

Seeing Sabrina, he brightened. He had to move out of the way for people coming in to buy lottery tickets.

"Did you shop this late?" Father Phil asked her.

"They have a lot of stores I looked at. What is it they are all buying?"

"Lottery tickets."

"How much is it for?" Sabrina asked.

"Eleven million," Nini said.

She took out a dollar.

At her elbow was this pack of Mob Stars cards on the counter, starring Joe Young, with the license plate around his neck.

"How many numbers do I need?" she said.

"Nine, plus the two tag numbers."

She pretended to be thinking, as she looked casually at the B number, the criminal number, on Joey Young's Mob Stars card.

She called out, as if attending a séance, "Eight three two . . . seven nine . . ."

"You'll see, this one will win," she said.

"Good," Nini said, punching in the numbers. "I won't jinx you by playing it. I sure —

"— Hey, no, no."

The black woman was off the streets again, and coming into his store.

"I told you," Nini said, looking at this woman in the doorway. "Across the street they give free lunch. The church basement. Go there."

"I be playin' a lottery," she said.

"You don't have food to eat, you want to bet lottery. We don't take food stamps for that," Nini said.

"Play a dollar," she said.

"How?"

She leaned against the wall and began to go through the purse. A couple of coins sounded. As her hand dug for them, her face showed pain at not being able to find them.

"Here!" Sabrina said, handing her lottery ticket to the woman.

"Oh, no. I be havin' a dollar in here somewheres."

"No, take it. Besides, I'm sure that you're going to win."

"Oh, thank you. I don't know how to thank —"

"That's fine. Now go across the street," Nini said.

Putting the ticket into her cracked purse, the woman walked out.

"Now what?" Nini said.

"I still want a ticket," Sabrina said, glancing at the Joe Young license plate card.

Father Phil looked at the same Joe Young card. "I need a couple of tickets."

She said, "Give me numbers eight three two . . ."

Reading off the rest of Joey Young's arrest number, B number.

"She better remember us if anything good happens," Nini said, punching the numbers into the machine.

Which did not react. There was no beep, no click.

"Wait a minute now," Nini said. "Give me the numbers again."

"Eight three two," she began.

He punched the numbers, and —

THE

MOTHER-

FUCKING

MACHINE

STAYED

DEAD.

60   There was banging twice on the corrugated metal door pulled down over the candy store entrance.

The first time was at a little before ten, when he heard Father Phil talking to the woman Sabrina. They obviously were back from dinner and expected to get their lottery tickets. They stayed outside for a short time, and then left. By now, it was too late to buy a ticket even if they found a machine that was working.

Nini took the phone off the hook. He could talk to them in the morning, tell them, I'm sorry I didn't get you a ticket, but no harm's done, it was a million miles away from winning.

The second time there came knocking was at five in the morning. A club or stick was being used. The corrugated metal door sounded like a mean church bell and must have startled people in the apartments over the store.

Nini stirred, then winced. He had been on the hard floor, flat on his back on the floor, unconscious for some time, no, for a precise time starting at 10:02 P.M., when on television this girl cheerfully danced around Ping-Pong balls popping up and calling out numbers, every single number of Joe Young's prison number.

He had no idea of time or why he was on the floor and when and why he had fainted and went down on the back of his head.

He pulled himself up and, not thinking, went to the corrugated door and pulled it open.

Standing in the light from the streetlight was The Fist in his courtroom blazer and flying saucer cap.

With eyes that would have made Frankenstein drop dead.

"I won," he said.

The fear exploded out of the origins of all emotion, most of which in Nini's case came from the place in his right pocket where he kept his cash.

"You give me my ticket," The Fist said.

Nini couldn't speak.

"Give me my ticket. You got any others, give them to me. I want all the moneys."

When Nini moved not, The Fist said, "I tell you something nobody ever heard twice:

"'No Ticket, no live.'"

It was amazing what Nini did. Hands frozen by fear grabbed the door handle. His knees bent for leverage. His whole frightened body brought the door down right in The Fist's face. There was a clang as the bottom hit cement. Without knowing what he was doing, Nini snapped a large inside lock. Then he went in the back of the store and sat on a straight chair with his head against a poker machine.

61

There were two cataclysmic events on this morn. The first came when a state lottery worker was putting posters all over the store saying, "We Sold an $11 Million Winner!"

"He's not even open," the lottery guy said. "He must of had some celebration."

The winning ticket was sold legally, so they had to pay even if Nini was in default with his payment.

"Do we know who won?" Father Phil said.

"We'd know by now if anybody else won."

"Not really. You get that when they come forward."

"It has to be," Fausti said.

"It sure doesn't look like it," Father Phil said.

She was on the church steps with her elbows on her knees. She smoked and stared at them. She was smoking a cigarette butt she got from the sidewalk.

Father Phil called Sabrina at Bellevue from the outdoor phone. "I know you're busy, but the woman we gave the ticket to —"

"Oh, lottery. I forgot all about it. When is the lottery? Last night."

He rolled his eyes. "The number you played," Father Phil said anxiously.

"Did it win? We think it might have. Yes, we think she might have the ticket. But you bought it. We have a case here. Sure it sounds impossible. I don't know what we can do. I hope it isn't true, but I know your ticket won," he said.

"How can you be laughing? Do you know what is involved?"

"How can I worry about something I never had? What about The Fist? He thinks he had the eleven million taken right out of his pocket. He wants the money. What? All right. Go ahea—"

He hung up. Then he called across the street to the woman on the church steps.

"Where's that lottery ticket the woman gave you?"

She shrugged. She called over, "Throwed it away. It doan win. Give me a cigarette?"

She stared at the glorious sight of the priest becoming a pinwheel as he erupted from head to toe.

On Thursday morn, the two hundred prospective jurors already had reported to the huge ceremonial courtroom on the first floor of the courthouse and were given long questionnaires. "There are forty-five pages," the judge said. The jurors shook their heads.

"Tell you the truth, this is most serious. You are the key personnel in the justice system of the United States. Treat all this like it's someone in your family being tried. This isn't a junior high school exam. You're not supposed to look at someone else or talk to them.

"Everybody has pens or pencils?"

In the laughter they began reading the questionnaires:

"Do you know anyone who is mentally ill (for example, schizophrenia, bipolar disorder, major depression)?

"Do you know anyone who has dementia?

"Do you know anyone who has suffered from a stroke?

"How much confidence do you have in psychiatrists/psychologists?"

There was a black woman in a blue shirt worn outside black pants, and with white Nikes. Next to her was a big guy in a green short-sleeve shirt and jeans. Kneeling on the carpeted floor in front of the first row was a man in a blue basketball jacket and dark pants and a young light-haired woman in a green polo shirt and khaki pants. They had the questionnaires on the floor and they read them, read them, read them, and all over the room there were people dressed simply but whose faces were complex, and the magnetic power of their act rose from the floor and caused the atmosphere of the huge room to become regal, to magnify Democracy.

The lawyers and prosecutors went over the written questionnaires for two weeks, reducing the number of jurors to eighty-five, who were told to assemble in the sixth-floor courtroom on June 23.

The next morning, at 9:15 A.M., Prospective juror number 17 came into the jury box in the sixth-floor courtroom to start the trial of *United States v. Dellacava*. After she was sworn in, the judge said, "This is a RICO trial. The defendant is Fausti Dellacava. He is seated at the table with his lawyers."

They stood and gave their names.

"Paul Marino."

"Vincent Ross."

The prosecutors:

"Arnold Benjamin."

"Vincent Greco."

The judge said to the woman, "Why don't you tell us something about yourself?"

"I'm forty-five, and I am happily divorced. . . ."

She laughed, the judge laughed, the news reporters laughed.

"Which newspapers do you read?" she was asked.

"Newsday."

That is the Long Island newspaper, which meant that she was one of the jurors brought in from Long Island. The federal Eastern District runs from the Brooklyn shore to Montauk Point.

Fausti was afraid to look around to see if anybody was giving him a death stare. The moment they did, he had decided that he would put it all on Nini. Exclusive. Him alone. Nini. He took the number under false pretenses. He hadn't paid his lottery machine bill and he still gambled that the machine would be on for The Fist's number, which it wasn't. Tell that to The Fist. He don't want to hear stories. He decides that he wins the lottery. If that's what he decides, then he is the winner. Where's the money? All the money, he wants.

It was fair to put it on Nini. He wasn't even going to be within two thousand miles of this place anyway.

When Nini left Sullivan Street, he wasn't sure of where he was going, but he was going that far, two thousand miles, and fast, on the dead run. Of course Nini left town. Left jobs and house and family and friends and clothes and anything else you want to mention. Fausti went with him to the Port Authority Bus Terminal on Eighth Avenue. Nini bought a ticket on the first intercity bus scheduled, which was going to St. Louis via Chicago, and then on to the South. Looking over his shoulder two or three times, he went downstairs to the lower level, where he plunged past a driver who was leaning against the side of the gate and smoking his last cigarette. Nini actually leaped on to the bus. He did not wave. Fausti was afraid to look around to see if anybody was giving him a death stare.

62 Had he known, had Fausti understood that over all the years this would be famous as one of the Mafia's greatest mistakes of all time, one for which young age still was no excuse, Fausti never would have had Nini and Al Hansen put Artie D'Amico onto his Mob Stars baseball cards.

Sitting in the court hallway early in the morning on this day, Fausti noticed these new guys, in somber federal lawman suits, coming off the elevators. Obviously, they had somebody in the building who was a big witness.

"He's on the witness list, that doesn't mean he gets up and talks," said one of them.

"He still must have some sense of honor."

"Sure. He sent his own son out to kill in a capital punishment state."

They were talking about Artie D'Amico, who at this moment sat with marshals in the courthouse basement, ready to take an elevator to the sixth-floor courtroom where he would try to sink the universe.

When Father Phil arrived, he frowned at the commotion in the hall.

"Who are they?" he asked Fausti.

"They got a big witness, they're saying," Fausti said.

Father Phil walked back to the defense room, where the lawyers were standing with bleak looks.

"Do you know what this D'Amico can say?" they asked.

"He would never say a word against us," Father Phil said.

"If it's the same as he was at the hearing, we're all right. But we keep hearing he is changing everything."

It all began, what, two, three years before this, back on the day when Fausti didn't listen to anybody and put this unknown, but unfortunately a living unknown, on one of their Mob Stars cards. And now Fausti sat in the hallways with a sinking feeling. He remembered every single solitary thing he had heard himself, or been told by others, about the cards being dangerous.

When Nini first saw the card, he dropped it as if it was burning. "Are you serious? You could get me and you killed. This guy, this guy here, he's a live guy. It's one thing to put pitcher cards out on dead guys or on big bosses can't do anything really. But you're using a live guy from the neighborhood. A made guy and that's all. I see him down Milady's bar. He could get mad."

The card said:

ART D'AMICO
BORN: Brooklyn, 1928.
MADE: November 1979 by Tony Corallo of Lucchese mob.
NICKNAME: Little Art.
RANK: Acting Boss of Lucchese mob.
ASSETS: Will say yes to any proposition.
LIABILITIES: Has made people very mad because of his son
   and man he guaranteed, Irwin Schiff.

All families could use him. Killing just another part of the day.

Had his own son go to an electric chair state on a hit. Has had himself into so many murders that no surprise if he goes himself as you read this.

D'Amico was on the corner of Spring and MacDougal when an old guy from the neighborhood, Frankie, came up to him and held out the card.

"You see this? You ought to see this. Where'd they get the picture of you?"

D'Amico stared at the picture. Pretty good one. He wasn't the least upset. He put it in his pocket. That night he was at a meeting of the Lucchese mob in a conference room of the Chief Executive Motel outside the entrance to Kennedy Airport. It was a sloppy meeting because they spent eight hours arguing over mob business, who owes what, who stole.

In the midst of which, D'Amico, looking for the business card of a shop steward in the Laborers Union, came out with the Mob Stars card. For no reason, he turned it over. Here is what happened as described in his own words when he came to court on this day.

Q. In this hotel room you thought or concluded that there was a plot against your life?

A. Yes.

Q. What convinced you of this?

A. When I read this card that you get with gum and took it as an advertisement to me that I am going to go.

Q. Was there somebody behind the plot, and the card?

A. The Fist Dellacava.

Q. How do you know this?

A. Because he is the Boss. No made man can be hit without his OK. And they were getting ready to hit me. I took it that The Fist himself was doing it.

Q. Then what happened?

A. I concluded Loscalzo was going to walk into that bathroom, get the pistol, and come out and shoot me.

And I stood up and put my hand in my pocket like I had a pistol, and they dogged it; they dogged the whole thing and I left.

Q. Where did you go?

A. To the federal authorities. Your place. FBI.

Q. And are you under protection?

A. Me and my family, Witness Protection Program.

Q. And in return you were to testify against —

A. Fausti Dellacava. The Fist.

63 The courtroom opened in the morning with six color television screens set up around the room. A technician speaking into a microphone said, "Mario, give us a voice test." Somewhere in the Midwest, Mario counted to ten on closed circuit television. The technician in the courtroom nodded.

They were getting ready for witness Domenico, who is in another city, under federal protection, and who is so sick with cancer of the stomach. He was going to testify on closed circuit.

The jury was in and the prosecutor called out:

Q. Can you briefly tell the jury what the circumstances were that led you to cooperate with law enforcement?

On the screen, grimacing, Domenico answered:

A. One of my partners had got arrested for cocaine, conspiracy to distribute cocaine, and he gave up a building where bodies were buried. They were going to charge me.

Q. What was the effect on you?

A. Bad.

Q. Mr. Domenico, still focusing on that same period of time, then, were you involved in the murders of Mr. Balsamo, Mr. Brocclie, Richard Scarcella, and Joseph Marino as part of Jerry Palermo's crew?

A. Yes — no. It wasn't Jerry Palermo's crew after a while on account of we killed him.

Q. Do you know what happened to Louis Napoli shortly afterward?

A. It wasn't shortly afterwards. I think the kid went to jail.

Q. Mr. Domenico, after he came out of jail did you speak to —

A. He got murdered.

Q. Did you inform anybody?

A. I reported this to Fist Dellacava.

In court, they were left with no defense.

The prosecutors said he was a big gangster.

The Fist described the scene in a mumble.

"Yez is all dirty cocksuckers!"

At 3:37, no voice called or whispered but suddenly they stood and filed into the courtroom, whose lights now seemed blinding. Moments like this recommend themselves. The judge's secretary was in front of the room in a brown striped shirt, tan skirt, and the smile of serious business.

"A note," she said to someone. She said it in a low voice, but it was heard all over the room. Verdict. Six marshals came into the room in severe dark suits. Father Phil rubbed his hand over his hair.

The judge came in wearing robes.

He nodded and they brought in the jury.

In they came, in a silence that sucked the air out of the room. No matter how often you sit through this, no matter how little or how great the doubt, it always is the same. The stillness causes all hearts to pound.

The judge asked the jury for the verdict, and the foreman rose and held the long jury ballot in his hands and read:

"Count number one, guilty. Charge one, not guilty, charge two, not proven.

"Count number two. Can't agree."

They went through six specific charges that were not proven.

On the ninth, involving Carlino testimony, they said, "Proven." The conspiracy to murder Gotti was "proven."

Then came thirteen provens, and everything to do with Domenico guilty, and at the end of thirty-six of such items the foreman stood quietly and the judge made a speech about the alertness and hard work and said, "You're discharged."

They smiled and walked out. They had just put an end to the Mafia as it is known on American streets and docks and truck stops and on film and in the lore of the country.

They wheeled The Fist through an alley in the crowd that was gathering more and more as the news of the verdict went through the building. The Fist had remained in the court after the verdict while they got continuance of his bail and set a sentencing date. He emerged into a hallway crowded with family and some friends and reporters and lawyers and people from other trials and court officers, all milling around, talking, then lapsing into silence and watching as The Fist went by, staring, mumbling to the end. One of his sons, his face straight and shaded with sadness, wheeled him to the office they had been using during the trial.

Sabrina Kalish came out of another office with another one of the prosecution doctors who had not been called to testify.

"I'm happy enough I wasn't involved," the doctor said.

"I guess I am," Sabrina said. She turned and saw Fausti. The eyes were bloodshot from tears.

She didn't say anything and neither did he. He walked straight for the office, his arms swinging, in a blue T-shirt and blue shorts and big white sneakers.

He opened the door and went into a room that was packed with relatives and lawyers. In the center of which was The Fist. He was facing outward in his chair so that he saw anybody coming in.

Sabrina stood in the open door and did not move. Nobody said anything to her and she said nothing to anybody else.

Fausti bent over his uncle and said, "I want you to know I'm sorry. I want you to know I'm truly sorry."

"Do you need anything?" The Fist said.

"No."

"If you need anything you let me know."

"Nothing," Fausti said. "I just want you to know how sorry I am."

Suddenly, Sabrina stepped up. She edged Fausti out of the way and she looked straight into The Fist's eyes.

"He does need something," she said. "He needs for your permission to get married. I know this is a very hard day for you and your family, but this young man has been penalized because of his name. I think that's more than enough. I know you have customs. But he has one girl he wants to marry. That's one great chance. If he loses her, it might never happen to him again. He would be losing a large part of his life here. Just the same as being sentenced. I hope you tell him to get married right away."

The Fist stared at her. Then he went away to the hospital ward at Westchester County Hospital, a federal storage site, until sentencing.

64

"Excuse me, excuse me, you can't go in there, what are you doing here anyway?"

The saleswoman at Kleinfeld's wedding dress store, a mean-faced saleswoman, stood in the doorway between the reception room and the large showroom and fitting room as if she ran a cell block.

Fausti kept walking.

"Would you please stop right there?"

Fausti was at the threshold of a blinding white room. Everywhere, wedding dresses were coming on and off young women, who then walked around in underwear while waiting for the next dress. Mothers hovered.

The saleswoman's outstretched arm was a gate.

"Only women can go in there with her."

"She doesn't have a mother. She's alone in there and she called me about some trouble with the dress. I want to talk to her."

"You can be with her when she has a baby. You can't be with her when she's trying on a wedding dress."

Kleinfeld's, which is the most thrilling building for women from all over the city and country, is in a large one-story building on the corner of Fifth Avenue and 79th Street in the Bay Ridge section of Brooklyn. Gray cables of the Verrazano Bridge hang in the air over the tops of the street's four- and five-story buildings.

For so long, since she had been ten, Concetta had imagined the dress that she had in her hands at Kleinfeld's after only two hours of search. It was in a trunk sale of a designer named Vera.

This dress cost four thousand dollars. She didn't have forty dollars. At the same time, she had a bride's mind: She was going to become a vision so breathtaking that every single solitary person in the church would be mesmerized, as if a plaster saint had just stepped from a pedestal and became a bride.

When she went up to Yonkers and asked her father for help, he sat at the dining room table in helpless silence while his wife recited the psalm of the stepmother:

"You're not getting any money from me. What's mine is mine."

"I'm not asking you. I'm asking my father."

"What's his is mine. So you get nothing here."

"Daddy, if you don't help me, what am I going to do?"

"I know what you can do," the stepmother cut in. "Why don't you go to the big-shot gangster family you're marrying into. Let them come up with the money for a wedding."

"Fausti is paying for that."

"I'll bet he is. With a name like that they probably make somebody else pay."

"I can't let him pay for the dress. What does it look like if I can't even get a dress?"

"Go ask them. You picked them. Your new in-laws. Mobsters."

Con left in tears. She remembers always her father holding the front storm door open and somehow hoping that she would kiss him, and she went past him without words and never looked back.

When she got to the apartment on Thompson Street, she was still crying.

Her brother said, "What are we supposed to do, die over — how much is it? —"

"Four thousand dollars," Con said.

That took some of the stand-up-guy bravado out of Pat's voice, but he did not waver beyond that.

"So what's that supposed to mean?" Pat said. "You're getting the dress."

Four thousand was about what he thought he had in a box in the closet. Every dollar came from a long season of selling peanuts from stands at all Catholic Church feasts in the city. The only times he spent any money was on trips down to Atlantic City, and he had in his mind what was left after them, and his mind said four thousand.

He miscalculated what he had in his box by two trips to Atlantic City. They took thirty-eight hundred. He had two hundred in the box. He clapped it shut. He couldn't let her know he was this bad off.

On Con's second trip to Kleinfeld's, the saleswoman told her that even if she was doing this in one day, this was her last look at the dress, which was part of a trunk sale by a designer who would rather leave town with the dress back in the trunk than have people pretend they were going to buy it.

Con called Fausti and was barely able to talk. She had a fear that was perfectly legitimate. Her brother Pat was a great friend. He also was a human being on Thompson Street. "It's one thing for Pat to say he'll pay. It's another thing for him to come up with four thousand today," she said.

While what once was the most common street scene, five hundred strolling shylocks, had been virtually wiped out, there still were one or two nice guys who could loan money and suck the blood out of your neck. I don't want him going near a loan shark, she said to herself.

An hour later, Fausti and her brother Pat came in. And Fausti, not allowed to go in and look for Con, asked the saleswoman, "Could you tell her I'm here?"

"I have customers all over that room. What's the name?"

"She is going to be Mrs. Fausti Dellacava. I'm Mr. Fausti Dellacava. Tell her to please come out and see me."

The woman indicated the couch in the reception room. She disappeared into the room of women in white. When she came back, she shook her head. "Nobody answers that name."

"She has to. That's going to be her name."

"We get plenty of them don't answer to the married name. Know what that means? The marriage is in trouble before the dress is fitted."

"The only thing men are good for here is to pay. You ought to get it done and pay for her dress and get out."

"You just told me you couldn't find her."

"She's my customer. She told me she don't answer to that name."

"It happens to be our name," Fausti said.

"She doesn't think so."

Fausti shrugged. "So we'll wait."

Con came out to the reception room. She had on a blue sweater and jeans and a face that showed she had been dazzled. "The dress is so beautiful," she said.

"Do you want it?" her brother said.

"Oh, geez, yes."

"So take it."

Uncertainty crossed her face.

"Get it put in a box," Pat said.

"Oh, no, I have to have some fitting done."

"But she got to pay first," the saleswoman said.

Pat Lauretano brought out a pack of folded hundred-dollar bills, straight from a shylock's cache.

"We don't take deposits on a trunk sale. You pay it all."

"That's what I got here. A whole four."

"You don't pay me. You pay the cashier." He did.

Fausti and Pat went outside and stood in the gray day.

The saleswoman came out into the doorway of a delivery entrance. Then she took out a pack of cigarettes. "I'm on my break.

"You might as well go over while you're waiting."

She pointed to Zeller's tuxedo store on the corner.

"Eighty-eight dollars for a tux," she said. "That's all the man is worth at the wedding. The bride costs a fortune. The groom's worth eighty-eight dollars. If you got kids, they get formals practically for nothing."

"We don't have kids," Fausti said.

"You don't have kids? What are you getting married for, you don't have kids?"

65 They still had no Boss and they had to vote one, but by now everybody was so hot, with their personal details following them, that they wouldn't dare try the Northeastern, whose comforts were by now dangerous. Gather there, the federals would bust any new Boss before he got across the lobby on the way out.

Father Phil spent two days finding the safe place. The Canal Street station has about every subway line threading through it on different tracks. Somewhere in the network of tunnels that are not connected to each other, people become exhausted by the amount of walking, and make mistakes that can bring you up to the street two and three times while looking for the right tunnel and train lines.

The meeting was set for 5 P.M. on a Thursday night, so the guys coming to the meeting could lose themselves in the throngs on Canal Street. As Father Phil came to the subway entrance, the sidewalk was a gigantic crowd of Chinese buying fish. There was a store with a thousand racks of sunglasses. Two young Asian women showed sunglasses to a pair of blond white women. The outside wall had a shallow recess in which there were hundreds of caps on shelves. A store down, two young men in white shirts and black pants sat on the two-step entrance to a store and smoked cigarettes. Behind them, two young Asian women in stylish denim overalls prowled and waited for customers. A group of eleven blacks, six of them children, went down the subway stairs in front of Father Phil.

He now went through crowded tunnels, then empty tunnels, then again crowded tunnels, and now he was at the signs for the N and R trains, going downtown, and he went through the tunnel under the tracks to the uptown side, and just before getting there he went down one flight, which had thick pipes on both walls and overhead. He came out of this iron house and into the chamber. There was the sculpture. A great black Viking standing in the front of a boat with a curved prow. He had a huge harpoon through a white man.

It took until ten at night for the guys to assemble. With the sculpture looming ominously in the shadows and the platform ankle-deep in filthy water, they sat on steps to name a new Boss. They got nowhere. Father Phil wanted to be named, and they knew it, but they also all were afraid that The Fist would get mad, and he could reach out from a jail as if he was signaling a turn.

At seven-thirty in the morning, Ozone Park representative Sal Meli stood up and put a hand on the shoulder of Big Fat Junior. He was the son of the Boss who was away forever.

"We nominate Big Fat Junior," Meli said. "Call the roll."

Ignatzio stood up and said in Italian that they should prepare to vote.

"His mother's Jewish. He can't be nobody," Fat Andy of Ozone Park yelled.

"His mother happens to be Russian," Meli said.

"Russian isn't Italian," somebody called out.

"Her parents couldn't go from Italy to Russia, some fucking war or something?" Meli said

"We nominate Big Fat Junior," Meli said. "Call the roll."

Of course Big Fat Junior is not Fat Tony. Nor is he Fat Andy or Fat Dom. He is Big Fat Junior and he is Sal Meli's candidate.

Ignatzio stood up and said in Italian that they should prepare to vote.

From the last row, almost at the top of the staircase, came Moishe Wolfe's voice, "Where does this leave us?"

"What?" Fish said.

"You told us we can't be made men, we got to be only associates because we're not Italian. He's half Jewish."

Big Fat Junior wheeled around.

"What's this half Jewish mean?"

"Your mother," Moishe said. "The mother is a beautiful woman. A lovely woman. She happens to be a Russian Jew."

"I'll go to the commission on this," Fish Cafaro muttered.

"You can't go to the commission. You're only the Acting Boss. You got to be the Official Acting Boss before you are allowed into a commission meeting," Pepe from Fish's home club called out.

Suddenly, one after the other, the guys got up and said that Salvatore Meli had done such a good job of leading, and getting Big Fat Junior off the stage so gracefully, and being that he was pure Italian and a known earner, and therefore he should be the new Boss.

Sal shook his head violently. "You're not going to do this to me," he said.

"Yes, we are," one of the captains said.

"Ignatzio!"

Old Ignatzio stood up for the roll call.

Salvatore Meli grimaced. The vote is a silent one. Each man nods. That is known as getting the nod. As Ignatzio started his benediction, Sal Meli could see heads nodding yes.

What do they think, that I don't know that Judge W. gives you a thousand years that are real? Salvatore Meli, in fear of prison walls, looked around. He heard a loud click. Overhead somewhere, a train was coming down the line. The Number L train to Canarsie was approaching.

Sal turned and went up the steep steps surrounded by pipes and then he started to run up the steps. They heard his footsteps sounding on the platform upstairs and the *shhhhhhhhh* of train doors closing.

Then as the captains milled around on the steps, Jimmy (The Spy) Sparacino bumped into Fish Cafaro's back and felt a gun. He was off the platform in one move. Now on the staircase he shouted, "Somebody got a gun!" This was a signal of the complete disintegration of the mob.

"I was afraid to come down here without one," Fish Cafaro cried. "You could get hurt here, some fuckin' Puerto Rican sticks you with a knife."

It didn't matter what he said. Everybody in the wet chamber fled. So did Fish.

Ignatzio and his notebook and Father Phil were alone on the steps. Ignatzio opened his oath book. By default there was a new Boss. To the sound of dripping water, he read the oath.

In Brooklyn, Sal Meli got off at the Atlantic Avenue stop and went into a fruit stand to buy a banana. Then he went across to a men's clothing store.

"Good morning," the clerk said.

"Stick 'em up," Sal said, holding out the banana.

The day was insufferably hot and airless, and the handcuffs were cold. Sal Meli was brought to Brooklyn Hospital, where he appeared to belong. Sabrina Kalish was not on duty when he was brought in. She would get to him when she arrived. She was late because she was home caring for a busted romance that she now understood to have been not much more than an illusion. The thought that she had fooled herself was intolerable. I meant so much to him that they are having a big wedding today and they don't even ask me, she said to herself, sarcastically. What if I could have found a man at the wedding?

At the hospital, she walked up to Sal Meli, while glancing at the file. "Did you really think the banana would frighten and intimidate people?"

Sal Meli shook his head.

"Then why do you think you did it?"

"I don't want to go to jail."

"But look where you are now."

"At least here won't be forever. What they wanted me to do would of got me life."

Sabrina looked through his file. She was perplexed.

"Were you brought here under arrest?"

"I didn't come in a taxi."

"I don't see an arrest warrant."

"Maybe they didn't make one out for you. The minute they get in here, they got a call and they run, the both of them."

"And they left you here like this?"

"I guess so."

"There is no hold on you."

"I told you, they got a call."

"If I don't commit you, then you are free to walk out of here."

Sal's hand went right to his tie. "Is there a barbershop around here? I got to shave before I go."

"Where would you go?" she asked.

"Sicily right away. Today, tonight. First plane to Taormina."

"I've heard it's beautiful," Sabrina said.

"Where I go it is. To the Boss's. The Boss of Taormina. I stay in his hotel, Lucky Luciano slept there. I sit in the café with him. He handles all the marriage beefs. They got way more men than girls."

"Where? There?"

"That's all they got, problems. The girl says she marries a guy, she changes her mind, says yes to another guy, even two other guys, says she'll marry them. You could have murders all over the place the Boss don't sit them all down."

"There are that many more men than women?"

"You know what a shotgun wedding is? Well, Taormina is the only place in the world where the girl has to be forced to marry some guy."

"That's where we're going. You'll be out of here and you can introduce me to all these poor lonely men."

"What do you think, you make a pimp out of me?"

"Precisely."

"I don't do that type a thing."

"It's either make introductions in Taormina or sit here until somebody finds the mistake and you get arraigned on a robbery charge."

"So I'm going to be a fucking pimp," Sal Meli said glumly.

"Starting when I get packed and come back here for you. What time is the plane tonight?" Sabrina said. "I said tonight," Sabrina said.

In the Westchester Hospital prison ward, a man scheduled for shipment to a state mental hospital for the dangerous was alone in a locked room at the end of the hall. One night, he let out a scream that did not end. Rather than understandable baying at the moon, it was deafening insanity. Through the night and into the next day and all through the next night he kept screaming. He never lost any of his insane and endless volume. It didn't matter what guards or orderlies, whose nerves were raw, said to him. He seemed not to see them even when they came into his locked room.

In his room down the hall, the Fist suddenly stood up and tapped on the window. The Fist nodded to a guard, who opened his locked door.

The Fist simply shuffled past the guard and went to the locked door leading to the end of the hall where the screamer was being kept.

"Open the door," The Fist said to a second guard.

It was the first time anybody had heard his voice.

The guard hesitated. The Fist stared at him. The guard opened the door.

The Fist walked down to the room where the guy was now in full insanely furious scream.

"Open the door," The Fist said to the guard.

Who opened the door.

The Fist stood in the doorway and locked those two big black searchlight eyes on the guy.

Shouting died.

The Fist spoke, not loudly, and certainly not threateningly.

He just spoke in his normal tone, all the while keeping those eyes riveted on the guy.

"You've got to stop this!"

The man who shouted sat on his bed in complete fear and silence. He never opened his mouth again.

The Fist turned and walked back to his room. He went in and fell asleep.

66 Con and Fausti were married in Miraculous Medal, under the smile and outstretched palms of Father Phil.

At the center of the ceremony, the priest called out, in gladness and emotion, "Do you, Fausti Dellacava, take —"

"— Blanfort Melton," Fausti said in a low voice.

The priest hissed, "Don't fool. This is a sacrament."

"I got it changed legally," Fausti said. The court paper crackled as he took it out.

"I hate that name," Con whispered.

"I got it changed legally," Fausti said.

"I told you, take my name."

"Fausti Lauretano? How does that sound?" Fausti said. He made a face. "It sounds like you made me take it," he said to Con.

It had just run up to the surface, this small nagging thing he had never really thought out, and now it suddenly exploded through all of him. He saw life in front of him with the name Fausti Dellacava. He wondered what his father would think of him kneeling here and changing the name he got when he was baptized right here in the same church.

"Fausti Dellacava," Fausti said. "I, Fausti Dellacava . . ."

"Do you, Concetta Lauretano . . ."

The reception was at Acero's, a banquet hall in the Whitestone section of Queens. The place has a terrace that runs right to the water of the East River where it broadens into Long Island Sound.

The first guests milled around two outdoor bars. They were busy congratulating each other for being there when Frankie California looked out at the water and saw this motionless boat. Two men in shirts and ties rocked on the waters and showed no fishing poles. One did put a video camera to his shoulder.

"They're makin' pictures!" Frankie called out.

"Why do they bother? They convicted the guy. What more can they do?"

"They can show it to the judge that the guy could go to a wedding, he could go for life. Anybody else here got a problem goes with him."

In the wedding suite, Fausti heard the excited voices and came out.

"Put something up so they can't see in at us," he said.

Frankie California said to the nervous banquet manager, "Get a *petition* up!"

The banquet manager said, "I don't see what that will do."

"I says get a *petition*," Frankie said.

The banquet manager came back with a couple of yellow legal forms. He signed his name on the first page and had waiters signing, too.

"What's that?" Fausti said.

"The *petition* against the agents."

Fausti said, excitedly, "A partition!"

"Put a blanket over the fence so they can't see through."

Soon busboys and porters were lugging out rolls of green netting that they place around new lawns. They attached them to the chain-link fence.

Inside, there was a stir. The Fist was wheeled into the reception. He was on a day pass from the jailhouse ward of the Westchester County Jail. Any hour now he would be off to serve his sentence. Right away he was in the center of a crowd of men waiting to greet him. The Fist was wheeled to a round table in a far corner of the banquet hall. He sat down and pointed at the ceiling.

"He wants the lights out," Frankie California told the waiter.

The waiter went to the light switches on the wall and shut off the ceiling lights over The Fist's head. He sat in the sudden gloom and looked around carefully. From the ceiling a few feet away came the hot light from a bulb embedded in the ceiling. The edge of its light washed up almost to The Fist's table. The Fist pointed again.

The banquet manager explained that he couldn't switch that one off because there were several bulbs attached to the one switch and if he did turn it off, then three or four tables would be in dimness, and, besides . . .

The manager's voice trailed off because he saw The Fist's eyes.

The Puerto Rican busboy came out with a tall ladder. Up he went with a pot holder around his hand. He made The Fist's table so dark that waiters stumbled. The Fist could not be seen from the dais, where his nephew sat with his new bride.

The waiters serving The Fist's table could carry only one tray at a time, as a free hand was required to guide them through the darkness and to the table without dropping chicken all over the place.

The reception proceeded wonderfully well until the band leader, getting too puckish for his own good, called out, "Here's a number for a special guest. The tune is:

"'Dancing in the Dark.'"

Out of the darkness came a deep, long growl.

Suddenly, the band leader said he wanted to play a different song. A loud tune had younger people rushing to the floor. Soon everybody was dancing, and The Fist sat in the dark and those who saw him said he seemed as pleased as he could be, being that he didn't want to go to jail.

67

The day after their wedding, Fausti and Concetta left for their honeymoon in New Orleans, employed or not. They had to sit in the taxi and wait. Blocking the car was a procession marking the end of the Feast of Saint Anthony. Once, they would have been there for an hour, and the parade would wind through all the streets, but now it was painfully thin. A priest walked first, and behind him were the last of the old neighborhood church women. A band in black berets and red shirts played an Italian march. The band had to be imported from Staten Island. After that came a float with a statue of Saint Anthony, and schoolchildren huddled around it. Then it was over. Once, there had been thousands marching. Now there were perhaps two hundred.

Fausti had the driver go down Sullivan Street, which was vacant in the afternoon shadows. Craning his neck, he could see that the club had a big silver lock showing on the door. The new Malocchio had gone to somebody's house in Jersey. He got out and went to the doorway over the club. On the slot for Apartment 1, the brass mailbox had scratched on it the initial "C." The building had no sound. Where was The Fist now? Somewhere between the detention ward at Westchester and the government medical facility at North Carolina. After that, where? Springfield, Missouri, or Rochester, Minnesota, or Fort Worth, or wherever they put prisoners with a medical problem. One thing was certain: He was gone from his street now. But one thing Fausti knew for sure: He'd be back. He'd be a lot older and maybe he wouldn't recognize the street, but he'd be back.

At his father's club, on West 3rd Street, Fausti stared at a place that was now split. A hairdresser was in one window. In a cubicle at the door was a locksmith. The next window was for Nails! Nails!

He thought he heard in the silence his father's shout over money or cops or Fausti's behavior while he cooked flounder in the back. The sound faded and the windows spoke of the power of a painted sign. Hang up a new name in the window and the eyes are immediately puzzled and old recognition is gone and, so quickly, memory is suffocated.

Young people were walking in and out of the Advanced Copy Center. Law students from NYU, only yards away, and others from schools all over the city brought papers to be copied that they hoped mightily would get them great degrees and huge careers. Simultaneously, from attics and cellars and tiny rooms came writers with plays and book manuscripts, all dreams to be doubled on paper while they wait at the counter.

The copy store, unnoticed on the street when the government suddenly made the Concerned Lutherans club so famous, now is known all over the city. It emerges as the busiest and best-known storefront on the block.

Fausti looked at the deserted front of the locked club, across at the crowded copy shop.

"You had it right from the start," he told his wife, Concetta. "You have to be crazy not to be legitimate."

He kissed her and they were off to the airport.